DEC 20

P9-CBX-854

# MARAUDER

A NOVEL OF THE *OREGON*® FILES

# MARAUDER

# CLIVE CUSSLER
## AND
# BOYD MORRISON

**WHEELER PUBLISHING**
A part of Gale, a Cengage Company

**LIBRARY OF CONGRESS CIP DATA ON FILE.
CATALOGUING IN PUBLICATION FOR THIS BOOK
IS AVAILABLE FROM THE LIBRARY OF CONGRESS.**

ISBN-13: 978-1-4328-8040-8 (hardcover alk. paper)

Published in 2020 by arrangement with G.P. Putnam's Sons, an imprint of Penguin Publishing Group, a division of Penguin Random House LLC.

Printed in Mexico
Print Number: 01     Print Year: 2020

# CAST OF CHARACTERS

**The Corporation**

**Juan Cabrillo** — Chairman of the Corporation and captain of the *Oregon*.

**Max Hanley** — President of the Corporation, Juan's second-in-command, and chief engineer of the *Oregon*.

**Linda Ross** — Vice President of Operations for the Corporation and U.S. Navy veteran.

**Eddie Seng** — Director of Shore Operations for the Corporation and former CIA agent.

**Eric Stone** — Chief helmsman on the *Oregon* and U.S. Navy veteran.

**Mark "Murph" Murphy** — Chief weapons officer on the *Oregon* and former U.S. military weapons designer.

**Franklin "Linc" Lincoln** — Corporation operative and former U.S. Navy SEAL.

**Marion MacDougal "MacD" Lawless** — Corporation operative and former U.S.

5

Army Ranger.

**Raven Malloy** — Corporation operative and former U.S. Army Military Police investigator.

**George "Gomez" Adams** — Helicopter pilot and drone operator on the *Oregon.*

**Hali Kasim** — Chief communications officer on the *Oregon.*

**Dr. Julia Huxley** — Chief medical officer on the *Oregon.*

**Kevin Nixon** — Chief of the *Oregon*'s Magic Shop.

**Maurice** — Chief steward on the *Oregon.*

**Strait of Malacca**

**Omar Jabal** — Captain of the oil tanker *Dahar.*

**Kersen** — Terrorist leader.

**Abdul Tanjung** — Terrorist.

**Melbourne, Australia**

**April Jin** — Former intelligence officer in the Royal Australian Navy.

**Angus Polk** — Former commando and Australian Department of Defence analyst.

**Lu Yang** — Former stepfather of April Jin.

**William Campbell** — Lu's attorney.

**Timor Sea**
**Sylvia Chang** — Scientist for the U.S. Defense Advanced Research Projects Agency.
**Roberta Jordan** — Cook.
**Lieutenant Commander Womack** — Executive officer of the *Ocean Protector*.

**Bali, Indonesia**
**Sinduk** — Terrorist leader.
**Oliver Muñoz** — Husband of Senator Maria Muñoz.
**Elena Muñoz** — Daughter of Senator Maria Muñoz.
**Emily Schmidt** — Wife of Senator Gunther Schmidt.
**Kyle Schmidt** — Son of Senator Gunther Schmidt.

**Australia**
**Leonard Thurman** — Doctor at Royal Darwin Hospital.
**Paul Wheatley** — Electrician.
**Harry Knoll** — Electrician.
**Sam Carter** — Royal Australian Air Force airman.
**Todd Wilson** — Royal Australian Air Force airman.
**Burt Gulman** — Nhulunbuy harbormaster.
**Sawyer** — American hunter.

**Bob Parsons** — U.S. Marine and hovercraft pilot.
**Renee Labelle** — Friend of Parsons'.
**Victor Ormond** — Archaeologist.

**Central Intelligence Agency**
**Langston Overholt IV** — The Corporation's CIA liaison.

**Ship Crews**
**Raymond Wilbanks** — Captain of the *Shepparton*.
**Gabriel Rathman** — Captain of the *Centaurus*.

**Ships**
*Salacia* — Roman bireme.
*Oregon* — The Corporation's flagship.
*Dahar* — Kuwaiti oil tanker.
*Namaka* — American research vessel.
*Empiric* — Australian research vessel.
*Ocean Protector* — Australian Defence Force vessel.
*Marauder* — Trimaran.
*Shepparton* — Australian cargo ship.
*Marsh Flyer* — Hovercraft transport.
*Centaurus* — Cargo ship.
*Thai Navigator* — Ore carrier.

# ONE

*Strait of Malacca*

Captain Omar Rahal tracked the small boat racing across the placid waters of the narrow strait. It was approaching his California-bound oil tanker from dead ahead, and far too quickly to be a fishing boat. He'd tried to raise them on the radio, but there was no response. It meant only one thing.

Pirates.

Using his binoculars, he could see that the boat was full of men armed with guns, but there was nothing he could do to avoid them. The *Dahar* was more than 300 meters long, and the strait between Malaysia and the Indonesian island of Sumatra was barely three kilometers across at its narrowest point. The ponderous ship would be impossible to turn around, and the speedboat would easily outmaneuver any attempt to ram it.

"Increase to full speed," he nevertheless

told the executive officer. "We're not going to make the *Dahar* an easy target." Such high velocity for a ship as big as theirs was risky in these tight confines, even with calm seas, but he couldn't let them hijack his ship without doing something.

As the XO ordered full power, Rahal activated the shipwide intercom. "Now hear this, men. We have hostiles off our bow. They are armed and mean to board us. Initiate emergency lockdowns and go to your action stations. Do not, I repeat, do not attempt to fight them." He didn't want any crew members to die on his watch.

The boat passed behind the bow of the *Dahar* so that Rahal could no longer see it. He went to the port bridge wing so he could watch for it over the side of the ship.

They came back into view, and he could now make out seven men clad in T-shirts and armed with automatic rifles. There had to be an eighth driving, hidden by the roof of the tiny wheelhouse. The boat circled around so it could match the tanker's speed. Rahal spied a man holding an extendable ladder.

He called to the XO. "Activate the SSAS alarm."

The XO flipped open a safety cover and pressed a large red button. The Ship Security Alert System was a silent alarm that contacted the ship's base of operations to inform them that a hijacking was in progress. It ensured that the hijackers would not be warned that help had been summoned.

A few seconds later, the bridge phone rang. Rahal picked it up.

"This is Captain Rahal on the *Dahar.*"

"Captain, this is operations headquarters. We are calling to verify that you have an emergency in progress."

"Affirmative. This is not a false alarm." Rahal recited the code sequence verifying his identity. "Seven or eight armed men are preparing to board us."

"Understood. We have your position and will contact the Malaysian Maritime Enforcement Agency and the Indonesian Sea and Coast Guard. Stay on the line as long as you can. Are there any ships in your vicinity that could render aid?"

"What do we have on our radar?" Rahal asked the XO.

The XO peered at the radar screen and shook his head in dismay. "The closest vessel looks to be a freighter thirty kilometers behind us."

"Even if we stop, it would take her two hours to get here," Rahal spoke into the phone. "What's my ETA on the Coast

11

Guard?"

"The MMEA is scrambling a helicopter in Johor, but the soonest they'll make it to you is ninety minutes. Stay calm and do not resist the hijackers. Help is on the way."

Rahal smirked at the XO. " 'Help is on the way,' he says."

"We're going to need it," the XO replied, pointing down at the deck.

The top of the ladder poked above the railing. Rahal dropped the phone and ran out to the bridge wing again. While some of the hijackers had their weapons trained on the railing in case anyone tried to push it away, others began climbing up, several of them carrying large backpacks in addition to their weapons. When seven of them were on deck, they ran toward the superstructure at the rear of the ship.

Rahal got back on the phone. "Headquarters, I have to hang up now. The hostiles are approaching the bridge."

"Good luck, Captain."

Rahal tried to calm himself for the sake of the rest of the bridge crew, but his insides felt like pudding. He hadn't been this shaken since the Iraqis invaded his native Kuwait when he was a teenager working on a fishing boat.

A few moments later, he heard feet pounding up the stairs.

"No sudden moves," Rahal said to his men.

The door was flung open, and three Southeast Asian men burst onto the bridge with their weapons at the ready.

"Don't shoot," Rahal said in English with his hands in the air. "We're unarmed."

A lean and wiry man with scarred flesh where his left ear should have been stepped forward with a menacing grin. He didn't have the rotted teeth of a drug-using robber. This man was a trained professional.

"You are Captain Rahal?" the man said in Indonesian-accented Arabic.

"Yes," Rahal replied in the same language, surprised that the man knew his name. "What do you want?"

"I want your ship. Now I have it."

"And my crew?"

One of the hijackers went to the controls and set the engines to full stop.

"If you and your crew behave, you will depart the ship with me, and we will ransom you. If no one pays, then we will kill you."

Rahal nodded. "We'll cooperate. And my company will pay your ransom."

"That's very good to hear," the scarred hijacker said. "Because if you give us any trouble, I'll leave all fifteen of you on board,

13

and you can go down with your ship when I blow it up in the strait."

# TWO

April Jin paced around her beat-up Ford as she waited in the parking lot of the Ravenhall Correctional Centre. Although the asphalt was already baking from the morning sun, there was no way she would set foot inside the prison doors again. She'd been coming here for three years now on weekly visits, and the sterile white walls inside reminded her of her own two-year stay at Dame Phyllis Frost Centre for women. Bile rose in her throat at the thought of ever walking back into the place.

The front doors of Ravenhall's main entrance finally opened, and she smiled when she saw Angus Polk strut out with a hardened look in his eyes. His erect posture and cropped hair hinted at his military background, marred only by the presence of a light beard. In his jeans and stretched T-shirt, he displayed a newfound bulk, thanks to his daily workouts in the yard, which had added definition to his tall frame. His face softened into a broad smile when he spotted his waiting wife.

Jin met her husband and melted into his arms. He lifted her from her feet as if she weighed nothing.

"You've lost weight," he said.

"Morning runs to stay in shape and light rations while dining alone."

Jin had a slim, slightly muscular figure. Her straight black hair was worn short, highlighting her lean face and dark, probing eyes.

After she gave Polk a long kiss, she said, "I can't believe they let you out."

"Free at last, thanks to my new favorite words — 'early release.' Apparently all that good behavior inside paid off." They put their arms around each other and walked toward the car. "Thanks for coming to meet me," he said. "I'll be glad to get home . . . wherever that is."

"You may not like our flat much better than your cell. It's the size of a birdhouse."

"As long as you are there, it will feel like a palace." They stopped as they approached the car. "Have you been managing all right?"

"The money's been tough, I won't lie. No

16

one wants to hire an ex-con who's sold out their government. I've found some freelance translation work, but it barely covers the bills."

"No support from our old patron?"

She shook her head. "Not a word."

"Some thanks. Well, I've got an old mate who left the service and started a small business. Maybe he'll give me some work until we sort things out." He patted the hood of the car. "Mind if I drive? I kind of missed it."

Before she could pass over the car keys, a limousine pulled into the lot and slowly cruised toward them.

"Now, that's how to depart the joint in style," Polk said.

To Jin's surprise, it stopped right in front of them. The chauffeur got out and opened the rear door for a man in a tailored pin-striped suit. An attorney for sure. Jin had seen enough in her life to spot one instantly.

He held out a card. "Mr. Polk and Ms. Jin, I'm William Campbell."

He didn't ask if that was who they were. He knew.

"What's this about?" Polk asked as he took the card.

"I represent the estate of Lu Yang. Would you please join me?" He gestured for them

17

to get in the limo.

"Did you say 'the estate' of Lu Yang?" Jin asked.

"Yes. I'm afraid he recently passed."

Jin and Polk looked at each other in surprise.

"I'm afraid I can't discuss any details here," Campbell said. "But I can assure you that this does not concern any of your criminal matters. In fact, I believe you will find the reason for our meeting most beneficial."

Jin looked at her battered truck, and Campbell said, "If you like, we can have your vehicle towed to a car lot for sale. When our business is concluded, you will no longer need it. Alternatively, you may drive to our offices on your own, but I think you will find the limousine more comfortable."

Jin and Polk looked around. Their past dealings with Lu Yang had always been highly secretive, and always through a third party. Sending a limo to pick them up, in front of a prison no less, was highly out of character. But then again, the man was now dead.

Jin and Polk climbed into the limo, settling into the luxurious leather seats across from Campbell.

As it drove off, Polk leaned over and asked his wife, "Did you know Lu Yang was ill?"

She shook her head. For ten years, her mother had been married to the Chinese tech mogul, though he didn't come into his extreme wealth until after they'd divorced. Jin's ex-stepfather had taken care of her mother, though, and supported Jin from afar, grooming her skills until he could put them to use for his benefit.

"When did he die?" Jin asked Campbell.

"He tragically passed away just a few days ago. More will be explained to you both when we reach Melbourne."

Jin glanced at Polk and saw a hopeful gaze in his eyes. He knew just as well as she did what that meant.

They were going to a reading of her stepfather's will.

It took thirty minutes to reach downtown Melbourne, where they stopped in front of one of its glistening towers. An elevator whisked them to the fiftieth floor. Campbell ushered them into a posh conference room, where they had an expansive view of the city skyline. He pushed a button, and wall panels folded back to reveal a huge TV.

"Please," Campbell said, indicating chairs along the mahogany conference table. A silver pitcher of ice water and some glasses

19

had been set out for them. He handed Jin a remote and a sealed envelope with her name on it. "Once I leave the room, just press play. You'll be asked for a code, which is contained in that envelope."

"You're not reading his will?" Polk asked.

"I'm afraid not. The video will explain everything."

He nodded and closed the door behind him as he left.

Polk turned to his wife and said, "What's going on here?"

"Let's find out." Jin opened the envelope and found a note card with nothing on it but a sixteen-digit number written by hand. She pressed PLAY on the remote and was prompted to enter the code.

When she did, an image of an elegant office came on the screen. At the center of the screen, seated at a desk, was Lu Yang. Jin felt her breath catch at seeing him, but she quickly saw that he was no longer the stern and strong disciplinarian she remembered.

Instead, his eyes were sunken, his hair was stringy, and the hands tented on the desk were skeletal.

"Hello, April," Lu said in English with a soft Shanghai accent, sending a jolt down her spine. "Mr. Polk, you must be there, too, as I'd required. We never met in person, but my name is Lu Yang. As you know by now, I am dead."

Jin reached for Polk's hand to steady herself.

"I realize the past few years have been difficult for you both, on account of a breach in security that was not of your doing. As you know, one of our operatives turned informant to the Australian Federal Police. He was eliminated before revealing the full extent of my operations in the country, but regrettably disclosed your respective data-gathering activities in the military's defense technology and intelligence arenas. Up till now, it has forced me to sever communications between us, for everyone's security. While you may have felt abandoned, that was not actually the case. Your defense attorneys were the best in the land, paid at my expense. And your respective early releases were no fluke. Let's just say that several members of the parole review board are sitting on thicker wallets today. But that is all in the past. Today, I need you, April. You and your husband are the only ones I can count on to carry out my last wishes."

"You're asking a lot, after what we've been through," Jin muttered.

"I realize you may be reluctant to do so," Lu said as if to answer her. "But you need me as much as I need you. Possibly more. Just five years ago, you were both models of your professions. Mr. Polk was a veteran of the Special Operations Command and a senior analyst in the Department of Defence. And April was Lieutenant Jin, an Intelligence Officer in the Royal Australian Navy, well on her way to attaining flag rank. You were both outstanding undercover operatives, acquiring the latest technological data for my company, and for China. But because those activities were exposed, you were stripped of your titles, fired from your jobs, and spent years in prison. This has left you destitute, with little, perhaps, except your fondness for each other. I intend to remedy that, but require a final request."

Lu began coughing and paused to take a sip of water, and Polk pointed irritably at the screen. "We know what happened. Are we just here to receive a lecture and another opportunity to get sold down the river?"

Jin put her hand up to quiet him. She wanted to see where this was going.

"Pardon me," Lu said, putting down the glass. "I have been diagnosed with pancreatic cancer, you see. I was well on my way to doing something truly epic with my life, but according to what the doctors are tell-

22

ing me, I have only a few weeks left. So I won't be able to carry out my vision. But you two can. You proved your loyalty during your criminal convictions by not revealing your ties to me. You also have the necessary talents to fulfill my objective. Mr. Polk, aside from your defense analytics, you were an accomplished commando leader, skilled at field tactics and leading men into battle. April, your naval experience gave you expertise in maritime weapons systems and counterintelligence. A perfect combination to make my operation a success."

Lu smiled. "Perhaps you are thinking, 'Why would I do anything more for my dying stepfather after what happened?' Well, let me give you two reasons. One, of course, is to help China take its rightful role as world leader by securing its military might. This you have both aided greatly with your past actions. The second is financial. Your lives and careers in Australia have been ruined. The government confiscated all your assets, including the hard-earned monies you earned from me. They even dissolved your military pensions, leaving you pariahs in your own country. You have few resources, and even fewer prospects ahead of you. But I can remedy your losses and allow you a future beyond your wildest dreams."

He winced as he lifted a case and placed it on the desk, opened it, and spun it around. It was piled to the brim with American one-hundred-dollar bills.

"This is one million U.S. dollars. I'm giving it to you, both for your past efforts and as an enticement. The lawyers will hand this case to you when you leave this room. You can take the case and run if you like, but we all know that a mere million dollars won't restore all that you have lost. I'm betting that it will only whet your appetite for what truly lies at the end of the rainbow."

Lu closed the case again, and Jin glanced at Polk. His eyes were glued to the screen.

"Because if you do as I request, using this case as seed money as well as additional resources I have provided for you to accomplish the task I have laid out, you will receive the rest of my fortune, valued at nine hundred and thirty-eight million U.S. dollars."

Jin gaped at her husband. They thought their lives were essentially over when they went to prison. Now they were getting a shot at more than they could ever imagine.

"The money is locked away in Croesus-Coin cryptocurrency. It will remain there until ten major newspapers from across the globe carry news articles confirming that you have completed your objective. I have designed a software program that scans the news websites and will release the lock on the cryptocurrency once the stories have been verified. To give you an incentive not to dawdle, I have provided a deadline. If you fail to complete the task by the appointed date, the account will be sealed forever. No one will ever get my money. It will simply vanish." He looked sternly into the camera. "As you know, I am not one to reward failure."

Lu smiled. "I suppose you may doubt whether my offer is legitimate."

Polk nodded. "The thought crossed my mind."

"The code you entered to start this video is also the account number. Look it up." He told her the login and password. "You may see the current balance, but you will not be able to access the funds in any way until the proper criteria are met."

With a trembling hand, Jin pushed Pause on the remote, freezing Lu's cadaverous gaze on them. She brought up the website for CroesusCoin on her phone and logged in. Just as Lu said, the balance was more than nine hundred million dollars. But the boxes for inputting wire transfer instructions were inaccessible, and there was a countdown timer.

It gave them just weeks before the account was locked permanently.

She showed the web page to Polk, who sat back in his chair to process what he'd seen. "I don't believe it."

"Believe it," Jin said. "My ex-stepfather wouldn't have gone to all this trouble for a prank. He was cruel, but never wasteful with his time. Whatever he's proposing, he's serious about it. He has no other heirs, so we are the logical recipients of his estate."

"But he's not just giving it to us. We have to earn it."

"Yes. But knowing how intelligent and precise he was, he will have planned his 'tasks' down to the last detail. As you can see, he has no shortage of resources to ensure its success."

Polk thought a moment. "I hate to say it, but he is correct. We're both nearing forty, our military careers are over, and we have no legitimate job prospects. We hitched our wagon to Lu Yang and lost everything; our Canberra home and our beach house on Bondi, our cars, even our investment account in Brunei that we thought was untouchable. Now that he's dead, we don't even have any contacts in China that could help us. A million dollars is a nice offering, but pales compared to a billion dollars."

"For this much money, he must be asking a lot. We have to assume it will involve great danger and risk." She squeezed his hand. "After waiting for you so long, I don't want anything to happen to us now."

Polk shrugged. "If we can trust him, we can pull off whatever he wants. And once we do, then we'll have all the protection money we'll ever need."

Jin nodded. "True."

"The question is, do you trust him?" Polk asked.

Jin thought a moment. "He's a harsh man, but he never deceived us, or my mother. And he's right about his ongoing support. We both should have served much longer prison sentences. I think we can believe what he says."

"We put our lives on the line for him in the past, for much less reward, and we're still standing. We know what's at risk, but we'll now have the resources to protect ourselves." Polk gazed at Jin with a confident air. "Let's see what he wants."

She pressed PLAY on the remote.

Lu Yang leaned toward the camera. "I'm glad you see it my way. Now, here's what I want you to do."

# THREE

Abdul Tanjung didn't want to wait on the boat while the others took control of the oil tanker, but he was the newest member of this cell of the terrorist group Indo Jihad, so he was left to ensure the boat was ready for their escape before security forces arrived. Now that the *Dahar* had come to a stop, there wasn't much for him to do but keep watch for any crew member who might attempt to escape by climbing down the ladder.

Tanjung had fought for the Islamic State in Syria and returned to Indonesia to help install a caliphate in his home country. With his connections in ISIS, it wasn't hard to find like-minded comrades in Jakarta. Their first mission appeared to be a complete success, and a second one planned for Bali would convince their enemies that the influence of the hated Americans was at an end in Southeast Asia.

28

Sinking a Kuwaiti oil tanker headed to the United States and causing a massive environmental catastrophe would strike fear into every government in the region. Encouraged by the tanker's sinking and the Bali operation, more jihadists would flock to their cause, and they would carry out even more headline grabbing attacks until the secular regimes were reduced to shambles.

Tanjung listened eagerly to the reports coming over the walkie-talkie and cheered at every small victory.

"We have all the crew accounted for," said Commander Kersen. "Bring them to the mess hall. Tanjung, what is your status?"

"Maintaining my position beside the ship. No activity out here."

"Good. We will lock the crew in the mess hall while we plant the bombs. When we're done, we'll bring them down to you."

"Yes, sir."

They had three bombs, which had to be placed carefully to sink a ship of this size, and they had to be detonated before the Coast Guard or defense forces could get there, presuming the *Dahar* had used the SSAS. Based on what they knew of response times from previous hijackings in the area, they had an hour to evacuate the ship and make a dash back to their shore base.

With the crew in custody, Tanjung could relax. He set down his assault rifle and sat on the deck to enjoy a well-deserved bag of klepons rice balls that his mother had made for him and his comrades. The sugary snack was covered in coconut shavings, and he brushed his fingers on his pants as he watched a cargo ship in the distance behind them.

Tanjung thought his eyes must be playing tricks on him because it appeared that the large freighter was racing toward them at an amazing speed. Every time he looked away and then back at the ship, it seemed closer.

He shrugged. It didn't really matter. A ship that size couldn't be doing more than twenty kilometers per hour. They would be long gone with the hostages before it got anywhere close to them. Not that a civilian cargo ship could threaten them anyway.

When he was done with his snack, he crumpled up the bag and tossed it overboard.

That's when his eye was drawn to something strange roiling the water. He rose and went to the gunwale.

The water bubbled from something rising up, almost as if a sea monster were emerging from the depths.

A long, flat object appeared next to his

boat, barely breaking the surface. It could have been a wayward piece of flotsam tossed overboard from one of the many cargo vessels that plied the strait.

Tanjung noticed that it wasn't entirely flat. Toward one end was a short cupola with windows. He was startled to see two eyes inside staring back at him. It was an older white man with ruddy cheeks and a fringe of reddish hair around a bald head.

For a moment, Tanjung wondered if someone had drugged his klepons. But his trance was shattered when a hatch flew open from the back of what he now understood to be a submersible that had come out of nowhere. A figure dressed in black and wearing a balaclava rose out of the opening like a demon and pointed a gun at him.

Tanjung turned to lunge for his assault rifle, but it was far too late. He heard a hiss and felt a needle plunge into his back. He tried to reach the dart to pull it out, but within a second his knees buckled, and he collapsed to the deck.

He didn't lose consciousness, but his head was fuzzy, and his mouth felt as though it were coated in cotton.

The man clad in black jumped over the gunwale and loomed above him like a giant. He bent down, plucked the dart out of

Tanjung's back, and turned him over.

The intruder tossed the assault rifle overboard before dropping to his knees, and Tanjung could see sharp blue eyes watching him intently. The man said something in English, which Tanjung didn't understand.

"No speak English," Tanjung heard himself reply, almost as if it came from someone else.

The man switched to Arabic, a dialect Tanjung recognized as Saudi.

"How many of you are on the *Dahar*?"

Tanjung tried to resist answering, but he felt compelled to tell what he knew.

"Seven."

"Don't bother trying to fight it," the intruder said. "The drug you were injected with not only disables you but it also acts like a kind of truth serum. Believe me, I've tried it myself. Now, what is your objective?"

"Bombs. Three of them. We're going to sink the tanker."

"And the crew. Are they still alive?"

"Yes. In the mess hall."

"Good. You're going to tell me where all the bombs are being planted."

The man yanked off his balaclava to reveal a blond crew cut and a handsome tanned face. He had intense, intelligent eyes, and

32

an innate authority about him that exuded confidence.

Even in his hazy mental state, Tanjung was surprised to see the man uncover himself.

"Who are you?" Tanjung asked, slurring the words as he spoke. For some reason, he felt the need to add, "I am Tanjung."

"My name is Juan Cabrillo, and I am about to put your terrorist friends out of business. Not that it really matters, I tell you." Cabrillo smiled like he was enjoying telling a secret he'd been keeping. "You see, the drug coursing through your veins also erases your memory. When you come to in about four hours with a splitting headache, you won't remember a thing about me."

# FOUR

Three people dressed in identical black clothes, body armor, eyeglasses, and balaclavas emerged from the submersible, leaving the driver behind, and joined Juan on the boat as he lashed the dazed terrorist's ankles and wrists with zip ties. Each of them had an MP5 submachine gun slung over their shoulders and dart guns in hip holsters. The only thing that distinguished them was that one was half a foot shorter than the other two.

"Looks like the sedative worked as advertised," the smallest of them said in a high-pitched, feminine voice.

Juan stood up and said, "With this stuff, I could make Colonel Sanders spill his secret recipes for both Original and Extra Crispy chicken. Tanjung here tells me there are seven hostiles on board armed with AK-47s. Use the darts only as long as we have the element of surprise." He checked his watch.

"I've got the bomb locations. Tanjung says we have about fifteen minutes left to deactivate the timers. He also mentioned that Kersen, the leader of their terrorist cell, has a remote detonator as a backup. Apparently, he didn't trust anyone else not to blow up the ship with him on it. You'll know him by his missing left ear."

Using his tongue, Juan clicked the molar mic embedded in his mouth. The transceiver not only allowed him to use his radio hands-free, it also played the sound inside his skull through bone conduction, which meant he could hear communications even in noisy environments.

"Is the deck clear?" He looked up, but the small gray quadcopter drone hovering above them was too high to be visible.

"No movement," came the reply.

"Anyone on the *Dahar*'s bridge?" It would be easy to spot Juan and his team coming over the railing if there were terrorists in that high perch.

"Maneuvering to get a better look." A pause. "It's empty."

Juan put on his balaclava and a pair of augmented reality glasses and fed in the bomb locations. They'd downloaded a detailed schematic of the tanker on their way to the ship so their glasses could guide

35

them through the corridors of its interior. In the corner of his eye, he could now see a deck by deck map of the *Dahar*'s layout.

"Let's go," Juan said.

He led the way up the terrorists' ladder. Juan felt it was his duty to be the first on the ship.

All of them were members of the Corporation, and Juan was its Chairman, an honorific many of his people used when addressing him. Technically, they were mercenaries, but Juan hated that term. Mercenaries hired themselves out to the highest bidders, no matter the cause or morals of their employers.

Instead, the Corporation was a company of private contractors made up of U.S. military veterans and former CIA operatives. They had an unusual set of skills and did work for the U.S. government when secrecy and plausible deniability were required. One such mission was a raid to sabotage a Syrian pharmaceutical complex producing sarin gas where they had acquired a limited batch of the tranquilizer serum they were now using. They also took jobs from friendly nations or non-government entities, but only if it served the interests of their home country.

Juan Cabrillo was not only the Chairman

of the Corporation but its heart and soul. A former CIA operative, he led the organization with fortitude and savvy, seemingly always one step ahead of his adversaries. He had helped assemble the top-notch crew around him and placed trust in every member of the Corporation to do their assigned job. In return, he was deeply respected and admired by all, most considering him a close friend.

The Corporation was unique in that it was based entirely on one ship, the *Oregon*. The new *Oregon*.

After the tragic loss of their previous ship, Juan and the rest of the crew had been eager to get back to sea to see what the new vessel could do. Their first voyage was meant to be a simple trial to test out her engines and a few of her other upgraded capabilities before returning to a Malaysian dry dock to finish prepping her for deployment. But intel about an imminent attack in the Strait of Malacca meant she had to set sail before she was fully outfitted. Now the *Oregon* was on her maiden cruise, and some of her crew weren't even on board yet.

The terrorists' plan was to plant the explosives and get off the ship with their hostages long before the authorities could arrive. But Indo Jihad didn't realize that their group had been penetrated by a mole from the Corporation, so they wouldn't be expecting anyone spoiling the party. Although Juan's team was outnumbered, their advantage was stealth and surprise.

When they all reached the oil tanker's deck, they split up into two pairs. Juan and Hali Kasim would take the engine room while the others would go to the bow.

The pair hustled to an access door set into the stern superstructure.

"How are you doing?" Juan asked as the two of them pressed themselves against the steel bulkhead.

Going on commando raids wasn't Hali's regular job on the *Oregon*. The Lebanese American was the ship's communications officer and had been responsible for catching the emergency alert sent out by the *Dahar*. Although the *Oregon* had a team of former special forces operatives who would normally take on a mission like this, they were all away on another job in Bali.

But everyone in the Corporation was trained for combat, and Hali had been on his fair share of dangerous operations in the past.

"Having a great time," Hali said. "That said, I'll be happy to be back in my nice comfy ops chair with a headset over my ears."

"Just follow me, and we'll be fine. Remember, don't take any chances."

Juan opened the door, and they found the nearest stairway. With the dart gun in his hand, Juan led Hali down, following the map displayed in his glasses.

When they reached the door to the engine room, Juan could feel the thrum through the steel. At least the terrorists hadn't shut the big diesels down when they brought the ship to a halt. The noise would help mask their approach.

Juan looked at Hali, who nodded in reply that he was good to go. Juan crouched and eased the door open. The sound of the loud turbines filled his ears.

The door was located on a catwalk overlooking the entire engine room, but the vast array of piping, ductwork, and machinery meant they weren't too exposed to anyone who might be below.

First, they crept to the control room, and Juan looked in the window. No one was inside.

Hali tapped his shoulder, and Juan turned to see two of the hijackers huddled over something they were attaching to the massive fuel line feeding the engines. Just as the terrorist on the boat had told them, the plan was to blow up the ship, igniting a raging inferno that would be seen for miles.

The hijackers twenty feet below them were so preoccupied with their task that they never looked up. Juan gave a signal to Hali that he would take the man on the right while Hali shot the one on the left.

They aimed through the catwalk railing. Juan fired. His dart hit the terrorist in the back of the neck. He turned at the same time that Hali's dart hit the other one in the back. Within three seconds, they both collapsed to the deck.

Edging around the catwalk, Juan and Hali scanned the rest of the engine room. No one else was there.

They went down the stairs to find the two terrorists huddled on the floor, mumbling to themselves. According to the man in the boat, there should have been two teams planting bombs in the engine room. He couldn't have been lying, so either he hadn't understood the plan or he hadn't been told the truth about it.

While Hali inspected the bomb, Juan spoke to the Indonesians.

"Where are your comrades?" he demanded in Arabic.

Both of them responded in a dialect of

40

Indonesian. Juan was fluent in Arabic, Spanish, and Russian, but Indonesian wasn't in his wheelhouse. He took out a small tablet computer loaded with translation software, chose Indonesian, and repeated his question.

The tablet spit out the audible translation. After a pause, the men responded, but the tablet flashed an error message.

*Language not recognized.*

He read it to Hali, who didn't look up from his examination of the bomb.

"Must be some unusual dialect that the computer can't interpret."

"Then we have a problem," Juan said. "Assuming there's a bomb at the bow, that still leaves one bomb missing." He checked his watch. "And now we have just ten minutes left to find it."

Hali stood. "I think we have a bigger problem."

"What's that?"

"I can't deactivate the bomb. It's a sophisticated design, and it's riveted shut, so cutting wires isn't an option. And if we start typing in random codes in an attempt to disarm it, that might set it off."

Juan bent over to look at the device. It was far more complicated than a typical pipe bomb, with a transparent polycarbon-

41

ate casing and a digital keypad. There was no countdown timer on it, just a set of blinking bars, like the battery-strength meter on a cell phone. There were currently four out of five bars left.

"Can we move it?"

"I'm no explosives expert, but I don't see any mercury switches. I think it's okay to move, but I'd like a second opinion."

"We'll get one soon. You stay here until we know we can move it. I'll start searching for the other bomb team." He took one last look at the device and saw it tick down to three blinking bars. "If it goes down to one bar, get out of here, and put the crew on the lifeboat."

Hali nodded as he warily eyed the bomb. "If you insist."

As Juan bounded up to the stairs to exit the engine room, he clicked his molar mic. "Linda, we've got a more complicated situation than we previously thought."

Nothing.

"Linda, do you copy?" he repeated.

The silence in Juan's ear was ominous, but he had to keep his mind on his task to find the third bomb. The team at the *Dahar*'s bow was three football fields away from him. If they were in trouble, there was nothing he could do to help them.

# FIVE

It wasn't that Linda Ross couldn't hear Juan. It was that she couldn't say a word. Even breathing might get her and Eric Stone killed.

The two of them were crouched in the shadow of a huge pipe, staring directly down the barrel of an AK-47. The terrorist with the gun didn't see them at the moment, but one move — one sound — and he'd realize someone was there and pull the trigger.

Linda was the Vice President of the Corporation and a Navy veteran. She'd seen more combat since joining the *Oregon* crew than during her entire time in the service, but she still didn't like having a gun pointed at her.

She was currently kneeling next to Eric beside the oil pumping unit closest to the bow. Neither of them had a clear shot at the man, whose attention had been drawn by the random clank of a metal chain behind them. A collection of pipes shielded his body, making a shot from one of their dart guns iffy at best.

The terrorist swept the area with his assault rifle, and when he was satisfied that he'd heard nothing unusual, he went back inside the shed to his comrade planting the bomb on one of the main release valves.

Linda finally drew a breath. "That was close," she said to Eric in a quiet voice that was high pitched but still radiated authority. She tapped her balaclava. "It's good I have this on."

Linda was known for regularly changing the color of her hair to suit her mood. Right now, it was styled in a pixie cut dyed a bright green that would have surely been seen by the terrorist if she hadn't been wearing the head covering.

"I intend to write a strongly worded letter to the *Dahar*'s captain telling him to make sure his crew locks down their equipment properly in the future," Eric said.

Eric had also been a U.S. Navy officer and was now the *Oregon*'s helmsman. Usually, he was dressed in a button-down shirt and khakis, not combat gear. He and his best friend, Mark Murphy, were the smartest people on the crew, so they were normally tasked with figuring out technical solutions to problems that the *Oregon* faced rather than taking down armed terrorists.

Like Linda, however, he had seen his fair share of fighting over his years with the Corporation, and the Chairman had made sure to keep all their operational and weapons training current while they finished constructing their new ship. She was glad to have Eric with her, not only for his expertise on the analysis of the bombs but also because he had strong tactical instincts.

Now they just had to plan how to approach the terrorists without being seen.

The pumping units were housed in a small shack that protected the valves from the elements. Pipes snaked from the structure in all directions to the massive oil tanks beneath their feet. A bomb going off in there would rupture a dozen pipes, igniting the oil feeding them and providing oxygen to the fuel vapor in the tanks that could cause a giant fireball to erupt. The blaze would be visible from the coasts of Malaysia on one side and Indonesia on the other.

"I'm too short to climb over those pipes," Linda said.

"I could give you a boost," Eric said. He wasn't a big guy, but Linda was tiny, so she had no doubt he could do it.

45

"Too exposed," she said.

"Going around will take too long."

"Then we go under." She pointed to a gap between the pipes and the deck. It was a narrow space, but they could belly-crawl through.

Juan's voice came over the line again. "Linda, do you copy? We've taken down two hijackers so far. That leaves five more."

Linda clicked her molar mic. "I read you, Chairman. We've got two hostiles here. About to make our move."

"Good hunting," he replied. They didn't say "Good luck" on the *Oregon*. Depending on luck was a fool's game. Although it didn't hurt to have some good fortune in a pinch, Juan preached that preparation, training, teamwork, and skill were far more important to a successful mission.

"We'll let you know when we've got the bomb in hand, Chairman," Linda said.

"Copy that."

She and Eric went to where the gap beneath the pipes was widest. Eric went first while Linda did her best to cover him with her MP5 submachine gun between the spaces in the pipes. The valve shed was ten yards away, and she wasn't going to risk a dart shot through such a narrow opening.

When he had squirmed through, he ran

46

over and crouched beside the shack.

Linda put the MP5 on her shoulder and got onto her belly, squeezing herself through. The distinctive smell of oil and grease filled her nose.

She was almost out from underneath when she saw one of the terrorists round the corner of the shed behind Eric. He was so surprised at finding someone there that he didn't shoot, which was the only thing that saved Eric's life.

Eric turned when he heard the footsteps and raised his MP5 to fire, but the terrorist knocked it from his hands with the butt of his AK-47. Eric didn't let him bring the assault rifle to bear. He launched himself at the terrorist and tackled him to the ground, and they began to wrestle for control of the weapon.

Linda wasn't out from under the pipes yet and couldn't reach her submachine gun. Instead, she drew the dart gun from her holster, but Eric and the terrorist rolled back and forth, keeping her from getting a clean shot.

At that moment, the second terrorist came around the shed from the other direction. He must have heard the commotion and simply came to see what it was, leaving his own AK-47 behind.

Still lying down, Linda snapped off a shot with the dart gun, but the angle was odd, and her dart hit the terrorist right in the leather belt he was wearing.

The man heard the sound but didn't realize he'd been hit. Then he saw Linda scrabbling out from beneath the pipes and sprinted toward her. She leaped to her feet just as he arrived and pinned her against the pipes.

He chopped the dart gun from her hand and pressed his forearm against her throat, cutting off her air. His hot breath on her face reeked of tobacco and curry. Linda tried to push his arm away, but the wiry man was too strong for her. It was only a matter of time before she lost consciousness.

She let go of his arm and ran her hand down his torso until she reached the belt. She grabbed the dart still jutting from the leather and yanked it out. With her vision tunneling, she jabbed the dart into the terrorist's neck.

His eyes went wide with shock, and he pulled out the dart, but it was too late. The injection directly into the artery made the effect of the drug nearly instantaneous. He sank to his knees and keeled over.

Linda took a huge breath and looked over

to see that the terrorist Eric had been fighting somehow had rolled away from him and next to the MP5. He picked up the submachine gun and was about to fire when Linda snatched the dart gun from the deck and shot him in the back.

The terrorist whirled around and tried to grab at whatever had stung him. He stared at Linda in surprise, and then his eyes rolled white as he went down in a heap.

Linda went over to Eric and held out her hand to help him up. Eric was rubbing the back of his head.

"Are you okay?" she asked.

"He got me good with the butt of the AK, but I'll be all right." Eric looked around and saw the two terrorists lying on the deck. "Looks like you got them both. Nice shots."

She grinned at him. "Didn't you know Annie Oakley was my great-grandmother?"

"I almost believe that."

"Come on. Let's take a look at that bomb."

They went into the shed and found the bomb situated directly under the main valve unit that the mass of pipes fed into. Linda shined her flashlight while Eric inspected it. There was an indicator with two bars blinking.

Linda clicked on her mic. "Chairman, our

hostiles are down, and the bomb is right in front of us."

"Good work. What's the word on the bombs? Can we move them?"

Eric, who could hear Juan as well, nodded. "That's affirmative, Chairman. I don't see any circuits or accelerometers that would be motion activated."

"Did you hear that, Hali?" Juan said.

"Copy that," Hali replied. "I'll come up with it now. Are we dumping them overboard?"

"I don't advise that," Eric said, picking up the bomb and putting it back in the sack that the terrorist had carried.

"Why not?" Juan asked.

"It may short-circuit as soon as it hits the water, which could put a nice big hole in the ship. The *Dahar* might not sink, but she could spill thousands of gallons of oil before it was brought under control."

"Might not sink?" Linda asked.

Eric shrugged.

"Is Eric shrugging?" Juan asked.

"Yes, he is."

"Then we need to find that third bomb and get all three of them as far away from us as possible before they explode."

# Six

Max Hanley, the driver of the *Oregon*'s submersible, grunted as he climbed out of the rear hatch. His youth serving on a Swift Boat in Vietnam's Mekong Delta was long behind him, and exercise wasn't really his thing, as evidenced by the generous paunch that Doc Huxley was always trying in vain to get him to reduce. Still, Max thought he was reasonably fit for a man his age, and his role as the Corporation's President and the *Oregon*'s chief engineer kept him busy.

The humidity caused sweat to bead on his brow now that he was no longer in the air-conditioned comfort of the *Gator.* The submersible was one of two on the *Oregon.* While the larger sub, *Nomad,* was built for deep dives, with an airlock and room for eight divers in full gear, the *Gator* was designed for speed and stealth. It was powered by a potent diesel engine for cruising fast on top of the water and by battery packs for operating below the surface to sneak up on ships, as they had done with the terrorists.

Max had been listening in on the comm link and heard that the third bomb had still not been found.

"Sounds like you're getting nothing out of the others, Juan," Max said over his molar mic as he tied the *Gator* to the terrorists' boat. "Maybe our friend Tanjung here can give us some more info."

"Tell me you're armed, Max."

"You worried about the old man?" Max joked. He and Juan were best friends, and together they had created the Corporation, not to mention designing and constructing both the old and the new *Oregon.*

"I do hear a lot of grunting. You sound like a grandfather hoisting himself out of his favorite easy chair."

Max made sure not to make any more noise as he heaved himself over the boat's gunwale.

"Don't worry. I've got a dart gun with me in case it seems like he's starting to come out of it. And if I'd wanted cracks about the sounds I make, I'd give one of my ex-wives a call. Now, are you going to help me translate or what?"

Max went over to Tanjung, who was dozing, and nudged him with a foot until he stirred. Max had a handheld radio that was tied into the comm system and held it up to Tanjung's face.

"Go ahead, Juan."

Juan spoke in Arabic, and for a moment it seemed like the young terrorist wouldn't respond. Finally, he spoke as if he'd chugged a fifth of whiskey.

"What did he say?" Max asked.

"He's convinced that what he originally told me is correct," Juan said.

"He seems like a newbie hired to drive the boat. Maybe he's out of the loop."

"Could be."

Before they could try another question, a different voice cut in. It was Gomez Adams, the *Oregon*'s expert helicopter and drone pilot and a veteran of the 160th Special Operations Aviation Regiment, the U.S. Army unit known as the "Nightstalkers," responsible for carrying Special Forces operators into combat. He was back on the *Oregon* providing them an eye in the sky.

"Oh, man, where did *they* come from?" His voice sounded both puzzled and angry, which was a bit concerning coming from someone as experienced as he was.

"What is it, Gomez?" Juan asked.

"I've got two guys on the deck walking

53

toward the ladder down to the boat. They'll be able to see over the side in less than ten seconds. Max, get under cover now."

Max may have been fit for his age, but getting back inside the *Gator* that quickly wasn't going to happen. His only choice was to duck into the boat's tiny wheelhouse.

He retreated under its roof and heard voices above him. The terrorists obviously thought they still had the ship to themselves because they didn't care how loud they were.

Then they fell silent.

"They're looking over the side of the ship," Gomez said. "They see the *Gator* and the man down."

"Where are you, Juan?" Max whispered.

"On my way up to you from the pump room," Juan answered. Max could hear him breathing hard as he ran up the stairs.

"Now they've got their weapons out, and one is climbing down the ladder," Gomez narrated.

"Great," Max muttered, pulling the dart gun from his waistband. What he hadn't told Juan was that the weapon had just one dart in it.

"Tanjung," the man coming down called out softly. "Tanjung."

The last thing Max wanted was for the

terrorist to spray the boat with assault rifle fire. The second-to-last thing he wanted was for the man to take a pot shot at the *Gator* and put holes in it.

"Gomez," Max said. "I could use a distraction."

"One distraction, coming down," Gomez said.

A couple of seconds later, Max heard a sound like an angry hornet approaching. The whine of the quadcopter's propellers was intended to be confusing to the terrorist, which was exactly what Max needed.

The drone whizzed by, which was followed by a surprised yelp.

"I think I've got his attention," Gomez said.

Max peeked out and saw the terrorist twenty feet above him holding out his AK-47 to try to get a bead on the flying menace. Max aimed the dart gun and fired. The dart hit the terrorist in the backside, causing him to swat at what he might have thought was a hornet's stinger. A moment later, his grasp on the ladder loosened, and he let go of the rung, falling the two stories onto the boat's deck.

Knowing that the man at the railing wouldn't take long to react to the strange events, Max scrambled over to the fallen man and picked up the AK-47. He pointed it up in time to see the terrorist above him swoon and fall back from the railing.

Juan peered over the side and smiled at Max.

"I see you've been making yourself useful," he said.

"All in a day's work," Max replied.

"That's seven of eight. One more hijacker unaccounted for. It must be Kersen. And he has the detonator."

Juan disappeared. Max heard him talking in Arabic to the man he had felled.

After a pause, Juan said, "He doesn't know where Kersen is, but he says the last bomb is inside the main pumping junction not far from here. They must have already been inside when we came on board."

"Not to be a nervous Nellie," Hali said, "but my bomb just ticked down to one blinking bar."

"Ours, too," Eric said. "Based on the time since the previous bar disappeared, I'd say we've got three minutes left before they blow."

# SEVEN

Hali dashed out of the *Dahar*'s superstructure with a duffel bag in hand and stopped in front of Juan out of breath.

"Where should I put this?" Hali asked.

Before Juan could answer, Gomez called out, "Movement on the bridge wing."

Juan looked up to see the final terrorist gaping at them from above. The mangled skin on the left side of his head identified him as Kersen, the leader of the terrorists.

The one with the detonator.

The distance was too far to use the dart gun. Juan snatched the submachine gun from his shoulder at the same time that Kersen fired his AK-47. Juan rolled across the deck, the bullets ricocheting behind him, and popped up to his knees to take aim, but the terrorist was already gone.

"He's left the bridge," Gomez said.

Juan sprinted toward the superstructure. "I'll bet he's heading for the free-fall lifeboat. As soon as he's at a safe distance, he'll blow the bombs with the remote detonator." If Kersen had been planning a suicide mission, he would have blown them already. "Hali, find the last bomb in the pumping junction and make sure all three get off the ship."

"Aye, Chairman."

Juan flung the door open and ran inside to the stairs, the emergency arrows pointing the way to the lifeboat station on the stern of the ship.

He burst through the exterior door and emerged onto the gantry in time to see Kersen jump into the orange lifeboat and yank the hatch shut behind him.

Juan stopped to aim his submachine gun, but the lifeboat was already sliding down the rails by the time he got any shots off. The bullets hit the polycarbonate windows but did nothing more than crack them. Kersen stared at him with dead eyes and then went out of view as the lifeboat dropped into the water.

Juan went to the railing and saw the bullet-shaped boat surface after its brief plunge and begin motoring away. A short distance away was a derelict freighter hugging the shoreline of an Indonesian island. Kersen had no time to wonder where the ship had come from.

Juan keyed his molar mic. "*Oregon,* you are weapons-free. Destroy that lifeboat."

"Weapons-free, aye," came the reply.

A round housing slid down from the top of the ship's forward mast, revealing a nasty-looking two-barreled Gatling gun called a Kashtan combat module. The Russian weapon's dual rotary cannons could fire 30mm explosive tungsten-tipped ammunition at a rate of ten thousand rounds per minute.

The twin Kashtan guns spun to life and swung around to aim at the lifeboat. Bright tracers lanced from them as the weapon system unleashed a torrent of fire, piercing the air with the sound of a giant buzz saw. The lifeboat was chewed to pieces, along with Kersen and the detonator. Within a second, it was nothing more than a burning hulk.

"All clear, *Oregon,*" Juan said, a jolt shooting down his spine as he saw his ship on the high seas for the first time.

Juan gazed at the tired vessel, knowing it was covered with a special metamaterial camouflage paint. Even though he knew what was coming, Juan was still in awe as an electrical charge was applied to the *Oregon*'s skin so it would change color. He watched as the rusty vessel changed appearance into a sparkling deep blue cargo ship with a white superstructure and black smokestack on the stern. She was less than a mile away off the *Dahar*'s starboard stern.

Juan had never viewed the new and improved *Oregon* from a distance because she had been boxed up in a covered dry dock during construction. He'd been waiting a long time for this moment, and he swelled with pride now that he could take her in from bow to stern.

The 590-foot-long break bulk ship, designed to carry any kind of cargo in containers, boxes, crates, or barrels, was equipped with four cranes on the deck. Each of the two pairs of cranes had their booms turned toward the opposite tower and secured together to form the crossbar of an H. The Kashtan gun was situated on top of the forward crane's tower. A sleeve rose back up to conceal it. No one seeing the ship would ever know that the Gatling gun was one of the many surprises hidden behind the ordinary-looking façade.

An object the size of a dishwasher took off from her deck amidships. It shot into the air and flew toward the *Dahar*. It was the *Oregon*'s cargo air drone, an octocopter that could lift up to one hundred pounds with its retractable claw.

Juan wrested his eyes away from the ship and headed back to the bridge.

"Status, Hali," Juan said.

"Gomez has the CAD on the way. All three bombs are ready for pickup. One minute left on the timers."

Juan reached the bridge at the same time the CAD swooped over the *Dahar*. The drone came to a stop over the bow, and Juan watched as it descended until Linda could latch her duffel onto the vehicle's claw.

As soon as it was secure, the octocopter leaped into the air and flew to Hali's position.

The drone hovered over Hali just a few yards from Juan, its blades wailing like banshees. Hali hooked up his duffel to the claw and backed away.

"Go, go, go," Hali yelled.

"I'm out of there," Gomez answered.

The CAD shot into the sky and out over the water away from both the *Oregon* and the *Dahar*.

Juan watched it fly toward the horizon and silently counted down in his head. Finally, Gomez said, "A thousand yards out."

"That's good enough," Juan said. "Get rid of them."

"Bombs away."

61

A speck dropped from the CAD, which sped off. As the package hit the sea, a bright flash erupted, throwing a huge geyser of water into the air. Three seconds later came a thunderclap that rattled the ship.

Juan had lost sight of the drone. "Did the CAD escape the blast?" he asked.

"All systems functioning perfectly," Gomez said. "Flying back as we speak."

Juan breathed a sigh of relief. After losing so much in South America during their last operation, he was glad to get out of this mission without casualties or destroyed equipment.

He went out onto the bridge wing and looked down to the *Gator*. Hali was already climbing back inside. Juan turned toward the bow and waved at Linda and Eric seven hundred feet away.

"Linda, are your hostiles secure?"

"They won't be going anywhere until someone unties them," Linda replied. "And we've retrieved the darts."

"Good. Then you and Eric get back to the *Gator*."

"On our way."

Juan wished he could collect all the terrorists in one place, but dragging them around a ship this size while sedated would be a chore, especially with the Malaysian

Maritime Enforcement Agency forces arriving by helicopter in the next thirty minutes. Besides, they had to erase all the video from the closed-circuit cameras before they left. Newer ships like this one had them all over the place.

"Tick-tock," Max said. "I don't want to answer awkward questions about what we're doing here in black clothes looking like the bad guys."

"You make a fine point," Juan said as he went back into the bridge to wipe any video recordings of their visit. "But we can't leave the crew locked up. On my way out, I'll pass by the mess and set a cutter on the locking mechanism. We'll activate it when we leave. Nice work, everybody. When we get back to the *Oregon*, margaritas are on me."

That brought a round of cheers.

"Let's keep the carousing to a minimum," Max said. "We have to be in Bali in two days, and we've got a lot of work to do tomorrow to get ready for the operation."

"You heard Commander Killjoy," Juan joked. "Only one drink apiece."

Now it was mocking groans.

"I didn't say what size the glass had to be."

More cheers. Juan didn't care how much it would hurt tomorrow. Tonight called for a celebration.

The *Oregon* was officially back in business.

When Captain Rahal and his crew heard the explosion outside, they knew it hadn't occurred on the ship. Too far away. Most of them thought that meant the helicopter coming to rescue them had been shot down, which didn't help morale. The preceding sound of a massive piece of equipment like a buzz saw only added to the confusion.

Fifteen minutes after the explosion, the locked handle on the door to the mess hall began to smoke. They backed away and were surprised when the door suddenly sprang open.

Rahal peered out into the corridor and found it vacant. He crept out. No one stopped him.

The XO was the next one out, and he stared at the scorched door lock in astonishment. "What do you think happened?"

Rahal inspected the melted metal lying on the floor. "I have no idea. Come with me. The rest of you stay here until we know what's going on."

Rahal and the XO made their way up to the bridge, tensing at every corner in fear that they might run into the terrorists.

But when they got to the bridge, it was completely empty.

The XO did a quick systems check. "All operations nominal. Engines, pumps, and cargo are intact, and everything's functioning normally."

"Where did they all go?" Rahal wondered out loud. "Is their boat gone?"

The XO went outside to the flying bridge and pointed down. "Captain, look."

Rahal joined him and saw a terrorist lying on the deck and two more in the hijackers' boat, all of them tied and motionless.

They went back inside and checked the shipboard cameras. Two more men were lashed to a pipe at the bow, and two were prone with their wrists tied to a railing in the engine room. The lifeboat had been launched. The remains of its shattered hull floated behind the ship.

"Was that the explosion we heard?" the XO asked.

Before Rahal could hazard a guess, he heard a call come over the radio in American English.

"*Dahar,* this is the *Norego* off your starboard stern. We've been alerted that you may be under attack by hijackers. Can we render any assistance?"

Rahal turned and was surprised to see a

65

ship just a mile away. It was a break bulk freighter a little more than half the size of the *Dahar.*

"*Norego,* we read you. Where did you come from? Our radar had you thirty kilometers behind us less than an hour ago."

"Must have been a faulty reading. We were only ten klicks behind when you stopped. Are you and your crew okay? We saw your lifeboat launch and then explode, and we've detected an inbound Malaysian security forces helicopter."

Rahal, still stunned by the fortunate turn of events, said, "We were attacked by hijackers, but they've all been subdued."

"That's great news. I'm sure your company and the Malaysian authorities will be impressed by your response to the emergency."

Rahal exchanged a look with the XO. They both knew that credit for saving their ship from certain destruction would earn them a hefty bonus.

"Yes, I'm sure they will be happy that the hijackers were stopped," Rahal answered.

"Well, you have a good day. Be careful out there."

"You, too."

Rahal replaced the handset and watched the cargo carrier with a puzzled look as it

66

passed by. He didn't know how this miracle could have happened, but he couldn't shake the sensation that they'd been saved by a guardian angel.

# EIGHT

*The Timor Sea*

Standing on the highest deck of the U.S.
research ship *Namaka,* Sylvia Chang
shielded her eyes from the midmorning sun
to focus on the sea-based drone that looked
like an unmanned Jet Ski. It was approaching her 300-foot-long ship from the east,
where the similarly sized Australian research
vessel *Empiric* idled a mile away, ready to
record the data that would decide if her
brainchild was a success or a failure.

Sylvia gripped the railing so tightly her
hand was going numb, and she struggled to
control her breathing. Since she was the
chief physicist on the project, her career was
riding on the experiment's outcome. This
test would prove whether a plasma shield
worked on the open ocean.

Ever since the USS *Cole* was nearly sunk
in a Yemen harbor by suicide bombers in a
small boat, the U.S. Navy had been search-

ing for a way to protect its ships from small-craft attacks. Once the technology was perfected, it could also be used by civilian vessels to ward off hijacking attempts. The report of a foiled attack on the tanker *Dahar* just two days ago in the Strait of Malacca only reinforced for Sylvia that her creation — code-named Rhino for the animal's protective hide — was urgently needed.

In principle, the idea was fairly simple. Rhino used lasers to project a dense shield of tiny plasma explosions, each equivalent to the power of a firecracker, in front of an approaching vessel or drone. Vessels would have to turn back so their crews would not be burned, and drones would be disabled because their electronics would fry.

At least that was the theory.

The tests on dry land had achieved the benchmarks required, but the most important test was on a ship at sea where the environment was less controlled. If she could show that Rhino worked in a real world situation, the Defense Advanced Research Projects Agency would fund her project for the next five years. If not, she'd risk being washed up before she was thirty.

Because the Defence Science and Technology Agency, DSTA, Australia's DARPA analogue, had technical expertise on important elements of the design, Sylvia joined forces with them on the project. They had suggested conducting the test in the open ocean two hundred miles west of Darwin, far away from all the main shipping lanes. The isolated location south of Indonesia meant they could do the experiments out of view of prying eyes.

She shifted her gaze to the *Empiric,* plucked the radio from her hip, and pressed the TALK button. "Mark, are you ready over there?"

"Does Crocodile Dundee carry a knife?"

Sylvia rolled her eyes, imagining Mark Murphy as she'd last seen him this morning: lounging in his chair at a computer terminal, drinking a Red Bull, and wearing a black T-shirt that read "And yet, despite the look on my face, you're still talking."

"I'm sure the Australians over there are loving your sense of humor," she said.

"That's what they're all saying. 'Murph may be a whinging yobbo, but he's no drongo.' I haven't looked those words up yet, but I can only guess that it's a compliment."

With multiple Ph.D.s, Murph was by far the most brilliant man on the *Empiric* even though he was also just in his twenties, so she had no doubt he knew that the phrase

70

meant he was whiny and obnoxious but no dummy. She was also sure that nobody over there had said any such thing.

Murph was on loan to DARPA from his real job. No matter how much she pried, she couldn't get much out of him about what that real job was, but his prior expertise had been designing weapons for the U.S. military. She'd requested him specifically for this project because his creative and analytical skills were unparalleled. To consult on the job, Murph had required only one condition, that DARPA supply key technology for the organization that he worked for. After some haggling, he joined the Rhino project, and his presence had proved invaluable.

"Let's get started with the test," Sylvia said.

"You're the boss," Murph said.

She turned to her research assistant, Kelly, and said, "Fire up the lasers."

Kelly called on her own radio, then replied, "Lasers are prepped, and the automated sensors are activated."

"Good." She called back to Murph. "Send in the drone."

"It's on the way." The drone, which had been making lazy circles, suddenly bolted toward them. "Don't worry, Sylvia. I've checked your math. This will work."

"Thanks, Mark. You're a sweetie."

"Hey, you'll ruin my reputation as a yobbo."

"Sorry."

This was the moment of truth. Sylvia's heart was hammering in her chest. She lifted the tablet hanging from her shoulder and saw that all the readouts from the Rhino equipment were normal. There was nothing else for her to do. All she could do was wait and watch.

When the drone was within three hundred yards, she heard the hum of the lasers charging in anticipation of a nearby threat. When the drone reached the two-hundred-yard mark, the lasers crackled to life.

She'd seen the Rhino in action before, of course, but to see it live always took her breath away. The air surrounding the drone lit up in thousands of tiny bubbles of prismatic fire, refracting the sunlight in a dazzling array of colors.

As the drone charged through the plasma shield, it shut down instantaneously and coasted to a stop a hundred yards away, slightly charred from the exposure to the intense temperatures. If it had been packed with explosives for an attack, the detonation would cause little or no damage to the ship from that distance.

"Sylvia," Murph called over the radio, "you rocked it. The feedback we got from the drone before the electronics died was exactly what we were expecting. If anyone had been on board the drone, they would have felt cooked and turned around pronto."

Kelly pumped her fist into the air and gave Sylvia a big hug.

Sylvia thumbed the TALK button at the same time she broadcast on the *Namaka*'s intercom. "Well done, people. We've made a huge breakthrough. I'm so proud of all the hard work you've done, and I thank you. Now let's bring the drone in and set up for the next run."

The *Namaka* turned and eased toward the drone to recover it.

Kelly got a call on her radio and said, "Sylvia, we may have to wait for the next test."

"Why's that?"

"We've got an unknown ship passing by."

"Out here?"

Kelly pointed north at a ship two miles away. Sylvia took out her binoculars, expecting a passing freighter or cruise liner.

Instead, it was an odd-looking vessel with three hulls. A trimaran slightly smaller than the *Namaka*. And it was heading in their direction at a high rate of speed.

"Who are they?"

"The captain says they won't answer his hails," Kelly said.

The trimaran abruptly turned and slowed, practically idling where it was.

"That's odd," Sylvia said. "What are they doing now?"

Kelly shrugged. "Maybe it's a billionaire's yacht. Those guys are weird."

A bright red flash from the ship's midsection caught Sylvia's attention. It looked like the muzzle blast of a gun. The *Namaka* was hit by a searing hot blast that tore through the bridge, setting it on fire. It couldn't have been a gun. No shell could have struck them that quickly from two miles away.

Sylvia was a scientist, but panic shoved aside any logical analysis.

"We need to get off the ship now," she called to Kelly, who was gripped by her own terror and ignored her boss. She ran to the nearest door and disappeared into the seeming safety of the ship's interior.

At that moment, the trimaran fired another volley.

Sylvia ducked her head as the burst from the unknown weapon made an impact right next to her and blew apart the door that Kelly had just entered.

The force of the explosion tossed Sylvia over the railing. The last thought that went through her mind before she plunged into the water was that her clothes were on fire.

# NINE

*Bali, Indonesia*

Raven Malloy couldn't see out of the van's windowless cargo area, but given how long they'd been on the road, she knew the terrorists from Indo Jihad were not going to the Denpasar conference center where the South Asia summit was being held. Despite her infiltration of the group, she hadn't discovered what the real target of their attack would be that day.

Indo Jihad operated in cells, which meant she had met only the five men in the van, but she knew there were more members of the group. Even if her cell was stopped, the attack would still go on. Her mission was to find out those plans.

"I thought we were going to kill infidels," she said in fluent Arabic as she pointedly cast her eyes around the van's interior. The sole object with them was a backpack, and when she'd placed her hand on it while getting in, she'd felt only soft clothes. They had no weapons.

"We are," said the terrorist leader Sinduk, who went by just his given name.

"But not at the economic summit?" Despite the heat, she had dressed in an expensive pantsuit and a headscarf as she'd been told to so she wouldn't seem out of place at the formal event. All the men in the van wore suits.

"That's where they think we will attack, which is exactly why I have chosen a more suitable target."

"Which is?"

Instead of answering, Sinduk paused as he peered at her. Finally, he said, "What do you think happened to our brothers who were caught hijacking the *Dahar*?"

Raven didn't hesitate to answer. "How should I know?"

However, she knew exactly what happened. Raven was the one who had warned the *Oregon* about the impending assault. In her dealings with the group, she'd come across a single cryptic text message on a phone that mentioned the *Dahar* and Malacca. The *Oregon* had been able to set sail and intercept the tanker barely in time to foil the attack.

"I think someone new to our group was

77

either careless or was spying on us," Sinduk said.

The two men on either side of him stared at her, stone-faced.

"And you think it's me?" Raven replied.

"No, not at all. In fact, we believe it was the boat driver. A man named Tanjung. We've since learned that his credentials claiming that he fought for ISIS in Syria were falsified."

That was fake information planted by the CIA after the hijackers were apprehended. The intent was to cast blame on someone besides Raven, and it should have worked. Before joining the Corporation, she had been a U.S. Army Military Police investigator and then an executive protection specialist. As a Native American, her reddish brown complexion and jet-black hair had regularly caused her to be mistaken for an East Indian, Arab, or Latina, allowing her to take on many different roles during missions. For this operation, her backstory was as a jihadist originally from Saudi Arabia now living in Jakarta. Her credentials were airtight.

Nonetheless, Sinduk seemed skeptical about her.

"You still suspect me?" Raven asked. "Even after all the money I've secured for the cause?"

"I'm a careful man."

Raven tensed, ready to fight if she had to. It would take time for the rest of her team to extricate her in an emergency.

"We're two cars behind you," came a honey-thickened Louisiana drawl in her ear. It was Marion MacDougal "MacD" Lawless, who'd been listening to her through the molar mic. "Be aware traffic back into the capital is moving slower than a Mardi Gras parade. If this is a fake-out, it'll take us an hour to get back to the conference center."

"So why bring me along?" Raven asked Sinduk.

"Because I want you to prove yourself. You need to show me that you're really invested in our cause."

"How?"

It couldn't be a suicide bombing. She would have felt a bomb in the backpack.

"The Americans sent two Senators to the summit. Certainly, those are the kind of highly priced targets that would get attention in the United States."

"But we're nowhere near the conference center," Raven said.

"The security around Denpasar is impenetrable. We wouldn't get within a half mile

79

of the conference hotel before we were stopped."

"But you want the attack to happen while they're here."

"It has to happen while they're here. The Americans are arrogant. They think they are invulnerable. But we will show them that they are not safe anywhere."

Sinduk picked up the backpack and unzipped it. He pulled out some clothes and tossed them to Raven.

"You'll wear that," he said.

She held up two small pieces of cloth. It was a blue and green bikini.

"You must be joking," she said.

"You're tall, but it should fit. You have to blend in with the tourists. Don't worry, I have a sarong for you as well." He handed her the sheer wrap.

The other men began removing their suits, revealing colorful tank tops and swim trunks underneath. She now realized they'd worn suits merely to throw her off.

"Don't worry," Sinduk said, misunderstanding her uneasy expression for shyness. "You won't have to change in front of us."

But she was more concerned that she would no longer be able to communicate with her team once she changed since the transceiver for her molar mic was cleverly embedded in her clothes.

The van turned and slowed as if they were approaching their destination.

At the same time, she heard MacD say in her ear, "What the what? What are these guys fixin' to do?"

The van came to a stop. Sinduk slid the door open, and Raven suddenly understood why MacD was confused.

They were stopped in a vast parking lot set along a seaside cliff. Above a crowded entrance pavilion was a large sign that said "Welcome to Ocean Land." A row of tall hedges stretched to either side, and Raven could see waterslides towering behind them.

"A waterpark?" she said.

"The newest and biggest on Bali," Sinduk said. "Very popular with foreigners."

"What's the plan?" She noticed that the entrance pavilion had metal detectors and guards checking bags. "We can't get any weapons inside."

"That is why we have cells independent of one another, so that you can't know enough to be a problem. There will be guns waiting for us inside along with more men. Besides," he added, ominously, "we have a backup plan."

For just a second, he glanced out to the channel separating them from a nearby

81

island covered in jungle vegetation, but all Raven saw was a single fishing boat collecting the morning's catch.

"And what's my role?"

Sinduk handed her a small ceramic knife. "You should get this through the metal detector without trouble."

"What do you expect me to do with it?"

"The American Senators' spouses are currently enjoying a day out with their children while the summit is going on," Sinduk said, eyeing her carefully. "To prove you are really one of us, you're going to use that knife to kill one of them."

# TEN

*The Timor Sea*

Sylvia Chang's clothes were in tatters, but she'd suffered only minor burns. She could do nothing but watch in horror as the *Namaka* was blasted apart while she clung to the experimental drone they hadn't recovered before the assault began. She couldn't fathom a reason for them being targeted, but she recognized the type of weapon the hostile trimaran was using to decimate the American research ship. As stunning as the realization was, she could come to no other conclusion. It had to be a plasma cannon.

Her own work with the Rhino plasma shield meant she was very familiar with the concept, but she had no idea someone had made such an enormous breakthrough. In any other context, the discovery would have been exhilarating. Now it was simply terrifying.

Of course, she had heard about the MA-

RAUDER experiments conducted for the Strategic Defense Initiative at Lawrence Livermore in the nineties. MARAUDER stood for Magnetically Accelerated Ring to Achieve Ultrahigh Directed Energy and Radiation, and the idea was to force super-hot ionized gas into a doughnut-shaped ring and shoot it out at ridiculously high velocities. Some estimates were that it would reach two thousand miles per *second*.

The project was a success in its early stages, which led to MARAUDER being classified by the military. But despite her own top secret clearance, Sylvia could find no further mention of a working plasma weapon, so she believed that the next phase had been a failure, and the project was disbanded.

Here, however, was proof that a plasma cannon was not only viable but devastatingly effective. The *Namaka* had been reduced to a burning hulk in mere minutes, sinking into the water by her stern. It wouldn't be long until she was completely swallowed by the ocean.

Strangely, their other research ship, the *Empiric,* was mostly spared. Only the masts of the ship had been melted, preventing any contact by radio or satellite.

What was even odder was the launch of a

different weapon from the trimaran. It shot a rocket toward the *Empiric* that detonated directly above it, dispersing a fine mist that settled over the ship. After that, the *Empiric* had been unmolested by the trimaran, but it made no effort to escape, and she could see no activity on her deck. The Australian research vessel just floated there, adrift, like a ghost ship.

Sylvia's idea to climb onto the drone to get out of the water was dashed when the unknown trimaran, instead of slinking away, motored toward her and the sinking *Namaka.* She kept the drone between her and the trimaran, with just her eyes peeking out from behind it.

The trimaran slowed to a stop only a dozen yards away, as if gloating over the *Namaka*'s bow as it disappeared below the surface.

She tried to look for any distinguishing markings, but the ship had no name stenciled on its hull, and it flew no flag. The only distinctive item she noticed was when four men were gingerly carrying a large plastic crate marked with a logo. It was a white A and a B layered stylistically one over the other and backed by a starburst pattern. The men seemed wary of its contents.

She couldn't tell what country they might

hail from. Two of them were talking, and she recognized right away that they were speaking in Mandarin. While her mother was of Irish descent, her father was originally from Shanghai. Sylvia had been born and raised in Northern California and understood a few Chinese words thanks to her dad, but the language was unmistakable.

The men were looking over the railings, searching for something in the water. Then one of the men pointed and shouted before firing an assault rifle into the sea.

An Asian woman in her thirties ran out onto the deck and ordered the man to stop firing. A white man the same age raced after her.

"What happened?" he asked in an Australian accent as the Chinese man slunk away in embarrassment.

The woman switched to English. "The lookout thought he'd spotted a survivor and shot at them. I told him we need to make this look like an accident."

"Was it a person?"

"No, thankfully. Just a piece of wreckage. Nobody has spotted a real survivor yet. Looks like the cannon did its job."

The white man looked toward the *Empiric.* "What about that ship?"

"It looks like the Enervum works just like we thought it would, but we'll make sure before we leave. They had no idea the real experiment today would be ours." She chuckled at that, which made Sylvia sick, reminding her of Kelly and all the others who had died on the *Namaka.* Her mind flashed to an image of Mark Murphy on the *Empiric,* and she agonized over his fate.

The man on the trimaran scanned the water and stopped to peer at the drone. Sylvia ducked behind it.

"What is it?" the Asian woman asked.

"That drone. I think we should sink it." Sylvia heard the snapping of a bolt on an assault rifle. She prepared to dive under, but she saw no other place to hide once she came back up to the surface.

"No. Accident, remember? Leave it there. It'll just make what happened here even more mysterious."

A few moments later, the trimaran's engines powered up, and it headed to the *Empiric* a mile away. Sylvia watched several figures board the Australian vessel, but they didn't stay long. A few minutes later, they returned to the trimaran. It sailed off in the direction of Darwin.

The fact that they left the *Empiric* intact gave Sylvia an uneasy sense of foreboding.

But she was glad it was still there, since it was the only ship visible on the horizon.

Sylvia left the security of the floating drone and began the long swim toward the *Empiric,* petrified about what she would find when she got there.

# ELEVEN

*Bali*

Eddie Seng, the *Oregon*'s Director of Shore Operations and a former CIA officer like Juan, sat in the front seat and watched the van with Raven inside. From the SUV's parking space a hundred yards away, Eddie could see Sinduk and the four men with him milling about the van as they waited for her to change clothes.

"Should we take them out here?" Raven whispered.

"No," Eddie replied. "Since they're not armed right now, there have to be more of them inside with the bombs or weapons. I contacted the State Department, but the Senators' families don't have a security detail in the park, just a guard in the car that dropped them off. All the focus is on the conference center downtown. If we call in a threat to the park, an evacuation might cause one of Sinduk's other cells to carry out their plan immediately."

"So what's the plan?"

"MacD has already gone in. He'll be keeping an eye on you. Linc and I will follow you in."

Sinduk banged on the van door and shouted something.

Raven's voice became even quieter. "I've got to go."

"One of us will have you in sight the whole time. Be ready for anything."

"Copy that."

The van's door opened, and she stepped out wearing a bikini sport top, a sarong around her waist, and flip-flops. The terrorists openly ogled her tall, fit frame.

She said something in Arabic, and Eddie noticed a couple of them back away from her. She probably warned them what she could do with that knife they gave her.

As the six of them walked toward the park, Franklin "Linc" Lincoln appeared at the SUV's window. Like Eddie, he was wearing a T-shirt and jeans, which wouldn't help them blend in, but they had nothing else in the vehicle to change into. Their attire was where the similarities between the friends ended. Eddie, who grew up in New York's Chinatown, was wiry and lean from his martial arts training, much of it done these days sparring with Raven. Linc, on the other hand, was built like The Rock's more muscular cousin and hailed from inner-city Detroit. He came to the attention of the Corporation because of his legendary exploits in the Navy SEALs as a deadly sniper.

Linc was grinning as he held two wristbands.

"Where'd you snag those?" Eddie asked as he got out.

"A couple of teenagers decided to make a quick buck by selling them to me at a steep markup," Linc answered. "Now we don't have to wait in line."

"You're full of good ideas."

"Full of something, all right. Were you able to get in touch with the Senators' families?"

Eddie shook his head. "They put their phones in a locker. Understandable in a waterpark."

According to their intel, Senator Gunther Schmidt of Iowa and Senator Maria Muñoz from Florida were attending the summit. Emily Schmidt and teenage son Kyle were enjoying the free day at Ocean Land with Oliver Muñoz and his fifteen-year-old daughter, Elena.

"How do we find them? It's a big place."

"We may have to let Sinduk lead us to them."

They walked to the entrance next to a family so they wouldn't be conspicuous. Sinduk and his men checked their surroundings frequently, but Eddie and Linc studiously kept their eyes off their target. The terrorists took Raven through the bag check and metal detectors without incident.

Before Eddie went through security with Linc, he briefly looked out to sea. A fishing boat was the only vessel he saw, but he knew the *Oregon* was hiding on the back side of the island, which felt reassuring. He hadn't seen the ship since a walk-through when it was still being built in the dry dock, so he'd never gotten a full view of it. He was eager to finish this mission and get properly acquainted with his new home.

First, however, his team had to live through the rest of the afternoon, and they had to do it unarmed.

He and Linc scanned their wristbands in the security line and entered the park, staying at least thirty feet behind Raven and Sinduk. MacD was nowhere to be seen.

"MacD, you there?" Eddie said into his molar mic.

"Ah have eyes on you and Raven," MacD replied. "Just let me know when to move."

"Will do."

The main promenade was jammed with tourists, most of them in swimwear, some of them carrying towels and bags. Staff wore distinctive yellow polo shirts and shorts, and cheerful music blared over the loudspeakers to mix with the screams and shouts echoing from the numerous rides. Everything smelled of chlorine and suntan lotion.

In the distance at the end of the broad walkway was the park's premier attraction, the Crazy Eights waterslide. The ten-story-tall octopus-themed ride had a wide central staircase around which eight tubular slides painted like blue tentacles snaked and coiled, leaving riders unsure where they would come out, which was part of the fun.

When they were halfway along the promenade, Sinduk stopped and spoke to two of his men, who peeled away and headed toward a walled-off section of the park that had a sign written in both Indonesian and English. It read "Coming soon. Feel the rush of Raging Rapids." A rendering showed thrilled riders on an eight-person raft careening down a white water course.

Sinduk pushed Raven forward with the remaining two men. The strays went through a door to the construction area that said "Employees Only."

93

"Where do you think they're going?" Linc asked.

"That must be how they snuck the weapons in," Eddie said. He keyed his mic. "MacD, Linc and I are heading into the Raging Rapids. We'll let you know what we find."

"Acknowledged. Ah'm on my own."

Eddie eased the door open and peeked through. No one was on the other side. He and Linc went in and found themselves on the pathway for the ride that was divided into two lanes, one for the majority of the attendees, the other for those who'd paid extra for the Super Pass.

The ride seemed nearly complete, with vines, fake trees, and artificial rocks adorning what was supposed to mimic a remote canyon. Eddie could hear water roaring just out of sight, which meant the ride was being tested in preparation for its opening.

A short way up the path, they crossed a bridge and could see down into the false gorge. An empty raft with eight barred seats around a flat center area was adrift on the seething water. It bounced and spun as its rubber sides slammed into the walls, soaking the craft with a gush of water every time it dipped over another mini-waterfall.

As they got closer to the ride loading area,

Eddie could hear several men speaking rapidly in Indonesian. He and Linc climbed over the path's railing and crept along the concrete simulated rocks until they found a hidden spot in the bushes where they could see who was talking.

Four bodies were lined up beside the control room. All of them were dressed in the characteristic yellow park uniforms, as were the terrorists, who must have secured their own supply of uniforms. Bullet holes were stitched across the dead men's shirts.

Huddled around two large metal boxes were six men, the two they'd been following and four more. One box was already opened and contained seats to be installed on more rafts. The other box was being pried apart. A pile of white towels lay on the floor.

They finished prying open the box and pulled out six submachine guns from between the seats, which they handed around, tucking them into towels so they could carry them out into the park unseen. Eddie recognized the weapons as Daewoo K7s. The South Korean–made guns were equipped with noise suppressors and were popular with the Indonesian military.

Eddie looked at Linc, who nodded. He'd noticed the same thing. If one box had room for six weapons, then the other opened one meant six more K7s might already be out in the park.

The four terrorists who were already dressed like employees took their towel-wrapped weapons and started down the path back to the main area of the park. The two left behind began stripping so they could put on their own uniforms.

This was the best chance for Eddie and Linc to procure weapons. Forty feet separated them from the terrorists, but there was a spot farther along the canyon where they'd only be ten feet away when they sprang from the bushes. Eddie pointed to the place, and Linc nodded again.

Before they could move, they heard voices coming from behind the ride's control room, causing the terrorists to freeze. There must have been an unseen passage from the employee area of the park. Two women in yellow uniforms came around the building and stopped, staring in horror at the corpses.

They looked up at the half-dressed men, screamed, and edged back the way they'd come. The terrorists scrambled to pick up guns.

Eddie and Linc responded instinctively, knowing that the women were dead if they didn't act. Both of them charged out of the bushes and rushed the men, distracting them long enough for the women to run.

The only thing that saved them was the terrorists' struggle to free their guns from the towels. Linc tackled his man, sending the submachine gun flying. They rolled across the loading area together and into one of the rafts that was moving along the conveyor belt toward the release zone into the rapids.

Eddie knocked his guy senseless and knelt down to retrieve the K7. He picked it up and turned toward footsteps pounding up the rider path. The four other terrorists must have heard the women's screams and came running back to investigate.

Eddie unleashed a volley from the automatic weapon and took down two of the men as they rounded the bend. The other two took cover and returned fire, forcing Eddie to dive behind the control room as its windows blew apart.

In the reflection of the lone remaining pane of glass, Eddie could see the shirtless terrorist he had flattened get to his feet and sprint toward the raft where Linc and the other terrorist were brawling. He leaped into it as the craft tipped down and plunged into the rapids.

# TWELVE

Raven heard the muted staccato gunfire coming from the direction of the rafting ride that was under construction, but no one besides Sinduk and his men reacted. To tourists, it would have sounded like construction equipment, but Raven suspected that Linc and Eddie had engaged the terrorists in battle. She had seen them out of the corner of her eye when they entered the construction zone.

"They must have encountered a couple of workers," Raven said.

"Then why is the gunfire still going on," Sinduk said. "They're supposed to take care of anyone who spots them quickly and with minimal noise. I don't like this. We can't wait any longer." He scanned the promenade. "There they are."

He nodded in the direction of the Crazy Eights waterslide. Raven saw Emily Schmidt, a forty-something brunette in a

98

black one-piece, and her son Kyle, a sun-burned redhead in long board shorts. With them was Oliver Muñoz, a reedy Cuban American covered by a loose swim shirt, and his look-alike teen daughter Elena, who was wearing a blue tank-top bikini.

The four of them were laughing, carefree, and dripping with water. They scanned their wristbands to use the Super Pass lane and began the long walk up the stairs to the top of the ride.

Sinduk raised his hand as a signal, and three men dressed in the park's yellow uniforms approached with loads of towels in their hands as if the bundles were an offering. By the menacing looks in their eyes and intense expressions, it was clear they were from the other Indo Jihad cell.

They abruptly stopped only a few feet away when a white man drunkenly staggered up to Raven. He was shirtless, wearing nothing but swim trunks and sneakers, and seemed proud of his ripped abs, bronzed biceps, and chiseled face that wouldn't have been out of place on a comic book superhero. He grinned at Raven as he gave a sloppy salute to the men with the green beer bottle in his hand.

"Ah have been waiting for you, beautiful," MacD Lawless slurred convincingly. He drained the rest of the bottle, which she guessed was water. "Where have you been?"

Raven played along with the act. "I think you have me confused with someone else."

MacD shook his head and burped. "It's time to go, babe. Eddie and Linc are busy right now, but they'll be ready any minute."

"Get out of here," Sinduk demanded.

Raven turned to Sinduk and put up her hand. "I can take care of him." She faced MacD again. "It's time for you to leave."

MacD smiled even wider, but his eyes flicked toward the men with towels. "Don't push me away, darlin'."

He took a step closer to Raven, and she understood what he wanted her to do. With both hands, she shoved him backward into the men holding the towel bundles.

MacD took a calculated stumble into the man in the middle, windmilling his arms in the process. He smashed the beer bottle into the head of the terrorist on his right, who dropped the towels he was holding. Two Daewoo K7 submachine guns clattered to the ground.

MacD swung the broken bottle in the other direction, plunging it into the chest of the second man.

Raven charged the third man as he drew a K7 from his bundle. She kneed him in the groin and jabbed the ceramic knife into his throat.

Before she could pick up one of the weapons, a fist slammed into her back like a pile driver. She dropped to her knees and saw Sinduk pick up one of the guns. He ran toward the waterslide with one of the other men from the van.

The third terrorist with Sinduk tackled MacD, and they began trading punches as they rolled around on the pavement.

The wind had been knocked out of Raven's lungs, and she struggled to catch her breath. At the sight of the fighting, blood, and guns, chaos erupted among the nearest parkgoers, with some running and shrieking and others craning their necks to see what the commotion was.

Raven finally stood and picked up one of the K7s to chase after Sinduk, but a hand reached out to trip her. She fell forward and saw that it was the man who'd been hit in the head by the bottle. Blood streamed down his face as he dragged Raven toward him.

The rubber flip-flops wouldn't do much damage, so she didn't bother trying to kick him. Instead, she whipped the K7 around by the barrel and bashed his head with the stock. This time he went limp.

Three terrorists down, with another still fighting MacD. Sinduk and his companion made a run for the Senators' families to complete the assassination mission.

The civilians took priority over helping MacD. In any case, Ocean Land security staff were sprinting from the entrance to break up what they thought was a simple brawl involving some of the guests.

They immediately pounced on MacD and the terrorist he was battling. Raven didn't stay to watch the outcome. She cycled the bolt on the K7 to make sure there was a round in the chamber and took off after the jihadists, who were waving their guns and weaving through the terrified crowd toward the Crazy Eights.

# Thirteen

The terrorists weren't expert marksmen, but they had Eddie pinned down from behind concrete poles holding up the roof of the Raging Rapids loading area. Every time he stuck his head up to take a shot, he had to duck back down under the withering cross fire.

Escaping the control room to either side was impossible without taking a bullet. Eddie couldn't stay where he was. He had to find Linc and get back out to the park to help Raven and MacD.

Out of the back door of the control room, he saw his one opportunity. An empty raft was passing by on the conveyor belt.

He crawled out of the building and flopped into the moving raft. He pressed himself to the floor as it passed out of the shadow of the control room.

He waited until the raft was nearly at the end of the loading zone, picturing the angles to where the terrorists were positioned. Eddie was counting on them still focusing their attention on the control room.

Once he had a clear view, Eddie popped up between two of the headrests and aimed at the terrorists from the side as they concentrated on the now empty building. He fired three-round bursts at each of them, and they crumpled to the ground.

Eddie scrambled out of the raft before it was launched into the river. His best chance for catching Linc was from the rider line bridge over the waterway.

He ran down the path until he reached the bridge. He spotted Linc's raft as it came around a bend toward him.

The raft was bobbing and wheeling as Linc fought against the two terrorists, who seemed to be trying to pitch him out of the raft. Linc was an expert brawler, but the unstable footing against two opponents who were smaller and more agile meant he was taking kicks and punches from both sides.

Eddie took aim, but the swirling raft made it impossible for him to get a clean shot without the risk of hitting Linc.

The bridge had a wire mesh screen to keep people waiting in line from dropping objects on the passengers fifteen feet below. Eddie climbed along the downriver side of the mesh. He had only a few seconds before the raft passed underneath the bridge.

He flipped down the outside of the barrier until his feet were dangling at the bottom of the bridge over the thirty-foot-wide chasm. As soon as he saw the lip of the raft emerge from beneath the bridge, he let go. At the same time, the raft was caught in an eddy and spun to the side. Eddie landed on the edge of the step into the boat, and he pitched backward to keep from falling out.

He landed right at the feet of Linc, who was pinned by the two terrorists. They looked down in astonishment at the new passenger.

"Nice of you to drop in," Linc grunted.

Eddie sprang to his feet and threw an elbow at the head of the closest terrorist, who barely dodged it. He twisted around, but Eddie latched onto his neck and put him in a headlock. The man clawed at Eddie's arm, helpless.

Now that Linc had only one foe to contend with, he used his colossal strength to wrestle the man over the side of the raft. The terrorist grasped the headrest to keep from falling into the foaming white water, but the boat lurched sideways as it hit a current, and he was crushed against the concrete wall.

The jolt forced the raft under a jet of water used to playfully drench the riders, but the combination of impacts allowed the terrorist to push Eddie back, and the two of them tumbled over the side.

Eddie still had his arm around the terrorist's throat as they fell, and the force of the impact as they hit the water was enough to snap the man's neck. He went limp, and Eddie let go as he swam to the surface.

He saw they were approaching the roughest leg of the journey, with whitecaps breaking and churning the water like a washing machine.

The raft bumped his head from behind, and he grabbed hold of the rubber tube. He tried to pull himself up, but the surface was too wide and slick. It was just a matter of time before he would be crushed between the giant raft and the canyon walls.

"Need a lift?" said a deep voice above him.

Eddie looked up to see Linc reaching down to him. He took hold of Linc's hand as the raft spun yet again, tilting toward a sure impact with the side of the channel.

As easy as if he were lifting a prize trout from a river, Linc yanked him out of the water and into the raft.

"And here's the catch of the day," Linc said as he leaned back against the closest seat to steady himself and catch his breath.

Eddie clutched one of the safety bars to keep from getting tossed around as they continued down the rapids.

"Thanks," he said. He keyed the mic with his tongue. "MacD, report please."

There was no response. He tried again with the same result.

All he and Linc could do now was wait in frustration until the raft was carried back to the end of the ride.

# FOURTEEN

If the crowds of shrieking guests hadn't been in Raven's way, she would have shot Sinduk before he reached the Crazy Eights. The terrorist leader and his comrade were making slow progress as they dodged panicked tourists, allowing Raven to make up ground as she ran after them through the cleared path they'd created behind them.

Halfway up the stairs of the waterslide, the Senators' families peered over the railing to check out what was causing the chaos below. Raven feared they would come back down the stairs right into Sinduk's path. She tried waving at Muñoz, Schmidt, and their two teens to keep climbing.

They weren't looking at her, but it didn't matter. Sinduk took a potshot at them, plastering the stairs with bullets too low to hit them. The Americans screamed and started running up the Super Pass side of the stairs.

Sinduk and the other man reached the stairs and sprinted up after them. Crowds of riders streamed past them down the main stairway. Luckily, Sinduk was so focused on his goal that he ignored the easier targets.

Raven got to the stairway moments later and took the stairs two at a time. There was a gap between the switchback stairs, allowing her to see Sinduk two stories above her. She stopped and took aim as they rounded a corner. She had Sinduk in her sights and fired.

The shots didn't hit him because the other terrorist stepped into the path of the bullets. The man went down without a sound.

Sinduk pointed his weapon over the railing and sprayed the stairway with rounds. They pinged off the metal, but Raven was able to duck back in time to avoid being struck.

When the hail of bullets stopped, she leaned back and saw that Sinduk had continued up, but he made sure not to present himself as a target again. Raven kept running.

When she passed the dead terrorist on the sixth level, she saw drops of blood spattered on the stairs leading to the top. She must have hit Sinduk. There was still a chance to catch him.

When she was on the eighth level, she saw him just above her, limping from a bloody wound on his thigh. He was wrestling his way through frightened guests pushing and shoving to get into one of the eight tubes of the waterslide and flee from the gunfire underneath them.

She bounded up the stairs, trying to reach Sinduk while he was distracted. She was still a flight down as he stepped onto the loading platform at the top.

When Raven turned the final corner, she saw that Sinduk had stopped and was pointing the gun at his quarry. The employees had long vanished, and the few remaining guests were piling into one of the eight tubes gushing with water. Oliver Muñoz shielded his daughter Elena while Emily Schmidt frantically pushed Kyle toward the waterslide.

The Senators' families were only a few steps away from him.

Raven couldn't take the risk of shooting with so many innocents in the line of fire.

In Sinduk's other hand was his phone. He tapped on it and dropped it to the floor.

"Death to America," he shouted in English, raising his weapon.

At that moment, Raven hit him in the back with her shoulder using all the power she could muster. The blow knocked them both to the floor. Sinduk dropped his weapon, and it went skittering into one of the waterslide tubes.

He leaped onto Raven, trying to snatch her gun away. Muñoz made a motion toward them, but Raven thought that was a good way for him to get killed.

"Go," she yelled. "Get out of here."

As Raven wrestled with Sinduk, Muñoz shoved Elena and Kyle into a tube, followed by Emily Schmidt and finally Muñoz himself.

Sinduk roared in fury as he saw his targets fleeing. He pried the gun from Raven's hand, sliding it away from them before slamming his elbow into her chin. Raven rolled away, shaking her head from the powerful jolt.

They both got to their feet, him on his bleeding leg, her with a swollen jaw. They faced each other with the gun lying halfway between them.

"Who are you?" he snarled in Arabic.

"I'm a guardian of decency," Raven said, drawing the ceramic dagger from its sheath that she had stuck into the knot of her sarong.

She could see the gears turning in his head. If he reached down to get the gun

111

with his bad leg, she'd be able to stab him before he could get back up. But he needed that weapon to complete his task.

He sneered at her. "You don't realize it, but you've already lost."

Instead of trying to pick up the gun, he reached out with his foot and kicked it into the waterslide tube where the Schmidts and Muñozes had gone down. In the same motion, he dived in after it. Raven didn't hesitate and plunged in headfirst right behind him.

The slick course twisted and corkscrewed down, with the translucent tube filtering the sunlight into a diffuse green glow.

Sinduk was only inches ahead of her. He clawed at the submachine gun that was sliding through the water just out of his reach.

Toward the bottom, as the slide leveled out, Sinduk was finally able to grasp the handle and pull it to him. He flipped on his back and pointed the gun behind him at his pursuer. There was nothing Raven could do to dodge the shot.

She didn't have to. As Sinduk pulled the trigger, he dropped into the pool at the end of the slide. Bullets tore into the sky until he was dunked under the surface.

Raven pitched into the water, the knife held out like a spear. It sank into Sinduk's chest, and he stared at her wide-eyed as blood billowed out into the pool. The life drained from his face, and the gun dropped from his hands.

Raven withdrew the knife and sheathed it back in her sarong before picking up the gun. She emerged from the water and realized that it was only three feet deep. As she stood, she scanned the area and saw the Schmidts and Muñozes scrambling out of the pool, seemingly unharmed.

Raven, however, knew they weren't out of danger yet. Sinduk said she had already lost. He had to be referring to something he'd mentioned to her at the van.

The terrorist leader had a backup plan.

# FIFTEEN

The Ocean Land security guards hadn't presented much of a challenge. MacD, however, was miffed that it had taken him a couple of seconds longer to free himself than it had the jihadist. He sprinted after the terrorist and caught him ascending the Crazy Eights.

MacD snagged the back of the terrorist's shirt on the third level and yanked him backward.

The terrorist wheeled around with his fist cocked. MacD was ready for him. He easily sidestepped the punch and leveraged the man's momentum to heave him over the railing. The terrorist fell still when he struck the pavement below.

MacD spotted Raven climbing out of one of the lower pools with a submachine gun in hand. Scarlet spread from a motionless body in the clear water.

Raven went straight to a group of three

people huddled around a fourth. Oliver Muñoz tended to his teenage girl, Elena, who was coughing like she had swallowed water, while Emily Schmidt and her son, Kyle, watched. They recoiled from the gun Raven was carrying, but whatever she said to them put them at ease.

"MacD, do you read me?" came Eddie's voice in his ear.

"Ah'm on the waterslide."

"We're coming out of the Raging Rapids." MacD saw Eddie and Linc jogging out of the rafting ride construction zone. Both of them were dripping wet. "Where is Raven?"

"She's at the bottom pool with the Schmidt and Muñoz families. All four of them look all right, and we've eliminated all the terrorists we spotted, but there may be more."

"Understood. We'll meet you there."

MacD sprinted down the stairs when a geyser of water erupted from one of the pools below him, followed by a concussive blast. A few seconds later, another one hit. Then a third.

MacD had experienced enough explosions to know that it was mortar fire coming from somewhere.

Raven and the families dived to the ground. MacD could see that the shells were closing in on them. He looked out from his high perch. His eyes were drawn to puffs of smoke emanating from the fishing boat out in the channel between the islands.

He saw Eddie on his phone and heard what he was saying.

"*Oregon,* we've got incoming mortar fire."

MacD didn't hear the reply, but he saw the result.

A rusty old cargo freighter with four cranes was rounding one of the islands at a leisurely pace. MacD recognized it instantly as the new *Oregon.*

He knew that the chameleon-like paint scheme that allowed the ship to change appearance from a brand new vessel to a decrepit tramp steamer at the push of a button was not her only upgraded feature. The *Oregon* was less than two miles away, and MacD could see a turret rising from the bow deck. The barrel of the ebony gun rotated until it was pointed at the fishing boat.

The weapon was a rail gun, but MacD hadn't seen it in operation until now.

Unlike a cannon that propels its shell with gunpowder, the rail gun used a powerful electromagnet to accelerate its rounds to hypersonic speeds. Although the shell was inert, its velocity of more than five thousand

116

miles per hour gave it the same explosive energy as the warhead of a Tomahawk missile.

As another puff of smoke indicated the mortar was letting off another round, the rail gun fired. Instantaneously, the fishing boat was ripped in two from stem to stern as if it were made of tissue paper, detonating the mortar rounds in a fireball. The two halves of the fishing boat sank into the sea, leaving nothing but burning oil on the surface.

The last round it fired, however, landed only a few yards from where Raven and the two families had been running away from the previous blasts.

The smoke from the explosion concealed them, so MacD couldn't tell if anyone had been injured. He looked out and saw the rail gun descend back down into the *Oregon*'s hull, where it was covered by a retractable deck plate. A huge white crest at the ship's bow showed that it was speeding away around the far island to get out of view of any curious onlookers.

Eddie and Linc had also disappeared in the mortar cloud. A moment later, the smoke cleared, and MacD could see Eddie and Linc kneeling over two prone figures.

Eddie called on the comm system.

"MacD, get down here pronto," he said with a grim tone. "We've got casualties."

# Sixteen

Raven, lying on her back, grimaced as Eddie put pressure on her shoulder wound to stanch the bleeding. She'd taken a piece of mortar shrapnel from the last round. It didn't look too serious as long as she didn't lose much blood.

"How are you feeling?" he asked her.

"I'll live. Is anyone else hurt?"

"Just one."

Emily Schmidt and her boy Kyle stood to the side, shaken up but unscathed. Oliver Muñoz, however, had taken a hit in his chest and was in shock. Linc tended to him while Muñoz's daughter Elena knelt beside them, crying.

"Please be okay," she sobbed. "Is he going to die?"

Linc shook his head. "Not if I can help it. But we need to get him real medical attention as soon as possible."

"It'll take an hour for an ambulance to

get him to a hospital," Eddie said. "We'll have to take him by air."

MacD arrived sopping wet from his ride down the slide, and Eddie handed Raven over to him.

"You're a mess," MacD said as he pressed his hand on her shoulder.

She rolled her eyes. "Nothing a little needle and thread won't fix."

Eddie called Juan, who was in the *Oregon*'s operations center.

"What's the situation?" Juan asked.

"We've got two wounded. Senator Muñoz's husband took part of a mortar shell in his belly, and Raven is also injured. I recommend we get them to the *Oregon*'s infirmary right away."

"Gomez is on the flight deck with the turbines at full speed. Doc Huxley is coming with him. Can you get Muñoz to the parking lot?"

Eddie scanned the area and saw an abandoned ice cream cart on wheels. They could lay Muñoz across the flat surface on top.

"We'll meet you there," Eddie said. "ETA three minutes."

They hoisted Muñoz onto the cart. Linc pushed while Eddie steadied the patient, and Elena held his hand. MacD pulled Raven to her feet and supported her as they walked, herding Emily and Kyle with them. Linc tried to steer over the smoothest patches of pavement, but every bump caused Muñoz to groan in pain.

They avoided the crowded main entrance and steered toward an emergency exit. By the time they reached the parking lot, Eddie could hear sirens in the distance. Thousands of guests had jammed the exits as they fled by car and on foot. Muñoz might be dead before the ambulance could even arrive through that chaos.

Even though the waterpark had been crowded, the outer section of the vast parking lot was free of cars, leaving room for their ride to land. As they reached the edge of the cars, Eddie heard the sound of rotors approaching. He looked up to see a sleek tiltrotor aircraft swooping toward them.

The AgustaWestland AW609 was a huge upgrade from the Corporation's MD520N helicopter, which had been destroyed when the previous *Oregon* sank. The tiltrotor had a range of more than eight hundred miles and could cruise at three hundred miles per hour while carrying a complement of ten passengers and crew. Now Eddie was glad they'd sprung for the more capable aircraft. There was no way they could have stretched out an injured man in the chopper.

The tiltrotor looked like any normal twin-engine private plane except the engines were situated on the ends of the wings to power the huge propellers. As it switched to hover mode, the engines turned vertically so that the propellers pointed straight up. The AW settled to the asphalt, the noise of its prop wash deafening.

The moment the tires touched down, Linc pushed the cart forward, and they all followed. Clamshell doors on the fuselage opened, with a short staircase on the bottom half.

A woman wearing green scrubs, her brown hair in a ponytail, hurried down the steps carrying a lightweight backboard. Normally, Julia Huxley had a gentle demeanor and soothing bedside manner that belied her experience as a trauma surgeon and chief medical officer at San Diego Naval Base. But right now she was all business as she zeroed in on her incoming patients.

She took a quick glance at Raven, who simply waved her off.

"Don't worry about me," Raven said. "We'll go find MacD a shirt." The Ranger smirked at her as he escorted her to the waiting helicopter.

Julia turned her focus on Muñoz, inspecting his torso before covering it with gauze.

"It's risky, but we'll have to move him," she said to Eddie. "He might not make it back to a hospital in Denpasar. The *Oregon* is closer. I'll stabilize him there."

The ship's infirmary, with an operating suite and a variety of diagnostic tools, was as well equipped as a big city hospital, and she and her staff could conduct any surgeries that didn't require a specialist.

They shifted Muñoz over to the backboard, and Eddie and Linc carefully lifted him through the door into the tiltrotor's passenger compartment. Once everyone was packed inside and buckled in, Eddie closed the door and went into the cockpit. He took a seat in the co-pilot's chair, strapping himself in with the four-point harness and donning a headset.

"Welcome aboard," George "Gomez" Adams said without looking away from his control panel. "Wish your first ride on the A-dub was under better circumstances."

Gomez, a strikingly handsome man with vivid green eyes and a handlebar mustache, came by his nickname because of a long-ago dalliance with a woman who looked just like Morticia from *The Addams Family.* The ace pilot was cocky about his flying abilities, but the self-assurance was well deserved.

"Me, too," Eddie said. "Doc says to get Muñoz to the *Oregon.* Let's go home."

Gomez increased the throttle, and the helicopter lifted into the sky as if it were borne aloft by a cloud. As he transitioned the tiltrotor to horizontal flight, the aircraft accelerated forward and gained altitude.

"This will be a quick trip," he said to Eddie. "Next time, I'll give you the full aerobatic demonstration. We've even got a hoist that we can attach for water rescues."

They banked away from the waterpark and out to sea. The stern of the *Oregon* came into view as it was rounding the nearest island. From this height, Eddie could see the landing pad between the two pairs of cranes amidships. It was marked by an H with a circle around it.

"You can fit this thing there?" Eddie asked, amazed at the tiny target where they'd be setting down.

"With room to spare," Gomez replied. "And the hangar below deck has enough space to do any maintenance work that's required."

The pad was designed to descend into the ship, after which it was covered by an identical pad that slid across the deck to conceal it.

Halfway to the *Oregon,* Hali called over

the radio. Eddie didn't like the sound of his urgent tone.

"Gomez," Hali said, "we've detected two incoming aircraft closing at a high rate of speed."

"The terrorists have planes now?" Gomez said.

"No, they're Indonesian Air Force F-16s. They think you're the jihadists fleeing the scene of the crime."

"Call them off. We've got kids aboard."

"I'm trying, but they're not responding to my hails."

"Those idiots. Our IFF transponder is broadcasting as friendly."

"They don't seem to care. The police reported seeing an unknown aircraft taking off from the terrorist event, and you fit the description." Hali paused and then called out, "Oh, no. Take evasive action."

Gomez responded instantly, sending the helo into a dive. "What's happening?"

"We've detected a missile lock," Hali answered. "They're preparing to fire."

# SEVENTEEN

Juan glanced at the radar projected on the wraparound screen of the *Oregon*'s op center. The high-definition flat-panel display could show a one-hundred-eighty-degree view of the ship's surroundings from any of the multitude of external cameras. Juan saw the tiltrotor diving toward the sea and the still smoking waterpark behind it in the distance. However, he was more concerned about the radar signatures of two F-16s flying toward them. They were forty miles out, but the AMRAAM air to air missiles carried by Indonesian fighter jets had a range of sixty miles. At that range, it would take less than a minute for a missile to hit the tiltrotor, and the jets were closing fast.

"Hail them again," he said to Hali Kasim, who had his eyes closed as he concentrated on whatever he was hearing over his headset.

"I'll try, Chairman."

Although the ship had a bridge at the top

of her superstructure like any other cargo carrier would, the *Oregon*'s was merely for show. The real heart of the vessel was the op center buried deep in the middle of the armored ship for protection. The op center had a tiered design, with the captain's chair at the center of a semicircle of workstations and the entrance at the room's rear. Cool lighting and smooth finishes made the space feel like the bridge of a futuristic starship. Except for a few dedicated switches and buttons for use in emergencies, all of the controls were touch screens, including one in the arm of Juan's chair, which allowed him to drive the ship on his own if required. Everything was controlled by computer, and the purpose of this shakedown cruise had been to test out their systems while supporting the Bali operation.

Hali shook his head in frustration. "The fighter pilots won't respond."

"Then tell Lang that the Indonesians are about to shoot down a plane with the families of two U.S. Senators aboard." Langston Overholt IV, the Corporation's CIA liaison, had given them this mission, and he was currently monitoring the situation. Their best bet to stop an attack was Overholt's backchannel connections to the Indonesian government.

"Aye, Chairman," Hali said.

"Stoney," Juan said to Eric Stone, who was seated at the helm, "all stop."

"All stop, aye," Eric said. Like the previous *Oregon,* the new ship was equipped with an advanced magnetohydrodynamic propulsion system that could push the 590-foot-long ship to speeds normally seen only in hydrofoils, while thrust-vectoring nozzles made her more agile than ships a quarter her size. The *Oregon* was powered by stripping free electrons from the seawater, providing a virtually limitless operating range.

Juan turned to Max Hanley at the engineering station.

"If those fighters fire their missiles, we'll have to give Gomez some help. Is the Kashtan software working yet?"

The dual Gatling guns that had performed so well to destroy the *Dahar*'s lifeboat had since developed a problem with their code that Max and Eric had been struggling to diagnose. There were three of the weapons systems on the *Oregon,* two in the crane towers, plus another hidden on the stern.

Max shook his head, even more frustrated than Hali had been.

"I've finally gotten the cannons operational, but now the sleeves covering them won't come down."

"Then we'll have to try out the LaWS."

Max frowned. "We haven't even had a trial run with it yet."

"Then this will have to be our first try. It worked with the rail gun."

"Yeah, and then it promptly overheated on the first shot. I'm working on that next after I get the Kashtans online."

"Then we're fortunate that Linda is a crack shot."

Juan's gaze shifted to Linda Ross, her green hair shining in the screen's light. She was seated at the weapons station, a spot normally reserved for Mark Murphy.

"We can't count on Lang getting to them in time," Juan said. "Bring the LaWS online."

"LaWS activating," she answered.

"Put it on-screen."

A portion of the exterior view was replaced by an image of the *Oregon*'s black smokestack, non-functional since there were no diesel fumes to exhaust. The top of the smokestack peeled back, revealing a white device that looked like a telescope. It rotated on a turntable and pointed up in the direction of the fighter jets.

LaWS was an acronym for Laser Weapon System. The defensive armament allowed them to target incoming enemy missiles and aircraft without revealing the origin of the attack. Although the *Oregon* would eventually be equipped with other weapons such as anti-aircraft missiles, anti-ship missiles, and torpedoes, they had to sail before any of those weapons could be installed.

"Linda, what's its status?" Juan asked.

"Functioning . . ." Linda hesitated as her attention was caught by something on her screen. "Missile in the air."

"Estimated time to impact?"

"Twenty-eight seconds. It's locked on. Second missile away."

The tiltrotor was flying barely above the waves, but that hadn't fooled the F-16's electronics. Gomez was an exceptional pilot, but even he couldn't avoid an air to air missile.

"Target that missile. Hali, tell Gomez to get as close to the *Oregon* as possible. See if he can hover behind the ship."

Hali and Linda both said "Aye" simultaneously.

Although the LaWS had a range of only three miles, its biggest advantage was its pinpoint accuracy. That was, of course, if it worked at all.

The tiltrotor was still a mile out. It would never reach the safety of the *Oregon*'s shadow before the missile impact.

"We'll have about four seconds from when the missile comes into range until it hits the target," Linda said.

"Do you have a lock on the first missile?"

"Locked and tracking. I have a firing solution."

She didn't have to tell Juan what he already knew, which was that the laser would begin firing as soon as the missile was in range. The LaWS worked by super-heating the warhead until it exploded.

"Put the missile on-screen," Juan said.

While half of the screen kept focus on the tiltrotor, the other half switched to a view of the sky. A pinpoint of light from the first missile's rocket motor was visible in the distance. The F-16s were still too far away to see.

"Ten miles out," Linda said. "Five seconds to LaWS firing."

She counted down. "Five . . . four . . . three . . . two . . . one . . . Laser firing."

Nothing changed in the view of the weapon itself. There was no gleaming finger of death reaching out like a movie special effect. The system's operation was completely invisible unless there was haze to illuminate the light's beam. Today was clear.

The missile's rocket was growing brighter

131

by the second. Juan held his breath as the AMRAAM streaked toward the tiltrotor seemingly unhindered.

Then without warning, the missile erupted in a ball of flame.

But Gomez and the others weren't out of danger yet.

"Targeting second missile," Linda said.

The tiltrotor circled the *Oregon* and came to a hover position behind the superstructure, which meant the second missile was now aimed directly at their brand new ship.

By now the second missile was even closer.

"LaWS activating," Linda said.

The missile seemed to be coming straight toward the camera. Juan leaned forward in his chair, literally on the edge of his seat, waiting to see if the laser would do its job.

Just when it seemed too late to work, the missile disappeared in a fiery explosion less than a half mile from the ship. Juan watched pieces of shrapnel peppering the superstructure and smokestack.

"F-16s approaching," Linda called out. "It looks like they're circling around to use their cannons."

Juan could easily shoot the two fighters out of the sky, but doing so against a friendly government would cause an international incident, not to mention killing two innocent pilots doing their jobs. However, he had to protect his people.

"Linda, keep an eye on their guns," Juan said. "If they open fire, target the remaining missiles they're carrying."

The two F-16s screamed out of the blue sky and dived toward the *Oregon,* but before they could get into position to fire on the tiltrotor, the jets banked away and flew off into the distance.

"I just got a call from the lead pilot," Hali said. "He said they were ordered to abort their attack."

Juan sat back in his chair, relieved that the friendly fire incident hadn't turned deadly. "Tell Gomez he can land."

"Aye, Chairman. And I've got Langston Overholt on video."

"Let's see him," Juan said.

A dignified older gentleman in a three-piece suit appeared on the view screen. Overholt, Juan's former boss at the CIA who had supported the creation of the Corporation, was seated in his stately Langley office.

"I'm glad you stayed at work so late tonight," Juan said, knowing that it had to be in the wee hours halfway across the world in Washington. "I suppose we have you to thank for calling off the Indonesian

Air Force?"

Overholt, trim and vigorous for a man his age, nodded. During his decades with the agency, he'd seen everything and knew every secret the CIA and its people held. Despite being well past retirement age, his experience and connections made it impossible to oust him before he was ready, which Juan didn't think would be anytime soon.

"I made a call to my counterpart in the Indonesian State Intelligence Agency. Now I owe him a favor, and I will expect to collect the same at a later date from Senators Schmidt and Muñoz. Are their families safe?"

"Oliver Muñoz is badly injured, but Julia Huxley is tending to him."

"Understood," Overholt said. "Keep me informed about his well-being. And good work on keeping the attack from being much worse than it was. I look forward to your briefing."

He hung up.

Juan stood. "I'm going to meet our guests. Stoney, you have the conn."

"Conn, aye," Eric replied, taking control of the ship.

Juan left the op center to rendezvous with the tiltrotor. He just hoped the delay in get-

ting them on board hadn't cost Oliver
Muñoz his life.

# EIGHTEEN

*The Timor Sea*

It took Sylvia longer than she thought it would to swim all the way to the *Empiric,* swallowing and spitting up seawater all the way in her panic. By the time she heaved herself up the dive ladder on the stern platform where the drone was launched, she was completely spent from the ordeal.

She lay on her belly while she gathered strength to stand. The ship was eerily quiet. All Sylvia could hear was her own breathing and water lapping at the ship's hull.

"Hello?" she shouted. "Is anyone here?"

No answer. She feared what she would find when she ventured into the ship.

Her thirst finally drove her to get up. She found a rinsing hose and slurped fresh water from it, careful not to drink so fast that she vomited it back up.

When she was sure she could move without collapsing, she found the nearest door to the interior and steeled herself to open it. She pulled the handle and peered into the corridor.

It was empty. No dead bodies. No blood.

"Hello. Can anyone hear me?"

In response, a moan came from deeper in the ship.

Even though it sounded as if the person was in trouble, Sylvia was momentarily elated. At least someone was alive.

"It's Sylvia Chang," she called out as she walked toward the groaning, which continued unabated. "Where are you?"

The person didn't answer, but the moan became more urgent.

Sylvia picked up her pace. "Tell me where you are."

No words, just moaning. Sylvia was becoming more distraught by the second.

Coming to an intersection of corridors, she stopped and called again.

"Who's there?"

Another moan to her left, from the direction of the galley.

Sylvia raced down the hall and entered the *Empiric*'s kitchen.

Sprawled on the floor was the ship's cook, Roberta Jordan, still wearing her apron. Sylvia knew her well from her time spent on the Australian ship. The normally jovial woman's face was a mask of pain, and she was jerking her arm. A large pot was over-turned on the floor, and water was pooled around her.

A burning stench filled the room. Smoke billowed from a pan on the stove directly into the hood fan, which had to be the only reason the fire alarm hadn't gone off. Sylvia moved the pan to the side and turned off the stove before kneeling beside Roberta.

Sylvia carefully lifted Roberta's hand, which elicited a wail from the cook. Her arm was already blistering from the burn she suffered when she was splashed with boiling water.

"Let me help you, Roberta."

Roberta looked at her with despair. The only sound she made was a pitiful groan.

Sylvia got up to retrieve the first aid kit hanging on the wall. She wetted a towel with cool water and took the kit back to Roberta.

"What happened to the ship?" Sylvia asked as she began tending to the wound. "Where is everyone?"

This time, the groan was more staccato, as if Roberta were trying to speak but couldn't.

Sylvia paused. Something was seriously wrong here.

"Can you understand me, Roberta?"

Roberta gave an effortful nod and made a noise like "Uh-huh."

"But you can't talk?"

"Uh-uh." *No.*

"Do you remember how this happened to you?"

Another No.

Sylvia ran her hands over Roberta's skull, but she couldn't feel any bumps. She took the injured arm, smeared it with antibiotic cream, and wrapped it with the towel from wrist to shoulder. The wound would clearly need care from a doctor.

"Roberta, do you recognize me?"

A groaned affirmative.

"Good. Do you know where you are?"

*Yes.*

Sylvia finished wrapping the wound and gently eased the arm down. Roberta looked more comfortable, but she didn't move.

"Roberta, can you sit up?"

*No.*

"Can you move at all?"

In answer, Roberta spastically moved her arms. Her legs remained immobile.

Sylvia's stomach knotted at Roberta's sudden paralysis. She had to find the other crew.

"Roberta, I'll have to leave you here for a

139

little while," Sylvia said, retrieving another towel and gently placing it under the cook's head.

Roberta groaned in terror. Sylvia wanted to stay and comfort her, but she had to go.

"You're safe now," she said, reassuringly rubbing Roberta's good arm. "I'll be back soon."

Sylvia went back into the hall and toward the center of the ship where the research staff would have been monitoring the results of the test run.

On the way, she passed an office. Two men were inside, both slumped on the floor. Sylvia checked on them, and they were breathing but immobile. She reassured them that she would get help and continued on.

Three more people she found were in a similar state. Sylvia now suspected that everyone on board had been affected with the same paralysis.

A sudden realization made Sylvia catch her breath. The gas from the rocket fired by the trimaran had to be the source of the condition. Which meant she might be affected as well.

She did a quick self-assessment of her body. She felt no difference in the function of her limbs, not even a tingling sensation. All her muscles seemed to work properly, and she had no trouble speaking. Whatever the gas was, it hadn't begun to affect her, at least not yet.

Given that people were still at their posts, they must have been affected quickly, but she had no idea how long it would take the gas to dissipate and become inert. She went to the nearest fire station, which held two gas masks. She put one on and went back to the galley to get a pair of latex gloves from the med kit. She checked on Roberta to make sure she was all right and found that there was no change in her condition.

Sylvia left the galley and didn't stop until she reached the control room.

The data control center was a long room with two rows of workstations facing a wall of monitors that still showed readouts from the experiment they'd conducted that morning.

There were ten people in the room, some of whom were still in their chairs. Most of them lay on the floor.

One of those still sitting was Mark Murphy. Angular and thin, with a wild mess of hair and wisps of stubble that he was desperately trying to grow into a beard, Mark was only a few years older than Sylvia, and he dressed like the skateboarder and heavy metal fan that he was. No one

141

seeing him in his all black ensemble of T-shirt and jeans would guess his intellect and academic credentials.

Mark was rigid in his swivel chair. Sylvia rotated it to face him.

"Mark, it's me, Sylvia."

As soon as he recognized who she was, he gave her a weak smile and moved his jaw, but only grunts came out.

She took his left hand. "I was so worried about you. Are you all right?"

He made a sound that clearly meant, "Are you kidding?"

"Sorry," Sylvia said. "Stupid question. I meant, are you in pain?"

He shook his head in jerks.

"Can you feel my hand?"

Mark moved his head in what Sylvia interpreted to be a nod.

She choked back a sob. Mark Murphy was her half brother, and they'd grown up together with their mother, who had Sylvia after she divorced Mark's dad and remarried. Despite their differences, her genius brother had always been her best friend and someone she admired. Seeing her sibling in this awful condition was heartbreaking.

She noticed he was rhythmically tapping on the right arm of his chair. No, it wasn't a rhythm. The index finger on his right hand made long and short taps in a pattern that she instantly recognized. Although she didn't know Morse code, she understood the message conveyed by three short taps, then three long ones followed by three more short taps.

SOS

Mark was trying to communicate with her.

"Morse code," she cried out. It was the first time she felt any hope since the trimaran had arrived.

Mark responded with a grunted, "Uh-huh."

Sylvia had to call for help, that was clear. If all forty-two people on board were in the same situation as the ones she'd already seen, they would be in dire straits soon. But the trimaran had destroyed the communications array, so a radio call was out.

"I can't send a distress call," Sylvia said. "All the antennas on the *Empiric* were destroyed."

He shook his head and began tapping again, this time with a different message. Sylvia knew Mark served on a ship, so it made sense that he knew Morse, but she didn't.

"I don't understand."

143

His eyes flicked to the desk that he was sitting in front of. Sylvia followed his gaze and saw his phone.

"You want me to pick up your phone?" she asked.

She got an affirmative response, and she realized why he wanted her to use it. She picked it up and held it up to his face to unlock it. Then she searched for the word "Morse" on his phone. It didn't have an internet connection, but she found an application that could translate audible Morse code into letters.

She held it close to Mark's hand and wrote each letter onto a notepad as it was translated. After a few mistranslations, she finally got it down correctly.

SATELLITE PHONE

"Of course," she said, feeling stupid for not thinking of it herself. "The satellite phone in your cabin."

She could make a call with it once she found it in the mess of his room. But who could she trust? The fact that they'd been found out in the middle of the ocean made it possible that the attack was an inside job. But why? What was the purpose?

The one thing she was sure of was that

144

someone had discovered where they were and targeted them specifically. This couldn't have been a random attack, not when it had been carried out so precisely with such advanced weaponry.

"Who should we call?" she wondered aloud.

Mark began tapping again. When he was done, Sylvia looked at what she'd written and said, "Are you sure?"

Mark nodded.

Although Mark had never mentioned a name to her, there was a man her brother had spoken of reverently on several occasions, so Sylvia had faith in Mark's judgment to trust him with their lives. She scrolled through the list of contacts on his cell phone until she found the entry, which had just a phone number and one word for the name. It matched the one in Mark's last message that she had scrawled on the notepad.

**CALL CHAIRMAN**

# NINETEEN

*Bali*

To meet the tiltrotor at the midship hangar bay, Juan used a transportation option not available on the previous *Oregon.* A broad corridor ran in an oval loop nearly the length of the ship. The corridor was divided into two halves by a yellow line. One side was dedicated to pedestrians, while the other side was reserved for an electric tram system. Each of the four open-air vehicles was large enough for passengers and cargo, and they were equipped with sensors that prevented them from colliding with anyone who might step into their path. They all moved in the same direction around the oval unless an override command told the vehicles to move in the opposite direction during an emergency.

Juan pressed the CALL button, and he didn't have to wait long for a tram to arrive. It was already carrying a gurney and two of

Julia's medical staff. He nodded to them and got on. The battery-powered cart accelerated smoothly with a soft whine from its motor and a hum from its rubber tires.

When they stopped next to the hangar bay, all three of them exited the vehicle and entered the large space originally designed as one of the cargo ship holds. Maintenance equipment, fuel hoses, and spare parts were neatly stowed along the periphery. The tiltrotor was resting on the descending helipad platform, its propellers pointed into the sky and lazily winding down. The plane's clamshell doors were already open, and Linc and Eddie were carrying Oliver Muñoz out through the doorway on the backboard, guided by Julia.

Before it had even finished lowering, Juan jumped onto the helipad and walked over to them. Julia's scrubs were stained with blood. Muñoz was barely conscious.

"How is he?" Juan asked.

Julia nodded, a positive sign. "It's good we didn't wait for the ambulance. He nearly coded on me. He has a tension pneumothorax — basically, a punctured lung — so I had to relieve the pressure with a needle during the flight over. Luckily, Gomez was able to give me a few seconds of gentle flying to do it." She waved the gurney over as soon as the platform was down.

"What happens now?"

"I get him to the infirmary and put a chest tube in. I'll give him a CT scan to look at the rest of the damage, but I think he'll require a cardiothoracic surgeon to remove the shrapnel and maybe put some broken ribs back into place. There are some excellent hospitals on Bali. I'd say the prognosis is good."

"How long do you need?" Juan asked as they loaded Muñoz onto the stretcher.

"It'll take me less than an hour to get him stabilized," Julia said, "assuming I don't find anything surprising."

Juan nodded. "We can be at a dock in Denpasar by then."

"I'll keep you posted."

Julia and her medical team wheeled Muñoz back to the cart. Juan was confident in Julia's assessment.

He took out his phone and called Hali.

"Tell Eric to set course for Denpasar. And ask Lang to have a CIA vetted doctor, a private ambulance, and a security team waiting for us at the dock to take Oliver Muñoz and the others to a hospital. He can tell the Senators to meet their families there."

"What should I tell Mr. Overholt about

the status of Mr. Muñoz?" Hali asked.

"That he's in the best care known to medicine, and Julia thinks he's going to make it."

"Aye, Chairman."

He hung up and saw Gomez exit the tiltrotor as the roof above them closed.

"Thanks for the assist, Chairman."

"I didn't want to lose you on our first mission."

"Me neither. There's no damage to my new baby, but it's a bloody mess in there," Gomez said. "We're going to have to do a biohazard cleanup." Gomez headed off to get the supplies while technicians secured the aircraft.

Both Eddie and Linc wore dour expressions, and their clothes were still wet.

"I hope Muñoz is going to be okay," Linc said.

"Me, too," Eddie added. "I wish we could have gotten them out of the park before the mortar shells came down."

"If it wasn't for you," Juan said, "all four of them would be dead, along with possibly dozens of other Ocean Land guests. Speaking of, where are they and MacD?"

"MacD took them to get some drinks and fresh clothes," Linc said. "They're pretty freaked out by the whole thing, especially

Muñoz's daughter."

"I thought it was better that they get them off the deck," Eddie said. "If Kyle Schmidt saw the tiltrotor descend into a hidden compartment on the *Oregon,* he would have been posting about it on social media the moment he got his phone back."

"Good thought," Juan said. "Come on. Let's get you into dry clothes before the debriefing. While you're doing that, I'll go find MacD and the others in the mess to give them an update on Oliver Muñoz."

As they walked to the tram, Linc said, "So far, I like the new ship, especially that laser. Came in handy."

"So did the rail gun," Juan said. "We used it to take out the fishing boat that was firing the mortars, although it looks like Max has to work out the bugs with some of the other new equipment. By the way, your new Harley made it into the hold before we set sail."

Although they hadn't lost any crew members when the previous ship sank in a Chilean fjord, many of their personal effects went down with it, including Linc's beloved custom motorcycle.

"Can't wait to see it," Linc said. "As soon as we get back to Malaysia, I'm going for a ride. I'm meeting an old Navy buddy in

Penang for Christmas." The *Oregon* was scheduled to be back in dry dock two days before the holiday.

They got on the next tram and headed back toward the crew quarters at the stern section of the ship.

"Wish I could have been there for the renaming ceremony," Eddie said. This *Oregon* was rebuilt from the frame of a break bulk cargo ship headed to the scrapyard, so they carried out the customary ritual for christening a ship with a new name.

"It was a little rushed because of Raven's call about the potential hijacking, but the Dom Pérignon went down well while we burned the old logbook. Just remember never to mention the *Oregon*'s previous name again. We don't want any bad luck." Juan knew that sailors tended to be a superstitious bunch and didn't want to anger the sea gods.

When they reached the crew quarters, Eddie and Linc headed to their cabins, and Juan walked toward the phony mess hall, which was distinct from the actual dining room for the crew. The *Oregon* had a portion of the ship meant to be seen by harbormasters, inspectors, and anyone else that needed to tour the ship. Those areas could be dressed up or made completely disgusting as the mission required.

But the hidden sections of the ship where the crew lived and worked were as elegant and luxurious as a five-star cruise ship. Since crew members spent most of the time on the *Oregon,* they were given allowances to decorate and furnish their cabins any way they liked. And the public areas were just as inviting. The dining service would have been Michelin rated if it were a restaurant, and the hallway Juan was walking through was appointed with plush carpeting, soft lighting, and original artwork rotated out from bank vaults where the Corporation's assets were held.

Juan reached the end of the corridor. To exit the ship's hidden inner sanctum, Juan pulled on the handle, and the door swung open to reveal a janitor's closet. When he closed it behind him, there was nothing to indicate that it was anything other than a wall with shelves of cleaning supplies. To open it back up, all Juan would have to do was press his hand against the white board next to the sink, and the palm print reader would automatically open it for him, as it would for any other authorized crew member.

He checked a camera view to make sure no one was outside and exited the closet into a hallway that was like any other generic cargo ship interior, with fluorescent lighting, whitewashed walls, and linoleum floors. If they wanted to make the environment less appealing to get visiting officials off the ship quickly, they could change the color of the wall paint. To make the illusion more convincing, the lights could be made to flicker, and a putrid smell could be pumped through the ventilation system.

Juan entered the public mess hall and saw MacD, dressed in a sweatshirt and shorts, talking to Emily Schmidt, who had her arms around her son Kyle and Elena Muñoz.

Juan went up to them and said, "I'm David Irving, captain of the *Norego*. I'm sorry we had to meet under such terrible circumstances, but we intend to get you back to Denpasar soon."

Elena looked up at him, tears in her eyes. "How is my father? Is he going to live?"

Juan nodded. "It looks like he will be all right. Our doctor is very experienced, and once he is stabilized, we will get him to a hospital for further treatment. Senators Schmidt and Muñoz have already been notified that the rest of you are uninjured."

Emily took his hand. "Thank you, Captain Irving. I don't know how your people were able to save us, but I'm so glad they were there."

"We were happy to help." Juan's phone buzzed. "Excuse me. I'll leave you in my crewman's capable hands. We'll let you know if there is any change in Oliver's status."

As he left the mess hall, Juan saw that it was Mark Murphy calling from his satellite phone.

"Murph, are you done with your experiment yet?" Juan said as he answered. "Max needs your help with some of the new gadgets on board."

"This isn't Mark," a woman replied in a shaky voice. "I'm Sylvia Chang, his sister. I didn't know who else to call."

Juan stopped. No one should be using Murph's satellite phone to call Juan except Murph.

"Where is he?"

"It's a long story."

"Is he okay?" Juan asked.

"No. That's why I'm calling you. He can't talk."

"Why? What happened?"

"I don't know exactly. He might have been poisoned."

"By whom?"

"I don't know. They were on a ship."

154

This call was getting more bizarre by the second. He worried that someone was spoofing the sat phone's number.

"How do I know this is really Sylvia?"

Juan was familiar with every crew member's bio. As he recalled, Sylvia was Murph's half sister on his mother's side. Her father had immigrated to America on a student visa before becoming a citizen. Sylvia was two years younger than Murph, and with Ph.D.s in physics and mathematics, she was his intellectual equal.

"I'm the lead investigator on the Rhino project," Sylvia said. "You're the Chairman, and you lent my brother to us in the hope that you'd be able to equip your ship with my plasma shield someday. He's the smartest, most infuriating, and goofiest person I know, and I love him. Mark told me that you saved his life one time in Albania."

That was actually one of many times, but Murph had kept his work aboard the *Oregon* confidential. Mostly.

"He also says you have only one leg, like Long John Silver."

That was also true. Juan lost his right leg below the knee during a mission long ago. He'd gotten so accustomed to wearing a prosthesis that no one knew it was there unless Juan showed it to them.

155

"Okay, Sylvia," Juan said. "You've got me convinced. Tell me what's going on."

For the next ten minutes, Sylvia explained the nightmare she'd been through. Juan interrupted only to ask for clarifications, getting angrier the more he heard, especially when he found out what had been done to Murph. When she was finished, Juan said, "You mentioned that you're in the Timor Sea. What are your coordinates?"

She told him, and Juan plugged them into the mapping function on his phone.

"We can be there in nine hours to take you and Murph aboard the *Oregon,*" he said.

"Nine hours?" she replied, incredulous. "How?"

"We're near Bali. It's only a few hundred miles from your position." This would be their opportunity to stress test the *Oregon*'s newly installed engines. "In the meantime, you need help with so many disabled crew on board. I'll call the Australian Navy and Coast Guard to rendezvous with you. You're going to have to trust them. If there's a U.S. Navy ship in the area, we'll get it there, too, since the *Namaka* and her crew were American."

"Thank you, Chairman," Sylvia said.

"Call me Juan. My name is Juan Cabrillo."

"Thanks, Juan. I'm glad Mark works for you."

"Call me if you need anything in the meantime. See you soon."

He hung up and headed back toward the op center to plot a new course south once they'd gotten the Senators' families to safety on Bali. He knew every crew member on board wouldn't hesitate to go to Murph's aid, but it still wasn't going to be fun telling them that their Christmas vacations were canceled.

# TWENTY

*The Timor Sea*

While she waited for help to arrive, Sylvia cared for the stricken crew members by treating wounds, bringing water to those who could drink, and making them as comfortable as possible. In addition to Roberta's burned arm, there were two men with head injuries, one with a broken arm, and a woman who had somehow sliced her leg with a knife.

As she tended to them, Sylvia kept the uncomfortable mask on, just in case, but she hadn't noticed any symptoms herself. The illness seemed to have affected people at different intensities. Some, like Mark, were almost totally paralyzed. Others had less severe debilitation but were still unable to speak clearly or move on their own. All of them would require round-the-clock care.

Ninety minutes after her call to Juan Cabrillo, she was startled to hear a ship's horn in the distance, far sooner than she expected anyone to reach the *Empiric.* She left the mess hall and went out onto the exterior deck to see who it was.

An unusual red vessel was about a mile away and approaching fast. It had its superstructure at the front of the ship and a helicopter pad mounted on a latticework of girders above the tall bow.

To come so quickly, they must have been fairly close by when Juan's call for assistance went out. Sylvia wrestled with what to do. If the people on this ship were in league with those on the trimaran, they would eliminate her as a potential witness. But she had nowhere to go. All she could do was follow Juan's advice and trust that they were here to help.

Sylvia took off her mask and watched apprehensively as the ship approached. When it was less than a quarter mile away, a voice spoke over a loudspeaker.

"*Empiric,* this is the Australian Defence vessel *Ocean Protector.* Prepare to be boarded."

The ship came to a stop and lowered a tender into the water. It motored over to the *Empiric*'s stern, and Sylvia went to meet them.

The boarders were already stepping onto

the rear platform when she got there. She was surprised to see that all six of them were wearing hazmat suits.

"I'm Lieutenant Commander Womack," a woman said. "Executive officer of the *Ocean Protector*. Who are you?"

"I'm Sylvia Chang. I was a passenger on an American ship called the *Namaka*."

"Is that the one that sank?"

"Yes."

"Any survivors of the explosion besides yourself?"

Sylvia thought that was an odd way to refer to the attack.

"No," she said. "I was the only one lucky enough to make it off the ship."

"And how many casualties on board the *Empiric*?"

"All forty-three."

"Dead?"

"None. They are alive, but something is wrong with them."

"What do you mean?"

"They were all stricken with a sudden paralysis."

"How is that possible?"

"I don't know. Apparently, they all passed out for a while, and when they came to, they couldn't move properly, if at all."

"We'll take care of them," Womack said,

nodding to her men. They fanned out across the ship. Sylvia moved to join them, but Womack stopped her.

"Just a minute," Womack said. "I want to know more about this accident."

"Accident?" Sylvia replied. "What are you talking about?"

"The distress call we received three hours ago said that there was an incident aboard the *Namaka* that caused a gas explosion, and before it sank, it released a chemical vapor that engulfed the *Empiric*. When we responded to the hail, we received no reply and came here at top speed."

"Distress call? That's not possible." Sylvia pointed at the melted communications array and then realized that the supposed distress call must have been sent by the people on the trimaran.

"Did that happen as a result of the explosion?" Womack asked.

"No, it happened when we were attacked."

"Attacked? By whom?"

"I don't know. It was a trimaran ship."

"In what way did they attack you?"

Sylvia couldn't say that she thought it was a futuristic weapon like a plasma cannon. Womack would think she was crazy.

"I'm not sure," Sylvia said. At least that was the truth.

"Why would someone attack you?"

"I don't know."

"What were you doing out here?"

"I can't tell you. It's classified."

"Which ship were you on when this attack happened?" Womack didn't mime air quotes around the word, but Sylvia heard them.

"On the *Namaka*."

"And you happened to be the only one who survived?"

"I fell overboard when the trimaran started blowing us apart. The trimaran stopped alongside the *Empiric* before it left, then I swam over here."

"And you wore that mask the whole time you were on board the *Empiric*?" Womack asked, pointing to the gas mask Sylvia was still holding in her hand.

"Well, no. I didn't know what had happened on this ship until I found some of the crew."

Sylvia went through the story once more, and Lieutenant Commander Womack looked as if she were restraining herself from rolling her eyes at Sylvia's story. It didn't help when one of the *Ocean Protector* crew members came up to them.

"We're treating some injuries," he said, "but everyone is paralyzed, just like she said. It's difficult to communicate with them, although many of them can respond to yes or no questions. Their condition must have been caused by the chemical release during the accident."

"It wasn't an accident," Sylvia insisted. "We were attacked."

Womack and her crew member shared a knowing look.

"I know what you're thinking," Sylvia said, "but I'm not hallucinating or making this up." Sylvia suddenly remembered the external cameras that the *Empiric* was using to record the results of the experiment. "I can prove it to you. There's video that will show the ship that attacked us."

"All right," Womack said before turning to her crewman. "Begin transporting the survivors back to the *Protector*. We'll evaluate them further over there. The first helicopter should be arriving any minute."

The man nodded and left.

"Helicopter?"

Womack nodded. "We'll be evacuating all of you back to Australia. The Royal Darwin Hospital is ready to treat you." She obviously meant Sylvia as well.

"Come on," Sylvia said. "I'll show you the recording."

She put on her mask and led Womack to the control room, where one of the *Ocean*

163

*Protector*'s crew was checking on the paralyzed occupants. Sylvia smiled at her brother, who was still seated in his chair, and gave his shoulder a squeeze.

"Help has arrived, Mark," she told him. "This is Lieutenant Womack of the Australian Defence Force. I'm going to show her what happened here, and then we'll get you to their ship."

He grunted in response. Sylvia sat down at a terminal to pull up the video files that had the time codes of the experiment.

She skipped past the part showing the plasma shield and played from the point just before the attack. She could see the drone dead in the water, and two people were standing at the railing of the *Namaka*, although the ship was too distant to identify that it was her and Kelly. She swallowed a sob at seeing her assistant.

"The person on the right is me," Sylvia said, pointing to herself on the screen.

A moment later, the bridge of the *Namaka* exploded. The light was so bright that you couldn't see the figures anymore, but she remembered her warning as Kelly ran into the ship. Another blast ripped apart the superstructure. That's when she went into the water. Seeing it from this perspective sent a chill down her spine.

Explosions continued to rip apart the *Na-maka* until it was a burning hulk, with a dense cloud of smoke drifting toward the *Empiric*'s camera. It sank into the water and disappeared.

"That was the attack?" Womack asked.

Sylvia heard the disbelief in her question and understood why. Only now as she watched the video did Sylvia see that the plasma projectiles were so fast that they weren't caught by the *Empiric*'s camera. To the untrained eye, it could look as if the *Na-maka* was blown apart from the inside.

"Where's the attacking ship?"

"It's coming soon," Sylvia said. She advanced the video to the point where the trimaran came to search for survivors, but the screen went black before she got there. There was nothing more. She had reached the end of the recording.

Sylvia's stomach went cold when she understood the reason there was no video evidence. That's why the killers from the trimaran had boarded the *Empiric*. They were erasing any proof they'd ever been there. Then they sent out a fake distress call to make it look like the whole episode was a freak accident. The *Ocean Protector* had been on its way long before Sylvia had called Juan Cabrillo because the attackers had wanted them found.

The question was why?

"Is that all?" Womack asked her.

Sylvia simply nodded. If she told the lieutenant commander that the video had been erased, it would just add to the idea that she was either hysterical or lying.

Womack took her by the arm and eased her out of the chair.

"We'll get you to safety," Womack said, her voice changing to that of a parent re-assuring a child.

"I want to stay with my brother," Sylvia said, standing next to Mark.

"This is your brother?" Womack asked skeptically.

"Yes."

"Can he corroborate your story?"

"No, he was unconscious like the rest of them."

Womack nodded as if she finally realized what was going on. "Do you think that's what happened to you as well?"

Sylvia sighed. "Possibly."

Maybe it was better that Womack didn't believe her, Sylvia thought. At least when she got to Darwin, she would be considered just one more victim of the accidental gassing. Otherwise, the man and woman aboard the trimaran might come after her to eliminate her as a witness.

Womack began helping her crewman tend to the other paralyzed occupants of the control room, leaving Sylvia by Mark's side.

He tapped on the armrest, and she translated the Morse code with his phone.

**I BELIEVE YOU. CHAIRMAN WILL, TOO.**

She appreciated his faith in her, but it was heartbreaking to see her brilliant older brother like this, robbed of his voice and mobility. Seeing that she could not convince Womack about what really had occurred that day, for now Sylvia would play along with her theory. She agreed that Juan Cabrillo might be the only person who would believe her besides Mark. But somehow, some way, she vowed to herself that she would find whoever was responsible for killing and injuring her friends and colleagues.

And when she did, she would make sure they never hurt anyone again.

# TWENTY-ONE

*Nhulunbuy, Australia*
Late December was smack in the middle of
monsoon season in the Northern Territory.
An afternoon downpour pounded April Jin
as she disembarked from the trimaran *Marauder,* named for the experimental plasma
weapon stolen from the Americans that
served as its main armament. It was docked
next to the cargo ship *Shepparton,* which
was awaiting its final load before sailing.
She hurried toward the temporary office set
up beside the concrete apron abutting the
shore.

The deepwater port was located next to a
giant aluminum factory that had permanently shut down a few years before, its
tanks and processing equipment now rust-
ing in the tropical humidity. Although the
local bauxite mine was still operating, the
closure of the refinery and the loss of its
jobs had hit the small town of Nhulunbuy

hard. The town on the Gove Peninsula was so remote that one had to drive the seven hundred kilometers of dirt road from the nearest paved highway to reach it. The townspeople were happy to get an infusion into the economy from a new business called Alloy Bauxite, a shell company created by Lu Yang.

Jin's stepfather had bought up fifty square miles of worthless land in the middle of a secluded swamp on the other side of the bay and built a secret facility there far from any prying eyes. The only difficulty was getting through the muddy marshland and shallow rivers to reach it where there were no roads at all, but Lu had thought of that, too. Jin's husband would be arriving on Lu's transportation solution momentarily.

She entered the office and shook out her raincoat before pouring herself a cup of coffee. She stared at the laptop on the desk, barely able to control her curiosity. The final piece of stepfather Lu's plan was to be revealed today. Jin was tempted to begin the video now, but she had agreed to watch it with her husband, so she surfed Australian news websites instead.

Their attack from the day before was all over the internet, exactly as planned. She scanned the articles for details. The Australian Maritime Border Command had responded to a distress call from two ships in the Timor Sea, one American and one Australian. There were survivors that were flown to a hospital in Darwin, but they were all seriously ill. Rumors were swirling that they'd been poisoned by some kind of gas in an accident, that the patients were paralyzed after exposure. According to reports, the ships had been performing a classified experiment in a joint operation between the U.S. and Australian militaries, so speculation was rampant that it was a chemical weapon test that got out of control. Preprogrammed bots set up by Jin on social media were fueling conspiracy theories that a secret Australian weapon was responsible for the tragedy.

Jin smiled in appreciation of Lu's careful planning. The seed of doubt and fear were already being planted in the public's mind. Even if the U.S. and Australia decided to reveal what those ships had been really experimenting on, the truth would be scoffed at as a ridiculous cover story concocted to deflect blame for the accident.

She was still savoring the irony when she heard the drone of huge propellers approaching. She rose and went to the window, looking not into the sky but out to the sea. Although the thick rain obscured the view, she could make out the white spray around the vessel racing toward the shore. It wasn't a ship. It was a giant hovercraft called the *Marsh Flyer.*

The rebuilt SR.N4 was the type of hovercraft used to transfer passengers and vehicles across the English Channel before the opening of the Chunnel made them obsolete. Its body was painted green, with windows where four hundred passengers would have been seated and large doors at the front and back for loading up to sixty cars and small trucks. On its flat top were a pilot's cockpit and four gigantic propellers on steerable pylons used for propulsion and navigation. A black skirt captured the air blown downward by the lift fan, which allowed the *Marsh Flyer* to cruise from the secret Alloy Bauxite facility through the swamps and across the bay back to Nhulunbuy.

The *Flyer* slowed as it approached the apron. Jin always enjoyed watching it float out of the water and onto land in defiance of all normal expectations. When it was on dry land, the hovercraft spun around on its axis until its tail was facing the docked *Shepparton.* Then the lift fan was shut down, and the skirt deflated, easing the *Flyer* to the ground.

A ramp lowered from the aft end, and trucks started driving off in the direction of the freighter's waiting cranes. When they were all unloaded, Angus Polk came down the ramp and trotted toward her through the rainfall.

As he came through the door, he said, "Did you watch it yet?"

"I was just about to, but I got caught up reading how the press is ablaze over the Aussie military's sloppy handling of their secret chemical weapons research. Pretty soon, they'll be wondering if the Enervum was actually a lethal nerve gas like VX."

"In a way, you could say it's a nerve gas," Polk said. "But as long as they blame their own government for it, I don't care what they call it."

"Did we make our quota of Enervum?" Jin asked.

Polk nodded. "The last batch of canisters is being loaded onto the *Shepparton* right now. It should be able to sail by nightfall."

"Good. And I'll leave for Port Cook at the same time."

"The press will go nuts when another 'accident' happens so quickly after the first one. Lu planned it out well." He noticed Jin frowning at him. "What's the matter?"

"I'm having concerns," she said.

"We're a little past the point of no return, if you're getting cold feet."

"I was just hoping for a single operation, and then we'd be finished. The risk grows with each step, and I would like to see the exit point."

"Lu has been right about everything so far. The factory, the gas, the *Marauder,* the plasma cannon, even how the press would react to our first attack with the Enervum. The locked cryptocurrency deposit has gone up in value by thirty million since we started this. We must be close to his final objective, he can't ask for much more. We have little choice but to see it through."

She took a deep breath and nodded. "I know. It's too late to back out now."

The fact was, their seed money had been spent quickly and their deadline was fast approaching. If they didn't go through with the plan, they'd be penniless and potentially wanted for capital crimes.

Polk nodded at the laptop. "Let's watch Lu's last video and find out what our objective is."

Up to this point, the final target for the Enervum had been held in secret by Lu. Today's date was the first time they could access the recording, when he would reveal the plan's endgame to them. Jin and Polk had been waiting for this moment ever since they saw Lu's first video in Melbourne.

"Let's do it," Jin said. She was too antsy to sit, so she got to her feet and typed in the code to play the video.

Lu came on the screen, unchanged from the last time they'd seen him, his body ravaged by the cancer that later ended his life.

"Good day, April and Angus," he said, his voice weak and gravelly. "I expect you've been eagerly awaiting this moment. I know I would be in your position. I would give anything to see your faces when I reveal what will happen." He took a sip of water and cleared his throat.

"He just loves his dramatic moments," Polk muttered, "even beyond the grave."

"You should have seen him when he was alive," Jin said.

"First, I would like to congratulate you on your success to date," Lu said. "There is still much to be done, but in just a few short days, your mission will be complete. You will have served China most honorably, and will inherit my wealth. While you may have to say farewell to your former lives in Australia, you will have friends in Asia, and the resources to live well anywhere else you desire."

174

"Okay, already, tell us what we need to do," Polk said anxiously.

Lu continued. "The carrot is still waiting for you. Hundreds of millions in crypto-currency will be yours at the end of this, as promised. You hold your end up, and I will do the same. Now for the objective." He went into another coughing fit and quenched it with a drink of water.

Jin and Polk looked at each other. It was all or nothing. Jin took her husband's hand.

"If you've followed my instructions, the *Shepparton* should be holding a full load of Enervum along with its delivery system," Lu said. "The amount of gas on board is enough to poison five million people, the entire population of Australia's largest city. You will take the ship, and at the stroke of midnight on New Year's Eve, nine days from now, release its cargo into the air in the middle of Sydney Harbour. That is your final objective. I hope you succeed."

# Twenty-Two

*Darwin*

After transferring a stabilized Oliver Muñoz and the two Senators' families to a hospital in Bali's capital, Juan had pushed the *Oregon*'s new engines to their limits to reach the *Empiric,* but Sylvia and Murph were long gone by the time they arrived. The ship kept going, and when they were within three hundred miles of Darwin, Gomez took off from the *Oregon*'s deck in the tiltrotor with Juan, Julia Huxley, and Eric Stone, who had insisted on coming when he heard about his best friend's condition. They landed an hour later, and Juan drove a rental van carrying Julia and Eric out of Darwin International Airport while Gomez stayed behind to refuel the plane.

"I can never get used to a hot Christmas," Eric said idly from the back seat as they passed a city bus plastered with an ad for a local bank. Its loan offer featured Santa on

176

his sleigh even though it was a hundred degrees in the midday sun. Yet the grass under the eucalyptus and palm trees lining the road remained green thanks to frequent downpours during the summer's wet season.

Juan glanced at Julia with a concerned expression, and she silently nodded. Eric was trying to distract himself from what he'd find when they arrived at the hospital.

"We'll do everything we can for him," she said.

"Maybe it's only temporary," Eric said. "He could be back on his feet by Christmas morning."

"Maybe," she replied with an air of hope. But the discouraged look she gave Juan made it clear she was dubious of that outcome. The holiday was only three days away.

The rest of the drive was quiet except when they stopped at a medical supply store to pick up an order Julia had called in. It was a motorized wheelchair for Murph to use. According to the reports they'd received from the Royal Darwin Hospital, he could still control one of his fingers enough to guide the chair with the joystick. Eric spent the rest of the ride attaching a custom-made device to the chair's armrest.

When they reached the hospital, they found it swarming with Australian soldiers as well as various government officials. Thanks to fake U.S. government IDs, the three of them were allowed to enter and went up to the fifth floor, where the patients from the *Empiric* were being cared for.

Julia stopped at the central desk and announced, "We're here to see Mark Murphy."

The duty nurse squinted at her and then looked at Juan and Eric. "I'm not sure he is allowed visitors."

A doctor who had been peering at a computer screen looked up. He was a trim man in his thirties with short black hair.

"I'm Leonard Thurman," he said. "Mr. Murphy has been under my care. Are you Dr. Huxley?"

She nodded. "How did you know that?"

"We've been expecting you. I received a most unusual phone call from my government an hour ago. The U.S. State Department apparently requested that I show you and your colleagues every courtesy. Mr. Murphy and his sister Ms. Chang are the only American survivors of the tragedy that brought them here. Please, follow me."

Thurman led Julia down the hall, and Juan and Eric trailed behind them.

"Dr. Thurman," Julia said as they walked,

"what is their latest condition?"

"Ms. Chang seems to have suffered no ill effects of what we think is a poison gas attack. The status of Mr. Murphy, on the other hand, has not changed since he arrived. He has not gotten any worse, which is good news, but he remains almost totally paralyzed from the neck down."

"Do you know the mechanism of the paralysis?"

"Not at this stage. None of the victims have sensory loss and can still feel pain, heat, and cold in their extremities. I'm truly puzzled. I've never seen such a quick onset of paralysis in a large group of people except from an unfortunate case of botulism at a family reunion."

"Could it be a form of curare?" Juan asked. "Central American indigenous tribes using the poison in blow guns. It causes paralysis."

"I don't think so. We've tried treating the patients with a cholinesterase inhibitor, but it had no effect. The symptoms show both upper and lower motor neuron involvement, like a combination of cerebral palsy and Guillain-Barré syndrome. Functional MRIs have shown that the neurons have become quiescent but are not dead."

"Is there a cure?" Eric asked.

"I suppose we might be able to synthesize an antidote if we could isolate the cause of the condition," Thurman said. "But that could take months or years of research. Barring that, I'm sorry to say that the paralysis may be permanent."

Thurman stopped at one of the rooms and gave a perfunctory knock as he entered. Murph was propped up in his adjustable bed in a hospital gown, and a young woman was sitting next to him with his right hand in hers. She looked at the new visitors warily, and then suddenly her expression changed.

"You're Mark's friends," she said, then paused for a moment before continuing. "He says your names are Juan . . . Eric . . . and Doc Huxley."

Juan noticed Murph's finger tapping on her palm and recognized the cadence of Morse code.

"You must be Sylvia," Juan said.

"I'm glad you came. So is Mark."

"How are you two?"

"I'm fine. Mark feels okay. He's just frustrated that he can't move."

Eric walked over to the bed. "Hey, buddy. Good to see you," he said, trying to keep the mood light.

Murph grunted and Sylvia interpreted his

rapid Morse taps. "He says, 'I know I sound like . . . Frankenstein's monster . . . but tell me I don't . . . look like him.' "

Eric smiled. "I'm sorry to say you still look like you. I brought a surprise. You'll be able to talk for yourself now. Sort of."

He put on a pair of augmented reality glasses, walked over to the motorized wheelchair, and rapidly manipulated the joystick with his finger like he was playing a video game. A voice that sounded like Stephen Hawking's halting robotic tone said, "I've modified the controls so that you can switch back and forth between operating the chair and speaking with the synthesizer app. The glasses let you see what you're typing."

"Don't worry," Eric added in his own voice. "That's just one of the four hundred voices programmed into it. Max and I threw this together when we found out what happened. You can sound like Mickey Mouse, Samuel L. Jackson, Marilyn Monroe . . . anything that's in there. I did, however, remove the Gilbert Gottfried and Kim Kardashian choices."

"Wow. That's amazing, Eric," Sylvia said. "Mark says he wants to try it out."

Dr. Thurman called for an aide to help get Mark into the chair, and while that was going on, Juan pulled Thurman and Julia

181

into the corridor.

"We would like to take them with us," Juan said. "It seems like Sylvia is uninjured, and Dr. Huxley has the resources and equipment to look after Mark."

Thurman frowned. "They just arrived yesterday. I'm reluctant to let him go so quickly in his condition."

"He isn't a threat to anyone since he isn't infected with a contagion," Julia said. "Is there any reason to expect Mark's status to worsen?"

"We don't really know anything about what's happening to him."

"Can you do anything for him here that my hospital couldn't?"

"I suppose not."

"Then I'd prefer to have him in my care," Julia said. "You did say that you were to show us every courtesy."

"I'll arrange with our State Department to authorize the transfer," Juan said, which meant going through Langston Overholt.

"Fine," Thurman said. "But I would appreciate you sharing any changes in his condition or progress in finding an effective treatment. I will do the same."

"Of course," Julia replied, and exchanged numbers.

Murph rolled out of the room in his

wheelchair and did a three-sixty. Eric and Sylvia followed close behind. When Murph came to a stop, he smiled the best he could, his eyes glittering with intensity behind the special glasses.

"Looks like you picked that up quick," Sylvia said.

He rotated to face her. The artificial voice spoke again, but this time it sounded like James Earl Jones's commanding basso. "I find your lack of faith disturbing. Now, before we leave and look for a way to get me free of this chair, can I please have my clothes?"

# TWENTY-THREE

Sylvia was amazed at how fast Juan Cabrillo could get her and Mark out of the hospital. She expected all kinds of red tape, but less than an hour later they were climbing on board a sleek tiltrotor aircraft at Darwin's airport.

"Where are we going?" she asked him.

"To the *Oregon,*" Juan said before climbing into the copilot's seat.

"She's a ship," Eric said as they strapped in. "Our home and base of operations. Mr. Overholt told us you have a top secret clearance, so the Chairman says we can show you around once we arrive."

"What does my security clearance have to do with it?" Sylvia asked.

Eric smiled at her. "You'll see."

"Can't wait to lay my eyes on it," Murph said. His artificial voice was now closer to his real voice. Even he was getting sick of constantly sounding like Darth Vader.

Once they were in the air, Juan joined them in the main cabin. Sylvia spent the rest of the ride briefing them on the attack by the trimaran. At Mark's urging, she even shared the goals of her experiment and a description of the plasma cannon that sank the *Namaka*.

When she was through with her story, Juan said, "The trimaran sounds like the design of a new patrol ship used by a lot of navies in this region, including the Australians. It's fast and has a long range for coastal and deep sea operations, so it could have come from anywhere. But the plasma weapon sounds too sophisticated for a terrorist group."

"It might be the Chinese government," Sylvia said. "I heard some of the crew on the trimaran speaking Mandarin."

"You also heard two of them speaking English with an Australian accent. Could you identify them if you saw them again?"

"Absolutely." Their faces were seared into her memory. Everything about the incident was.

"Eric, take her to see Kevin Nixon. He can draw up a composite sketch of them." Juan turned back to her. "Is there anything else you can remember to help us narrow our search for the trimaran?"

185

She nodded. "I don't know if this means anything, but there was a logo on a metal crate aboard the ship. It was an A and B over a starburst."

"No name?"

She shook her head.

"Okay. Kevin can draw that up, too. Tracking down this trimaran and the chemical weapon they used might be the only way of discovering an antidote."

The pilot, a handsome man with a handlebar mustache, announced, "Chairman, we're approaching the *Oregon*."

Juan returned to the cockpit. Then he called back. "We'll do a flyby so Murph can get a look at her."

Sylvia went to the window beside Mark's and gazed out. She saw nothing but open sea lit by the fading sun.

"There she is," Mark said. "Awesome."

An ordinary-looking freighter appeared on the water below. Sylvia thought he was joking with her. "That's it?"

"Looks can be deceiving," he replied, not taking his eyes off the vessel.

The tiltrotor settled onto a landing pad in the middle of the deck, and to Sylvia's astonishment, the aircraft was lowered into the ship.

Juan opened the door and said, "I'm going to the op center. Eric, when Kevin has any actionable info, let me know." With that, he was gone.

"I'm going to take Murph to the infirmary for my own assessment," Julia said.

"Are you going to be all right?" Sylvia said, taking Mark's hand.

"Don't worry," Mark said. "We've got the best medical bay on water."

Sylvia was uneasy about letting her brother out of her sight, but she could see he was in good hands.

"Come on," Eric said. "I'll take you to the Magic Shop. Then we'll find you a cabin."

He took her to a corridor where they got on a tram car, surprising her yet again with the technology on this ship. They were whisked toward the stern.

"What is the Magic Shop?" she asked.

"It's the place where we make fake IDs, uniforms, makeup and wigs, props, and any other disguises and gadgets we need for our operations. It's run by Kevin Nixon, who is an award-winning special effects expert and makeup artist from Hollywood."

"What *are* your operations?"

"We take on difficult jobs that our government can't do itself. Secret jobs, the type where they don't want publicity. We're kind of the last resort. If we can't do it, it probably can't be done."

"So you're spies. I knew it. My brother is a spy."

Eric shrugged. "More like special ops."

"Whatever you call it, I had no idea he worked in such an amazing place with such talented people."

"I'm glad I could finally meet his sister. I've heard a lot about you."

"Was I what you were expecting?"

"Exactly."

Their eyes locked for a moment, and then Eric adjusted his horn-rimmed glasses and looked away with flushed cheeks. She'd have to grill Mark later about why he'd never introduced her to his charmingly awkward best friend before.

The tram came to a stop and Eric led her down a series of plush halls more suited to a luxury yacht than a cargo ship. Then they entered a large room crammed with racks of clothing, storage bins and shelves full of props, several mannequins outfitted with military uniforms in various stages of tailoring, and four swivel chairs set in front of a wall of mirrors.

A slim man with a thick brown beard was tinkering with a prosthetic leg propped on the counter. He was sucking on a lollipop and so intent on his work that he hadn't noticed them come in.

"Kevin," Eric said, "the Chairman told us to see you."

Kevin jerked his head around and nearly knocked over the artificial leg.

"Jeez," he said, grabbing his chest. "What are you? Ninjas?"

"Kevin Nixon, this is Sylvia Chang. She's Murph's sister."

"And yes, Eric, the Chairman told me to expect you." Kevin turned to Sylvia. "I hope Murph gets better soon."

"Thanks. That's why we're here, if you're not too busy."

"No, I was just making some adjustments to the Chairman's combat leg."

"He lost his real one in a ship battle a long time ago," Eric said.

It looked more advanced than any prosthesis Sylvia had ever seen, but before she could ask about it Kevin put it aside and said, "How can I help?"

She told him about the people she saw on the trimaran and the logo she'd spotted on the crate.

"Let's start with the logo. That'll be easier to figure out than the faces." He took out a laptop and pulled up a drawing app. "What did it look like?"

She described it for him, and they fiddled

with it until it was an exact match for the AB logo as she remembered it. The recognition of it sent a shiver down her spine.

"I'll send it to you so you can do a reverse logo search," Kevin said to Eric.

While he was doing that, they moved on to the two Aussies she'd seen, detailing their features, which Kevin plugged into his app. Within thirty minutes, she was looking at an eerie facsimile of the faces of the man and woman who had hurt her brother and killed the crew.

"That's them," she said.

"We can try a facial match with the CIA's database," Kevin said. "If my drawings are close enough and they're in the system, they should pop up."

"The logo has popped up," Eric said, looking at his phone. "At least, I've narrowed it down to three possibilities."

He showed them to Sylvia. They were all similar, but her eye was immediately drawn to the image in the center.

"It's that one."

"Alloy Bauxite is the name of the company," Eric said. "According to their corporate filings, they process aluminum."

"What could that possibly have to do with an attack on the *Namaka* and *Empiric*?" Sylvia wondered.

"I don't know. But if we want to find out, we don't have to go too far. All their operations are based in one small town in the Northern Territory. It's called Nhulunbuy. We can be there by tomorrow morning."

# TWENTY-FOUR

*Port Cook, Australia*

After a hot afternoon spent replacing a burned-out transformer on a utility pole, electrician Paul Wheatley was looking forward to tossing back a cold beer at his favorite pub. The only problem was that his loony workmate would probably join him.

"Mate, I'm telling you," Harry Knoll said from the passenger seat of their maintenance truck. "They have aliens in there."

"You're daft."

"Then why would they build this place out in woop-woop?"

Wheatley rolled his eyes. He'd had this conversation a hundred times with Knoll. The transformer they'd fixed had been near Royal Australian Air Force Base Talbot, which was located in the far north of Queensland and was the service's newest "bare base." Situated on the west coast of the Cape York Peninsula, it was used in earnest only a few times a year by training squadrons headquartered at other bases. The rest of the time, Talbot had a skeleton staff of four and served as a backup base in case someone tried to invade Australia, which Wheatley thought was about as likely as Knoll suddenly abandoning his paranoid delusions.

"Last year, they had trucks going in and out from the docks," Knoll rambled on when Wheatley didn't answer him, "and planes were coming and going. We never saw what was in them, did we?"

"They told us what was happening," Wheatley said. "They temporarily used the base as an immigrant detention center. They've built several of them."

"That's what the government wanted us to think. But the military could be doing anything in there. Didn't you hear about that research ship they found west of Darwin? I heard all those scientists are vegetables now from some secret Navy experiment."

"The news said they were paralyzed."

"Same difference. Don't you think it's possible they've got a team of boffins inside the base tinkering with some unholy technology not of this earth?"

"No. I reckon it's got four blokes bored

out of their noggins waiting for something interesting to happen. Besides, there are only three hundred and twenty people in Port Cook. Good luck keeping something secret from that gossipy lot."

They were almost back to town when a thunderclap split the air.

"Where did that come from?" Knoll wondered. "There's not a cloud in the sky."

Something in the rearview mirror caught Wheatley's eye. Dense black smoke was soaring skyward from the air base two miles behind them.

"There's been an explosion at Talbot. We need to get to the station." Wheatley stepped on the gas. Both he and Knoll were members of the volunteer fire brigade.

Knoll twisted in his seat and gaped at the column of smoke. "It had to be the alien technology. Maybe we'll get a chance to see it now."

"Don't be a dipstick. One of their ammo dumps must have blown up."

As he drove, Wheatley kept one eye on the fire burning behind him. He had no idea what set it off, but the light breeze coming from the sea would be fanning the flames.

Then from that direction, he saw something new, a bright light streaking toward them.

"What is that?" Wheatley asked.

Knoll turned in his seat. "It looks like a missile. Maybe it cooked off when the ammo dump went up."

The missile shot over them just as they were entering the outskirts of Port Cook. Wheatley craned his neck to watch it through the windshield as it changed course and angled down toward the ground.

Five hundred feet above Port Cook, the rocket detonated, emitting a puff of white mist that seemed to quickly dissipate.

"That's lucky," Knoll said. "Looked like it was going to land in the center of town."

As they were crossing the bridge over the river that marked the edge of town, Wheatley saw several of the townspeople outside on the main street watching the smoke in the distance. Without warning, each of them collapsed and slumped to the ground.

"What's going on . . ."

That was all Wheatley got out before he lost consciousness.

When he came to, the first thing he noticed was the smell of brackish water. His legs and nose ached. He vaguely remembered that there was an accident at Talbot, and his last memory was of a missile shooting toward them. After that, it was black.

He opened his eyes and saw that the

windshield was cracked and the hood crumpled. It was also sideways. In front of him was the bank of the river. Somehow they had plunged off the bridge, but he didn't recall that happening.

Wheatley turned his head with effort, but his legs wouldn't move, and he could only flail his arms. Knoll was below him, water from the river threatening to submerge him.

Wheatley tried talking, but he could croak out nothing more than a few unintelligible groans. Knoll responded with a terrified keening. The river's surface was creeping higher as the truck settled into the river's muck, and it didn't look like he could move either.

Wheatley fumbled in an attempt to unhook his seat belt, then thought better of it. His seat belt was the only thing keeping him from dropping into the water beside Knoll.

The feeling of complete helplessness was horrifying. He could only watch as the water rose to Knoll's neck. A similar fate would follow soon for Wheatley unless someone in town came to their rescue.

The two of them remained like that for what seemed like an eternity, but for all Wheatley knew, it could have been mere minutes. He heard nothing but the gurgling of water until the air was split by the screech of brakes.

The water was nearly up to Knoll's mouth, so Wheatley did his best to shout, but it sounded more like the cry of a wounded animal.

"What is it, Wilson?" a man said from above. Wheatley recognized the voice as Sam Carter, one of the young airmen stationed at Talbot. The other man had to be his buddy Todd Wilson.

"Looks like a truck went over the side of the bridge," Wilson said. "There are two guys inside."

"Who is it?"

"Wheatley and Knoll." He called to them as he clambered down the riverbank. "Oy, there. Are you hurt?"

Both Wheatley and Knoll responded with groans to the question.

"Come on, then, Carter," Wilson said. "Give me a hand before they drown."

Wilson yanked the driver's door open. As Wheatley felt hands gripping his shoulders while his belt was unclipped, he was overwhelmed with relief at being rescued.

Wilson and Carter grunted with effort as they carried him back up to the road.

"Why do you think the fire brigade didn't answer when we called?" Wilson asked.

"It certainly wasn't because they were

helping these fellows."

They laid Wheatley roughly on the warm grass next to their Humvee so they could go back for Knoll.

As they went back down, Wilson said, "Crazy day. First, the storage depot goes up in smoke for no reason, and now we find these two in the river."

They disappeared back down to the river while Wheatley could only look out at the placid ocean. The next few minutes of exchanges from below were about how to get Knoll out of the truck. Wheatley wasn't sure they had succeeded until he saw them carrying Knoll over the embankment. They laid him next to Wheatley. Knoll was soaking wet but still breathing, his eyes wide with fear about his near-death experience.

"Why can't either of them talk?" Carter asked.

"I don't know," Wilson said. "Concussions, perhaps?"

Wilson dropped to his knees to check them for wounds while Carter tried his phone.

"Still can't get anyone," he said after a moment. He turned toward town. "Maybe they . . ." His voice trailed off. "It can't be."

"Huh?" Wilson asked without looking up.

"I was so focused on the damaged bridge

railing, I didn't see them."

"See what?"

"Bodies. They're everywhere."

Wilson's head snapped around, and he leaped to his feet. He gaped for a moment, then yelled to Carter.

"Call Canberra. Tell headquarters we've got a major incident here." Wilson turned back to Wheatley and Knoll. "Don't worry, fellas. We'll be back as soon as we can."

Wheatley tried to protest, pushing himself up awkwardly with his arms, but his moans didn't stop the two panicked airmen from jumping in their Humvee and speeding away.

Exhausted from that small movement, Wheatley lay back down, waiting for them to return. He tried to distract himself from his predicament by watching an odd trimaran ship hurtling past Port Cook before abruptly turning out to sea.

# TWENTY-FIVE

*Nhulunbuy*

Although he was the harbormaster for a small Northern Territory mining town, Burt Gulman took his ship inspection task seriously, part of his plan to get a transfer to a prestigious job at the giant port in Melbourne. The captain of the docked cargo vessel *Norego,* a fit-looking American named John Cable, was trying to impress Gulman with the technology on the ship's state-of-the-art bridge, but the harbormaster played it like he'd seen it all before.

"The control panel looks functional," Gulman said as he checked off an item on his clipboard. In fact, it was sleek and high-tech. The only object that seemed out of place was a vintage brass coffeemaker, attached to the back wall, that was giving off a tempting aroma.

"All the latest software," Cable said proudly. "We can control everything in the ship right here, from navigation to fire suppression to cargo transfer. If I didn't need to eat, I could probably run the ship myself."

Cable let out a hearty laugh, but Gulman didn't join in.

"After we finish here, I'll need to see the engine room and then the cargo holds."

"Of course. I'll be happy to show them off, but you can see them from these monitors, too."

Cable punched some buttons and pointed at one of the many high-definition display panels. Cameras switched between multiple views of an immaculately clean engine room holding two giant turbines. A single worker could be seen checking one of the instruments.

"That's our chief engineer, Michael Wong," Cable said. "Loves vehicles of any kind. He was especially keen on that hovercraft we saw arriving this afternoon. Very unusual to see that here." He pointed at the giant craft on the tarmac, where it was being loaded with trucks from a nearby warehouse.

"That's the *Marsh Flyer*," Gulman said as he ticked off more items on his checklist. "Alloy Bauxite brought it in to access their production facility."

"I'll have to ask the pilot if Mike can take a peek."

"I doubt it. Bob Parsons is a friendly sort, but he knows who butters his bread. AB is very protective of their proprietary information."

"Too bad. Mike has been talking about it nonstop."

"If your engineer wants to chat him up, Bob can usually be found at the Lazy Goanna when he's off work."

"The Lazy Goanna?"

"Our local tavern. All he has to do is buy Bob a drink."

"Thanks," Cable said. "Mike might just do that while we're here. Speaking of a drink, I'm going to pour myself a cup of coffee. Do you want one before we continue the inspection? It's a special Vietnamese blend. I highly recommend it."

"Don't mind if I do," Gulman said.

Cable filled a tall cardboard cup and handed it to Gulman. "Be careful. It's hot." He nodded to a cupholder next to the control panel. "You can put it there to cool off if you need to."

"Appreciate it." Gulman took the cup and was about to take a sip when it began to warm up in his hand. Cable wasn't kidding about the heat. Gulman had to put it down before it burned his fingers.

He crossed quickly to the cupholder and was about to place it in the receptacle when the cup seemed to leap out of his hand as if he had a sudden muscle spasm.

Gulman could only watch in horror as the cup landed on the control panel and splashed steaming coffee across the instrumentation.

Alarms blared, and lights flashed on a number of screens.

Cable rushed over and looked like he was going to tear his hair out.

"What did you do?" he yelled. "Oh, no. The fire suppression system was activated." He tapped furiously on one of the touch screens.

"I'm sorry," Gulman sputtered. "I don't know what happened."

Cable calmed down and waved him off. "It was an accident. No worries."

"But —"

Gulman was interrupted by a man on one of the video screens. He was covered in fire retardant foam and gesticulating in fury from what looked like the engineering control room.

"What is going on up there?" he demanded. It was Michael Wong, the chief engineer. "My engine room is soaked with foam. It'll take us two hours to clean this up."

The screen switched to the view of the engine room, and Gulman's stomach sank when he saw foam all over the formerly pristine machinery.

"We had a malfunction up here," Cable said with a wink at Gulman. "Must have been a software glitch."

"A glitch. If I find who made that bonehead mistake, I'll make sure he never works in this business again."

Wong stormed off, and Cable turned off the screen.

"I . . . I don't know what happened," Gulman said. "I must have slipped when I put the coffee down."

"I'm sure you did," Cable said with a surprisingly understanding and magnanimous tone. "Look, you seem like a nice guy. I don't want to make you a laughingstock in the community or put a blot on your job record. We'll get this sorted out. I'm sure no serious damage is done. Now, you've seen enough to know the *Norego* is shipshape." He chuckled. "I mean, our fire suppression system obviously works. What do you say we wrap up the inspection here and forget the whole thing?"

Gulman nodded vigorously. "That's

mighty kind of you, Captain. I don't think I need to see any more. Everything seems to be in order. My apologies again."

He quickly signed the necessary forms and hustled off the ship as fast as he could, his stomach in knots hoping the *Norego*'s captain would keep this incident private. They would never trust him with the Melbourne posting if anyone found out about his embarrassing blunder.

"It worked," Juan said as he watched the harbormaster scurry down the gangway. "You can come out."

Eddie emerged from the adjacent room in fresh clothes, toweling the last of the fake fire retardant foam from his hair with one hand and carrying a tablet in the other.

"Did the harbormaster look as red in person as he did on camera?" Eddie asked. "I thought he was going to transform into a tomato right in front of me."

"At least now we know our little ruse works."

When docking in ports where oversight was lax and the underpaid administrators were corrupt, Juan could get inspectors to cut short their visits by buying them off or making the ship so disgusting that they couldn't wait to leave. But that trick

205

wouldn't work in countries where the standards were higher and the harbormasters well paid and principled.

The new *Oregon* could be made to look like a brand new technological marvel, allowing her to call on ports that were never available to the Corporation's previous ship. To get past an inspection that might come uncomfortably close to revealing some of its hidden secrets, they had to come up with a new technique to get inspectors off the ship prematurely.

Since the *Oregon* was actually controlled from the op center, the non-functional bridge could be made to look like a shambles or, as it was today, it could be dressed up to seem as if it were fresh from the shipyard. The process for embarrassing Gulman enough to make him leave before finishing the tour had several segments.

The video of the fake engine room being doused with fire retardant foam had been filmed weeks ago on a movie set. The only part that was live was Eddie's appearance on the monitor in his costume. The trick spill cup had been rigged up by Kevin Nixon. It had a hidden heating element that induced Gulman to put it down, and tiny neodymium magnets embedded inside pulled it over once he got it close to the control panel. The rest was theatrics and Juan's improvisation.

"Any more word on that incident in Port Cook?" Juan asked Eddie. News had been trickling out about a situation that sounded suspiciously similar to what happened on the *Empiric.*

"The Australian military began flying in teams this morning," Eddie said. "The latest is that they have five hundred and eighty-four casualties. Of that total, there were seventeen deaths, and the rest are paralyzed like Murph."

"Anyone not afflicted?"

"Just the four airmen who were the skeleton crew of the nearby base. The rumor on the internet is that a gas leak at the base was caused by a fire in a top secret storage depot. A lot of Australians are convinced that both Port Cook and the *Empiric* are the fault of their own military."

"Or it was made to look that way. I don't buy that the military could have two similar 'accidents' a thousand miles away from each other in just a few days. Port Cook and the air base are right on the coast."

"Do you think it was another attack like the one Sylvia Chang described?" Eddie asked.

"Maybe. But we don't have anything

concrete to connect them. Eric and Murph are still working on the facial recognition of Sylvia's mystery couple. The only lead we have is a crate she saw with a logo of Alloy Bauxite, and that's pretty thin. Do you have the satellite photos of their facility?"

"Right here," Eddie said, tapping on his tablet. "But it doesn't look like it's going to be easy to get to."

The image from a few days ago showed a large rectangular building in the middle of a green expanse dotted with muddy bogs. It had a small annex attached to it. The structure looked more like a warehouse than a smelting factory. The *Marsh Flyer* was parked next to it, and several other vehicles were scattered nearby. Eddie zoomed out, and there was nothing but swampland for miles around, with just a corridor denuded of trees for the hovercraft to navigate to and from the bay.

"We can't go in by air," Juan said. "The tiltrotor is too noisy. Can we get there by boat?"

"Only part of the way," Eddie replied. "Then it would be a long slog wading through those marshes, which happen to be filled with snakes and crocodiles. Exfiltration would be just as difficult."

"Not to mention that they might have

guards patrolling the perimeter. Some of those smaller vehicles look like hovercraft as well."

"If they're connected with the gas attack, we have to assume they have armed security," Juan said. "And whatever that building is, it's not configured like a bauxite processing plant. Which is why we need to see what they're actually doing in there."

"Before we try to sneak in, some firsthand intel about the place would be helpful," Eddie said.

Juan looked out at the giant hovercraft being loaded with trucks. "I think it's time for me to have a chat with the pilot of the *Marsh Flyer*."

# TWENTY-SIX

When Juan entered the Lazy Goanna with Max, it took a few seconds for his eyes to adjust to the gloom. Unlike the upscale bar and grill up the street, this tavern was the kind of dive bar where people came to either drown their sorrows or celebrate making it through the day. Tacky signs and knick-knacks were nailed haphazardly to the walls, and in front of the mirror behind the bar there was a large neon Foster's logo with half the letters burned out. The place reeked of beer, sweat, and testosterone.

It was around dinnertime, and the place was filled with bauxite miners, mechanics, fishermen, and other working folk. The only group who looked out of place was a table of four men in their twenties doing shots and whooping it up, giving away their status as tourists every time they shouted taunts at each other in their American accents.

"You think this is where they got the idea

for *Crocodile Dundee?*" Max asked.

"This might be where they filmed it," Juan said, scanning the room now that he could see more clearly.

"I don't see Parsons."

"Neither do I. But the harbormaster was pretty certain he'd be here."

"Might as well have a brew while we wait," Max said.

They took two stools at the end of the bar. The only woman in the place was a pretty blonde bartender wearing a tight tank top.

"What can I get for you fellows?" she asked in a chipper twang.

"Two Victoria Bitters, please," Juan said.

"You got it."

As she filled two glasses from the tap, one of the Americans lurched over to the bar.

"Four more Jagerbombs for me and my mates," he said in an exaggerated Aussie accent.

"You boys aren't driving anywhere, are you?" the bartender asked.

The guy leaned toward her. "Why? You want to join us?"

"No, thanks."

"Come on. We're going hunting tomorrow at a private ranch. It's my Christmas present. Wild boar, water buffalo, maybe even a camel." He reached out and grabbed her arm. "It'll be more fun with you there."

Juan was about to tell him to back off when a thick finger tapped the American on the shoulder.

"I think you should let go of the lady," he said with an Australian drawl that was dragged through gravel. "Right now."

The man was in his forties, six feet tall, his ropy arm muscles covered with sleeves of tattoos and his crew cut shot through with silver. The creases on his forehead made him look a bit older than the photos from his service record that Juan had seen, but it was definitely Bob Parsons.

The American released the bartender, who said, "Never mind him, Bob. I've handled worse."

"You heard her, Bob," the American slurred. "Why don't you leave us alone?"

"I know you don't need my help with him, Mindy," Parsons said as he took a seat on a stool one down from Juan. "I just don't like to see someone treat you rudely. I was hoping these loudmouths would be gone by the time I got back from the dunny. Just my luck that I have to keep hearing this one brag about the expensive vacation his daddy gave him." He took a swig from the beer bottle that Mindy set out for him.

Max leaned over to Juan and whispered,

"I'm beginning to like this guy already."

The young American glanced at his friends and then snarled at Parsons. "Are you looking for a beating, old man?"

"You tell him, Sawyer," one of his buddies yelled.

Parsons grinned at Sawyer. "Why would I want to give you a beating?"

"Okay, tough guy. Let's go outside and see who's smiling after I smack you around."

The three other Americans stood up at hearing the challenge.

"All right," Parsons said. "You go out and practice falling down while I finish my beer."

Sawyer looked at the other Americans, all of whom nodded like they were giving him permission to knock the Australian out. Parsons, meanwhile, kept drinking his beer, his eyes focused straight ahead.

With a wicked grin, Sawyer reared back to deliver a sucker punch to the side of Parsons' head, but his fist found nothing but air as Parsons leaned forward out of its path. The mirror behind the bar had made it easy for Parsons to anticipate the right cross.

With a single motion, Parsons was off his stool and grabbed the back of Sawyer's head. He slammed it onto the bar, causing the other three to launch themselves at Parsons.

With impressive speed, precision, and power, he whipped the beer bottle around and smashed it into the head of the lead guy, kicked the second in the groin, and hammered the kidney of the third with his elbow. All of them went down, holding their various injured body parts and wailing in pain.

By then, Sawyer had shaken out the cobwebs and plucked the neck of the broken bottle from the floor, wielding it like a dagger. Parsons was so occupied with the others that he didn't see the guy coming. Juan, who was already off his stool by this point, snagged Sawyer's wrist and used a foot sweep to knock his legs out from under him. The tourist landed hard on his back. Parsons turned in time to see Juan bend Sawyer's wrist until he dropped the bottleneck.

"That's not very sporting of you," Juan said, letting him go and kicking the weapon away.

The other three Americans staggered to their feet, but it was clear that they were all mouth and no spine. The fight was gone from them. They yanked Sawyer to his feet and carried him out the door.

"Thank you, sir," Parsons said. "I didn't mean to get you involved."

"Happy to help a Marine."

"You're American."

"Not all of us are snot-nosed brats. My name's Juan. This is Max."

"You recognized my tat?" Parsons held out his right arm, which was emblazoned with the Marine Corps logo: an eagle atop a globe laid over an anchor.

Juan did notice the tattoo, but he had also read up on Parsons before venturing out to the Lazy Goanna. Although Parsons had been born in Australia, his American mother had taken him to California when he was ten years old after his father died. He had been a Marine for five years, serving two tours in Afghanistan, before transferring to the Navy and becoming a LCAC pilot. The Landing Craft Air Cushion vehicles were giant hovercraft used to ferry tanks and personnel to shore during amphibious assaults.

"We're both veterans," Juan said, which was close to the truth. "Navy."

"Well, I appreciate the backup," Parsons said, sitting back on his stool. "Let me buy you two swabbies a drink."

After swapping sea stories over three rounds, Juan and Max were laughing with Parsons like they were old pals. Juan even showed him his prosthetic leg and made up a story about how he'd lost it in Iraq.

"How long have you been in this town?" Juan asked, finally getting around to his job now that they'd gotten friendly with him.

"Nhulunbuy?" Parsons said. "Oh, about a year now. Alloy Bauxite needed a hovercraft pilot, and I was the only one in these parts who could fly an SR.N4. Not too much different from an LCAC." He pronounced it "L-Cack."

"Where did they find a Mountbatten-class transport like that?"

"Ah, you know your hovercraft. They bought a scrapper that used to cross the English Channel and refurbished it. Even upgraded the controls so I could fly it without a navigator or flight engineer."

"She's a beauty," Juan said. "Too bad you have to be working so close to Christmas."

"I can't complain," Parsons said. "You wouldn't believe what they pay me to drive through that swamp. Besides, tomorrow's my last run and then I'm off for the holidays."

"Seems like an odd place to build a factory," Max said. "What do they make in there?"

"I don't know. I just move the trucks in and out." Parsons tossed back the remainder of his beer and let out a huge belch. "And

216

even if I did know, I couldn't tell you no matter how drunk I got."

"Why not?" Juan asked.

"Because they made me sign one of those non-disclosure agreements. Top secret and all that. If I so much as make a peep about what they do in there, they'd sue me so hard, my grandchildren would be bankrupt. And I don't even have kids."

"We wouldn't want to get you in trouble."

"Anyway, I think they're closing up soon."

"Why do you say that?" Max asked.

"Because the *Shepparton* left Nhulunbuy with a huge shipment, and my contract is up in a few days."

Juan and Max looked at each other knowingly. A huge shipment. They needed to find out what kind of cargo was already out to sea.

Parsons got off his stool and said, "It's been fun, gentlemen, but I need to sleep before my last flight of the year. Juan, Max, good to know ya."

"Nice to meet you, Master Chief," Juan said.

"Anchors aweigh and semper fi," Max said.

"Oorah," Parsons answered with a crisp salute and staggered out the door.

"He probably won't even have a hang-

217

over," Max said enviously. He turned to Juan and furrowed his brow. "I know that look. You've got an idea."

"We've been looking for a way into that factory," Juan said. "Parsons is taking his giant hovercraft over there in the morning. The *Marsh Flyer* seems pretty roomy. Why don't we just hitch a ride?"

## TWENTY-SEVEN

It was three in the morning when the operation began. Max, Hali, Eric, and Murph were in the *Oregon*'s op center watching the hovercraft on the large screen at the front of the room. The *Marsh Flyer* sat in the center of the concrete apron abutting the defunct aluminum refinery, a hundred yards of open space on all sides. One guard was posted at the bow while two other guards circled it on patrol.

"They're well trained," Murph said with his artificial voice. He was now out of his hospital clothes and wearing jeans and a black T-shirt that said "I can explain it to you, but I can't understand it for you."

"Their pattern is random and properly spaced," he continued. "No way to get past them without being seen."

"Where is the team?" Max asked from the command chair.

Hali was on the radio with Raven. "She

says they're in position."

Raven, still mending from her shoulder wound, had taken a rigid-hull inflatable boat through the harbor to the opposite side of the tarmac where she ran it ashore out of sight of the guards. Juan, Eddie, Linc, Linda, and MacD were prepared to dash to the hovercraft, but they needed a distraction to get across the open ground.

"All right, Murph," Max said, "lock on target with the laser."

Eric cleared his throat. Max was so used to Murph at the weapons station, he'd spoken without thinking.

"Sorry, Murph," he said. "Eric, you ready?"

Eric zoomed in the view on the main screen until they could see a patch of grass growing out of a crack in the concrete. "Locked on."

"Fire."

In an instant, the grass erupted in a blaze of light, ignited by the laser's invisible but intense beam.

The guard at the front of the hovercraft jerked his head around at the small fire and got on his radio. The other two guards came running. He sent them over to check it out, and they approached the flare-up cautiously.

Murph switched his voice to make it

sound like a curious teenager. "How did this fire start way out here with not a soul in sight? Strange."

"Tell Juan they're clear," Max told Hali.

Hali relayed the message, and Eric split the screen so it showed five black-clad figures sprinting toward the hovercraft. They disappeared behind it and a minute later reappeared atop the fuselage, dwarfed by the giant propellers. One of them eased open the external door to the cockpit, and they all quickly went through it into the darkened craft.

The guards lost interest in the smoldering grass and continued their patrols, none the wiser that they'd just failed at their jobs.

Juan was the last one through the door and closed it behind him. The cockpit was too cramped for all of them to fit, so Linda and MacD were already down the ladder leading to the car deck. There were two pilot seats, but only the one on the left showed wear. Touch screens surrounded the flight controls, making it look like the interior of a new airliner.

The windows gave a three-hundred-and-sixty-degree view, but the cockpit was situated well back from the sides of the hovercraft, so the guards next to it were out of sight.

"Hali, we're in," Juan said into his molar mic. "Let us know if anyone is coming on board."

"Roger that, Chairman."

He followed Eddie and Linc quietly down the ladder. The car deck was pitch black, so he flipped on his night vision goggles. The clamshell doors at the stern were closed. The guards outside almost certainly couldn't hear them, but Juan kept his sound-suppressed MP5 submachine gun ready just the same. Although this was a recon mission, all of them were fully armed. In addition to his MP5, MacD also carried his trusty crossbow.

The deck contained twenty two-axle box trucks, the kind used to deliver packages or carry small loads of freight. They were all facing the rear doors. Even with that cargo, the space was so cavernous that it was only half full.

"If the cargo ship is gone," Linda asked in a whisper, "what are these trucks going back to the factory for?"

"Good question," Juan said. "Raising the doors will make too much noise right now. We'll find out when we get there."

Hiding in the car deck wasn't an option.

They'd be spotted at first light. Juan led Eddie and Linc into the port passenger area, while MacD and Linda went starboard.

Surprisingly, the seats were all still in place, as if the vessel were ready for another run across the English Channel. A center aisle split three-abreast seats on either side. Together, the passenger cabins had room for four hundred people, plus toilets and galleys.

"It's still a few hours till dawn," Linc said. "Might as well get some shut-eye."

Sleep being a precious commodity, they each took a seat far from the windows and dozed off, knowing that the *Oregon* would warn them if someone boarded the craft.

Juan woke when he heard Hali in his ear. He blinked as sunlight streamed through the glass.

"Chairman, there's an SUV coming toward the *Marsh Flyer*."

"Understood," Juan answered. "Everyone to your hiding spots."

Eddie and Linc squeezed into the galley together while Juan closed himself in the port toilet. MacD and Linda would be doing the same on the other side. They reasoned that no one on the transport would be using the facilities for such a short trip.

The lack of odor in the bathroom confirmed that it hadn't been used recently. Juan donned his augmented reality glasses and switched them on, showing him views from the two wireless cameras he had hastily attached to the exterior of the cockpit on the way in.

He could see the SUV park at the edge of the tarmac. A man got out and walked toward the *Marsh Flyer* with a powerful gait. It was Bob Parsons, dressed in a flight suit and mirrored sunglasses. He gestured to the guard and kept going.

"Parsons and the three guards are all getting on," Hali said.

A few minutes later, Juan felt the engines start up, and the propellers began to spin.

"We'll lose radio contact with you once you cross the bay," Hali said.

"I've got my sat phone in case we need you to send in the cavalry," Juan said.

"Max says, 'Happy hunting.' "

"See you soon."

The propellers came up to full speed, and the hovercraft lifted up atop the cushion of air filling its rubber skirt. The *Marsh Flyer* rotated until it faced the shore before accelerating off the concrete and onto the water.

Within moments, the hovercraft was racing across the bay, a white mist of seawater billowing behind them. Ten minutes later, it completed the bay crossing and reached the vast swamp of Arnhem Land, slowing to half speed as it approached the greenery.

The thick grasses and reeds of the marsh would have fouled any boat trying to navigate through, and no wheeled vehicle would have made it a hundred feet from the coast. But the *Marsh Flyer* floated across the muddy bog as if it were the smoothest asphalt. Low trees dotted the landscape to either side, but there was a wide-open swath cut through them.

The ocean was far behind them when Juan finally spotted a large white building in the distance. It was two stories tall with what looked like sophisticated air-handling units on its roof.

"The factory is up ahead," Juan told the rest of the team.

"Is it okay to come out?" MacD asked.

"Let's wait to see if anyone comes into the passenger areas. If they do a search, be ready to fight."

As they got closer, Juan could now see the vehicles he'd spotted on the satellite image. Parked on the tarmac were a couple more trucks like the ones on the car deck. Next to them were half a dozen four-person

225

hovercraft likely used for patrols or for carrying personnel back to Nhulunbuy.

Behind all of them was a helicopter, a Bell JetRanger, the kind used for sightseeing trips.

Juan saw a group of men waiting for them on the apron, all wearing uniforms and caps, many heavily armed.

"We've got a lot of potential hostiles out there," Juan said. "I count at least twenty, and they're packing assault rifles by the look of it."

"Must be something important inside," Eddie said.

The hovercraft came to rest on the tarmac, and the engines powered down. A small tractor trundled toward the hovercraft with a metal ramp to attach to the stern, and the clamshell doors swung open for unloading the trucks.

"How are we getting off?" Linda asked.

"We can't sneak off without being seen," Juan said. He'd been hoping that they could slip into the swamp undetected, but there was too much open space to cross.

The first truck drove off the hovercraft toward an open garage door in the building. Juan didn't hear any sounds in the passenger cabin, so he cracked the toilet door open. The cabin was empty.

"We're clear on this side."

"Same here," Linda said.

Linc and Eddie joined him. They could hear voices out in the car deck before each of the trucks started up and drowned them out.

"Any ideas over there?" MacD asked.

Eddie peeked over the bottom edge of the window.

"All the guards are Chinese. They're speaking Mandarin."

"Chinese?" Linc said. "I thought this company was supposed to be a contractor to the Australian military."

Juan shrugged. "That's what the intelligence said."

"At least we have a way in now," Eddie said. He had grown up in New York's Chinatown and spent years embedded in China as a spy for the CIA, so he spoke the language like a native. "I'll wait until one of them is alone and call him in here."

They went to the door leading to the car deck, and Eddie pulled it slightly ajar. He said something in Mandarin and backed away.

A curious guard poked his head in, and Juan slammed the butt of his gun down. The guard slumped to the floor, and they pulled him inside.

They quickly stripped him, zip-tied him, and locked him in the toilet while Eddie put on his uniform and cap and traded his submachine gun for the assault rifle. With his head down, Eddie could now easily pass for one of the guards.

"You drive the next truck," Juan said. "We'll get in the back."

Eddie went out into the car deck. When the space was clear, he waved for them to hurry out. Linda and MacD exited from the other side, and they quickly scrambled into the back of the truck, pulling the roll-up door down behind them. MacD and Linda both lit small flashlights.

Six crates were secured to the floor. Each of them was stenciled with the Alloy Bauxite logo.

"I thought these trucks were empty," Linc said. "What are they carrying in?"

"Let's take a look," Juan said. He used a multi-tool to pry the lid off of one of the crates. As Eddie started up the truck and rolled it out of the hovercraft, Linda shined her light on the box's contents.

MacD whistled in awe. "Now, what are they planning to do with those?"

Juan had no idea, but it couldn't be good. The crate was filled with sticks of dynamite.

# TWENTY-EIGHT

From his office on the second floor of the factory, Angus Polk watched the trucks stream in one by one, directed to their designated spots along the assembly line. They were spaced out evenly throughout the building. Now that all the Enervum they needed had been produced and installed in the rockets that would distribute the nerve gas, it was time to cover their trail.

The dynamite would erase any trace of their involvement, but Polk had to leave false evidence as well. Specific documents and objects had been carefully planted around the structure to survive the blast. When the inevitable investigation was conducted, all the clues would point to a secret operation by the Australian military, giving more proof to the country's citizens that their own government was responsible for the catastrophe that was about to befall them.

His phone buzzed, and he saw that it was his wife on video chat. He tapped on the phone, and April Jin appeared, smiling.

"Have you seen the news lately?" she asked.

Polk nodded. "People love conspiracy theories about Air Force bases."

Jin had used her plasma cannon to set one of RAAF Base Talbot's storage buildings on fire, then purposely sent the rocket carrying the paralysis chemical over the base before it detonated above the adjacent town. Any witnesses would be convinced Talbot had been the source of the gas.

"Between Port Cook and the *Empiric,*" she replied, "the Australian media is in overdrive. Social media is full of speculation about all kinds of secret experiments going on that have been hidden from the public. The public is calling for an independent investigation into the incidents."

"Blowing up this factory will only accelerate the chatter. How's the *Shepparton?*"

After gassing the town, Jin had taken the *Marauder* trimaran to rendezvous with their cargo ship after the attack on Port Cook to check in on it.

"Captain Rathman has her on course. All the modifications have been made to the ship, and preparations are on track for when she arrives in Sydney." The captain didn't know what the cargo was, and he was paid amply not to ask questions. "I'm on my way to Cairns now to meet you."

"We're supposed to be watching Lu's last video today," Polk said.

"I know. That's why I called, so we could watch it together."

Polk sat at the office desk and opened his laptop. He typed in the command to start the video and pointed his phone at the screen so Jin could watch as well.

Lu appeared. Though he looked haggard, his expression was almost buoyant.

"If you are watching this, congratulations. We are nearing the endgame, and after this you will hear from me no more. If you have been careful to date and have executed my plan to perfection, then the final actions should be completed without issue. You will be heroes to the cause and the beneficiary of my estate."

"I am so glad this is the final one," Polk muttered.

"Me, too," Jin added.

"I think it's time for you to know the purpose of all your efforts. By now you realize that I intend to cause five million Sydneysiders to suffer some form of paralysis. The fact that you're watching this video means that you agree to carry out my plan despite the enormous implications. It also means that I have chosen my agents wisely."

Lu cleared his throat and took a sip of water.

"My motive is not revenge. I bear no ill will to Australia's citizens. Yes, millions may die and millions more will endure a lifetime confined to a wheelchair. But the round-the-clock care the survivors will need is not a by-product of my plan, it is the entire goal. It's the only way China will break out of its confines of regional dominance in Asia and replace the United States as the world's preeminent superpower."

"How so?" Polk said.

Jin waved her hand at him. "Shh. We're about to find out."

"I am a patriot, and for too long it has been easy to isolate China. Yes, my country has been exercising its financial might throughout the world, but it's not enough. It is too timid. I've argued for a long time that we should have a bolder strategy. The Party resisted my calls for expanding the empire by invasion, considering it too risky. They declined despite having decisive new weapons I developed for them like the plasma cannon, whose design was long ago stolen from the Americans and perfected by my company. So I took the weapon back, built the *Marauder,* and devised my own plan to extend China beyond its borders without the Party's knowledge."

"He wants to invade Australia," Jin said breathlessly.

"How is that even possible?" Polk asked.

"What do you think will happen when five million Australians are suddenly incapacitated?" Lu said. "The government can't let them all die where they are. It would be inhuman. No, they would do everything in their power to save those unfortunate souls. But Australia doesn't have the manpower. Overnight, twenty percent of their population would need special attention. I estimate at least half of them would die within days if the country didn't undertake a massive effort to care for them. Who would they turn to?"

"The United States?" Polk mused.

"Not the United States," Lu seemed to answer him. "It's too far away and doesn't have enough people to send. My projections are that Australia will need at least one million caregivers immediately. And what's the only country with the resources, manpower, and proximity to provide them? China. Thanks to some recent airline bankruptcies, a hundred spare airliners are ready to be deployed at a moment's notice, and there are a million contract employees available to the Chinese government when they are requested."

Polk paused the video and looked at his wife. "You've got to admit, it just might work."

Jin nodded. "Australia will have no choice but to take the help."

"And with a million Chinese citizens suddenly entering the country, China has a foothold on another entire continent."

"Lu knows the Chinese government will want to extract concessions in return. It's a backdoor invasion. And because the Australians already think that their own military is behind the disaster, there would be virtually no resistance to bringing them in. They'd be welcomed as saviors."

Polk continued the video.

"Of course, the Chinese military will need to send units as well, purely for coordination purposes," Lu said. "And once they are in the country, I doubt they will be leaving. In any event, a good portion of Australia's residents will at that point be Chinese. The invasion will take place right under the Australians' noses, and China's land area will double in the space of a week, giving it a larger total land area than Russia. More than enough room for a billion more Chinese."

Lu leaned back in his chair with a satisfied look, as if he had already accomplished his goal.

"Perhaps you disagree with my plan or simply don't share my goals. It doesn't matter. My name will go down in history, but Lu Yang won't be remembered as a monster. I will be known not only as the person who saved millions of Australian lives but also as the visionary of a new era for the Chinese people. For all our sakes, I hope you complete your task and become billionaires by the beginning of the new year. Good luck and good-bye."

"That guy is certainly audacious," Polk said.

"What do you think about his plan?" Jin asked. "Is it worth the risk?"

"He's provided all the resources to get us this far. It's just a matter of delivering the goods now and making our escape." He looked his wife in the eyes. "I see no reason not to finish the job."

"Fair dinkum. My stepfather might not care about revenge, but I will love seeing the Australian military raked over the coals for this debacle. Serves them right for throwing us in prison."

"I'm just glad I don't ever have to listen to him again."

"How much more do you have to do there?"

"Not much. All the factory workers are already taken care of. Now I'm just packing up. Then I'll blow the place and get back to the airport outside Nhulunbuy. Lu's jet is waiting there."

"Don't forget the antidote," she said.

"It's already on the helicopter. Let's hope we don't need it. Makes me ill to think about being paralyzed like that."

"See you soon, my love," Jin said.

It was time to purge all the on-site computer servers along with his laptop since the files had already been backed up to the main computer on the *Marauder.* Polk pressed the button to begin the deletion procedure. A window popped up saying that the entire database would be wiped clean in fifteen minutes.

He stood up and walked over to the window. All of the trucks seemed to be in place.

No, he counted only seventeen out of the eighteen that were to be taken out of the hovercraft. The other two left on board would blow the *Marsh Flyer* to bits.

Where was the last truck? These ex-soldiers hired by Lu were supposed to be top notch. Not the smartest apparently, but fanatical in their loyalty to Lu and his vision.

Polk took a SIG Sauer pistol from his desk, shoved it into his waistband, and left his office to find out what was going on. The gun was so he could tie up one other loose end, namely the *Marsh Flyer*'s pilot.

He had to kill Bob Parsons.

---

## TWENTY-NINE

The dynamite truck rolled to a halt, and
Juan could hear the muffled voice of Eddie
talking to someone in Chinese outside the
truck. The conversation got heated, so he
had MacD, Linda, and Linc ready to fire if
the rear door was opened for an inspection.
But a moment later, the truck started up
again. After a few turns, it stopped.

Eddie hauled the door open, and they all
got out. It looked like they were on a narrow concrete strip between the rear of the
building and the swamp. There were two
doors, one into the main factory and another into what looked like an office annex
or living quarters with windows facing the
swamp.

"Sounds like we had a close call," Juan
said.

"The guy wanted me to drive into the factory," Eddie said, "but I convinced him that
I was told to go around back. We probably

don't have a lot of time until they wise up."

"Then let's check it out. When we're done, we'll steal one of those Qingdao hovercraft and get out of here." Though the speedy Chinese-made vehicles were built to carry four people, he felt sure they could squeeze an extra person on board.

"Eddie and I will take the factory. Linda, MacD, and Linc, use the annex door. Remember, this is a recon mission. Engage only if you have to. We'll rendezvous back here in ten minutes."

As the three others went into the side building, Juan cracked the factory door open. A quick scan showed that they were in the clear.

He and Eddie ducked inside. It was a vast room containing robotic machine tools, laboratory equipment, and stacks of crates marked with the Alloy Bauxite logo. Other than the guards that Juan could hear farther along the building, there didn't seem to be any workers. Wide aisles allowed room for the forklifts that were parked along the back wall. Now the trucks from the hovercraft were jammed into the free space.

Juan assumed all the other trucks were packed with dynamite as well, which meant they were getting ready to destroy the building.

Eddie tapped his shoulder and pointed at an enclosed stairway leading up to what looked like an office, perhaps the factory foreman's. It might be a good place to find information about what had been going on in here.

They climbed the stairs, and at the top peered through the glass in the door to see that the office was empty. They crept in low so they couldn't be seen through the window overlooking the factory floor.

The file cabinets were pulled open, and every drawer was empty. The high-capacity shredder was still warm, and several garbage cans were overflowing with minced paper.

The only remaining intact item was a laptop on the desk.

"Take a look at it," Juan said to Eddie. While Eddie inspected the computer, Juan went to the window and peeked over the sill.

From this vantage point, he had an excellent view of the sprawling facility. Most of it looked automated, so it could be operated with minimal personnel.

One odd element stood out, however. Just below him were lab benches crammed with all kinds of scientific equipment, flasks, test tubes, and chemical hoods. Next to it was a huge glass tank of water, and inside it floated a cloud of jellyfish that were pulsating with light.

At the opposite end of the factory, several of the guards had gathered around a man who was obviously in charge. Juan couldn't see his face clearly, but he could tell the guy was tall and muscular, with sleeve tattoos on his arms. Walking toward that group, escorted by two additional guards, was Bob Parsons.

"Chairman, they're deleting their files," Eddie said.

Juan went over to the desk and saw a progress bar on the screen. It read "Erasing remote files: 68% complete."

"Can you cancel it?" Juan asked.

"No, but I'm trying to download as many files as I can before it completes the task." Eddie had inserted a flash drive into the laptop's USB port. It was a special device created by Eric and Murph for this kind of data extraction.

"Can't we just take the computer with us?"

"I don't think it would do much good. The hard drive looks virtually empty. There must be a server stack somewhere in the building."

Juan switched on his molar mic. "Linc, we've found a laptop erasing all of the local computer files on a server. They're getting ready to wipe this place from existence. Tell me you've found something useful."

Linc, MacD, and Linda had found something, all right. Dead bodies. Twenty-two of them haphazardly piled one on the other.

"I think we've located the factory workers, Chairman," Linc said. "We saw nothing but empty offices and bunkrooms in here before we stumbled onto a cold storage unit and discovered twenty-two bodies stacked inside. It's not pretty."

"Now we know the type of people we're up against here," Juan said. "Call me when you've finished your sweep."

Linda bent down to examine one of the corpses. They were all men, half of them Caucasian and half Chinese.

"No gunshot wounds or blunt trauma," she said. "No bruising or scratches. Not one sign of struggle."

"Do you think they were poisoned?" MacD asked.

"No, I don't think so. See the splotches in the eyes? It's called petechial hemorrhaging. He likely was suffocated."

MacD quickly scanned some of the others. They showed the same effects.

"They all were," MacD said. "How do you

suffocate twenty-two men, and not a single one fights back?"

"Maybe they *were* poisoned, with the paralyzing gas used on Murph," Linc said. "Then they were finished off when they couldn't move. Some kind of sick test that also got rid of the potential witnesses. Let's keep going."

They left the storage locker and continued down the long corridor. They found two more bare offices before coming to a room filled with computer servers. Lights blinked as if they were processing reams of data.

There was a lone terminal in the room. Linc tapped on the keyboard, and the screen powered up. It was asking for a password.

He typed PASSWORD just to see what happened, and it blared PASSWORD DENIED.

"You'll never break into that," Linda said.

"At least not in the next few minutes," MacD added.

"Chairman," Linc said, "we've found the server room, but we can't get into the system. Should we unplug everything to stop the disk wipe?"

"No, let it keep running," Juan said. "We're trying to get as much info as possible before it's erased."

"Roger that."

"Meet us back by the truck. We're leaving in four minutes."

"Understood."

They went back into the hall to complete their search. As they moved to the next room, the door at the other end of the corridor opened. A guard entered, calling out in Chinese as if he were looking for someone.

For a moment, he stared in shock at the three strangers standing in the hall. He recovered quickly and raised his assault rifle.

Before he could get it to his shoulder, MacD snapped off a shot with his crossbow. The bolt went through the guard's eye, and he keeled over backward.

"He was probably looking for the truck driver," Linda said.

They hurried to the door. Linc looked out, but there was no one there. However, a voice was calling on the radio attached to the dead guard's belt. The tone was getting increasingly urgent.

"Chairman," Linc said into his mic, "we had to cap one of the guards, and I think someone is about to come looking for him."

# THIRTY

Although he'd needed Parsons to pilot the
*Marsh Flyer,* Polk had never liked the swag-
gering Marine. He was too much of a Boy
Scout. Just last week, when one of the factory scientists injured himself while loading
the hovercraft, Parsons insisted on taking
him to the infirmary in Nhulunbuy instead
of letting them patch him up at the swamp
facility, despite the severe breach of security
protocol. The action ended up saving the
man's life — at least for a few more days —
but it was clear Parsons could be trouble. If
Polk had any other choice of pilots when it
happened, he would have killed Parsons
then and there.

Now Polk would get his wish.

"I'm happy to tell you that your services
are no longer needed, Parsons."

Parsons smirked at him. "You've found
someone else to pilot the *Flyer* back to Nhulunbuy?"

Polk fixed him with a stony stare. "No."

"So you're just going to leave it here?"

"More or less. Not all in one piece."

Parsons finally got it and looked at the guards surrounding him. "I'm not getting any severance pay, am I?"

"No need for it." Polk nodded at two of the guards, then pulled out his pistol and leveled it at Parsons' chest. The guards bound Parsons' hands behind his back with a zip tie.

Parsons gave a rueful chuckle. "I should have known you would do something like this. What a great Christmas present. And I suppose Miller isn't your real name?"

"No, it isn't."

"I guess it doesn't really matter at this point. Would you believe me if I said that I've kept a record of everything I saw here, and it'll get out if anything happens to me?"

"We've been observing you. You haven't spoken to anyone outside of Nhulunbuy about your job since you started working for us, and my men have already searched your rental and examined your phone. They found nothing."

"You tapped my phone?"

"You shouldn't have left it unattended in the hovercraft cockpit."

Parsons looked at the gun and sighed. "I

guess I'm too stupid to live then. Get it over with."

"As much as I'd like to shoot you, that's not what's going to happen. A bullet in your head would ruin any appearance of an accident here." Polk motioned to two of the guards. "Take him to the cold storage room and lock him in. When we're ready, we'll find an appropriate place to put him along with the other bodies. He'll be another casualty of the explosion."

Parsons glared at Polk while the two guards shoved him away.

"Now, where's my missing truck?" Polk said in Mandarin to a guard holding a walkie-talkie. While he waited for an answer, he climbed into the bed of the nearest one and opened the box holding the timer for this truck's detonator. He set it for two hours, plenty of time to get everything in order before they left. All the trucks were loaded with dynamite and spaced so close together it would set off a chain reaction that would reduce the building to fragments.

The guard spoke into his radio several times asking about the truck, but he got no response. "I don't know where it is, sir. I sent a man around the building to locate it, but I can't reach him."

"Then send more men to find both of them."

"How's it coming?" Juan asked Eddie from his spot at the window.

"It was a race to the finish," Eddie replied as he unplugged the USB drive from the laptop, "but I was able to download the remaining files before they got erased. We won't know if any of them are readable until we get this back to the *Oregon*."

"Hold on," Juan said. He saw Parsons being escorted by two of the guards. The hovercraft pilot had his hands tied behind his back. "We've got a new problem."

Eddie joined him at the window. "It looks like Parsons is going to get the same treatment as the other workers."

The guards were escorting Parsons through the laboratory area in the direction of the living quarters where the rest of the team was.

"Linc," Juan said, "you're about to have some company. A couple of guards. Be advised there is a friendly with them. It's a guy named Bob Parsons, a Caucasian with a crew cut."

"Got it," Linc answered. "We'll give them a proper welcome."

As Parsons and the two guards passed the

tank holding the jellyfish, he suddenly turned and head-butted one of the guards, who stumbled from the impact and fell to the floor. Then Parsons threw his shoulder at the other guard, and they smashed into the tank. He kneed the guard in the groin, but the guard slugged him in the jaw with an elbow, and Parsons reeled back from the punch.

The furious guard raised his assault rifle. Juan smashed the window with the butt of his MP5, distracting the guard long enough for Eddie to shoot the man with a three-round burst. The guard went down, but one of the bullets went all the way through his torso and hit the tank glass, causing a series of growing cracks.

Seeing what was about to happen, Parsons backed away quickly.

Just as he got out of harm's way, the tank shattered. The second guard staggered to his feet at the same moment that a gush of water enveloped him and tossed him to the floor. One of the jellyfish landed on his head. He convulsed in agony and let out a piercing scream as he clawed at the venomous tentacles draping across his face.

Parsons looked up at the office, dumbfounded.

Juan pointed at the back door and yelled, "Go."

Parsons didn't hesitate and ran.

"We're hearing gunfire," Linc called out. "Are you okay in there?"

Drawn by the sound of the battle, more guards sprinted in their direction.

"Change of plans, Linc," Juan said. "Parsons is on his way, and he's alone. Get the truck started. It's time to leave."

# THIRTY-ONE

By now additional guards were approaching, so while Eddie ran for the stairs, Juan fired at them to pin them down. When Eddie got to the bottom, he took over firing, and Juan joined him. Together, they ran for the back door to the factory.

They got outside to find Linc in the driver's seat of the truck and Linda and MacD in the back with Parsons, whose hands were now untied.

"Never thought I'd see you out here, mate," Parsons said as Juan and Eddie jumped in the truck's bed. "Glad I did, though."

"How long to start up the *Marsh Flyer*?" No way they'd get the open-topped Qingdao hovercraft up and running before they were under a hail of gunfire.

"I'd say about a minute to get her off the ground and moving," Parsons said.

Juan thought they could defend it that

long. "Linc, get this truck back onto the *Marsh Flyer*."

"On our way."

The truck lurched forward, but not before the rear door to the factory burst open. Juan and the others immediately cut down the first two guards through, but a third managed to get off a volley before he was shot.

The guard's bullets raked the back of the truck. As it sped around the building, Juan yelled, "Anyone hurt?" It was only then that he saw a round dent in one of the boxes holding the dynamite and realized they were lucky it hadn't penetrated and set off one of the sticks.

All the answers were no except Parsons, who was cradling his right hand, blood oozing through his fingers. He looked more annoyed than hurt.

"Look at this mess. I'll need help piloting the *Flyer* now."

Linda took a field dressing out of her med kit and wrapped it around the wound.

"Never mind me," Parsons said. "Take care of him." He was pointing at Juan's right leg.

Juan looked down and saw a bullet hole in his pants below the knee.

"It's all right," Juan said, lifting the pant leg to show off his combat prosthesis, which now had a slug embedded in it. "Remember, I'm a vet like you."

The truck rounded the building. Scattered gunshots peppered the side of the truck as it accelerated across the concrete. When they had a view of the building from the rear bed, Juan and his team opened fire, holding back the few guards who had come out this way.

The truck passed the row of Qingdaos, then flew up the rear ramp and onto the car deck of the *Marsh Flyer.* It screeched to a halt, and when Juan jumped out, he saw that Linc had stopped mere inches from one of the other two trucks.

"Linc, you take the right passenger compartment. Eddie, the left. MacD and Linda, stay on the car deck. I'll help Parsons fly this thing."

"What's your name again?" Parsons asked as he climbed the ladder to the cockpit.

"Juan Cabrillo."

"I can't wait to hear how you ended up in this place."

"A story for another time," Juan said, following him up.

He could already hear sporadic gunfire and the sound of the small hovercraft outside starting up.

Angry about the last-minute incursion on the factory, Polk ordered his men to go after the intruders and kill every last one of them, including Parsons. He didn't bother going back to his office. Now nobody would believe the evidence he'd carefully arranged to be planted around the building. It was more important to destroy the facility and its contents and get out of there as soon as possible.

He went back to the truck with the detonator and reset it to two minutes. Then he sprinted for the helicopter.

While in Australia's Special Operations Command, Polk had taken rotary wing flight training, so the Bell JetRanger was a cinch for him to fly. He jumped in and started up the engine without even going through the checklist.

At the same time his overhead rotor began spinning, so did the giant propellers on the *Marsh Flyer.*

"Do not let them leave," he ordered into his radio.

One of the Qingdao hovercraft with four men aboard rose up on its skirt and hurtled across the tarmac. Bullets sparked off the fuselage, and one guard went down, but not before the craft was able to shoot up the rear ramp of the *Marsh Flyer* and onto the car deck.

A second Qingdao was only moments behind, but the giant hovercraft was lifted up by its own skirt, causing the temporary ramp to slide off. The second Qingdao bounced off the rubber without going in. Instead, it flipped over, crushing the guards on board.

The *Marsh Flyer* accelerated off the concrete and over the swamp, but Polk could see the flash of gunfire through the open rear clamshell doors. The four remaining Qingdaos, now holding the only surviving guards, took off after it.

With his rotor at max speed, Polk lifted the chopper off at full throttle so he could quickly gain speed and altitude and put some distance between him and the factory.

He checked his watch, which was counting down in sync with the timer on the detonator.

. . . *three* . . . *two* . . . *one* . . .

The first load of dynamite went off right on time, blowing a hole through the roof of the Enervum factory. It was followed in quick succession by a series of gigantic blasts that rippled across the building until it was one huge fireball. The shock wave tossed the JetRanger around, but Polk was able to get it under control.

The destruction wasn't exactly the way he wanted it to happen, but he thought it might be good enough to serve their purposes.

But he couldn't celebrate just yet. He banked the chopper around to watch the four small hovercraft racing to catch up to their far larger cousin. From this angle, it looked impossible for them to take out a hovercraft the size of the *Marsh Flyer*.

He silently patted himself on the back for having the foresight to arm his security team with rocket-propelled grenades.

# THIRTY-TWO

Linda was crouched beside MacD on the car deck behind one of the trucks near the *Marsh Flyer*'s bow. She could make out three of the guards from the Qingdao that had made it on board, but she didn't see the fourth one. They took cover behind their hovercraft, which had crashed into the rearmost of the three trucks. The space echoed with the deafening sound of gunfire.

"Where is he?" MacD yelled between bursts from his MP5. The invading gunmen carried high-powered Norinco assault rifles.

"I don't know," Linda called back, "but if one of those rounds hits the dynamite, we won't have time to regret our life choices."

"We've got to ambush them now," Linc said over the comms. "Eddie, are you in position?" Both of them were standing behind the doors to the passenger compartments on each side of the *Marsh Flyer*.

"Ready."

"Linda and MacD, distract them."

"Here goes," Linda said.

She and MacD jumped up and unleashed a barrage in the direction of the three guards. They were so focused on the incoming bullets that they didn't see Linc and Eddie burst onto the car deck behind them and open fire. All three were dead before they hit the deck.

Linda and MacD edged forward, checking under the trucks for the fourth guard.

"Do you see him?" Linda asked.

"No," MacD replied.

"Neither do I," Linc said.

"Hold it," Eddie said. "The rear door to the truck we came in on. Was it closed?"

Linda looked at MacD, who shook his head.

"We didn't close it."

They joined Linc and Eddie quietly outside the rear of the truck. While Linc and Eddie held their weapons on the door, Linda and MacD put their hands on the handles. Linc nodded, and they threw them open.

The remaining guard whirled around with something in his hand, reaching for his Norinco, but before he could reach his rifle, he was riddled with bullets.

Linda picked up the object that he

dropped. It was a small detonator with a countdown timer set at twenty seconds. There was a keypad labeled in Chinese characters. She handed it to Eddie, who tapped on it. The LCD screen went blank.

"I've canceled the timer," he said.

The crate beside the guard's body was open. A pocket in the lid the size of the detonator was empty.

"The detonator must already have been in there," Linc said.

While Eddie, Linc, and Linda opened the other crates, MacD ran to the next truck and came back a few moments later holding an identical one in his hand.

"It looks like each truck has only one detonator," Eddie said.

"Too bad," Linda said, looking through the open rear door at the Qingdaos that were quickly gaining on them. "It would have been nice to dump these crates behind us one by one like depth charges. I'm already low on ammo."

"Me, too," MacD said.

"That's actually a good idea," Eddie said. He peered at the pursuing hovercraft and nodded his head rhythmically.

"What do you mean?" Linda asked. "What are you doing?"

"I see where he's going with this," Linc

said, getting into the driver's seat and starting up the truck.

"They're seven seconds behind us," Eddie said. "Plus give us an extra ten seconds of safety."

He typed seventeen seconds into the keypad of the detonator.

Linc reversed the truck, with them inside, until it was near the rear edge of the car deck, and Linda understood.

The whole truck was going to be the depth charge.

"Trim the starboard props and make sure they aren't over-revving," Parsons said from the pilot seat of the *Marsh Flyer,* his good left hand on the steering yoke.

Juan followed the instructions, and the huge hovercraft slewed away from the edge of the swamp track through the trees.

"Nice work," Parsons said. "You're a natural."

"It's just point and click."

Steering the *Flyer* must have been challenging for Parsons, even with both his hands and at half the speed. But with a bullet hole in his right hand and the throttle at maximum, he needed Juan's assistance to keep it from spinning out of control.

Juan pulled out his radio and called the

It was patched through to Max. "Where are you? We don't see the *Marsh Flyer* yet."

"You will soon," Juan said. "Tell me you've already cast off from the Nhulunbuy dock."

"As planned."

"Good, because we're coming in hot. Be ready for hostile forces."

"Roger that."

The updated *Flyer* cockpit had screens showing the view from cameras on all four corners of the craft to give a view of the surroundings, including the mushroom cloud of smoke rising behind them from the remains of the factory. While Juan helped Parsons with the instruments, he also served as eyes for the rest of the team.

He had an image of the car deck on his view screen, so he'd seen the entire gun battle. Linc was still in the driver's seat of the truck he had driven to the stern of the hovercraft, and MacD and Linda were on either side of it. He couldn't see Eddie.

"We've got four Qingdao hovercraft approaching fast from the rear," Juan said. "Can you see them?"

"We've got an idea," Eddie replied.

A guard in the lead Qingdao had a launcher for a rocket-propelled grenade on his shoulder. Linda and MacD took a few shots, but the driver of the hovercraft swerved to avoid them.

"They've got an RPG," Juan said. "Whatever you're planning, do it now."

Eddie came into view and waved to the rest of them. Linc jumped out of the cab as the truck started to roll backward while the rest of them pushed. The truck fell off the lip of the car deck and flipped backward into the swamp.

"Bombs away," Eddie said.

The Qingdaos easily went around the truck, and the guard with the RPG lined up for his shot. At the same time that he fired, the truck erupted in a massive explosion. It was too far behind the hovercrafts to destroy them, but it threw off the aim of the guard.

Instead of flying into the car deck, the RPG went high. At first, Juan thought it would miss them completely, but it struck the starboard rear propeller. The broken blades went flying into the sky.

The stump of the pylon was on fire, and the *Marsh Flyer* immediately began turning to starboard, threatening to send them crashing into the jungle.

Parsons strained at the wheel to pull them back on course.

"Cut back power on the port engine," he

shouted, pointing with his bad hand at a handle near Juan's knee. Juan pulled back on the control, and the engines lowered the speed of the propellers on the port side to compensate for the one that was now missing.

Parsons was able to keep them straight now, but their speed was cut in half.

"Can we put out the fire?" Juan asked.

"Not without flaming out the engine."

A guard in one of the other Qingdaos now had an RPG ready to fire.

A second truck in the car deck rolled to the stern, this one facing the opening. The tires squealed, and Linc rolled out of the driver's door as the truck sped through the doors.

The truck exploded seconds after it landed in the water. Two of the hovercraft were going around it as before, but this time they were catapulted into the air. One of them blew up in midair when the RPG misfired, and the other somersaulted across the swamp.

"There's the bay," Parsons said. The swamp was beginning to thin out as they approached open water.

The drivers of the last two Qingdaos learned the lesson and went wide, quickly pulling alongside the *Marsh Flyer*. If they could damage the skirt, it would be over. The giant hovercraft would be dead in the water.

There was one truck with dynamite left, but it wouldn't do any good if they couldn't get it into the path of their pursuers.

"Can you spin this thing?" Juan asked Parsons.

"Are you crazy?" Parsons said. "I'm barely keeping it together as it is."

"We won't be here at all if they can pick us apart with those RPGs. Can you spin it?"

"Maybe once. Why?"

"Because we're going to turn the *Flyer* into a slingshot."

Polk was watching from two thousand feet up. The *Marsh Flyer* was burning as it crossed into the bay back toward Nhulunbuy, but it was still moving. His men should have destroyed it by now, but their tactics had been sloppy. He told them to stop following behind the hovercraft and shoot at it from the side. Once they deflated the skirt, the surviving guards could sink it and kill everyone who jumped overboard, then meet him at the airport for their flight to rendezvous with the *Marauder*.

One of the Qingdaos matched the speed

of the wounded *Flyer,* and a man stood with an RPG to cripple his target. It seemed like an easy shot.

But to Polk's surprise, the *Flyer*'s propellers rotated, sending the gigantic hovercraft into a horizontal spin on its own axis. The centrifugal force flung something out the back as the stern aligned with the Qingdao, and Polk realized it was another truck like the last two.

Neither he nor the Qingdao pilot could do a thing as it splashed into the water and exploded, sending a geyser into the air that disintegrated the small hovercraft and severely damaged the *Marsh Flyer.*

The aft skirt was ripped to shreds, and the *Flyer* plowed into the water. The propellers on top continued to turn, but it wasn't going anywhere. It was already beginning to list. The buoyancy tanks must have been punctured. It wouldn't stay afloat for long.

Polk radioed to the last Qingdao.

"Make sure no one gets off alive."

Low rain clouds were starting to roll in, so he wouldn't be able to watch for much longer, but he wanted to be sure they finished their task.

He'd been so focused on the hovercraft that he hadn't noticed a ship entering the bay until he banked around for another pass. It looked like an ordinary bulk cargo ship, although it was spewing a huge wake behind it like it was a speedboat.

Then something odd happened. The tower on one of the ship's cranes seemed to come apart, revealing some kind of device. It was only when the mechanism swiveled around and aimed at the Qingdao that Polk recognized it as a twin-barreled Gatling gun.

A torrent of rounds poured from the weapon, obliterating the small hovercraft in an instant.

A moment later, a boat sped out of a gap in the ship's hull.

It wouldn't take long for the *Marsh Flyer*'s rescuers to realize Polk was involved in the attack. He turned the chopper sharply and flew for cover into the nearby cloud bank.

As he flew toward the airport, he called ahead to the pilot to make sure he was ready to take off the moment Polk arrived. Then he phoned his wife.

"How did it go?" she asked. "Are you on your way?"

"I'm on my way, but we've got a big problem," Polk said, fuming about the debacle he had just witnessed. "Our operation has been compromised."

"Compromised? By whom?"

"That, my dear, is the right question."

# THIRTY-THREE

Despite his injured hand, Bob Parsons didn't need any help getting into the *Oregon*'s rigid-hull inflatable boat. He stepped over the gunwale easily from the top of the sinking *Marsh Flyer*. MacD, Linda, Eddie, and Linc were right behind him, followed by Juan, who was the last off. As Raven steered the RHIB back to the ship, the giant hovercraft turned turtle with a huge splash and disappeared into the depths.

Parsons gave the *Flyer* a crisp salute, then watched the crane sleeve on the *Oregon* return into place, covering the Kashtan Gatling guns. He was equally interested in the gap in the hull of the ship where the RHIB had emerged. The boat garage was located at the waterline and contained all their surface craft, including Zodiacs, Jet Skis, and the special operations boat they were now on.

"I know my U.S. Navy ships," Parsons

said, "and that isn't one of them. I'd say you've got yourself a Q-ship."

Q-ships, warships disguised as tramp steamers, were most frequently used against U-boats during World War II. They would act as decoys to lure submarines to the surface where they were vulnerable to the hidden armaments.

"You're looking at the *Oregon*," Juan said, "and I'm her captain. As you've already seen, she has a few hidden tricks."

"You work for the Americans?"

"Mostly. This job, however, has a more personal aspect. Your employers injured one of my crewmen, and I want to know why."

"How did you know they were going to kill me?"

"We didn't. We just happened to be in the right place at the right time to give you a hand. No pun intended."

"No worries," Parsons said with a chuckle. "If it hadn't been for you, I would be part of the factory wreckage."

"Do you know what they were doing in there?"

"I wish I could tell you. They were pretty tight about security, although I did catch a few bits and pieces from some of the workers there."

"Like what?"

"I transported a load of ammonium perchlorate to the factory. I looked it up. It's mainly used to make rocket propellant."

"How much?"

"I don't know. A lot."

"Anything else?" Juan asked.

Parsons shrugged. "Just that some of the people working in there were biochemists, although I don't know what that would have to do with rockets."

"Who did you work for?"

"A guy that called himself Miller, although that wasn't his real name. That was the one who was about to have me wasted. He worked with his wife or girlfriend, but I never got her name. I think she was a ship's captain like you."

"Why?"

"I saw her giving orders to the crew of a trimaran."

"A trimaran?" Juan took out his phone and showed Parsons a screenshot of the two sketches that Kevin Nixon had drawn from Sylvia Chang's descriptions of the man and woman she saw during the attack on her ships.

"Is this the couple?"

Parsons' face darkened when he saw them. "One hundred percent. Who are they?"

"The sister of our injured crewman had an encounter with them that was even worse than yours. It took a while to run them through every photographic database we could find, but we finally spotted them in the records of the Australian prison system. Their names are Angus Polk and April Jin."

"They're convicts?"

Juan nodded. "Married to each other and released over a year ago. Polk is a former police detective, and Jin is a former Royal Australian Navy officer. They were convicted of embezzlement and fraud. They were also investigated for the murder of two people who discovered their scheme, but there wasn't enough evidence to make those charges stick."

"So why are they operating a factory way out here in the middle of nowhere?"

"We don't know for sure, but we think it's related to the incident in Port Cook. It's looking more like it was an attack than an accident."

Parsons nodded. "I heard that six hundred–plus people were paralyzed. You mean, I might have been a party to that?"

"Yes. Unwittingly."

Raven pulled the RHIB into the boat garage, where Julia was waiting with a medical kit.

"I'm Doctor Huxley, Chief Parsons," she said as he stepped onto the loading platform. "Let me take a look at that hand."

"I appreciate it," he said mechanically, still frowning over his innocent role in Polk and Jin's plans.

While everyone else exited the RHIB and the hull plate closed behind them, Julia removed the blood-soaked bandage and examined the wound.

"It looks like a through and through," she said. "It hit the fleshy part of his hand and missed the tendons. We'll get you to the sick bay and patch you up."

"Wait," Parsons said to her and turned to Juan. "If you're going after them, I want in. I know a lot of people in Australia who might be helpful, and you've seen that I've got some skills of my own. Just tell me what I can do."

"I may take you up on that," Juan said. "The most important thing is finding the last ship they were loading. You said it was called the *Shepparton*?"

Parsons nodded. "It took them two days to load it. Dozens of truckloads of cargo."

"Do you know its destination?"

"I have no idea. I wish I did."

"All right. We'll find her."

"What do you think this is all about?"

271

Juan shook his head. "Now I'm the one with no idea. But rest assured that we won't stop until we find out."

Julia escorted Parsons to the infirmary, and Juan called Max as he left the boat garage.

"I'm going to my cabin to shower and change," Juan said, "then I'll join you in the op center. Have you found the *Shepparton*?"

"She's listed on the Vesseltracker website as heading toward Jakarta, though her port of origin is listed as Brisbane, not Nhulunbuy. Right now her transponder has her due north of Darwin."

"They must have tampered with her records. I'm guessing Polk and Jin will try to divert the ship now that they know someone is onto them. The best way to stop them is to intercept the *Shepparton* and seize her cargo. How far away is she?"

"If she keeps loafing along, we can catch her in twelve hours."

"That puts us there in the middle of the night," Juan said. "Perfect. Set a course at maximum speed. I'll tell Eddie to let the team know they should get some food and sleep before we suit up again. Looks like we've got another mission tonight."

# THIRTY-FOUR

The *Oregon*'s spacious board room gave Sylvia Chang and Eric Stone plenty of room to spread out printouts and work on their laptops. A giant screen on the wall showed a view of the sunset so crisp that it looked like a picture window. This morning it had given her a front row seat to the sinking of the *Marsh Flyer*. Now she and Eric were working together to decipher the computer files brought back by Eddie Seng.

"I'm just glad to know everybody is now sure that I'm not crazy," she said.

"Why would anyone think you were crazy?" said Eric, who was sitting next to her.

"I had no proof of what happened until Bob Parsons made my story plausible. I was beginning to wonder myself if I had hallucinated the whole trimaran attack."

"I never doubted you. You're too smart and resourceful to make up something like that. I'm still in awe of how you survived the sinking of your ship. That was a long swim, and then you immediately started taking care of everyone else on the *Empiric*. It's pretty inspiring."

Sylvia put her hand on Eric's. "That's sweet of you. I'm glad I've gotten to know you over the last few days. This has been hard on Mark, but it's comforting to know he has you as a friend here on the ship."

Eric looked down and turned red, but he didn't take his hand away. "And I'm happy you're here for him. Besides, without you I wouldn't have decrypted nearly as many files as we already have."

"At least we may have found something to help him."

"I know he hates being locked to that chair. I've already promised to help him set up his skate park on deck when he's recovered."

"He skateboards here?"

Eric nodded. "I even got him a new board for Christmas, but it seems like a bad idea to give it to him now."

Sylvia squeezed his hand. "I bet he'll love it. It'll give him some hope."

The door to the boardroom opened, and Julia walked in followed by Murph in his wheelchair. Eric snatched his hand out from under Sylvia's.

"How did the checkup go?" she asked.

"No change," Julia said. "His condition seems stable."

"Stable meaning still stinks," Murph said through his voice box. "What are you two doing?"

"We're just working on the download from the swamp factory," Eric babbled nervously. "Nothing different. Why would we be doing anything else? The only reason I'm sitting here is because it's easier if we're close. That is, we can see each other's screens. Otherwise, I'd be sitting over there."

"Jeez, what's your problem?" Murph said. "I only meant what's the latest?"

"I heard you had some new information for me," Julia said, taking a seat.

"We haven't decrypted everything yet," Sylvia said. "It's kind of a mess because even some of the files that got downloaded are partially overwritten."

"But we have found something that might be useful regarding the paralyzing gas," Eric said. "It's called Enervum, and it's made from jellyfish venom."

"We even know what species of jellyfish," Sylvia said. "*Chironex welleri.* It's a rare type of sea wasp that normally lives deep in the ocean, but it sometimes rises to the surface to breed."

"Since they're mainly found in the open sea, they're not usually dangerous to humans. But we found an article about a storm in Indonesia twenty-three years ago when thousands of them washed up on a remote island. A fishing crew was discovered there a week after the gale. All six were dead from dehydration."

"From dehydration?" Julia said. "Not from the venom?"

"No stingers were found embedded in their skin," Sylvia said. "It was a mystery why they died."

"Apparently, the wasps emit a gas when they rot," Eric said. "It has a paralytic effect."

"How horrible," Julia said.

"So the fishermen laid there, unable to move, until they died of thirst," Murph said.

"It seems like it," Sylvia said. "The Enervum seems to be a weaponized version of that gas. But we do have good news."

"You could have started with that," Murph said. The voice box didn't accurately convey the snark that Sylvia knew was there.

"There's an antidote," Sylvia said. "We found extensive documentation of the testing they did with it."

Julia sat up at that. "Do you have the

formula?"

Eric nodded and handed her several pages of printouts.

She quickly scanned them.

After a long pause, Murph asked, "So can you make it?"

"I could if this formula were complete," Julia said. "I have everything I need to replicate the process, except for a single chemical ingredient. Here it's simply called nuxoleum."

"Nuxoleum?" Eric said. "It sounds like a brand of engine grease."

"If my Latin is correct, that means 'nut oil.' I need to know what kind of nut, and I need enough of it to make the antidote for the six hundred people who've been afflicted."

"There's no description of it in the files we've found so far," Eric said.

"We're still looking, though," Sylvia said. "I'm sure we'll find something helpful."

Julia stood. "I'll get back to the infirmary and start setting up a production system. I want to be ready to crank out the antidote once we have a supply of this mystery nut."

Eric got up abruptly. "I'll go with you. I've got some more info to help with your setup. It's easier just to show you."

He gave a slight nod to Sylvia and left with

the doctor.

"He's acting weird," Murph said.

"I think he's nice," Sylvia said.

"What do you mean nice?"

"I don't meet a lot of cute young intellectuals in my line of work."

Murph glared at her. "You do know he's my best friend."

"And an adult. So am I."

"You're my little sister."

"And your point is?"

Murph sighed. "I thought this situation couldn't get any worse."

"I'm not saying I'm going to do anything with him, but if I did . . ."

"La-la-la-la-la-la, I am not listening. Please put my hands over my ears."

"Relax. I won't tell you if anything happens. Deal?"

"I think I'll have a talk with Eric."

"You'll do no such thing. If it's that big of a problem, let me know now."

"Fine," he said after hesitating. "But I don't want to know a thing. Now, let me help decipher the rest of the data. You know I can still help."

"I welcome it."

Sylvia didn't mention the real reason Eric was acting strangely when he hurried off with Julia. He had to tell the doctor one other troubling piece of information he and Sylvia discovered, a fact that they didn't dare share with her brother.

According to the experimental research in the files, if they didn't inject Murph with a dose of the antidote within a week, his condition would become permanent.

# THIRTY-FIVE

*The Timor Sea*

As Linda piloted the *Gator* toward the *Shepparton,* Juan glanced at his watch. It was just after midnight.

"Merry Christmas, everybody," he said.

Eddie, Linc, MacD, and Raven repeated the sentiment, and the response was genuine, if a bit halfhearted. This was not the Christmas Juan had envisioned for his crew. They should have been away with their families instead of in the middle of the ocean about to silently infiltrate another ship. Still, all of them were pros. They knew the stakes.

For now, the best thing they could do was to seize the shipment of Enervum. At least they would be able to prevent the same thing from happening to anyone else. Raven had insisted on being part of the assault team, convincing Juan with a steady gaze that she was ready to return to action. He only relented after quietly checking with Doc Huxley.

The semi-submersible matched the speed of the slow-moving freighter and pulled alongside. As with the boarding of the *Dahar*, all of them were equipped with tranquilizer dart pistols. It was important to capture the crew unharmed so they could be questioned. Juan hoped it would lead to Jin and Polk as well as the antidote they needed for Murph and the rest of the nerve gas victims.

Juan opened the hatch and went up on the *Gator*'s flat deck. He wasn't worried about being seen. In the darkness, no one would be able to spot them even if they looked straight down from the railing above.

Linc handed up a special device that Max had created for ship-in-motion assaults. It was a carbon fiber telescoping ladder, very lightweight but incredibly strong. He extended it until the top was even with the ship's deck and activated the heavy-duty magnets on the top rung. It latched on to the steel hull, securing it in place.

Juan started climbing. When he got to the railing, he looked over the top and didn't see anyone. He pulled himself over and ran to the shelter of the nearest crane.

While he waited for the others to join him,

he scanned the deck of the *Shepparton,* a break bulk freighter similar in size and layout to the *Oregon,* except the *Shepparton*'s cranes were on the side of the ship instead of along the centerline. Unlike a containership, the bulk carrier's cargo was carried below deck, protected from the elements. Once they had the ship stopped, they would be able to search the cargo bays thoroughly for the gas.

When they were assembled, Juan sent Linc and Eddie to secure the engineering compartments while the rest of them went for the crew areas.

With MacD and Raven's help, it didn't take long to dart the crew sleeping in their quarters. They went up to the bridge and found two men on the night watch, tranquilizing both of them and tying them up. When Eddie and Linc called to say that the engine room crew was subdued, Juan told them to head to the nearest cargo bay and check it out while he took MacD and Raven to the captain's cabin.

He darted the captain in his bed before he even knew that anyone was inside. Juan flipped on the light to see a white man in his forties flailing about on his bunk as the drug coursed through his blood.

While MacD and Raven stood behind

him, Juan took a seat at the captain's desk.

"What's your name?" he asked.

"Raymond Wilbanks," the captain said with a slurred Aussie accent. The truth serum had already taken hold.

"Do you know the real contents of what's in your cargo hold?"

"I don't understand."

"Are you in on Polk and Jin's plan or are you just a mule for them?"

"Who?"

"Parsons did tell us that Polk used a fake identity," Raven interjected.

"The people who hired you," Juan said. "They probably didn't use their real names."

"I don't understand," Wilbanks said.

"I'll make this simpler for you. What cargo did you bring on board in Nhulunbuy?"

"I don't understand."

"Is this the dumbest ship captain we've ever met," MacD said, "or is he more loopy from the tranq than he should be?"

Juan shook his head. "Something is wrong. Wilbanks, you were in Nhulunbuy two days ago, yes or no?"

"No," Wilbanks said.

MacD frowned. "That doesn't make a lick of sense."

"Is he lying?" Raven asked.

"He can't," Juan said. "Not with this drug."

"Then why is he giving us such screwy answers?" MacD asked.

"Maybe he hasn't understood because I've been asking the questions with the wrong assumption." Juan turned to the captain. "What is currently in your cargo bays?"

"Nothing. They're empty."

"What is your port of origin?"

"Brisbane, Australia."

"Why are you going to Jakarta?"

"To pick up a load of lumber to bring back to Australia."

"That matches the online manifest," Raven said.

Eddie called on the comm system.

"Chairman, Linc and I are down here in cargo bay five. It's as bare as a bachelor's refrigerator."

"Check the others to make sure," Juan said, "but I think you'll find the same thing."

"Acknowledged."

"What's going on here?" MacD asked. "The Nhulunbuy harbormaster confirmed that the *Shepparton* was docked there."

"And when we approached this ship, Parsons said it looked like the one he'd seen in Nhulunbuy," Raven said. "Do you think they unloaded the cargo en route?"

284

Juan shook his head. "Transferring cargo from ship to ship in the middle of the ocean is a delicate process that would take a significant amount of time. They would never have gotten this far if they'd stopped on the way."

"Besides, Wilbanks here would have spilled his guts about it," MacD said. "You didn't transfer cargo at sea, did you, Captain?"

"No," Wilbanks said.

Raven sighed. "Then there's only one other possibility."

"The freighter in Nhulunbuy wasn't the *Shepparton*," Juan said as he stood, banging his hand on the desk in frustration. "We've got the wrong ship."

# THIRTY-SIX

*The Coral Sea*

Five hours after leaving Nhulunbuy, Captain Gabriel Rathman had the name *Shepparton* painted over and replaced with the ship's true name, *Centaurus.* The need for secrecy had been made abundantly clear by April Jin, backed up by the million-dollar paycheck he was getting for transporting this shipment.

He didn't know what cargo he was carrying, and he didn't want to know. All he had to do was bring it to Sydney in time for New Year's Eve. If he was late, he would forfeit his fee. The storm and heavy seas they were plowing through right now were threatening the schedule, but Rathman planned to make his date no matter how big the waves got.

Lu Yang had hired him for this job more than a year ago, even going so far as to supply him with a Chinese crew that was to follow his orders to the letter, though by the weapons they were armed with, they seemed there primarily for security.

He didn't really care. This was a one-time job. And according to the post-death recording Lu left for him, Rathman had something in common with the billionaire's stepdaughter, having also been chucked from a seafaring career.

Rathman had been an able seaman, but he was notorious for being a brutal taskmaster, driving crews to their breaking points. The final straw that cost Rathman his certification was when he was ratted out to the authorities for locking his crew in the freezer as punishment whenever one of them failed to complete a task as ordered.

He hadn't commanded a ship since then until Lu came calling. Apparently, Lu liked Rathman's reputation. He said it was exactly what he'd been looking for.

Now as he sailed along the Great Barrier Reef on Christmas morning, Rathman felt at home in his captain's chair, despite knowing his time as a shipmaster wouldn't last past this voyage. Although the bridge pitched up and down as rain lashed the windows, there was nothing better than being master of a ship, whatever the size. With the money he'd make on this sailing, he was going to buy his own charter boat, maybe run fishing trips off the Gold Coast for rich businessmen and their model girlfriends.

Then the bridge officer said something that shook him out of his bikini-filled reverie.

"Captain, we've got a problem with crane two."

Rathman groaned. "What is it?"

"It seems the boom wasn't locked down securely." The man pointed at the crane a hundred yards from the bridge, and Rathman could see the horizontal boom clanging against the adjacent crane arm with every wave crest. If it wasn't locked in place properly, the storm could rip it from the tower, causing untold damage to the ship and its cargo as well as delaying their arrival.

"There's a safe harbor fifteen miles west where we could shelter to make sure it's secure," the officer said.

Rathman exploded out of his seat. "We are not changing course. Get a man out there right now and up into that cab to reposition the boom and lock it down."

"Aye, Captain."

The officer made the call, and a minute later a crewman went out on deck, holding on to the railing with a death grip as he pulled himself through the fierce wind and rain. Rathman noticed that the idiot wasn't even wearing a life jacket, but he wasn't going to bring him back now and cause a further delay. With each wave, the boom banged even harder against its neighbor. If the cables snapped, the whole thing could come tumbling down.

The deckhand finally made it to the crane tower and climbed the stairs inside. Rathman couldn't see when he reached the cab, but it was obvious that he'd made it when the crane swung around and nestled against the one beside it.

Rathman breathed a sigh of relief that his payday was now as secure as the crane.

The crewman exited the tower and started pulling himself along the deck back to the safety of the stern superstructure.

As Rathman settled back into his chair, he looked back out to sea and gasped when he saw a wall of water the height of a six-story building barreling toward them from dead ahead.

He activated the shipwide intercom. "Rogue wave approaching. Secure all stations."

Rathman had heard about the phenomenon of a rogue wave, but he had never experienced one in person. On rare occasions in a storm like this one, normal-sized waves intersecting at just the right moment could combine into one giant superwave. Many mariners thought they were myths until they became well documented by North Sea oil rigs.

Now one was about to hit his ship. He braced himself for the impact. The bow of the *Centaurus* rose into the air, carried aloft by the slope of the wave. Before it could reach the peak, the crest of the wave broke over the ship, sending a massive surge of water across the deck.

The crewman who'd been struggling to make it back inside disappeared for a moment. As the water subsided, the crewman's yellow rain jacket was visible as he hung from the railing, his feet dangling over the open water. For a moment, it looked like he could climb back over, but his grip gave, and he fell into the ocean.

"Man overboard," the bridge officer called out automatically. He looked to the captain for orders, but Rathman remained silent as he thought about what would happen next.

Stopping to turn around and search for the man might take hours or days in this weather. And calling it in to the Coast Guard would mean that he'd have to assist in the rescue attempt and answer uncomfortable questions. Either of those options would make their chances of arriving in Sydney on time non-existent.

The officer seemed to understand his thinking. "If we throw a life buoy into the water for him to find, he might be rescued by a passing ship. If we don't, it's likely he'll never be found. Nobody would know what happened here."

The rest of the bridge crew watched him expectantly, but none of them looked particularly concerned about their fellow crewman. They knew their substantial pay was dependent on completing the voyage on time.

The captain nodded. "Stay the course. I'll alter the manifest to take his name out." First, of course, he'd have to find out what the man's name was.

Rathman felt justified in his decision. After all, it wasn't his fault, and no careless fool was going to deny him what he was owed. He put the lost crewman out of his mind and thought ahead to sailing into Sydney on New Year's Eve when he'd toast his new life while watching the famed fireworks show from the middle of the harbor.

# THIRTY-SEVEN

*The Timor Sea*

The *Oregon* stayed in the vicinity of the *Shepparton* until Juan was sure that the crew had recovered and the ship could continue on its way to Jakarta safely. The problem was that they had no idea where the Alloy Bauxite cargo ship was now. Vessel-tracker and the other marine traffic databases had no record of a ship leaving Nhulunbuy on that date. It was clear her name had been changed, so they couldn't possibly track her.

Out of leads for the moment, there didn't seem to be much to celebrate, but Juan made sure the chef put together a huge midday turkey dinner for the entire crew. At least for a few hours, they distracted themselves with good food, wine, and gift exchanges. Everyone especially loved Murph's new skateboard from Eric, ignoring the grim possibility that he might never use it and instead focusing on the hope it brought everyone.

Toward the end of the meal, while the rest of the crew was still enjoying the festivities, Juan returned to his cabin alone. To lend his quarters a classic vibe, he had re-created the furnishings from his cabin in the previous *Oregon* that evoked the style of Rick's Café Américain from the movie *Casablanca*. He could hold small meetings in the anteroom with its authentic 1940s dining table, sofa, and chair, while his bedroom had a rolltop teak desk and a large vintage safe holding the *Oregon*'s valuables, including cash, gold bullion, and cut diamonds for untraceable purchases, as well as Juan's personal weapons. An original Picasso oil painting on one wall was one of the pieces of artwork that was saved when the old ship went down. The large television screen on another wall currently displayed portholes straight out of a nineteenth-century ocean liner.

Juan took a seat at the anteroom table to review the files on April Jin and Angus Polk, looking for anything that might point out how to find them. Two convicts little more than a year out of prison couldn't possibly be funding such an expensive operation without help from someone with deep pockets. Using their experience in the police and military, they certainly had the skills to carry out their attacks, but why? What was the ultimate target? Who was behind it all?

There was a knock at the door, and Juan said, "Enter."

Maurice, the *Oregon*'s elderly steward, glided in holding a silver tray with a coffeepot, cup, and a slice of pumpkin pie with whipped cream.

"You left before dessert was served, Captain," Maurice said, setting the dishes on the table. He was wearing his standard pristine white uniform with a napkin draped over his arm, an affectation he'd brought over from his decades in Britain's Royal Navy. He also insisted on calling Juan Captain instead of Chairman to maintain naval tradition.

"Thank you, Maurice. How are our guests doing?"

"I'm doing my best to make Ms. Chang and Mr. Parsons comfortable. I believe the young Mr. Stone has taken a shine to Mr. Murphy's sister."

Despite Maurice's elegant demeanor, he was the ship's go-to person for onboard scuttlebutt. If something was happening on the *Oregon,* Maurice knew about it.

"I hope it doesn't cause a rift between Eric

294

and Murph," Juan said. "I'd hate to see their friendship blown apart by something like that."

"I've been assured that nothing has occurred but flirting. They're more concerned with Mr. Murphy's unfortunate medical condition at the moment."

"So am I."

"Nonetheless, I am glad that Mr. Murphy has his sister with him at this difficult time. It's always more comforting to go through something like that with family, although I like to think we are all his family. Now, if you'll excuse me . . ."

Maurice left as quietly as he'd entered, leaving Juan to ponder his last words.

Who but family would trust disgraced felons like April Jin and her husband with a well-armed ship and a huge factory pumping out poisonous gas?

He rechecked Jin's file and there it was, buried in a footnote. For several years, her stepfather had been a Chinese billionaire named Lu Yang. According to an internet search, Lu had died almost eighteen months ago. No information about his beneficiaries was available, but Jin had to be the recipient of the bulk of his estate.

He called Eric. "Stoney, I know it's Christmas, but I have a question for you to investigate."

"Actually, Chairman, we're already back at work." He didn't have to say why. Julia had already told Juan about their time crunch related to the antidote for Murph.

"I believe Lu Yang, April Jin's stepfather, might be the source of their funds. Check to see if Lu has any link to Alloy Bauxite or ever purchased a trimaran in the same class that Sylvia and Parsons described."

"We're on it," Eric said and hung up.

Ninety minutes later, Eric, Sylvia, and Murph appeared at Juan's door, and he asked them in. All three were still wearing the Santa hats they'd put on at the party.

"I guess you found something," Juan said.

"You were right about Lu," Murph said, his voice box mimicking Samuel L. Jackson. "He's neck-deep in this, which is appropriate since he's dead."

"Alloy Bauxite was created through a series of Australian shell companies," Sylvia said. "The intent was to make it look as if the Australian military had funded it."

"But they forgot to completely cover their tracks on the purchase of the hovercraft," Eric said. "Guess who Alloy Bauxite bought the *Marsh Flyer* from."

"If it isn't a subsidiary of Lu Yang's

companies," Juan said, "I'll be very disappointed."

"Exactly. Not only that, the same organization that bought the hovercraft also supplied trimarans to various navies around the world, including China and Australia."

"So now we know who we're up against."

"But that's not the best part," Murph said.

"We kept looking through the computer files you found at the factory," Sylvia said. "Something very interesting popped up. A reference to an archaeological dig in Western Australia."

"Apparently, it's the source of the antidote," Eric said.

"What did they find?" Juan asked.

"We don't know," Sylvia said. "Most of the file was corrupted. Just that it involved ancient ruins of some kind and that the archaeologists were all lost in a plane crash returning from the dig site. None of them survived to report their findings."

"Then how did Jin and Polk know about it?"

"We asked the very same question ourselves," Murph said.

"Perhaps the archaeologists communicated their findings before they left the dig site," Sylvia said.

"Or the plane crash was faked and they

did make it back," Eric said. "We've seen what this couple does to their own employees."

"None of this sounds very helpful yet," Juan said, "which means you're about to tell me something good."

Sylvia and Eric looked at Murph, giving him the chance to deliver the news. He smiled, the happiest Juan had seen him since picking him up in Darwin.

"And you thought we didn't get a present for you," Murph said. "The file contained the GPS coordinates of the dig site. The ruins they found are along the Ord River on the northwest coast of Australia. We can be there by tomorrow morning."

# THIRTY-EIGHT

*Horn Island, Queensland*

The *Marauder* finally made it to the Torres Strait Islands late on Christmas Day. The archipelago was located at the tip of the Cape York Peninsula, the only place within two hundred miles with an airport large enough for Polk's jet to land and refuel. He was agitated as the launch made its way to the anchored trimaran.

When he stepped onto the ship, he was met by his wife, who looked equally distressed.

"How could this have happened?" she asked as she hugged him. "Everything was going so smoothly."

"I don't know," Polk replied, looking around at the men idling on deck. "Let's talk in your cabin."

They went below decks and locked the door behind them. They didn't want to give the sense that they were losing control of the situation, even though that's exactly what had happened.

"Do you think Parsons arranged the attack?" Jin asked him.

"He's no actor, and I could see he was surprised when I told him he was about to die. No, it was someone else."

"Who?"

"I don't know. But they had an armed spy ship. It had guns mounted on a crane, and I saw a boat deployed from its hull."

"A spy ship?"

"That's what it looked like to me," Polk said. "The Australian Navy doesn't have anything like that."

Jin shook her head. "I don't know who does. What did it look like?"

"Big cargo ship. Maybe five hundred feet long. Four cranes."

"Did you catch the name?"

"I checked with the Nhulunbuy harbor-master. It was called the *Norego*."

Jin paced the small room. "This doesn't make any sense. If the military was onto us, they would have mounted a full-scale raid on the factory, not sneak in with a minimal force."

"It must have been a recon mission."

That made Jin stop pacing as she looked at Polk in horror. "Did they get away with any intel?"

Polk shrugged. "Doubtful. I set the computer servers to overwrite the drives, but I didn't have time to see if they took any with them."

"This is potentially damaging."

Polk nodded. "I wasn't expecting last minute visitors. I had to blow the factory as soon as possible in case another team showed up."

"Who could possibly know?"

"Hard to say. Perhaps there's a leak with Lu's people," Polk said.

"He may have made a mistake somewhere along the way that led these people to us. So what do we do?"

"We try to find them."

"How?"

"Where would they go next?" he asked rhetorically. "The logical place to start is with our cargo ship. But they would know it as the *Shepparton*. They have no idea its real name is the *Centaurus*. I'm confident our shipment is safe."

"Yes, I think so, too," Jin said.

"The most damaging info that they could have gotten from the computer files is about the Enervum and its antidote."

"If they learn that there *is* an antidote, they'll need the nut oil to make it."

"Since there are only two places in the world to obtain those nuts," Polk said, "I could take a strike team to destroy the existing supply. I'll go to Jakarta first."

"That's a good idea," Jin said. "But what about the archaeological dig Lu sent us to?"

"It's so remote, I never thought anyone would find it."

"We can't make that assumption anymore. I'll take the *Marauder* there. Since it's closer than the original nut source, the people on that spy ship — the *Norego* — might send someone to check it out or the whole ship might go. Maybe I'll come across them on the way there. If not, I'll be waiting to eliminate them."

"I want you to be careful," Polk said, taking Jin in his arms. "That Gatling gun I saw them use was pretty powerful."

"Maybe. But we've got some weapons of our own."

# THIRTY-NINE

*The Ord River Estuary, Western Australia*

Juan had the *Oregon* anchor in the wide Cambridge Gulf, bordered on the west by high sandstone hills and on the east by mudflats and thick mangrove colonies. The northern part of the gulf let out into the Timor Sea, while the southern end was dominated by Adolphus Island. It was bounded by arms of the Ord River, now swollen to more than a mile in width by the heavy seasonal monsoons.

Juan piloted the RHIB up the eastern arm of the river, while Eric guided him toward the GPS coordinates that they'd obtained from the factory computer. Since Juan didn't expect any trouble on this expedition, Sylvia had joined them, holding a camera that linked back to Murph on the *Oregon* so he could participate. Juan also asked Bob Parsons to come along since he was familiar with the outback flora and

303

fauna as well as its geography. Julia Huxley rounded out the team. If they found any clues about the antidote, Juan wanted her there to work through the formula.

Even this early in the morning, the summer heat and humidity were oppressive. The breeze as the RHIB motored along the river helped, but Juan's shirt was still soaked with sweat.

Sylvia leaned over the gunwale for a better view to show Murph the scenery, and Parsons tapped her on the shoulder.

"I wouldn't be doing that if I were you," he said.

"Taking video?"

"Putting yourself out over the water. You make a tempting meal."

He pointed at the river. What looked at first like drifting logs were actually massive crocodiles.

Sylvia leaped back from the edge, nearly dropping the camera. Eric reached out to steady her and then self-consciously pulled his hands away when he saw that Juan noticed his protective gesture.

Sylvia gave a quick "Thanks" to Eric and gazed all around her. The river was infested with crocodiles.

"They're everywhere," she said breathlessly. "That is horrifying. Mark, are you seeing this?"

"For once I'm glad I couldn't go along with you," Murph replied over the comms that everyone was linked to.

"Saltwater crocs are common in every tropical river and swamp in Australia," Parsons said. "Nasty buggers. They can grow up to six meters long and a thousand kilograms."

"They also have the strongest bite force of any animal on earth," Murph chimed in. Eric had rigged his finger joystick so that he could type into his computer as well as speak, using a predictive keyboard like the ones found on satellite phones. Drawing on his skills as a video game wizard, Murph had become adept at typing with one finger at lightning speed.

"It says on this website that their bite is three times as strong as that of a Bengal tiger," Murph continued, "and may be equivalent to the bite of a great white shark, though that's never been measured in a lab for some odd reason."

"I'd like to see them try that test," Eric said.

"The crazy thing is that their jaws only are strong in one direction," Parsons said. "You can hold them closed with duct tape. I've seen them transported that way."

"Let's not test out what their bites can do," Julia said. "I don't want to figure out how to patch you up with a chunk taken out of any of you."

"We've got a couple of M4s in case the crocs get frisky," Juan said. He didn't mention his doubts about how well the assault rifle ammo would penetrate the reptiles' rhino-like hides.

All of them kept a watch on the water as the boat snaked up the desolate river until they were as close as they could get to the coordinates. Juan beached the RHIB on the shore and kept guard with one of the M4s as everyone got out.

Eric led the way up an embankment and through the greenery. The moist air smelled of fragrant flowers and rotting vegetation, and birds of all types chirped and cawed in a variety of distinct rhythms.

As they got farther from the river and climbed higher, the shrubbery thinned out, and picturesque sandstone formations abutted their path. Finally, two hundred yards from the Ord River, Eric stopped.

"This should be it," he said.

Juan looked around but saw nothing obvious that would indicate there had been an archaeological expedition here. No ruins, no uncovered pottery or tools, no structure of any kind. Only an expansive view of the river below.

"Spread out and look around," Juan said. He was already worried they'd come all this way for nothing.

They spent nearly an hour combing the area for any signs that someone had been there when Parsons called out to the group.

"I think I've got something."

They all converged to an outcropping where a rockfall had covered the slope. Parsons pointed to a dark hole in the middle of the rock pile just big enough for a cat to squeeze through.

"I think there's something in there," he said. "Feel it."

Juan put his hand over the opening. Cool air streamed from the hole.

"It's a cave," he said. He stepped back and looked farther up the hill. There was a deep scar in the sandstone along with some charring.

"The rockfall happened deliberately. Someone set off explosives to cover this up."

"What do you think is inside?" Sylvia asked.

"Only one way to find out," Eric said.

"Then I guess we need to start moving some stones," Juan said.

They began moving whatever rocks were

small enough to pick up or leverage away from the others. The work in the awful humidity was backbreaking and required frequent rests for water. Two hours later, they finally had a hole big enough to squeeze through.

Juan went first after making sure the *Oregon* knew where they were in case a new rockslide trapped them in. He shimmied through the opening and stood up once he got inside. The cave had to be huge since his light couldn't penetrate far enough to see the back wall.

He waited until everyone was inside. Then he led the way into a wide chamber with a domed ceiling.

Juan heard a gasp and turned to see a frightened Sylvia standing over seven skeletons lined up side by side. Their clothes were torn and bloody, as if they'd been savaged by animals.

"How many archaeologists were presumed killed in that plane crash?" Juan asked.

"Seven," Eric said. "Five men and two women."

Julia bent over to examine the remains.

"Based on the body size, clothes, and jewelry," she said, "I'd say there are five men and two women here."

"Were they eaten?" Sylvia asked as she

filmed them for Murph to see.

Julia nodded. "Picked clean by dingos or other scavengers that got into the cave after they were already dead." She pointed at several broken rib bones. "These people were shot."

Juan picked up a spent rifle shell that was among the clothes of one of the victims.

"More like executed," he said.

"It makes me sick to think I worked for anyone involved in this," Parsons said, turning away from the carnage.

"What does this all have to do with the poison gas?" Julia asked.

"Maybe it's related to this writing." Parsons pointed at the cave wall.

Juan turned his light on the stony surface, and deep etchings came into view. He'd been expecting some aboriginal art or primitive drawings. Instead, it was lettering.

He stepped closer. Not only was the writing made up of letters, they were recognizable as the Latin alphabet. There were rows and rows of the letters, carved neatly into the rock.

Juan traced the writing to its starting point and saw a single line at the beginning set apart from the others.

AUC DCCII.

"Murph, are you getting this?" Juan asked as he motioned for Sylvia to focus her camera on it.

"I'm looking up the translation now."

"If these are Latin letters," Eric said, "the last part could be a number."

"Seven hundred and two?" Julia asked. "Seven hundred and two what?"

"I found something for AUC," Murph said. "It stands for *ab urbe condita.* That's Latin for 'from the founding of the city.' "

"What city?" Parsons asked.

"Rome," Murph said. "It's how they wrote years."

"The number of years since the founding of Rome?" Julia said in astonishment. "You mean this is Roman writing?"

"What is AUC 702 in our years, Murph?" Juan asked.

"Rome was founded in 753 B.C. If that date on the wall is to be believed, the conversion means that the writing dates from 51 B.C. You're looking at evidence of a Roman settlement in Australia older than the Colosseum."

# FORTY

Translating the writing was a tedious process because the letters were strung together without gaps in the tradition of ancient Roman writing. Normally, it would take mere seconds for the computer to give the English interpretation, but it wasn't programmed to tell where words began and ended. With Sylvia and Eric's help, Murph input the letters manually, segmenting them into words that were translated one at a time.

In the meantime, Juan, Julia, and Parsons conducted a thorough search of the cave for any other information or relics. They came up empty-handed.

"How could these archaeologists know that the etchings are authentic?" Julia wondered as she ate one of the sandwiches they'd brought along with them. "Someone could have been playing a prank. It's happened before."

"They wouldn't be dead over a prank,"

Parsons said.

"I think she means that the writings wouldn't have been enough to convince them," Juan said.

"Right," Julia said. "There must be actual ruins somewhere around here that they were excavating that proved Romans really came to Australia."

"And I think we might have some insight into that now," Murph said. "The translation is complete. Sending it to Sylvia now."

"Got it," she said.

"So how did Romans get all the way to the other side of the world two thousand years ago?" Julia asked.

"This was written by a man named Flavius," Sylvia said. "He wrote it as a record for his son. I won't go through it word for word, but it says Flavius was captured by the Parthians and enslaved by them."

"Who are they?" Parsons asked.

Eric was on his own tablet, which was linked to the *Oregon*'s computer system.

"Parthia was an empire in Persia, now modern-day Iran. The Romans lost twenty thousand men killed and a whole legion of ten thousand soldiers taken captive. It was the greatest Roman defeat up to that time. The losing commander was Marcus Licinius Crassus."

"Crassus?" Juan said. "Why do I know that name?"

"He was the general who defeated Spartacus."

"And crucified him," Murph added.

"Lovely," Julia said. "Sounds like a wonderful guy."

"He was also the richest man in the Roman Empire," Eric continued. "After the Parthians killed him, they poured molten gold down his throat as a symbol of his greed."

"So our friend Flavius here was in the Army and got captured with this lost legion," Juan said. "I seem to remember a story that they were brought to northwest China and settled there."

"Flavius claims that only half of the captives went with him to a southern port city called Charax," Sylvia said. "Maybe the other half went to China."

"Does it say how they escaped the Parthians?"

"Flavius stole ships the Romans were forced to build for the Parthians. They sailed across the unknown ocean, finally settling on an island far from here. It seemed like a paradise until a storm arrived. Then a sickness struck."

"What kind of sickness?" Julia asked.

"They couldn't move," Sylvia said. "He used the word 'Enervum.'"

"That's the name Polk and Jin used for the nerve gas," Juan said.

"The situation matches the story about the fishermen who were found on an island a few years ago," Julia said. "Does he mention jellyfish?"

"Not by that word," Sylvia said. "But he does say that there were poisonous sea creatures that washed up. He says the survivors fled on the only ship they had left and eventually landed here."

"What does this have to do with an antidote?" Parsons asked.

"There's a love story in here, too," Sylvia said. "His wife was one of the people who was paralyzed. She was with child at the time, and Flavius wanted to cure her. He was convinced that the answer lay in why only the soldiers were unaffected by the illness."

"Smart guy," Julia said. "Most people at the time would have just chalked it up to the will of the gods."

"He realized that the soldiers were the only ones who drank a bitter liquid as part of their regular rituals. It was infused with the oil of a particular nut found on their island."

"Did he save his wife?" Eric asked.

"Yes," Sylvia said. "They had brought a supply of the nuts with them. Flavius made the drink for her, and she eventually could move again in time to give birth to their son. That's where the story ends."

"No," Julia gasped. "Does it give the name of the nut?"

"It's called *nux viridi lucus.* It means 'green-eyed nut.' "

"Eric, can you find any nut with that name?"

"I'm looking but don't see anything."

"It's probably called something else now," Julia said. "Without a picture of it, the nut may be impossible to find."

"We don't even know what island they were on," Murph said. "It could be any one of thousands in the Indian Ocean. It's not looking good. Maybe I should get used to this chair."

Sylvia sniffled, and Eric put a reassuring hand on her shoulder.

"Don't give up yet," Juan said. "We'll try out every single nut in existence if we have to. I know we'll find the antidote."

Julia didn't look as confident about his reassurances because of the time pressure, but she didn't say anything to Sylvia. They would never be able to replicate the antidote in a week if they didn't know the key ingredient.

"Let's get back to the ship and see what we can come up with," Juan said.

"Before we go, I want to get photos of the dental work on these skeletons," Julia said. "It will help their families get closure if we can identify the bodies for the authorities."

She knelt beside the bones and gently lifted each skull one by one to take the pictures.

On the fourth person, something fell to the ground when she picked up the skull.

"What's that?"

Juan bent over and focused his light on a blue plastic object the shape of a piece of gum.

It was a USB thumb drive.

"How did that get there?" he wondered as he picked it up. The case was still intact and unharmed.

"This man must have had it in his mouth when he died," Julia said. "There must be something on it that he didn't want the killers to find."

# FORTY-ONE

Eric plugged the USB drive into his tablet.

"There are a lot of files on here," he said. "Here's one that's a translation of all this text on the wall."

Murph cut in. "That would have saved us some time."

"Do a search for 'nux viridi lucus' and 'green-eyed nut,' " Julia said.

"Searching. It looks there are several mentions of them."

"Any pictures?"

"No images that I see. Just text files. Here's one called Daily Log. It looks like this thumb drive was the property of the expedition leader, a guy named Victor Ormond."

"He knew that his team was in danger and hid the files," Juan said. "Too bad it didn't help him, but it might help us. What do the references to the nut say?"

"Here's a file where he talks about researching the nut's origin, but there are no conclusions."

"What about the daily log?" Julia asked.

"It says they found amphorae sealed with beeswax. Three of them were marked 'N V L,' etched in the wax. It looks like they brought one of them back to their headquarters here, but the log ends before it mentions what they found inside."

"Sounds like there's more to this site than this cave," Parsons said.

"Where did they find the amphorae?" Juan asked.

"They were stowed on a ship, a Roman bireme called the *Salacia* that ran aground. The archaeologists were in the process of excavating it from the mud."

"That's incredible," Sylvia said. "A Roman vessel came to Australia eighteen hundred years before the first European settlers. This would have been the discovery of a lifetime for any archaeologist."

"I bet we find out that Lu Yang had something to do with this expedition," Juan said. "Maybe he even funded it. And when his lead archaeologist reported back what he'd discovered, Lu sent a hit team to cover it up."

"The big question is, where's the ship?" Julia said. "If there are two more amphorae on board with nuts inside, we might be able to use them to make the antidote."

"Even if they're two thousand years old?" Sylvia asked.

"It depends how well the ceramic and beeswax preserved them. I've read about butter thousands of years old found in barrels recovered from Irish peat bogs that is still edible. Maybe we'll get lucky. At the very least, we can identify the exact type of nut it is and secure a fresh supply."

"There's a lot of mentions of the bireme," Eric said. "I'm looking to see if they have a map to its location."

"I know new ships, not old ones," Parsons said. "What's a bireme?"

"It's a Roman single-masted galley with two rows of oars on either side for propulsion to supplement the wind," Juan said. "They were used both as warships and to transport cargo."

"Here it is," Eric said triumphantly. "The one they found is thirty meters in length. About a hundred feet long. They've even included a helpful layout of the ship."

Eric turned the tablet around so everyone could see it. A drawing showed a diagram of the bireme with notations for each of the sections. One outlined a weapons room. Another showed where tools were stored.

In the middle of the ship, there was an area marked "Ceramics."

"That has to be where all the amphorae are," Juan said. "It sounds like there might be hundreds of them. Does it give any more detail about where the two we're looking for are?"

Eric took the tablet back and after a few moments of typing, shook his head.

"We'll just have to search through them until we find the ones that have the nut label."

"Does it give the location of the wreck?"

"There is a GPS coordinate." Eric sent it back to Murph on the *Oregon.*

"Got it," Murph replied. "It's two hundred yards from your current position, right along the riverbank."

Before they left, Julia finished photographing the archaeologists' teeth while Sylvia made a thorough video recording of the wall etchings. They headed back out of the cave and down toward the river, guided by Murph.

They walked along the bank, making sure to keep well back from the rain-swollen water's edge.

"All right," Murph said. "Stop there. You should be able to see it."

They looked around, but there was no

320

evidence of an archaeological dig.

"Could it have gotten overgrown with plants in just a year?" Sylvia said, examining the shrubbery beside them.

Parsons shook his head. "This isn't a jungle where vines could cover ruins in a week. If they dug it up, we'd still see it."

"Unless Lu's men blew it up as well," Eric said.

"Then there'd be a crater here," Juan said. "Murph, are you sure this is the spot?"

"Wait a minute," Murph said. "If these numbers are correct, you're still about forty yards away."

"Okay. Which direction should we go?"

"Directly north. Apparently, it's right on the bank of the river."

"We're already on the bank of the river," Juan said.

"Oh. That's a bummer."

Then it dawned on Juan. This wasn't the normal riverbank. The monsoons had considerably widened the Ord.

"You mean the ruins of the bireme are underwater?" Julia asked.

"And it probably will be for a few more weeks," Parsons said. "This is the wet season."

"Then we'll have to dive on the *Salacia* to recover the amphorae," Juan said.

At that moment, a huge feral pig on the opposite bank of the river crept down to the water to take a drink. It had gotten through a single slurp when a crocodile lunged out of the water and clamped its jaws around the pig's head, dragging it into the river as the prey futilely thrashed to get free. The twenty-foot-long croc shook it like a dog's toy. As soon as the pig went limp, the croc disappeared under the surface with its prize.

Parsons shook his head at Juan's intention to go into the water. "You were saying?"

# FORTY-TWO

By the time the shore team got back to the *Oregon,* there wasn't enough daylight left to prep and execute a wreck dive, so they planned to go at sunup the next day. The launch point for the operation would be the moon pool.

The large chamber, which smelled of seawater and grease, was situated in the center of the ship. The *Oregon*'s two submersibles, the *Gator* and *Nomad,* were stowed in cradles in the ceiling, and a gantry crane moved them around. The water surface of the large pool at the bottom was even with the ocean level outside, which was why the room didn't flood. Large doors in the keel slid apart to allow subs and divers to emerge from the ship undetected.

Today it was *Nomad* that was being lowered into the moon pool while the *Gator* remained suspended in the air. With the Ord River full of crocodiles, diving off a boat like the RHIB would be an invitation to a smorgasbord. Juan thought using *Nomad* instead would give them a better chance to explore the wreck without being noticed by the hungry predators.

Although *Nomad* was designed to dive to a thousand feet, for this mission it would simply be floating on the surface of the shallow river. The sub's key feature was its two-person airlock, which had a hatch in its belly. Juan and Linc would emerge from *Nomad* underwater, conduct the search of the *Salacia* to recover the amphorae, and return to the sub without drawing attention to themselves from the crocs sunning on the surface.

That was the theory, at least.

Linc was in the process of checking their dive gear, part of which included two suits made of titanium chain mail. They were intended to be used for diving in shark-infested waters and were so heavy that a diver would sink like a brick without a buoyancy vest. They covered nearly the entire body, from hood to gloves to boots, all of which were secured by Velcro straps. Only the face was exposed.

"I never thought we'd be using these for diving with crocodiles," Linc said as he packed up the suits. They would don them once they were on site.

"Don't depend on them too much," Juan replied. "Their teeth might not penetrate the mesh, but they could rip apart our scuba gear and hold us under until we drown."

"That's why we have these."

Linc pointed to the knives sheathed in the leg of each suit. They were Wasp injection knives. The handle contained a cartridge of $CO_2$ compressed to 800 psi. When the blade was stabbed into a target, one press of the button on the hilt forced enough freezing cold gas to fill a basketball into the body, killing most animals instantly.

They would be wearing full-face masks to fit over the augmented reality glasses they'd have on. The muddy river water had a visibility of less than five feet, which would severely hamper their search of the wreckage. The glasses would display the images revealed by sonar signals sent from *Little Geek,* the remotely operated vehicle that Eric would be directing from *Nomad.*

Rounding out the team were Max, *Nomad*'s pilot for the mission, and MacD and Raven, who would be standing on top of *Nomad* with assault rifles to ward off any crocs that ventured too close.

*Nomad* was now free-floating in the moon pool. Eric popped out of the hatch and said,

325

"Max has finished his pre-dive checklist and says he's ready to go when you are."

Linc and Juan lowered their gear to MacD and Raven through the hatch and got in, closing it behind them. Max filled the ballast tanks, and *Nomad* sank beneath the surface. He goosed the electric motors, and the sub eased away from the *Oregon* for its journey upriver.

As the *Marauder* neared the entrance to the Cambridge Gulf, Jin sat on the bridge drinking a cup of coffee and poring over a map of the area. The eastern arm at the southern end of the gulf was the outlet for the Ord River. The western arm was the navigable waterway that led to Wyndham, a port town that served the mining communities nearby.

That was the destination for the ore carrier *Thai Navigator,* which she watched entering the gulf to pick up a load of iron or nickel. The ship looked a bit like the *Norego,* but it didn't have the cranes that Polk told her about. Besides, there was no way a ship that size could have beaten her here.

It was possible that the intruders from the *Norego* had simply flown out here to search for the dig site. If that was the case, the plan was simple. She would anchor the trimaran at the mouth of the Ord and take a strike team upriver to the cave and wipe them out.

If there was no one there, she would simply lie in wait for the *Norego* to arrive and blow it out of the water. And if neither of those happened in the next couple of days, they could be confident that the site hadn't been compromised.

Jin consulted the depth charts for the Cambridge Gulf and saw nothing unusual. Still, she might as well take advantage of the ship that sailed these waters on a regular basis.

"Follow the *Thai Navigator*," she ordered her helmsman.

It wouldn't take more than an hour to reach the southern end of the gulf.

Sylvia was honored that Juan Cabrillo trusted her enough to let her into the inner sanctum of the *Oregon*'s op center while they monitored *Nomad*'s mission on the Ord. She was seated next to Murph, who was grunting in frustration instead of using his voice box.

"What's the matter?" she asked.

"I should be out there," he said. "*Little Geek* is *my* toy."

"I'm sure Eric won't break it. You'll be

327

back out in the field in no time."

The big view screen showed a shot from *Nomad,* which was cruising on the surface as it approached the Ord. Black clouds loomed in the background.

Linda, who was sitting in the command chair, asked Hali, "What's the weather forecast?"

"It looks like there is a squall line coming in," Hali said. "Intermittent periods of heavy rain."

"That shouldn't affect the dive."

"I do have some ship traffic to the north on radar."

"Identity?"

"According to her AIS signal, it's an ore carrier called the *Thai Navigator.* She's gotta be bound for Wyndham and is about fifteen miles out."

Hali switched the screen to a camera on the *Oregon.* The oncoming freighter was nothing more than a dot on the horizon.

Sylvia leaned over to Murph. "What's AIS?"

"Automatic Identification System," Murph said. "It's a transponder signal that all commercial cargo ships transmit. We change ours as necessary for the mission. The *Thai Navigator* is reading us as the *Norego* right now."

"We're anchored far out of the shipping lane," Linda said. "It shouldn't be a problem."

# FORTY-THREE

Careful not to ground the sub on the riverbed, Max drove *Nomad* back and forth over the site of the GPS coordinates from the archaeologist's diary and used the side-scan sonar to verify that the wreck was indeed under the water. They all crouched around Eric's screen, watching for any sign of the bireme.

"There it is," Juan said, nearly an hour after they'd left the *Oregon.*

Out of the irregular river bottom, he could make out the defined shape of a boat. The top deck had eroded away, exposing the cargo holds underneath. Most of the wreckage had been excavated from the riverbank, and at the center of the vessel were dozens of objects that looked like flower vases.

"Those are the amphorae," Eric said.

"Looks like we may have to go through a bunch of them," Linc said.

"Then we better get started," Juan said.

330

"Let's suit up."

While they put on their shark suits, MacD and Raven, both dressed in rain gear, climbed through the upper hatch with their weapons. Steamy air washed through the air-conditioned cabin until the hatch was closed again.

Max spoke over his shoulder from his cockpit seat. "I've gotten you as close as I can while still giving you room to open the belly hatch. You'll have to swim about twenty yards. I'm releasing *Little Geek* now."

A compartment on *Nomad*'s exterior opened, allowing Eric to guide the remotely operated vehicle from the sub's underside using its battery-powered propellers. The ROV, connected to the sub by a fiber-optic control cable, was the size of a suitcase and had been specially outfitted with a mini-sonar. Juan and Linc would swim beside it, and the echo reading would be displayed on their augmented reality glasses through additional fiber-optic lines linked from their suits to *Little Geek*.

With the full-face masks on, Juan and Linc would be able to talk to each other and to *Nomad* through the comm link in the ROV.

Once they had their heavy gear on, Juan and Linc entered the airlock. Linc's bulk made the fit a tight squeeze, but they were only inside long enough for it to cycle and fill with water.

When it had equalized with the river water, Juan opened the hatch and lowered himself through the opening. His feet touched the muck of the riverbed before his head was out of the airlock, which meant the depth was no more than fifteen feet. He inflated his buoyancy vest so that he could float. Otherwise, the chain mail suit would anchor him to the bottom.

He grabbed a handrail on the side of *Little Geek* and attached his fiber connection. As soon as Linc was on the opposite side, Juan said, "We're ready to go." The ROV whirred into motion, dragging them along.

As they'd expected, visibility was poor, even with the headlamps. Juan could see *Little Geek* and make out the shape of Linc next to him, but they were hazy. The sonar signal sent out by the ROV was too high pitched for the human ear to hear, but it seemed to be working because Juan could clearly see the contours of the river bottom rendered on his glasses as if he were looking at a movie special effect.

"There's the bow," Linc said.

A remnant of the *Salacia*'s prow jutted out of the silt. Its ram had broken off, but the wood was surprisingly well preserved after two thousand years. The floodplain's clay that had covered the ship obviously did a fine job of protecting it from rot.

They passed over a large cache of ancient weaponry that Juan would have loved to examine if they had more time. Swords, spears, and arrows were exposed, and Juan was sure there were more artifacts still to be uncovered.

They continued on to the center of the ship, and Juan could now see the pile of amphorae that poked out of the silt. It looked like they had been painstakingly dug out to minimize damage to them as they were prepared for collection.

"Okay, Stoney," Juan said. "You can stop here."

*Little Geek* came to a halt and settled onto the riverbed. They would have to search carefully now by hand, making sure not to puncture the beeswax lids on the ceramic jars.

"You start on that side," Juan said, "and I'll begin over here."

Using his dive light, he peered at the first amphora, but there was no lid on it. Same with the second one. The third had a lid, but it said "HERBIS."

The next three containers were shattered,

as if they'd been hit by something heavy during the recent flooding. Their contents were long gone, swept away by the current.

He picked up the necks of each one. The second one had a beeswax seal. It read "N V L."

"Great," Juan said.

"Did you find something?" Linc asked.

"Yeah. A broken amphora with the label we were looking for."

"That stinks. Since they took one of the amphorae away, there's only one left down here."

"Right. Keep your fingers crossed it wasn't damaged like this one was."

Juan dropped the piece, which stirred up the silt, exposing something that glinted yellow in his light. He momentarily paused his search to brush away the mud to reveal more of the object.

He was astonished to see a gold eagle's head sticking out of the muck. He levered it loose of the silt that had piled up around it and plucked the weighty relic free. It must have been the item that crushed the ceramics.

Juan didn't bother examining it further and placed it into a small mesh bag on his belt. There would be plenty of time to look at it once they'd found the container they were searching for.

In addition to the noise of the bubbles emitted by his mask's regulator, a new sound penetrated the gloom. It was like the muted crackle of static on the radio.

It was rain. There was a downpour up above.

"We got the fun part of the job, didn't we?" MacD said as huge droplets pounded him and Raven while they stood watch atop *Nomad*. Water sluiced down his hood and rain jacket.

"Don't be such a crybaby," Raven replied. "Showers like these don't last long."

"At least Ah can't get any wetter. It's already like a sauna in this thing."

"That's funny."

"It's not *that* funny."

"No, I mean it looks like that croc in the middle of the river is heading this way."

She pointed, and MacD saw a huge crocodile moving steadily in their direction.

"That's a big sucker," he said. "Do you think he's interested in *Nomad*?"

"None of them on the other side of the river seemed to pay any attention to us while we were cruising back and forth looking for the shipwreck."

The croc was making a beeline for the

wreck. "Something's attracting him. Can he hear the divers?"

"I don't know," Raven said before calling Juan. "Chairman, we've a crocodile coming toward us with purpose."

"How long do we have?" Juan asked.

"Not long. Maybe a minute."

"Good to know."

She and MacD took aim with their rifles, but they wouldn't be of any use. Like a U-boat readying its attack, the croc disappeared below the surface.

# FORTY-FOUR

Jin was getting impatient with the slow speed of the *Thai Navigator,* so she ordered the helmsman to overtake the ore carrier. The *Marauder* came along her starboard side only three miles from Adolphus Island.

As they were passing the *Thai Navigator,* a new ship came into view. It had been blocked both visually and on radar by the large cargo freighter.

The ship seemed to be stationary, an odd place to drop anchor. She picked up her binoculars and walked out to the bridge wing.

At this distance, she couldn't read the name stenciled on the ship's stern, but when she focused the binoculars, her stomach knotted at the sight of the four cranes on a break bulk carrier. It was exactly the configuration of the ship that Polk had described defending the *Marsh Flyer.*

It couldn't possibly have arrived here

before she had. She had estimated it would take at least another day or two for it to get here. No ship that size could hope to match the speed of her trimaran.

She dashed back into the bridge.

"Tell me the name of that ship?" she asked.

The first officer checked his screen. "It's called the *Norego.*"

It couldn't be the same ship, but there it was.

She suddenly realized that the *Thai Navigator* had shielded her approach, giving her an opportunity for a sneak attack. But she couldn't have the crew of the ore carrier as witnesses.

"Activate the plasma cannon," she ordered. "And arm two Enervum rockets, one aimed at the *Thai Navigator,* and the other at the *Norego.*"

Sylvia stood and gaped in horror when she saw the zoomed-in close-up of the trimaran on the *Oregon* op center's view screen.

"It came out of nowhere," Hali said. "It must have been directly behind the *Thai Navigator.*"

"Is that the same ship, Sylvia?" Linda asked.

Sylvia nodded. She was amazed at how

calmly Linda responded, especially since it was just her and Hali on the bridge with Sylvia and Murph.

"Cutting anchor loose," Linda said, tapping on her armrest.

"Missiles in the air," Hali said.

Two rockets launched from the trimaran. One detonated moments later over the *Thai Navigator.* The second was on its way toward the *Oregon.*

"Activate the laser," she said.

"Locking on," Hali replied.

"Fire."

Sylvia and Murph could only watch as the missile streaked toward them. Suddenly it erupted in a flash of light, white gas thrown into the air halfway between them and the trimaran.

"Engines coming online, activating exterior camouflage," Linda said. "Hali, uncover the Kashtans and prepare to fire."

Sylvia knew those were the *Oregon*'s twin Gatling guns. She also knew that the trimaran was at the edge of those guns' effective range.

On the other hand, the *Oregon* was well within the effective range of the plasma cannon that was emerging from its protective shell on the deck of the trimaran, its wicked barrel swinging toward them.

■ ■ ■ ■

Jin was shocked to see the rocket explode before it reached the target. She was even more surprised when she lost sight of the *Norego* for a moment.

"Where did it go?" she blurted.

She squinted, then made out the profile of the cargo ship. It had seemingly turned from blue to brown, blending into the sandstone cliffs behind it.

"It's still there," she said. "Use your last target lock and fire the plasma cannon."

"Firing."

The *Marauder* shuddered as the plasma cannon charged, building up enough power to release its superheated ammunition. The whole ship was enveloped in a hum of energy, and then a crack like a bolt of lightning ripped the air.

In the distance, a fiery explosion atop the *Norego* meant they'd hit the target. Smoke marked their new bull's-eye.

"Power up for another shot," she said. She preferred survivors that she could question, but if she had to completely destroy the ship and kill everyone on board, so be it.

"Damage report," Linda called out.

"The Kashtan command module is out," Hali said. "We can't fire them."

"What about the rail gun?"

"Coming online, but our stern is to the trimaran. By the time we turn to get a bow shot, it might be too late."

As if to punctuate his statement, another explosion rocked the *Oregon.*

"That one took out the bridge," Hali said.

"Aim the laser at their bridge," Linda said. "It might buy us some time."

"Firing."

They couldn't see what effect the laser was having, but the firing of the plasma cannon stopped for a moment.

"Squall," Murph said.

"What?" Sylvia asked.

"Aim for the squall." He was looking at the screen.

She followed his gaze and saw what he meant. The dark clouds were only a few hundred yards away directly ahead of the *Oregon,* and a curtain of rain was gushing from the sky.

She turned to Linda and pointed at the screen. "The plasma cannon is a fair-weather weapon. If we can get into those heavy showers, they will attenuate its effectiveness."

Another ball of plasma shot by, scorching

a line along the *Oregon*'s deck.

"I'll take your word for it," Linda said. "Brace yourself."

Sylvia gripped the nearby control panel just in time to keep herself from falling. The *Oregon* surged forward and raced for shelter before they were all blown apart.

# FORTY-FIVE

At the same time that the call came in from Raven that a croc was coming their way, Linc found the last remaining amphora containing the nuts they were looking for. He brought it over and handed it to Juan. The mark on the wax seal was worn down, but it clearly said "N V L."

"Let's get back to *Nomad,*" Juan said, cradling the ceramic container in his hands as he grabbed on to *Little Geek* for the short ride back.

Halfway to the sub, its cylindrical form came into focus in the sonar image displayed on the inside of his glasses. Then another more ominous figure appeared beside it.

The shape resolved quickly into the body of a huge crocodile, its powerful tail swinging back and forth behind it.

He and Linc weren't going to make it back to the airlock in time. Juan drew his Wasp injection knife, ready to stab the croc as it raced toward them.

It opened its jaws wide but seemed to aim right between them. To Juan's surprise, the croc clamped down on *Little Geek,* and he realized that its sonar signal must have attracted the animal.

The croc quickly realized its mistake and let go of the inedible meal. But it now sensed a more tasty alternative nearby.

It lunged for Juan, who twisted out of the way, just missing the snapping teeth. Unfortunately, the motion brought the amphora he was holding into its path.

The croc's jaws crushed the heavy ceramic like it was made of fine crystal, shattering the container. Juan could make out a swirl of objects that scattered into the water along with the pottery shards. He reached out and snagged one. The rest were lost in the swirl of water.

The croc, still unhappy about not finding a meal, lunged for Juan, who jabbed his prosthetic leg into the reptile's massive maw. The croc's jaws snapped shut, and it began shaking its head viciously, tossing him around like a rag doll in an attempt to drown its prey.

Linc appeared out of the murk with his own knife and thrust it into the croc's head. But with the animal twisting so quickly, the blade glanced off, its load of deadly compressed air wasted as bubbles in the water. The knife itself was knocked out of his hand and went spinning into the gloom.

The croc wasn't deterred and kept its death grip on Juan's leg. In another situation, Juan would be wearing his combat leg, which — along with its hidden compartment holding a .45 ACP Colt Defender, ceramic knife, and C-4 packet — contained a shotgun slug that could be fired from the heel. But for the dive, he had on his normal, unarmed artificial leg.

Linc grabbed the croc's skull in a bear hug to keep it from opening its jaws to take another bite. Juan remembered what Parsons had said about how easy it was to keep a croc's mouth closed. Linc must have known that fact, too, and continued to ride him like a bucking bronco.

Still holding his own knife, Juan contorted himself so that he could reach the croc's upper jaw. He timed his strike to match the angle of the crocodile's next head twist and slammed the Wasp between its teeth.

The Wasp's blade didn't sink far into its soft palate, but it went deep enough. Juan pressed the button on the hilt, and air blasted out of the hole in the steel into the croc's lower jaw. At the same moment,

345

Linc's grip gave out. He was flung out of sight.

The croc released its hold on the prosthesis, taking the knife and Juan's flipper with it. The wound didn't seem fatal, but blood spewed into the water. The crocodile must have had enough of his prey fighting back because it turned to swim away.

However, as it did so, its massive tail swung around, catching Juan's buoyancy vest and air hose. The sharp edge of its hide tore through both, filling Juan's mask with water and evacuating the air from his vest.

Without the buoyancy, the chain mail weighed him down so much that he couldn't rise to the surface. His lungs were soon screaming for air.

With one hand, he used the quick release to unclip his vest and shed his tank to free up some weight, but the exertion from fighting the croc had used up all his oxygen. It would be a close race to see if he could get light enough to get up to the surface before he drowned.

Still, he had to try. He got the shredded buoyancy vest off, but he had an overwhelming urge to suck in water. His chest was burning with the need for air.

Juan felt a pair of strong hands grab his shoulders and propel him upward. Together, he and Linc broke the surface, and Juan gulped in fresh air. He looked up to see a hand reaching down to him, and he took it.

With a mighty heave, MacD and Raven yanked him up onto *Nomad*'s deck. They turned to pull Linc up beside him.

He sat next to Juan panting.

"Thanks, Linc," Juan said. "I wasn't going to make it another second."

Linc nodded. "I didn't think you could wait for the airlock to cycle. After that, I think I'm qualified to join the rodeo."

"It's good you got out when you did," Raven said, pointing at a flotilla of crocodiles heading toward *Nomad*. "All that blood and thrashing has attracted attention."

"What's that?" MacD said, nodding at the gold relic on Juan's hip.

"I don't know. I found it among some broken amphorae."

"Speaking of that," Linc said, throwing the broken lid of the container onto the deck in disgust. "I saw the croc chomp through the container. We lost our chance to find out what the antidote's secret ingredient is."

"No, we didn't," Juan said.

Throughout that ordeal, he had never let go of what was in his hand. He held out his clenched fist and opened it. In his palm was a single green nut the size of a golf ball. It had a pattern on it that looked like the iris of a human eye.

Juan didn't have time to savor his victory.

Eric poked his head out of the hatch with an anxious look on his face and said, "We need to leave right now. Hali says the *Oregon* is under attack."

# FORTY-SIX

The *Norego* had escaped into the narrow channel east of Adolphus Island, protected by a curtain of heavy rain, so Jin ceased firing the plasma cannon. The weapon was rendered ineffective by the showers, but it also meant that the spy ship's laser had stopped painting her bridge with its blinding light.

"Captain," her XO said, "the *Thai Navigator* is on a collision course with us."

"Move us out of the way," Jin said, "but don't get any closer to the *Norego*. What's the *Thai Navigator*'s heading?" The ore carrier wouldn't be stopping, not with her crew incapacitated by the Enervum gas.

"Looks like she'll hit the rocks on the west side of Adolphus Island."

"Good. Then she won't be in our way when she sinks."

It would only be a few minutes before the squall passed, allowing her to press her attack and finish off the ship. But she still wanted survivors to question.

"Hail the *Norego.* Tell them to call our encrypted satellite number so we won't have anyone listening in on our conversation."

A few moments later, the XO said, "They're calling us."

"Put it on speaker."

"This is the captain of the *Marauder,*" Jin said. "Who am I speaking to?"

"This is the acting captain of the *Norego,*" a woman replied in an American accent. "You must be April Jin."

Jin controlled her surprise. "Why would you say that?"

"Because we know who you are and we have witnesses who identified you and Angus Polk as the people responsible for a series of poison gas attacks. We know about your production facility in Nhulunbuy. It's only a matter of time before we shut down the rest of your operation."

"And who is 'we'?"

"I'm Linda. That's all you need to know."

"Actually, I need to know more. That's why I'll make you this one-time offer. Surrender now, and I won't destroy your ship."

"That is a tempting proposal. We'll have to think about it and get back to you."

"Don't think too long," Jin said. "It

350

expires as soon as those rain clouds go by."

"April, I have to tell you, I'm not a big fan of the hard sell."

"I've disabled your Kashtan control system, and your anti-aircraft laser is nothing more than an annoyance. Face it, you've already lost."

"You know what?" Linda said. "You're right. Come on over, and we'll bring you on board for tea and cookies."

"Very inviting, but I'll give you something else to think about. If I don't see your crew up on deck with their hands in the air by the time the rain stops, I'll light up your ship like a Roman candle. Got that?"

Before Linda could respond, Jin drew her finger across her throat, and the connection was cut.

Based on what she'd heard, Jin didn't actually think they would give up. A shame, really. She was quite curious about who she was going to kill.

Linda was hoping that her dialogue with April Jin had bought enough time for Sylvia to get comfortable with the stern Kashtan Gatling gun's manual targeting system. Without the automated targeting, the guns were tricky to aim. Although she was a weapons expert like her brother, Murph had to give her a crash course on its operation.

If Linda had been able to turn the ship around, she could have brought the bow's powerful rail gun to bear. But the channel was so narrow, she was afraid they'd run aground and become a sitting duck.

On the screen, she could make out the trimaran through the haze of the downpour. The *Thai Navigator* was now past, giving the *Marauder* a clear shot at them.

"Not to hurry you guys," Linda said, "but the rain is starting to let up."

"I'm ready," Sylvia said.

"What's the range to target?"

"Two miles," Hali replied.

"That's at the edge of the Kashtan's range," Linda said. "The counter says we're down to four hundred rounds on that gun. We'll only get one or two salvos out of it before it's dry."

At the Kashtan's ten-thousand-round-per-minute firing rate, it was barely enough ammunition for two seconds of shooting.

"She can do it," Murph said.

Sylvia nodded in agreement, her gaze focused on her control panel.

"Then target that cannon and take it out before it blows us out of the water," Linda ordered.

Sylvia activated a burst, and a second of

tracer fire poured from the double barrels of the Kashtan. They missed to port.

"This is tricky," Sylvia said, re-aiming the weapon.

Then as if a knob on a shower had been turned off, the downpour ended abruptly.

Sylvia fired again. This time the rounds made a direct hit on the *Marauder,* causing the deck to spark and smoke.

At the same instant, the *Marauder*'s plasma cannon spit out another blast. The superheated gas hit the Kashtan, knocking out its targeting camera.

"Weapon is down and ammo is gone," Sylvia said.

If the plasma cannon was still functioning, their only play now was to back out of the channel and try to turn before they were blown apart. She reversed course and brought the engines to full power, bracing herself for the next impact.

It never came.

"The *Marauder* is turning tail and running," Hali said. "Sylvia must have disabled the plasma cannon with her shot."

On-screen, the trimaran swung around and shot forward, rising onto hydrofoils as it sped away at a velocity even the *Oregon* couldn't match.

"The rail gun," Murph said. "Before she

is out of range."

The rail gun could fire much farther than the Kashtans, but the fleeing trimaran was no longer Linda's priority.

She switched the camera view to the *Thai Navigator,* which was closing on Adolphus Island.

"That cargo ship won't stop before she hits something," Linda said. "Not when her crew is suffering the effects of that gas."

"They won't be able to evacuate if she starts sinking," Hali said.

As the *Oregon* cleared the channel, Linda turned the ship toward the *Thai Navigator* and set them on a rendezvous course at top speed.

"Hali," she said, "call Eddie and tell him to get ready to jump ship."

# FORTY-SEVEN

A minute after getting the urgent call from Hali, Eddie rushed up to the starboard side of the *Oregon,* where a gangway was emerging straight up out of the deck. When they were beside the *Thai Navigator,* the gangway would rotate to a horizontal position and extend out over the ore carrier. Eddie would then traverse over. That was the plan anyway.

The problem was that the gangway was intended to be used for boarding a ship that was stationary, not one traveling at ten knots in an increasingly narrow gulf. The *Oregon* would have to get within fifteen feet to make it work, overcoming the wakes both ships were producing.

Adolphus Island loomed ahead. Eddie could make out the rocky shoals that would tear the hull wide open. There would be no time to evacuate all the paralyzed crew before it sank.

Eddie had no experience operating a large cargo ship, but he was the only person available for this mission. The Chairman and his team were still in *Nomad* on the Ord River. The ore carrier would be at the bottom of the gulf long before they could return. Eric Stone, who was a skilled sailor, would talk him through the procedure for stopping the ship. He put in his earpiece.

"I'm topside," he said. "You there, Eric?"

"I'm online," Eric said. "Let me know when you're on the bridge."

"Roger that. Linda, I'm ready to go over."

"Not yet. We've done a quick calculation here. You'll have to wait."

"Why?"

"Because it's too late for the ship to avoid a collision, even at full reverse."

"Then what are we going to do?" Eddie asked.

"We'll get between the island and the *Thai Navigator* and give her a little nudge," Linda said. "Brace yourself. This is going to get rough."

Eddie understood what was about to happen and backed away from the railing to grab hold of a lashing chain. Linda was going to use the *Oregon* herself to push the *Thai Navigator* off its current course like a tugboat.

But with two ships over 500 feet in length, it was a hazardous maneuver at best. If Linda came in at the wrong angle, the *Oregon*'s armored hull could cave in the steel of the ore carrier, causing as much damage as the rocks. And she was running out of time. They had only minutes before both ships ran aground. It was like they were playing a futile game of chicken with Adolphus Island, and the winner was already decided.

The *Oregon* came alongside the *Thai Navigator,* matching her speed. Slowly but steadily, the *Oregon* eased over until the ship lurched, accompanied by the piercing shriek of grinding metal. The noise continued unabated as the two ships rubbed against each other.

The *Oregon*'s venturi tubes were thrust vectored, meaning the jets of water produced by the magnetohydrodynamic engines could be pointed in different directions to steer the ship. Right now, they were straining to shove the cargo ship off her heading, with the *Thai Navigator* and her fixed rudder fighting back the whole way.

Eddie wasn't sure it was going to work until he noticed the *Oregon*'s bow gradually starting to point away from the island.

"It's going to be close," Linda said.

She wasn't exaggerating. Eddie could no longer see water between the *Oregon* and the shore. The island's sandy cliffs towered over them. At times, he could hear a scraping sound coming from the island side of the ship.

Then they passed the promontory of the island's peninsula and were back into the open water of the gulf. The *Oregon* backed away from the ore carrier, and the grating noise stopped. In places, the ore carrier's hull had been stripped down to bare metal, but there were no holes visible.

"You okay up there?" Linda asked.

"No problem for me," Eddie said. "Nice driving. Other than needing a touch-up on the paint job, I don't think the *Thai Navigator* suffered much damage."

"Thanks, but we're not home free yet."

The flat mangrove-fringed shore on the opposite side of the gulf was now directly in front of the *Thai Navigator*. At their current speed, Eddie estimated they had less than five minutes to bring the ship to a stop.

Linda kept a parallel course and lowered the gangway until it was hanging out over the water. Eddie walked out to the far end of it, ready to jump onto the *Thai Navigator* as soon as it was in place over the deck.

The *Oregon* crept closer until the gangway

was five feet above the other ship's deck. Eddie tensed to jump and made his leap just as the *Thai Navigator* was bumped just a fraction off course by some unseen force.

Instead of tucking and rolling onto the deck, Eddie had to reach out and snag the railing with one hand to keep from dropping into the churning wake below. He dangled there, his fingers cramping from the effort.

"Eddie," Linda yelled. "Hold on. We'll get the gangway under you."

"No," Eddie grunted. "I've got this."

He swung himself around and latched onto the metal railing with his other hand, pulling himself up until he could put his foot on the deck. He hopped over and headed for the bridge.

When he got there, he found four men lying on the deck. They were all conscious but immobile except for a few arm and hand movements.

"Don't worry, guys," Eddie said. "I'm here to help you."

He got only unintelligible moans in return.

The mangrove shore was much closer now. "Eric, I'm here, and we don't have much time. What do I do now?"

"I found the bridge specs on that ship design," Eric said. "Steering is going to be

359

too complicated for you to handle by yourself. We're just going to stop the ship."

"How?"

"In the center of the console, there should be a lever labeled Engine Order Telegraph. It'll look a lot like the handle on the RHIB's thrust control."

Eddie scanned the controls until he spotted it. It was above a semi-circle sticking out of the console marked with STOP, DEAD SLOW, SLOW, HALF, and FULL on both AHEAD and ASTERN. It was currently set to HALF AHEAD.

"Got it," Eddie said.

"Good. Linda thinks that you won't be able to stop in time to avoid grounding on the shore, so you're going to have to set the engines at full astern."

There were several other buttons and knobs to set, and Eric guided Eddie through them. Then Eddie yanked the lever all the way back.

The *Thai Navigator* shuddered as the screw came to a stop, and even as it began rotating in the opposite direction, the inertia of the huge ship was still carrying it forward. The trees were growing closer with each passing second.

"We're still moving, but we're slowing," Eddie said. "Is there anything else I can do?"

"I'm afraid not. Just hang on."

While he waited, he dragged each of the crewmen so that they were lying against the front of the bridge.

As he finished bracing them, Eddie felt the bow rising as it crunched across the sandy bottom of the marsh. He took the captain's chair and watched as the ship sliced through the stand of mangroves.

To his surprise, the *Thai Navigator* came to a gentle stop on the shore.

He switched the throttle to STOP, and the vibrations ceased.

"We ain't going anywhere," Eddie said. "Better get Doc Huxley over here. She's got some new patients."

"She's on the way," Linda said.

"What about the *Marauder*?"

"The trimaran turned east after leaving Cambridge Gulf, but it's now out of the rail gun's range and off our radarscope. April Jin got away."

# FORTY-EIGHT

By the time Juan got back to the *Oregon* with *Nomad* and his team, the entire crew of the *Thai Navigator* had been evacuated and brought on board. He oversaw their transfer to the nearby port town of Wyndham, where they'd be treated by an incoming military medical team familiar with the symptoms.

None of the men on the ore carrier remembered the attack, so it was easy to pass off the *Oregon* crew as Good Samaritans who happened to be in the vicinity and came to their rescue. With the story they'd made up about how they'd found the stranded ore carrier, the questions from the authorities didn't take long to answer, and they were allowed to leave.

As they left the port, Juan was on the *Oregon*'s deck with Max inspecting the damage from the battle with the *Marauder*. The stern Kashtan gun was out of commission, as was the automated control module on the superstructure, the fake bridge would need extensive repairs, and the hull was scorched in several places, requiring new paint to fill in the gaps of their active camouflage system.

"We couldn't keep her clean for even a week," Max grumbled. "It's like driving your brand new sports car off the dealer's lot and being sideswiped by a garbage truck before you can get home."

"I'm sure you'll patch her up nicely until we can get back to Malaysia and finish outfitting her," Juan said. He pointed at two of the *Oregon*'s technicians whose cutting torches were showering the deck with sparks. "I'm more worried about the hangar doors. How long until we can get them open again?"

One of the blasts from the plasma cannon had fused several hinges on the doors that allowed the tiltrotor to rise out of the ship. That's why they hadn't sent Gomez to keep an eye on the trimaran as it fled, and their short-range drones didn't have enough battery power to track a ship that could be more than a hundred miles away by now.

"I'd say another three hours before we can crank them up," Max said. "The mechanism will be held together by spit and baling wire, but it'll work."

"You're an engineering genius, Max," Juan said, clapping him on the shoulder. "I don't know what I'd do without you."

"Supergenius, I think you meant. And you'd do what you always do. You'd find a way to get the job done, just like you did with that croc."

"That was mostly Linc. All I had to do was not get eaten. Let me know when the repairs are complete."

As he left Max, they were passing the stranded *Thai Navigator,* the front third of it surrounded by mangrove trees where it had plowed ashore. It would take a very high tide and several powerful tugboats to get it floating again. He'd already been briefed on what it took to save the crew, and he felt a swell of pride in what his well-trained team could accomplish.

Back inside, he headed to the boardroom and found Sylvia and Eric waiting for him. They were huddled closely together and didn't notice Juan enter.

"Find out anything interesting?" he asked.

Instead of being embarrassed by their proximity, Eric seemed comfortable with it. He smiled at Sylvia and said, "A few things. We're just waiting for Murph and Doc Huxley to get back to talk about some of them."

Juan took his seat at the head of the table where the golden eagle he'd found in the shipwreck was on display. It had been cleaned, and its wings gleamed as brightly as the day it had been buried two thousand years ago. The letters SPQR were etched over crossed swords.

"Can you tell me what this idol is?"

"We think it's an *aquila,* which is the Latin word for 'eagle,' " Sylvia said. "It was a battle standard carried by a Roman legion, worshiped by them as a symbol of Jupiter."

"You *think* that's what it is?"

"None have survived," Eric said, "so we have nothing to compare it to. At least none until now. The closest we've found are some imperial seals. But the SPQR definitely confirms it's Roman. The letters stand for *Senātus Populusque Rōmānus.* 'The Roman Senate and People.' This might be the only one still in existence."

"How did it get to Australia?"

"They must have hidden it from the Parthians to protect it when they were taken prisoner," Sylvia said. "It was considered a shameful disgrace and a terrible omen for an *aquila* to be captured in battle. When the Romans lost three of them in Germania, they spent the next thirty years trying to get them back."

Eric nodded. "So we think Flavius and his men either kept the eagle hidden from the Parthians or they stole it back when they escaped."

"It must be priceless," Juan said. "But the formula for the nerve gas was apparently worth more."

"Which leads to our next finding," Eric said. "There was one more useful item in the files you took from the swamp factory. The file refers to an upcoming operation using the factory's output that was loaded onto the cargo ship in Nhulunbuy."

"Do you know where the op will take place?"

"Unfortunately, no," Sylvia said. "It's an inventory spreadsheet titled 'Canisters for 12/31 *Shepparton* mission.'"

"New Year's Eve," Juan said. "That's only five days from now."

"That's not the worst part," Eric said. "The spreadsheet has a column heading called MR-76 and another for Enervum canisters, followed by a list of production dates."

"Enervum is the name they used for the gas. What's MR-76?"

"It's a Swedish-made rocket used by the militaries of many countries," Sylvia said, "including Australia. That must be what they are using to disperse the gas."

"How many?" Juan asked.

"The total at the bottom for each is two hundred and ninety-six," Eric said.

"Used all at once, it would be enough gas to saturate an entire city," Sylvia said.

Juan sat back in his chair at the grim news. "So we know there is going to be a nerve gas attack on New Year's Eve, but we don't know the place where it will happen or the actual name of the ship carrying the rockets, and we have no antidote."

"We've made progress on that front," Julia said from the boardroom door. She walked in and took a seat, followed by Murph trailing her in his motorized chair.

"Can you make it from the nut I found?" Juan asked.

"No, it was too old and desiccated to be viable. But we've identified the source."

"Yes, we did," Murph said, and then played a chorus of cheers from his audio translator.

"The Romans called it the green-eyed nut," Julia said, "but the tree is known today as *arenga randi,* or Rand's palm. It's found on only one island in the world."

"Christmas Island," Murph said.

"Fitting for this time of year," Juan said. "The one in the Indian Ocean, I assume, not the one in the Pacific?"

"Correct. It's an Australian territory. About fifteen hundred miles from here."

"The tiltrotor could make it with a stop in Indonesia," Juan said. "How many nuts do you need?"

"I estimate it will take three nuts to provide enough oil for each dose," Julia said. "Given that we have more than six hundred people affected by the gas, we'll need approximately two thousand nuts."

"And I volunteer to be the first to try the antidote," Murph said.

Sylvia reached over and took his hand. "Are you sure? There could be side effects."

"I may look cheery, but this sucks. If there is a potential cure, I'll try it."

"First, we need to make sure we can find the trees," Juan said. He called Hali on the speakerphone.

"Yes, Chairman?"

"Connect me with Bob Parsons."

"I'll track him down."

A few moments later, Parsons said, "What can I do for you?"

"You mentioned that you have connections all over Australia," Juan said. "Do you have any on Christmas Island?"

There was a hesitation. "Well . . . not really."

"It sounds like you do. This is important. We need a guide who might know the island's flora."

Parsons sighed. "All right. I do know someone. Renee LaBelle. She runs an eco-tourism business there. If she can't help you, she'll know someone who can. But she might not want to hear from me."

"Why's that?"

"We had a fling a few years back and it didn't work out."

"Listen, we're sending a team there, and we just need an introduction."

"Better I go with you, then," Parsons said. "I should do it in person."

"You're on the team," Juan said before switching back to Hali. "Tell Gomez to get the tiltrotor ready to fly. As soon as Max has the hangar doors fixed, we're heading to Christmas Island."

# FORTY-NINE

*Jakarta, Indonesia*

It was near midnight as Polk drove his black Toyota SUV behind two other identical vehicles through the city's central business district, its dazzling array of skyscrapers awash in a variety of colors. Their destination was far less glamorous — the manufacturing region east of downtown known as Cikarang.

He had the vehicle to himself so he could speak to Jin freely.

"Are you all right?" he asked when she told him about the sea battle with the spy ship.

"Just a few scrapes from some shrapnel," Jin said. "We lost four crew and the plasma cannon was damaged, but I was able to get away."

"And we still don't know who we're up against?"

"The only person I spoke to was a cheeky

woman named Linda. Their ship had more advanced features than we realized."

"Like what?"

"Like an anti-missile laser and some sort of camouflage system."

"You're joking."

"There are only a few countries in the world with the resources to fund something like that. But it was odd, as the woman spoke English with an American accent. I'd say the United States must be involved."

"How much do you think they know?" Polk asked.

"I wish I had an answer. But they obviously found out about the archaeological dig. Who knows what they discovered there."

"Then it's good I came on this trip. We can't have them making their own antidote."

"Be careful. They seem to be a step ahead of us."

"Do you think Lu is playing some sort of game with us?"

"I don't think so," Jin said. "But that's why we have our backup plan."

They had never put all their confidence in the cryptocurrency payout for accomplishing their objective in Sydney. If the money didn't come through as Lu had promised, they still had a way to profit from the paralysis of five million Australian citizens.

When Polk flew away from the factory near Nhulunbuy, his helicopter was carrying ten gallons of Enervum antidote, enough for nine thousand people. The containers were now sitting on his jet, ready to fly to Sydney for rapid deployment after the gas attack. The city's rich and famous would pay anything to reverse the effects, and Polk figured they could sell the doses for at least fifty thousand dollars apiece on the dark web, netting them close to half a billion dollars.

Whether Lu delivered or not, they would come out of this with enough money to change their identities and build a new life.

"Where are you going now?" Polk asked.

"We're on our way back to Marwood," Jin said. "I don't think repairs will take more than a couple of days. Then we'll head down to Sydney to rendezvous with you."

"You be careful, too. The location of our base wasn't in any of the records at the factory, but we've been surprised before."

"Don't worry. I'll make sure the guards are on full alert. Hope your raid goes well."

"Thanks. One more stop after this and then I'll head to Marwood. See you soon, luv."

Polk hung up. He could see their target up ahead. It was a giant manufacturing plant owned by Blovex pharmaceuticals.

The drug company was the only place outside of Christmas Island with a supply of nuts from the Rand's palm tree. They'd been experimenting with them trying to make high-priced health supplements. Polk and Jin had attempted to buy out their inventory, but they'd refused to sell. Jin had convinced Polk to leave them alone and not raise any further suspicions about their interest in the nuts, but now that storehouse was a threat.

The nut supply had to be destroyed.

Although Blovex security was decent, it wasn't a military base. Polk had anticipated this day and toured the facility as a prospective business partner months ago to get the layout and location of the nut storage units.

He drove forward and took the lead, pulling a balaclava over his head to prevent his face from appearing on any security camera footage and putting a suppressed Glock pistol on his lap.

When he reached the guardhouse at the front gate, he didn't wait for the two guards to leave their shack. He shot each in the head while they were still trying to figure out why they could only see his eyes.

He got out and punched the button that opened the gate. He checked his watch to note the time. They had a good five minutes before they could expect any kind of police response.

The storage unit was contained in the third building past the guardhouse. While one team waited outside the building for any Blovex security guards who might show up, Polk took the other men inside, all four of them rolling hand trucks behind them.

They found the storage unit marked "Rand's palm." Inside were forty canvas sacks filled with nuts harvested from a wild grove on Christmas Island.

"Load them up," Polk said.

It took several trips to transfer all the bags to the SUVs with the carts.

By the time they were leaving the facility, they could hear sirens in the distance. Polk led them to a vacant lot on the shore of the Citarum River. The toxic waterway was considered one of the most polluted rivers on earth, so choked with garbage and human waste that you couldn't see the water. His balaclava kept the worst of the stench at bay.

One by one, Polk sliced open each bag of nuts with a knife and had his men pour the contents into the river. He was sure no one would find them in that noxious stew.

When they were done, Polk said, "Back to

the airport."

They'd get some sleep and fly out first thing in the morning.

It wouldn't be so easy to dispose of the trees that bore the nuts. Polk made a mental note to call ahead and make sure they could transport the amount of petrol they needed once they landed on Christmas Island.

# FIFTY

*The Coral Sea*

After a week in Fiji, Gary Bonner wasn't eager to get back to his dentistry practice in Cairns, but he wished the five-knot wind would pick up a little. They'd already been delayed by the storm that had blown through a couple of days before, and he had to go over the accounting books before the new year.

Still, the bright morning sun and calm seas made for a pleasant cruise on his new fifteen-meter sailing yacht, *Tooth Ferry*. His wife, Vivian, was lounging on the deck in her bikini with a coffee and a romance novel, while their twelve-year-old son, Cameron, sat astride the bow, where he liked to dangle his feet above the rushing water.

Something seemed to have drawn Cameron's attention away from his phone, which Gary thought was a triumph. Maybe he'd spotted a pod of dolphins.

Gary called out to him. "See something interesting?"

Cameron stood as if to get a better look. "I don't know. What is that?"

He pointed, and Gary followed the line out to a point about a mile away. A yellow object was waving in the breeze.

Except it was going back and forth rhythmically, not fluttering in the wind.

Gary picked up his binoculars to take a closer look.

He was shocked to see a man floating in the ocean. He was frantically trying to hail them with a yellow piece of clothing.

"Viv, get up," Gary yelled, turning the yacht. "There's a guy over there in the water."

"What?" she said, sitting up. "You're pulling my leg."

"Cam spotted him. He must have eyes like a falcon. Come over here and take the wheel, so I can douse the sails. Cam, put down that phone and give me a hand."

Cameron had started to film the rescue, but he pocketed the phone while they quickly took down the sails. Vivian started the motor and drove them full speed toward the yelling man. Cameron took his phone out again and continued the video recording.

As they got closer, Gary could tell that the man was Asian and yelling in a foreign language. The yellow item was a jacket, and he clung to a white piece of Styrofoam.

"Did he fall off a ship?" Cameron asked.

"Probably," Gary answered. "He was a lucky bloke to find that piece of flotsam." He retrieved their life preserver and tied it to a rope to haul the man on board when they got close enough.

As they approached, Gary saw a fin surface fifty meters behind the shouting man. It sliced through the water on a direct line toward him.

A shark.

Gary's stomach went cold when he realized what had happened. The man had been floating motionless since the storm, drawing no notice to himself. But as soon as he started waving at the passing yacht, his thrashing and yelling simulated the movements and sounds of a fish in distress, exactly the kind of motion that would attract a nearby shark.

Gary waved his hands in what he hoped was a universal gesture to calm down.

"Stop moving. There's a shark in the water."

He pointed at the oncoming predator, but the man didn't understand him and continued shouting, waving, and splashing the water with joy at having been saved.

The fin reached the man when they were within a boat length of him, and his joyous call turned to a bloodcurdling scream. He was yanked underwater for a moment, and then he surfaced amid a sea of crimson.

Gary threw out the life preserver, and the man desperately grabbed hold of it.

"Come on," Gary cried out and pulled with all his might.

Vivian rushed toward him and gave him a hand. With their combined effort, they were able to get him up onto the boat.

One of the man's legs had been bitten off mid-thigh. Blood cascaded across the deck.

"Whoa," Cameron said breathlessly, though he didn't stop filming.

"We need to put tourniquets on," Vivian said, rushing below to get the medical kit. Gary was never more glad that she was an intensive care nurse, which also explained why Cameron wasn't traumatized by such a horrific sight. He loved hearing her gruesome stories about car crash victims and lawn mower accidents.

The injured man was babbling, repeating the same words over and over, but Gary didn't understand them.

"Do you speak English?" he asked.

The man shook his head and continued his chant, almost like a mantra. They got progressively softer until he went silent.

Vivian returned and saw that he was turning pale. She knelt and put her fingers to his neck. After a few seconds, she pulled them away slowly.

"He's gone," she said. "Poor fellow. He's been floating out here in the ocean for who knows how long and then dies just as he's being rescued."

"I didn't know someone could bleed that much," Cameron said, lowering his phone.

Gary sighed and put his hand on his son's shoulder. "I'm sorry you had to see that. Are you all right, sport?"

"I'm fine. You have a hard job, Mom."

"Some days harder than others," Vivian said.

"At least we can give his family some closure," Gary said. "We'll take him back to Cairns with us so his body can be returned home."

"I'll go radio the Maritime Border Command," Vivian said. "Better to let them know now than show up at port with a corpse. Then I'll get a sheet to wrap him with." She went below.

"Let's see if we can find out who he is," Gary said.

He went through the man's pockets. He didn't find any ID. Just a pack of Chinese cigarettes and a matchbook that had an image of two clinking glasses of beer. It read "The Lazy Goanna, Nhulunbuy."

"I wonder what he was saying," Gary said.

"Maybe I can find out," Cameron said and began tapping on his phone.

"How?"

"Jeez, Dad. You can do anything on the internet now." Their satellite connection and Wi-Fi system meant that even out in the middle of the ocean they could stream movies and browse the web.

Gary could hear the man's last words on the phone.

"What are you doing?"

"Playing the recording for a translation app," Cameron said. After a few moments he frowned at the phone.

"What was he saying?"

"That can't be right. Maybe this app doesn't work."

Gary looked at the phone's screen and agreed with his son. The app couldn't have translated the phrase correctly. Why would a man with mortal wounds keep repeating the words "the centaur left me"?

# FIFTY-ONE

*Christmas Island*

After a stopover in Surabaya, Indonesia, to refuel, Gomez landed the *Oregon*'s tiltrotor at Christmas Island's airport at eight in the morning. In addition to Parsons, Juan had brought along Raven, MacD, Eddie, and Linc. As they climbed out, Juan noted that the only other airplanes on the tarmac were an Indonesian airliner and a private jet.

They couldn't go around brandishing assault weapons on this small island, but Juan didn't want to travel unarmed, not after the surprise attack on the *Oregon*. False bottoms in their bags were good enough to fool the customs agents, allowing them to at least have pistols with them.

At the airport's exit, a beautiful woman with a blonde ponytail rushed toward them and threw herself into Bob Parsons' arms.

MacD held out his hands toward the doors as if expecting his own enthusiastic greeting. When no other women came in, he joked, "Don't we all get one?"

She extricated herself. "Bob, it's so good to see you."

Parsons looked shocked. "I thought you might not want to see me."

"That was a long time ago. And I was the one who broke up with you, remember?"

"Because I wasn't ready to settle down."

"That doesn't mean I stopped loving you."

Parsons suddenly noticed the five others looking at him. He cleared his throat.

"Renee LaBelle, I'd like you to meet your new friends."

He introduced each of them, but Renee was more interested in the bandage on his hand.

"What happened to you?"

"Actually, that's why we're here. Without my knowing it, I was part of a plan that has made a lot of people ill, and now I'm trying to make amends. There might be a tree nut on Christmas Island that can help cure them, and we need to find it."

"What is it?"

"Rand's palm."

Renee nodded slowly as she was thinking. "It's endemic to the island. Rather rare. The trees are scattered throughout the national park, but there's only one large grove I

383

know about."

"Can you tell us where it is?" Juan asked.

"Even better. I can show you." She smiled at Parsons. "I took the day off so we could catch up."

As they walked out to the parking lot, Juan said, "Did you see who got out of that private plane?"

Renee shook her head. "When I got here, I asked if that was your plane, but the security guard said it was government types headed out to the immigration detention center. We get them here from time to time to transport some of the detainees to other locations." She stopped at a silver Mercedes SUV. "You can borrow my G-Wagen."

"Is there room for all of us?"

"No. That's why I had a friend drop it off here for you. Bob and I will drive my other car."

She pointed behind the SUV to an exquisite Jaguar convertible with burgundy-colored paint, a tan and red leather interior, and wire-spoked wheels.

"Now, *that's* a car," Linc said.

"It's my toy, a 1955 Jaguar XK140. It has the Special Equipment engine option, which is good for two hundred kilometers per hour. Mostly, I just take it for spins around the island with the top down on nice sunny days like today."

Parsons leaned over and whispered to Juan. "I didn't mention that her family is rich, did I?"

"You left that part out."

"Smart, beautiful, and rich. I was an idiot for letting her get away."

"I can't disagree with you on that one."

"Shall we?" Renee said, hopping into the Jaguar's driver's seat.

"We shall," Parsons said, squeezing into the passenger seat.

The rest of them got in the Mercedes. Juan drove with Eddie beside him and the others in the back.

The Jag took off with a throaty roar, shaking the SUV's windows with the exhaust note from its twin tailpipes. Juan had to step on it to keep up.

Other than the small town of Flying Fish Cove at the north end, the island was sparsely inhabited. Soon they were driving through a dense tropical rain forest.

According to the research they'd done on the flight in, Christmas Island wasn't a huge travel destination since there were very few beaches. Most of the shoreline consisted of jagged rocks. Tourists who came were most interested in the biodiversity, including the massive annual red crab migration. Apparently, the *Oregon* team had missed it by only a couple of weeks.

The only other industries were several phosphate mines, with some quarries dating from the 1800s, and the immigration detention center on the west side of the island.

Renee led them on a winding course through the island until she stopped along the side of the road just past a metal overpass. Juan came to a stop behind her and got out.

"We can leave the cars here. Everyone knows them, so no one will bother them." She turned and pointed at the overpass behind them. "That's for the red crabs to cross the road during the migration. Otherwise, they'd get squashed by cars."

"I'll try to come back and see it sometime," Juan said. "How far are we from the grove?"

"I'm not sure exactly. I haven't been out here in a while. There are several trailheads in this area where you can park, but I think this is the closest one. The paths crisscross the entire national park, so we may need to fan out to find the one leading to the grove."

"We'll be able to talk to each other through our earpieces."

While she went back to her car, Juan and his team hid pistols under their shirts and got out fifteen balled-up nylon sacks to carry as many nuts as they were able to find.

They began the trek into the jungle, led by Renee, who took Parsons by his good hand.

"Be careful not to step on the crabs," she said. "They live on the forest floor. You could say they're our local treasure. And if you see any small tree with broad heart-shaped leaves, don't touch it."

"Why not?" Raven asked.

"It's another plant unique to our island called the jelutong, or stinging tree. One of its leaves rubbed against my arm once. It felt like being scalded with acid. If you so much as brush your hand against it, you'll be in agony for days."

"I hate jungles," Linc muttered and kept his hands close by his side as he picked his way through the foliage.

They reached a fork in the trail. The path went in three directions.

"This is where we'll need to split up. The trees are in a clearing that was supposed to be a phosphate mine, but they never started digging after cutting down the trees. The flora is just now starting to come back. I think that's why the Rand's palms started growing so well there. Otherwise, they're difficult to locate."

Eddie and Linc took the trail to the left, while Raven and MacD went to the right. Juan stayed with Renee and Parsons and kept going straight.

They walked for another five minutes before Renee asked, "How did you two meet?"

Juan looked at Parsons, who said, "I have to be honest with you. Juan and his friends saved me from some unsavory people."

"The ones who hurt you and those others that you need the cure for?"

"Yes. This is related to the *Empiric* and Port Cook incidents. And they might come here, so after we find the trees, Juan has asked you and me to leave and wait for them back at the airport."

"Absolutely not," Renee objected. "If my little island can help, I want to do my part."

"My dear, we can't —" Parsons started, but Juan put his hand up to stop the two of them.

"Do you smell that?" he said.

Renee sniffed the air. "Is that petrol?"

Although they were surrounded by thick jungle wilderness, the breeze carried the unmistakable odor of gasoline.

# FIFTY-TWO

At the same moment that Juan called Eddie to tell him about the gas smell, he and Linc noticed it, too. There seemed to be an opening in the trees up ahead, and voices soon accompanied the odor.

They got off the path and crept forward. Eddie almost stepped on one of the red crabs that Renee had mentioned. Crunching its hard shell underfoot would certainly draw attention. He pointed it out to Linc to keep him from making the same mistake.

They kept going until they could see into the clearing that Renee had described. There were a dozen squat palm trees loaded with ripe nuts, many of which had already tumbled to the ground. There were more than enough to supply antidotes for everyone who had been affected by the Enervum gas.

But the stench of gasoline had gotten stronger as they'd approached the clearing, and Eddie now saw why. A Chinese man only twenty yards away was unloading the last of a plastic gas tank onto the ground near the trees. Three more tanks were discarded nearby.

As Eddie and Linc drew their pistols, the man backed into the trees and took a cylindrical object from his pocket. Eddie couldn't tell what it was until the man took the top off and struck it against the remaining segment.

It blazed to life. A road flare. The man was going to toss it into the gas-soaked clearing and burn up their best chance at developing an antidote.

The man reared back to throw the flare. Eddie and Linc didn't give him a warning. They both shot at him through the trees until one of their bullets took him down. The flare fell harmlessly at his feet in the damp jungle.

Eddie's eye was drawn to another flare lit up on the opposite side of the clearing.

It was Polk. Only his head was visible over the palms. He was staring back at Eddie and grinning. Three men were spread out beside him, all armed with pistols. A fourth was farther along the clearing and struck a flare as well. They were making sure they set the entire grove on fire.

Eddie and Linc opened fire to stop them, but it was too late. Polk and the other man threw their flares. They arced up in different directions and came down in the clearing.

The petrol fumes ignited even before the flares landed. The entire clearing went up in flames, creating so much heat that Eddie and Linc had to back away into the jungle. Smoke billowed into the sky.

"Good thing it's the wet season," Linc said. The surrounding lush jungle was in no danger of catching fire.

Eddie could barely make out Polk through the growing flames. He paused for a moment, as if appreciating his handiwork. Then he waved for his men to follow him, and he turned and disappeared into the jungle.

Cutting across the burning clearing was impossible, so Eddie and Linc would have to go around to chase them down.

"Chairman," Eddie called on his comm unit, as he and Linc struggled to get through the dense foliage. "We were too late. The Enervum cure is up in smoke."

Polk was pleased with his impeccable timing. He'd been surprised by the gunfire, but he supposed he shouldn't have been. These people had been thorns in his and his wife's

391

side for days, and for once he had gotten the better of them.

Still, as he and his men followed the trail back to their vehicles, he couldn't help wishing he'd been able to take one of them captive. The operation wasn't complete yet, and he didn't have any idea what else they knew. They could still pose a threat.

He had left a man with the Range Rovers where they'd parked. Since he hadn't heard gunshots from that direction, Polk had to assume the SUVs were safe.

"Be alert," he said to his men as they made their way down the path quickly but cautiously. "There may be more of them."

# FIFTY-THREE

The dense black smoke drifting above Raven blotted out the sun, darkening the jungle. She and MacD had come to another fork in the trail and were headed north when they'd heard the gunshots behind them.

Not wanting to blindly rush toward the flames and shots, she and MacD stopped for a sitrep. They crouched down on either side of the path and listened in as Eddie described to the Chairman what had happened.

"We counted four of them with Polk," Eddie said.

"Where are they going?" she asked.

"They were on the other side of the clearing," Eddie answered. "Going north."

"Then they're headed toward us," MacD said. "Are any of you close by?"

"It'll take us a while to get there," Eddie said.

"Renee said there were other parking spots around here, so they must be going back to their cars," Juan said. "I'm going to take Renee and Parsons back to our vehicles. Rendezvous there and we'll chase them down."

"Since they'll be coming past us," Raven said, "we could lay an ambush."

"Not when you're outnumbered two to one. Get back here."

"Aye, Chairman."

Raven and MacD stood, but she immediately waved him back down. There was movement from up ahead, and silhouettes visible against the bright flames. She pointed them out to MacD, and each of them melted farther into the trees. She saw one of the broad-leafed stinging trees she'd been warned about and steered clear of it.

"We can't get there right now," Raven whispered as she knelt behind a towering palm tree. "They're going to pass right by us."

"Let them through," Juan said. "Follow them quietly if you can."

Raven saw the four men walking down the trail, holding their pistols at the ready and scanning the surroundings for enemies. Shooting all four of them through the trees would indeed be difficult.

She kept an eye on them until she heard a crunch come from MacD's direction. She immediately knew what it was — one of the jungle's numerous red crabs being squished by a boot.

Raven whipped around to see that it wasn't MacD who'd made the gaffe. A fifth man had snuck up behind them. He must have seen MacD and was closing on his position to kill him.

MacD had heard the same warning sound and turned to see the man just twenty feet away. Before Raven could react, he rose and exchanged gunfire. He hit the hostile in the chest to take him out, but the sound drew the attention of Polk and his other men.

They starting shooting in MacD's direction, and one of the rounds hit him in the arm. He went down.

"MacD?" Raven called on her comm unit.

"Ah'm all right," he responded, though she could tell he was in pain.

Raven stood and fired at the men in the path, but they had now taken flanking positions, and she didn't have a clear shot.

Polk and two of his men converged on MacD's location, while the other two took on Raven.

"What's happening over there?" Juan asked.

"Taking fire," Raven said. "MacD's down."

"Linc and I are on the way," Eddie said.

Not soon enough, Raven thought.

There was a short fight, then she saw Polk order his men to pick up MacD. Blood was coursing down his shirt. They herded him down the path at gunpoint. Polk commanded the other two in Chinese. She had no doubt the order was to stay behind and finish her off.

Raven had only two magazines, and her first one was almost out. She couldn't get into a prolonged firefight with them.

They were circling around in opposite directions to get her in a deadly cross fire. She emptied her mag at one of them without success and reloaded.

She kept the tree between her and the first man, focusing on his companion. She didn't want to waste bullets shooting through the thick greenery. The second man continued to edge toward her.

When he got within ten yards, she unloaded a volley at him. The final round hit him square in the chest, and he went down.

The first guy took that as a cue to rush her. Raven turned just in time to see him crash through the bushes and launch himself at her.

She caught his gun wrist with her free hand, and he did the same with her, locking them together in mortal combat.

Raven was a tall, strong woman, but the man was her equal and had an iron grip. She needed an advantage and remembered the nearby stinging tree. It was just to her right, only a couple of yards away.

She wrestled him to the side, trying to maneuver him into the plant. But to get him to move, she had to shift her weight, and the motion gave him the leverage.

He swept her right foot out from under her, and they toppled to the ground only inches from the stinging tree's leaves. The pistol dropped from her hand, and the man landed on top of her.

She clamped both her hands around his arm, but he used his body weight to slowly inch his gun toward her head. His finger was wrapped around the trigger. In a few more seconds, she was a dead woman.

One of the large leaves dangled over her face. She was so close she could make out the tiny hairs covering it.

She kneed the gunman, causing him to pitch forward just enough for his face to brush against the leaf.

He let out a hideous shriek and jumped to his feet, clawing at his face in pain.

Raven rolled over and picked up her gun. Before he could focus again, she put him out of his misery with a shot to the forehead.

Careful to steer clear of the pain-inducing leaves, she leaped to her feet and ran for the path in pursuit of MacD.

Up ahead through the trees, she saw the road. There were two Range Rovers. Polk's two henchmen tied MacD's hands behind his back with a jumper cable. She raised her pistol, but again she didn't have a clear shot.

MacD was stuffed into a Range Rover with Polk and one guy, while the other got into the second SUV. They took off just as she reached the road. She got off two shots before her gun went dry. The Range Rovers skidded around a corner and were gone. If she was right about her orientation, Polk would be passing their parked vehicles in a minute or so.

"Chairman," Raven said into her earpiece. "Polk has MacD. They took off in two Range Rovers and are coming your way."

# FIFTY-FOUR

Juan was at full sprint now to get back to the road, leaving Renee and Parsons behind him to catch up.

"Gomez, do you read me?" he said as he ran.

"I'm here, Chairman."

"What's your status?"

"I'm refueling now. I can be ready to take off in ten minutes."

"What's the private jet doing?"

"It's taxiing out to the runway."

"Can you block it?"

"From taking off?" Gomez asked.

"With the tiltrotor."

"Depends how long they wait at the end of the runway. They're almost there."

"They won't take off yet," Juan said. "Do what you can."

He ran out onto the road with his back to the crab bridge and saw the two Range Rovers racing toward him. Juan drew his pistol.

399

MacD would be in the back of one of the SUVs, so Juan's best chance was to take out the drivers as they passed him.

He stood behind Renee's Mercedes and took aim at the lead driver. From this distance, he couldn't make out his face or tell which vehicle MacD was in, so he'd have to be careful about his sight lines. He couldn't take the chance that one of his stray bullets would hit MacD.

The Range Rovers approached at high speed, one closely following the other. As the lead SUV came closer, he could tell the driver was a Chinese man, not Polk. He took aim and fired three quick shots at him.

One of the rounds hit him, causing the Range Rover to swing off the road. At the same time, he saw Polk in the driver's seat of the second vehicle. Juan squeezed off a shot as it flashed by, but he missed. MacD grimaced from the back seat, where he was being guarded by another man.

The lead Range Rover with its dead driver struck one end of the crab overpass, severing it from its base, and flipped into the trees.

The bridge, now supported on only one side, came crashing down just as Polk's vehicle drove safely underneath it. The bridge settled onto the roadway at an angle, reducing the clearance to only four feet high, far too little to allow the Mercedes G-Wagen to pass below it and chase them down.

A gargling rumble came from behind him. Juan turned to see Renee squeal to a stop next to him in the low-slung Jaguar.

"Get in," she shouted and pointed at the narrow gap under the collapsed bridge. "We can make it through there."

"I can't ask you —"

"It will take twice as long to intercept them in the other direction with the Mercedes," Parsons called out as he jogged up. "And you have the gun. She won't take no for an answer, believe me."

Juan didn't argue any further. He hopped over the door, and Renee took off before he was all the way in his seat.

Renee gunned the engine, and it felt like the sports car was shot from a cannon. She threaded the Jag neatly under the bridge remains and floored it in the hope of overtaking the Range Rover.

"How many different ways to the airport on this road?"

"Just two, but they won't take the scenic route along the coast."

The speedometer needle was already pushing ninety. At this rate, it would take only a few minutes to cross the small island.

"Thanks for doing this," Juan shouted over the rushing wind as he loaded a fresh mag.

"Don't let them get away with harming our island."

The Jag screamed around a corner and onto a long straightaway. The Range Rover was a half mile ahead. Renee deftly cycled through the gears until they were at well over a hundred miles per hour.

Juan couldn't risk shooting through the cabin and hitting MacD, so he was going to aim for a tire. It would delay Polk long enough for Eddie and the others to intercept them.

But Polk's Range Rover was slowed by another vehicle that he had to pass, and the Jag closed the distance. They were only a few car lengths behind when the man guarding MacD started shooting at them.

MacD slammed his body into the man, throwing off his aim, so Renee easily dodged the bullets. Juan leaned over the side and carefully sighted down the right rear tire of the Range Rover. He squeezed off a round, and he saw a puff from the tire. A direct hit.

But nothing happened. The rubber didn't fly apart, and the tire didn't deflate.

"You hit it dead-on," Renee said in astonishment. "Why didn't that work?"

"It must have run-flats," Juan said, "so we can't stop them before they get to the airport. Our only chance is to stop the plane from taking off."

"I'll ram their landing gear if I have to."

Juan still had half a magazine left. "Let's hope it doesn't come to that."

They reached the end of the straightaway.

"The entrance to the airport is just a kilometer around this curve," Renee said.

But instead of following the road to the left, the Range Rover made an abrupt right, smashing through a barrier onto a dirt road.

"Why is he going in there?" Renee wondered as she slowed.

"What's in there?"

"It's an old phosphate mine. Unused now since the airport was built."

Juan remembered seeing it from the air as they'd come in for a landing this morning.

"The mine is at the end of the runway. Follow them."

Renee turned the Jag onto the dirt track, which was now covered with a dust cloud thrown into the air by the Range Rover. She kept on their trail for a few twists and turns until the road became little more than a rocky track for heavy machinery. There was no way the old Jag would be able to navigate through it.

Renee came a stop, and through the dust, they could see a path where the shrubbery had been flattened by the Range Rover. Juan jumped out and ran through it.

He came out the other side to see the private jet idling at the end of the runway a hundred yards ahead. The Range Rover skidded to a halt next to it, and MacD was hauled out and roughly pushed up the stairs by Polk and his henchman. In the distance beside the airport terminal, the tiltrotor's propellers were turning, but it would be several more seconds before they were fully up to speed for liftoff.

The door to the jet closed, and the twin engines whined as they came to full power. Juan sprinted across the grass, too far away to take a decent shot. Before he could get close, the jet rolled down the runway, leaving the Range Rover behind. It lifted off and turned east. Juan watched it vanish into a cloud bank.

This morning when the tiltrotor had arrived, his team had been in a good mood, expecting to find the essential ingredient to the cure for Murph and the others who had been paralyzed. Now not only had they lost their best chance at an antidote, but they'd also lost MacD in the process.

But Juan wasn't the type to give up easily, and he still had reason for hope. All the *Oregon* crew were implanted with GPS trackers in their thighs for just this eventuality. When activated, the tiny chip broadcasted a location signal every minute.

They would be able to tell exactly where Polk was taking MacD.

# FIFTY-FIVE

By the time the Gulfstream jet reached
cruising altitude, MacD's injured arm had
been bandaged by the Chinese man while
Polk kept a pistol aimed at him. When first
aid was complete, his hands were tied
behind his back again, and Polk spoke in
Mandarin to the medic. MacD flexed his
arm and winced, but he'd been through
worse.

"Mighty nice of you to patch up your
hostage," MacD said. "Ah'll take a mimosa
and a Vicodin while you're at it."

Polk put the pistol away and leaned back
in the opposite chair. "He says the bullet
went through the muscle in your shoulder.
You'll need stitches when we arrive at our
destination. In the meantime, I didn't want
you bleeding all over the plane."

MacD looked out the window, but all he
could see was water. Judging by the sun's
position, they were heading east.

"And what is our destination?"

"A secluded location."

"They'll track us there."

Polk shook his head, smiling. "Not with the plane's transponder off, they won't." He sat forward. "Which brings me to my first question. Who are you and who do you work for?"

MacD stared at Polk as he considered how to respond. He knew the *Oregon* was tracking him, so he had to stay alive long enough for a rescue. And now that the secret ingredient to the antidote was destroyed, the only chance to cure Murph was for the Corporation to find Jin and Polk on the chance that they'd created their own supply.

When the pause went on too long, Polk said, "We dressed your wound, but that doesn't mean I'm above torturing you to get what I want to know."

"That wouldn't do you much good," MacD said, a delaying tactic forming in his mind.

"Why is that, tough guy?"

"Ah'm tough, but torture can break anyone. No, it's just that Ah went to Ranger school, and Ah know that someone who is tortured will say just about anything to get it to stop. You can't be sure it's the truth."

"I'm willing to try."

407

"What Ah'm sayin' is, Ah'm happy to tell you what you want to know. MacD Lawless is my name, and Ah work for an organization called the Corporation."

Polk chuckled at that. "Can you be more specific?"

"No. That's our name. It's intentionally vague because we're mercenaries."

"You don't work for the U.S. government?"

"We work for anyone who pays us."

"Then who's paying you to interfere with our operation?"

Here's where MacD had to be careful. A good lie was always close to the truth, and he was about to spin a whopper.

"Interfere with it? We want you to succeed."

"What are you talking about? You've been fighting with us for days. The factory at Nhulunbuy, the battle between the *Marauder* and the *Norego,* Christmas Island."

"It all comes back to Lu Yang."

Polk narrowed his eyes. "What do you mean?"

"Lu was an arms dealer, among other things. You've got the Enervum gas courtesy of Lu. Am Ah right?"

"So?"

"So we were hired by one of his competitors to find the formula so y'all didn't have exclusivity on that little weapon."

"But you said you wanted us to succeed."

"When we found out that there was an antidote, we thought that might be more valuable than the weapon. So we've been trying to develop it ever since. And if you carry out more attacks, it makes the antidote worth even more."

Polk looked dubious. "So you've been searching for the antidote to sell it?"

"Of course. We do this for money."

"How do I know you don't work for the authorities?"

MacD let out an exasperated sigh. "Have you seen any military or police forces in any of our dustups? We want to stay clear of them as much as you do."

Polk hesitated as he thought about MacD's story. "I'm not convinced. Give me something valuable."

"All right," MacD said. "You've seen our ship, right? What do you want to know about the *Norego*?"

"What weapons does it have?"

MacD started with the items he knew April Jin had seen in combat. "Anti-aircraft laser, Kashtan Gatling guns, counter-illuminative paint." Then he added items from the previous version of the *Oregon.* "A

120mm cannon, torpedoes, surface-to-surface missiles. She's not just a spy ship. She's a warship."

"Built by the Americans."

"Not at all. Built for us at a Vladivostok naval base under Admiral Yuri Borodin. Unfortunately, Borodin is currently dead, so you can't fact-check that with him."

Which was all true, but not for the version of the *Oregon* that Jin had fought against. It was the previous ship that had been constructed in Russia.

"What do you know about our operation?" Polk asked.

"We know you have a lot of that gas. We beat that info out of Bob Parsons."

"How did you know about the factory?"

"We've got some good tech people. They traced Alloy Bauxite back to Lu."

"Do you know anything about our future plans?"

MacD shrugged. "Ah don't know your target. Ah'm just a grunt. They don't tell me everything."

"If you don't have the antidote, then why do you want our operation to succeed?"

"Because we do have the formula for the antidote. That makes it worth something on the black market. Ah'm sure my boss would be willing to make a business deal with you.

410

You do whatever you're doing, then we connect you with the right people and get a commission on the sale. He might even be willing to help you get your mission done for the right price."

"How do I get in touch with him?"

"Get me wherever we're going, stitch me up, give me a hot meal, and then Ah'll tell you who to call."

"Give me a name."

"Ah can't do that. You can call him Chairman."

"And if he won't make a deal?" Polk asked.

"Ah wouldn't be telling you all this if Ah didn't think he'd be interested," MacD said, knowing how much was riding on Polk believing this tale. "If Ah'm wrong, you won't have any more use for me."

Polk nodded. "That is the only thing you've said that I know for sure."

411

# FIFTY-SIX

The fire and dead bodies caused quite a stir on Christmas Island, but Renee LaBelle was able to convince the authorities that Juan and his team were friends of hers, and their arrival just before the chaos was purely coincidental. Given that the corpses seemed to be Chinese nationals and that their jet had taken off without permission after leaving a vehicle on the runway, the local police had their hands full taking the investigation of the event in other directions.

Inside the airport, Juan said good-bye to Renee and Bob Parsons. The rest of the team had made it back in the Mercedes and were waiting for him on the tiltrotor.

"Thanks for all your help," Juan said to Parsons. "You sure you don't want a ride somewhere?"

Parsons looked at Renee, then shook his head. "I've got a bit of catching up to do here. Besides, I don't have anywhere else to go at present."

"We'll keep looking for more of the Rand's palm trees," Renee said. "It's rare, but if we find any that are nut-bearing, we know how to get in touch."

"I'm sorry about MacD," Parsons said. "I hope you get him back."

"Me, too," Juan said. "And I'm sorry your island has been damaged."

"Luckily, it's not the dry season, so the fire is already out," Renee said. "The land will recover, as it always does. It'll make quite the story around here for years to come."

Juan said his good-byes and watched Renee and Parsons walk toward the parking lot hand in hand.

Juan headed to the tiltrotor, and as soon as he was on board, Gomez took off.

Raven, Linc, and Eddie didn't look dejected. They were seething.

"It's my fault they got MacD, Chairman," Raven said. "I should have seen that guy sneaking up on us."

"It's no one's fault except Polk's," Juan said. "Let's focus on getting MacD back. Polk took him either because he wants info about who we are or he's going to use MacD as a bargaining chip. That means he'll keep MacD alive at least a little while."

413

"Then we'll have to act fast."

"Any idea where they're taking him?" Eddie asked.

"We'll know soon enough. When we do, we'll need to come up with a way to rescue him."

"What about the antidote?" Linc asked. "All the nuts were burned up in the fire. If that deadline is correct about how quickly the antidote is needed, Murph and the others are running out of time."

"I think there's still hope. Jin and Polk had that antidote formula for a reason. Maybe they made some of it for themselves. I suggest you all eat and get some sleep on the flight back to the *Oregon.* We might be pretty busy between now and New Year's Eve."

Juan took a couple of sandwiches from a cooler and went to the cockpit. He handed one to Gomez, who had already set the tilt-rotor to autopilot.

"Thanks, Chairman," Gomez said. "Wish I could have gotten airborne and in that Gulfstream's way before it took off."

"It might not have worked anyway. The way Polk has been tearing through every place he goes, there's no telling what he might have done."

Juan put on a headset and called Max to

414

fill him in on what happened at Christmas Island.

When he was done, Max said, "It's going to be tough to break it to Murph that we have no antidote."

"We still might have a chance if we can find Jin and Polk. Since they knew exactly where the trees were, it's possible they made some antidote for themselves."

"Then we need to capture one or both of them alive."

"That's the plan," Juan said. "And now we might have a way to find them. Do you have MacD's tracker?"

"Yes. He's eastbound over the Timor Sea. He might even pass right over us."

"We'll never catch them. That Gulfstream is twice as fast as the tiltrotor. Where are you now?"

"We got a tip that a trimaran passed through the Torres Strait at the northern tip of Queensland, so we kept going in that direction. We're almost there now, but of course the *Marauder* is probably long gone. They could be partway across the Pacific, heading down the east coast of Australia, or heading north toward the Philippines."

"All of their operations have been centered around Australia, so I'd guess they'll stay in this vicinity."

"We only have three days until New Year's Eve," Max said. "What do you think their target is?"

"That's the million-dollar question. It's also another reason we need Jin and Polk alive. If we can capture one of them, we can make them tell us where that Enervum gas is headed and how they intend to use it."

"It would help if we knew the new name of the *Shepparton.*"

"I've asked Lang to keep his eyes and ears open for any leads on that front."

Langston Overholt would be able to inform them if any key words providing clues about the cargo ship popped up on any communications networks.

"So we've got nothing except MacD's tracker to go on," Max said, his frustration evident.

"We do have that satellite number that Linda used to call Jin," Juan said. "Did you have Eric, Murph, and Sylvia see if they could trace it?"

"They tried but hit a dead end. The signal is routed through a dozen satellites, completely masking where the end user is."

"Don't worry," Juan said. "If I know MacD, he's talking Polk's ears off right now with some wild story. Sooner or later, they'll be calling us."

# FIFTY-SEVEN

*Marwood Island, Queensland*

As she brought the *Marauder* into its home port, Jin was glad to finally be back at the base Lu had chosen for the trimaran. Not only would she be able to finish repairs to the plasma cannon they had begun at sea, but she would also be able to see her husband, who had arrived with their prisoner the day before.

Located near the Whitsunday archipelago off the central coast of Queensland, Marwood was home to an abandoned World War II naval base that Lu refurbished when he bought the property. The island was shaped like Mickey Mouse's head, with a circular harbor where the mouth would be and a narrow opening to the ocean at the chin.

The setting was ideal because of the fair weather year-round and the calm seas protected by the Great Barrier Reef. Although most of the island was mountainous, there was enough space for the restored runway that ran through some high hills on Mickey's left cheek. One end stopped at the sea, the other near the dock. A cluster of concrete buildings at Mickey's nose served as the base quarters and facilities. The ears were peaks covered with eucalyptus trees and hoop pines.

The Gulfstream was chocked at the end of the runway, and men on ATVs towed equipment to the dock to complete the repairs on the trimaran.

After she had tied up the *Marauder,* she asked where she could find Polk. She was directed to the main office building.

He was inside at a desk, looking at a laptop with his back to her. She leaned against the doorway.

"So busy you couldn't come to greet your own wife on her triumphant return?"

He turned and smiled at the sight of her, bounding over to give her a kiss.

"I was just checking the weather in Sydney for tomorrow night. Hot and dry. Perfect for the operation."

"Is Rathman in place?"

"The *Centaurus* is on schedule to arrive this evening."

"I hope you take some Enervum gas grenades with you this time, just in case."

418

They'd tested the grenades on the scientists back at the Nhulunbuy factory and found them effective.

"Those definitely would have come in handy at Christmas Island," Polk said. "I'll put some on the plane. What do you think Lu's plan is to get the Australians to ship in a million Chinese so quickly?"

"He's probably got more triggers set up to react to the news stories of the attack. But that's someone else's problem."

"I wonder how the attacks have impacted Lu's financial worth."

"Let's take a look."

They'd both memorized the password, but the account number was so long that Polk had to copy it from the notepad app on his phone. He typed the info into the crypto-currency's online platform.

"The balance is up to nine hundred and eighty million," Polk said.

"It might even go up in value after the attack," Jin said. "People take their money out of the stock market after terrorist incidents and they've got to put it somewhere."

"And if not, we've got the antidote in the Gulfstream as a backup."

"This MacD. Did you find out anything about him?" Jin asked.

"I was able to verify that he really was a U.S. Army Ranger."

"I want to talk to him before we give his Chairman a call."

"He's down in the bomb shelter. I'll have him brought up." Polk called for two of their men to retrieve him.

"When do you leave for Sydney?" Jin asked.

"In a few hours," Polk said. "I wish we were going together."

"Me, too, but I've got to get these repairs done if I'm going to set sail by tonight. I want to be in Sydney Harbour in time to see the fireworks."

The plan was for Polk to go down and complete the preparations on the *Centaurus*. After the gas was launched, he would transfer over to the *Marauder*.

"What about the antidote?" Jin asked.

"I'm not sure whether to believe this guy's story. It might be better if we split up the doses. I'll take half with me to the *Centaurus,* and we'll put the other half on the *Marauder.*"

"A sound move."

Jin turned as a strikingly handsome man with a bloodied bandage on his left shoulder was escorted into the room. She nodded and the two guards sat him forcefully in a chair.

"You must be MacD," she said.

"The one and only."

"Your boss has been trying to call me."

"Ah told your husband that he'd make a deal with you."

"To leave us alone?"

MacD shook his head. "We're not mobsters running a protection racket. The Chairman's got connections all over the world. He can make a market for you."

"A market for what?"

MacD shrugged. "Plasma weapons, Enervum gas, the antidote you've got. Whatever you want to sell."

"We'll see about that."

She took out her satellite phone.

"They blocked their number when I talked to Acting Captain Linda two days ago. How do I call your Chairman?"

MacD told her the number.

"I am going to put this on speaker," Jin said, eyeing MacD. "If you say one word without my okay, I will kill you. Do you understand?"

"Couldn't be clearer," MacD said.

She dialed the number that he gave her.

"Is this April Jin?" a voice answered.

"Yes, it is. Is this the Chairman?"

"Speaking."

"Your man here, MacD, says you might be interested in a business proposition."

"I might be."

"Before we get started, I don't do business with anyone if I don't know their name."

"Juan Cabrillo, captain of the *Norego.*"

"Tell me, Juan, why have you been after us?"

"What makes you think we're after you?"

"Then why do we keep running into each other?"

"You have something we want."

"The Enervum?" Jin said.

"As well as the antidote. Obviously, we failed to get either."

"MacD claims you can make a market for our products."

"They would fetch a high price on the black market," Cabrillo said. "Of course, they'd be tricky to unload without drawing unwanted attention."

"That's an intriguing thought. Listen, we've got a busy couple of days ahead of us. Why don't we circle back in the new year and talk a deal."

"And my man?"

"We'll keep him with us. I don't know how fond you are of him, but it can't hurt to have a hostage to make sure we're getting our money's worth. If you get in our way again, we'll kill him. Bye-bye."

She hung up.

"Told you," MacD said with a smile.

"Don't get too happy yet," Polk said. "Captain Cabrillo needs to come through for you to ever get off this island." He waved for the guards to take MacD back to his cell.

"He'll come through, all right," MacD said over his shoulder as he left. "Ah guarantee it."

# FIFTY-EIGHT

Eight hours after Juan got off the phone with Jin, the *Oregon* approached Marwood Island from the north, MacD's tracker leading them there. Juan was concerned that the signal would start moving quickly again, indicating he was back on a plane. But it hadn't left the island. In fact, they were no longer getting a signal at all, which meant he was probably underground or in a shielded room in the group of buildings they'd observed on the satellite image of the old World War II base.

They couldn't recon the layout of the buildings, and no blueprints existed from that time period, so they needed real time info. From his chair in the op center, Juan watched the main video screen showing the feed from a drone that Gomez was flying low over the trees to avoid detection. It had an oblique view of the harbor.

"There's the *Marauder* at the dock," Sylvia said from the weapons station. During the past few days, Murph had been training her on the *Oregon*'s weapons systems to take his place while they were short-handed, and to no one's surprise, she had already mastered the basics of operating the rail gun and laser.

"No Gulfstream, though," Murph said from his chair next to Sylvia.

Eric, who was at the helm, said, "Does that mean Polk is gone? He's the one who's been flying around on it."

"We only need one of them," Juan said. "Gomez, switch to the infrared camera and see if the *Marauder* is hot."

The screen changed to black and white. Heat bloomed on two sections of the trimaran.

"The midship hot spot has to be the charged plasma cannon," Sylvia said.

"And the stern section is the engine," Eric said. "Looks like they're not staying long."

"Then we still have an opportunity to capture April Jin," Juan said. "We have to assume she's commanding the *Marauder*."

As soon as they'd known that Marwood Island was their destination, they'd developed a two-pronged plan. The first part was a rescue of MacD. Max had already taken the *Gator* to the west side of the island to a

425

tiny beach between the Mickey Mouse ears. From there Eddie would lead a team of Raven, Linda, and Linc to come at the base from the direction of the setting sun. They would sneak into the building where MacD was being held, free him, and exfiltrate back the way they'd come before anyone knew they were there.

In the second phase of the operation, Juan would lure Jin and the *Marauder* out of the tight confines of the harbor, where the *Oregon* would have little room to maneuver. Once the trimaran had left the safety of the port, Sylvia would use the rail gun to disable the *Marauder,* and they would force Jin to surrender for questioning with the use of their tranquilizer. She would tell them everything they wanted to know about the upcoming operation with the Enervum gas.

They were holding steady at the east end of Marwood's runway so that low hills blocked the view of the *Oregon* from the buildings and harbor.

"Stoney," Juan said, "prepare to swing around to the harbor entrance."

"Affirmative," Eric replied.

Juan hoped repositioning the *Oregon* would allow a few free shots with the rail gun before Jin could bring the plasma cannon to bear.

Juan turned to Hali. "Tell Max to commence his operation."

Eddie, dressed in forest green camos like Linda, Raven, and Linc, was having his team do one final check of their gear when Max turned to them from the cockpit.

"Juan says they're in position. You ready?"

They confirmed their comms were working, and Eddie said, "Take us in."

This mission was all about stealth. The tree cover ended a few hundred yards from the base buildings, a lot of open ground to cover in daylight. Eddie, Linda, and Linc were carrying suppressed M4 assault rifles, but gunfire would alert the entire facility to their presence. After using up most of their limited supply of tranquilizer serum during the raids on the *Dahar* and *Shepparton,* they were down to only a few darts left. Instead of a dart pistol, Linc was armed with a tranquilizer rifle. He would tranquilize any guards between them and the buildings. Raven had brought MacD's crossbow instead of a gun.

Once they subdued the guards, it would be a simple matter of questioning one of them to find out where MacD was being held. Speed was of the essence. A missing guard would rouse suspicions just as much as gunshots would.

Max brought the *Gator* close to shore, making sure there was no one around to observe them before he surfaced. He got as close as he could to the beach. They climbed out and waded to shore. The *Gator* moved back to deeper water and resubmerged, where Max would wait until they returned.

The sun was starting to set behind them. If their timing was right, they would be hard to spot coming out of the trees.

"Let's move," Eddie said.

Based on the recon from the drone, they hadn't seen any security precautions on this side of the island. Nevertheless, they made their way carefully through the forest as they climbed, wary of any motion sensors or cameras.

When they reached the top ridge, they had an expansive view of the harbor below. Eddie used a pair of binoculars to watch the movements of the guards. None of them seemed to be on an active patrol pattern. Instead, they were busy moving equipment from the buildings to the ship, with the clanging of metal and shouts of instructions in Mandarin drifting up the hillside.

"Looks like they're getting ready to leave," Eddie said. "We need to hoof it."

They double-timed it down the ridge until

they were at the tree line closest to the cluster of buildings, nine of them in all.

Beside the one farthest from the dock, a lone man was leaning against the wall taking a smoke break. If they could get to the edge and take him down, they had a clear path to the buildings.

They moved along the trees to a point where Linc had a clear shot from a hundred yards away. He put the scope to his eye and held his breath as he aimed.

He pulled the trigger, and the rifle puffed as the air cartridge ignited. The guard grabbed his chest where the dart hit him. He dropped his cigarette and slumped to the ground.

Eddie said, "Come on."

The four of them sprinted across the open ground in a two-by-two formation. They had nearly reached the tranquilized guard when a second one rounded the corner of the building. He was carrying a rifle in his hands. Detecting a noise, he had come to investigate.

When he saw the four of them running toward him, he raised the gun to fire. Raven stopped and snapped a shot with the crossbow. The bolt went through the man's cheek before he could get his finger on the trigger.

Linc dragged the body over to the still living guard, and Eddie knelt beside the man.

"Where is your prisoner?" Eddie asked him in Mandarin.

"The American is in the main building," the man slurred, his eyes barely open.

"Where in the building?"

"The bomb shelter in the cellar."

Eddie translated for the others.

"That explains why we couldn't read his signal," Linda said.

"How many guards are here besides you?" Eddie asked.

"Twenty-two," the man said. "Some are already on the *Marauder*."

"Why?"

"I don't know where we're going, but in fifteen minutes, we're leaving the island."

# FIFTY-NINE

The repairs to the *Marauder* took less time than Jin had expected, and she was preparing to set sail, never to return to Marwood. After completing their task in Sydney, they would go to Hainan Island in the South China Sea. The *Marauder* and her plasma weapon would be turned over to the Chinese government in return for protection from any possible extradition. Jin and Polk already had their eye on a twenty-million-dollar seaside mansion on the outskirts of Haikou.

Her husband had flown out after lunch. He texted her that he'd landed in Sydney and was on his way to the *Centaurus,* which was anchored near Shark Island in the harbor.

By traveling at top speed, she expected to join him by nine the next evening, in plenty of time to watch the world-famous fireworks show launched from the Sydney Harbour

Bridge. At the same time, two hundred and ninety-six rockets loaded with Enervum gas would be fired from the *Centaurus.* Most people would be focused on the bridge, but anyone seeing the launch from the cargo ship would simply think it was part of the show.

Once the operation was complete, she would use the *Marauder* to sink the *Centaurus* and put to sea. By the time any authorities came from other parts of the country, she and Polk would be long gone. She would upload her video recording of the launch to the internet, leaving no doubt as to what had happened. News organizations around the world would carry the story, unlocking the cryptocurrency account.

Jin could practically taste how close she was to her new life. She didn't want to wait any longer than she had to for the end of this mission.

"What's the status of the plasma cannon?" she asked her XO.

"All tests are complete," he said. "The weapon is fully operational."

"What about our fuel and supplies?"

"Topping off the fuel now. The last of the supplies are being loaded."

"Then make ready to cast off as soon as we have everyone aboard," Jin said. "Have two men go get the American."

MacD's cell was bare, but at least its underground location was keeping him cool in the tropical heat. There was a single bulb in the ceiling lighting the concrete ceiling, walls, and floor.

A heavy blast door was locked from the outside. He'd tried opening it numerous times, but nothing short of a blowtorch would get it open from his side.

The stitches under the bandage itched. They were made with thick black thread by someone who seemed to know what he was doing. It wasn't a bad job, but it would leave a nice jagged scar to match his others.

Propped against the wall, he tried not to move his arm, which was now aching. A sling would have been nice to keep it immobile, but he would have settled for an aspirin.

Besides some water and a bowl of noodles, he hadn't eaten anything since he left Christmas Island, and his stomach was grumbling. Still, it wasn't his worst time in captivity. Afghanistan beat this experience by a long shot.

In the stairwell outside, he heard the echo of two Chinese men speaking as they descended the stairs. Keys jangled. They were coming to get him for something. Whether it was for more negotiations, a trip, or an execution, he had no idea.

MacD stood, grimacing from the jostling of his shoulder. The key was inserted into the door.

Then he heard two thumps. It sounded like the men had fallen over.

Moments later, the key turned. The door opened to the vision of Raven standing over two dead guards, one with a crossbow bolt in his neck, the other with a knife in his back. MacD's crossbow was cradled in her arms.

"Aw, you brought me a present," he said with a grin. "You shouldn't have."

"I didn't," Raven said, retrieving the knife and cleaning it off. "Now I know why you like it so much. I might decide to keep it."

"Over my dead body. Gimme."

She nodded at his shoulder. "What are you going to do, hold it one-handed?" She picked up one of the dead guards' pistols and handed it to him.

MacD took it and sighed. "Ah guess this is better than nothing." Eddie and Linda entered behind her, and Raven gave back Eddie's throwing knife. "Nice to see y'all here. Wherever here is."

"Marwood Island," Linda said, "near the

Great Barrier Reef."

"Are you all right?" Eddie asked, eyeing his wound.

"Ah could use some water," MacD said.

Linda gave him her canteen. He drank half its contents in two gulps while Eddie and Raven pulled the drugged guards into the room.

"How's the arm?" Linda asked.

"Ah'm not going to be swinging a golf club anytime soon, but it's not too bad considering Ah got shot. Did everyone else make it off Christmas Island?"

Raven nodded and locked the door behind them. "No casualties besides you. I think you just wanted to play the damsel in distress."

"Not likely. Next time Ah'll be sure to duck."

"Let's get out of here," Eddie said, leading them up the stairs. "Are you up to taking a hike with us?"

"Absolutely. Ah could use the fresh air."

At the top of the stairs, Linc was keeping watch. He glanced at MacD and said, "Nice to see they decided not to mess up that pretty face."

MacD smiled at him. "Not this silver-tongued devil."

"We'll go out the back door," Eddie said.

They went low to avoid being seen from the harbor through the windows. At the rear of the building, Eddie eased the door open and looked out.

As he did so, someone cried out in Mandarin from a few buildings away.

Eddie shook his head and looked at the rest of them. "I don't think you need a translation to know someone found the dead —"

Before he could finish, bullets ripped into the door above his head. They all dived to the floor as a klaxon began to wail.

# SIXTY

"Where's that gunfire coming from?" Jin demanded.

"From the main building," said the *Marauder* XO, who was on the phone. "One man reported dead, another incapacitated."

"They're here."

"Who?"

"Juan Cabrillo's people. Send everyone available to track them down and kill them."

If they had gotten this far into her base, then his ship must be close by.

"Relay that order," she said. "Throw off the moorings. Now."

While the XO went out onto the bridge wing to give the command to cast off, she took the phone and called the leader of her guard unit. She had to know if the harbor exit was clear before walking into an ambush.

"Get someone on an ATV and send them to the end of the runway. Make sure he has a phone so he can make a video call. I want to see what he's seeing."

"Yes, Captain."

A man on the dock jumped onto an ATV and raced down the runway at top speed.

The XO ran back inside. "Mooring lines are cast off."

"Take us away from the dock."

The *Marauder*'s engines increased power and pushed them into the harbor.

"Shall I take us out of the harbor?" the XO asked.

"No. Go out two hundred meters and turn the ship around."

"Captain?"

"Do it."

He gave the order to the helmsman, and the trimaran moved out into the harbor and rotated.

"Bring the plasma cannon online."

"What is the target?"

Jin raised binoculars and watched dust rising from the impact of bullets around the central office building. It was the one where MacD was being held prisoner. She couldn't tell if her men or theirs were winning.

"Our target is the whole base," Jin said. "Starting with the main building. We can't afford anyone surviving."

"But our men . . ." the XO protested.

"Will be making a great sacrifice for the glory of China."

Eddie and Linc took up a defensive position at the front door while Linda, Raven, and MacD took the rear door. They were taking fire from all directions. Sprinting for the hills now would just get them all killed.

"Hali," Eddie said into his molar mic, "we're taking heavy fire."

"Can you make it to the *Gator*?"

"No, we're pinned down at the base."

Two of the guards ran toward the office building from the direction of the dock, and Linc took one down, but the other ducked safely behind the corner of an adjacent building.

"What are they doing?" Linc wondered aloud as he looked out into the harbor.

Eddie didn't understand the question until he turned and saw the *Marauder* pivoting so that its bow was facing the base complex.

The barrel of the plasma cannon was swinging around to aim right at them.

"She wouldn't," Linc said. "Not with her own men so close."

"She would," Eddie said. "Time to go."

"I think you're right."

They dashed toward the back of the building. They made it halfway when a momentous crack pulsed through the room. Linc dived and pulled Eddie down with him. The opposite side of the building was smashed, raining pieces of sizzling concrete around them. Searing heat seemed to boil the water vapor in the air, causing steam to instantly appear along with the dust.

Eddie and Linc scrambled to their feet and kept going.

"What was that?" Raven shouted.

"Jin's firing the plasma cannon at us," Eddie yelled back. "We have to get out of here now."

A second blast pulverized the front of the building where he and Linc had just been standing, reducing it to particles.

"Where should we go?" Linda asked.

"Anywhere's better than here," MacD said.

Eddie pointed at a barracks fifty feet away. For a moment, the gunfire had stopped, giving them a brief opening to make a run for it.

Eddie nodded, and they burst out the door, Linc firing in one direction with his assault rifle, and Eddie giving covering fire in the other. Raven used the crossbow to take out one man who poked his head around a corner, while Linda and MacD took point.

Before they could get a quarter of the way, a third shot from the plasma cannon utterly wiped out the remainder of the office building. The impact threw them all to the ground.

The plasma cannon began to tear apart the barracks, systematically blowing it to pieces. The wooden roof was a blazing inferno.

"Back to the main building," Eddie yelled. Maybe if they took refuge amongst the rubble, they'd be spared while she destroyed the rest of the complex.

They sprinted back to the ruined building, which looked like it had been shelled by artillery. At least the jagged concrete debris provided protection from the guards who continued to fire at them.

"Hali, a little help, please," Eddie said. "The *Marauder* is about to annihilate us."

# SIXTY-ONE

Even before Eddie's call, Juan had ordered Eric to bring the *Oregon* into Marwood Island's harbor. Gomez's drone gave them a bird's-eye view of the *Marauder* pounding away at the base facility. But with the hills between them and the trimaran, they had no way to use the rail gun against her.

"How long until we're in position to fire?" Juan asked.

"The harbor entrance is one minute out," Eric replied. "There isn't much clearance between those headlands for us to get through. I need to swing out before we enter to get a straight course."

"Prepare to raise the rail gun, but stand by for my order."

Juan turned to Sylvia. "Are you ready to fire?"

She looked nervous, but she nodded. She'd taken only a couple of practice shots out at sea to conserve the limited ammunition they had on board. According to Max, he thought he'd fixed the overheating problem they'd encountered in Bali. They were about to find out if he was right.

"Remember," Murph said to his sister, "no need to lead."

"I know," Sylvia said.

Normally, artillery cannons had to lead the target if it was moving. They had to be aimed at where the target was going to be. But the hypersonic rail gun shells were so fast that, at these distances, the rounds would reach the target nearly instantaneously.

"We need Jin alive," Juan reminded her. "Try to avoid completely destroying the ship if you can."

"I'll target the plasma cannon turret," Sylvia said. "But the *Marauder* is between us and the buildings where your team is. If I miss, the shell could hit them."

"Then hold your fire until you're all the way in the harbor," Juan said.

"I've got the *Marauder*'s current position as a reference."

"Take her in quick."

Jin had already decimated half the buildings on the base when the man she'd sent out on the ATV called in on a video chat.

443

"I'm at the end of the runway," he said. "There's a ship out there."

"Show me," she said.

He flipped the phone around. It showed the open ocean and the blue sky. The camera swung around until an object came into view.

It was a ship all right, a break bulk freighter with four cranes, but it moved at the speed of a light craft.

The camera shifted more, and land came into view. Jin recognized it as the headland of the harbor.

She ran out to the bridge wing and looked toward the harbor entrance. At first she saw nothing. She squinted, flipping between the image on her phone screen and what was out her window. Suddenly, she saw the ship round the headlands and turn toward the harbor entrance.

She ran back into the bridge and shouted at the XO, "We have an enemy at twelve o'clock. Turn us around and prepare to fire."

"What about me?" the man on the ATV asked.

"Get back to the base and help the others finish off those intruders." She hung up.

"She's not fully clear of the landscape," the XO said. "I can't get a firm lock just yet."

"Then we'll have to aim manually," Jin said. "I'll do it myself."

"They're coming about," Juan said.

The nimble trimaran was turning quickly, as was the plasma cannon. It would now be a race to see who could fire first. The *Oregon* wasn't in the right position yet to eliminate the threat of an errant shot hitting the building that Eddie and his team were in, but they couldn't wait any longer.

It was as if they were two World War I dreadnoughts about to stand off at point-blank range.

Juan gave the order. "Sylvia, activate the rail gun."

"Activating," she said.

The rail gun rose into place on the forward deck, its menacing black barrel rotating as soon as it was clear of the hull.

"Fire at will," Juan said.

"Weapon is charged," Murph said.

Juan could see the aiming reticle on the main screen. It was locked on the plasma cannon turret, which was now facing them dead-on.

It launched a salvo a moment before Sylvia fired the rail gun.

The plasma round hit the *Oregon*'s armored hull, its energy rocking the ship just enough that the rail gun shell missed the turret. Instead, it blew through the crew section of the ship, shattering every window on the trimaran, including the bridge.

"Keep firing," Juan said.

Sylvia's second shot grazed the turret and tore up the hillside behind the base, knocking down a dozen trees in the process.

The *Marauder* fired again. This time the ball of plasma went right between two of the cranes, melting the paint as it went by.

"Now I've got it," Sylvia said as she loosed a third round.

The tungsten projectile slammed into the turret, ripping a gaping hole in the metal. The plasma cannon's barrel was torn free and catapulted into the water.

Sylvia slumped in her chair, thinking that the battle was over. Eric reached over with his hand in the air, and she returned a weak high five. Murph's voice box played the sound of a cheering crowd.

"Good job," Juan said to Sylvia. "But stay alert. The *Marauder* may try to ram us. That's the only play they have left."

"Don't worry," Sylvia said. "I think I've got this thing figured out now. It won't get any closer to us."

Juan used his armrest control to focus the external camera on the bridge of the *Ma-*

*rauder.* He wanted to see who he was up against.

As the camera zoomed in, no one was visible. Then someone rose into view with a staggering motion.

The person slowly turned toward the *Oregon.* It was April Jin. The left side of her face was covered in blood.

"That's her," Sylvia said through clenched teeth. "That's the woman who sank my ship and paralyzed Mark."

Juan turned to Hali. "Radio their ship. Tell Jin to surrender or we'll destroy them."

# SIXTY-TWO

The last few stragglers on the base kept fighting, even one who showed up on an ATV. Eddie guessed there were three or four of them left, all of them concentrating their fire from behind the razed barracks.

"Your ship has been defeated," he yelled in Mandarin. "Put down your weapons."

No response except for the automatic fire that continued unabated. Eddie's team was pinned down.

"Sounds like they're not interested in quitting," Linc said. "And I'm out of grenades."

"Anyone else have any?" Eddie asked.

They all shook their heads.

MacD pointed at the wide expanse between them and the next closest building. "There's an awful lot of ground to cross to circle around them."

"I wouldn't advise charging them," Raven said. "At least a couple of us are liable to get hit."

"We've already got the solution," Linda said, nodding at the *Oregon.* "Let's call in a strike."

"Good idea," Eddie said. "Hali, we need some artillery support."

"What's the target?" Hali asked.

"Third pile of rubble from the north."

"There's a lot of rubble over there. Sylvia doesn't want to hit you. Can you mark your position?"

Eddie took a smoke flare from his pack and popped it. Orange mist belched from the canister.

"Do not," he said, "repeat, do not shoot at the orange smoke. The hostiles are behind the debris of the building next to us on your right."

"Understood. Take cover."

"Get down," Eddie said. "Open your mouths so your eardrums don't rupture."

They hit the floor and put their hands over their heads.

A massive shock wave shredded the air as a round traveling at Mach 7 went by. A deafening explosion seemed to occur simultaneously. Concrete particles fell on them like snow, and a cloud of dust mixed with the orange smoke.

There was no more gunfire.

Eddie sat up, his ears ringing but his hearing intact. As the dust cleared, he could see that the ruins hiding Jin's men had been scoured away as if by a broom.

"That's all of them," Linc said, getting to his feet.

"That rail gun is a nasty weapon," Raven said.

"Max, are you there?" Eddie said into his comm unit.

"Loud and clear. Still on station where I dropped you off. Sounds like I missed the party. Is everyone okay over there?"

"We all made it through, but I don't think any of us feels like taking a walk right now. Why don't you come and get us."

"On my way."

Eddie took a seat on a broken piece of concrete. "We might as well get comfortable and enjoy our front row tickets."

"Too bad we don't have any popcorn," MacD said as the rest of them joined him. "I can't wait to see what Captain Jin is going to do."

Jin wiped her sleeve against her head, but all it did was smear the blood around. Everyone on the bridge had been sliced with glass when the windows shattered.

A voice was calling from the radio.

"I repeat, this is the *Norego.* You are ordered to surrender your vessel. Shut down your engines, come on to the deck with your hands in the air, and prepare to be boarded."

She picked up the microphone and said, "Acknowledged, *Norego.* Shutting down engines."

Jin initiated the shutdown procedure, then helped the XO to his feet. "Gather the men and take them out to the deck. I'll join you in a minute. I have to make a phone call first."

The executive officer made a shipwide announcement to muster topside and then escorted the bridge crew outside.

When she was alone, Jin took a deep breath and typed in some last commands into the control pad. After she was done, she took out her phone and called her husband.

The phone rang four times and then went to voicemail.

"Honey, it's me. We've had some trouble here, and I think I'll be late to Sydney. I wish I could be there to see the launch. You'll do great, and I want you to know that I love you. Whatever happens, I know this will lead to a better life. Good-bye, my dear."

She hung up. It rang almost immediately, and she answered without looking at the number.

"Darling," Jin said.

"I don't think we're to that stage of our relationship yet," Juan Cabrillo said.

"What do you want?"

"I want you to come out on the deck like we asked."

"You were never planning to make a deal, were you?"

"Sure I was. It's just that the terms may not be to your liking."

"You're either here to commandeer my ship and kill us," Jin said, "or you're going to take us all to prison. I told myself a long time ago that I was never going to set foot in prison again. I intend to keep that promise, Mr. Cabrillo."

She watched the needle on the temperature gauge for the plasma cannon's power generator rising toward the redline. As soon as it reached the critical limit, the weapon would self-destruct, blowing the *Marauder* apart.

# SIXTY-THREE

Even though it wasn't dusk yet, the harbor was in the shadow of the island behind the *Marauder,* giving the scene an eerie cast.

"What makes you think I want to send you to prison?" Juan said, getting out of his command chair. He took Hali's headset and switched to its audio mic, but the entire op center could still hear Jin.

Her crew was lined up on the deck outside, but she was sitting in her own high captain's chair on the bridge, talking with the phone in her palm and watching the *Oregon.* The image was enlarged enough that he could see her hair blowing with the breeze through the broken windows. It seemed as if she were looking directly at him.

"I'm glad to have someone to talk to at the end like this," Jin said. "I wish I knew what you looked like. You have a nice voice."

"That sounds like a woman who doesn't

intend to be taken alive," Eric said.

Sylvia gasped. "Can you put that infrared video feed back up?"

Juan nodded, and Eric switched the camera to the black and white image of the *Marauder*. The highlight at the stern was now fading as the engines cooled, but the center of the ship was almost white with heat.

"I thought we destroyed the plasma cannon," Hali said.

"Just the gun," Murph said.

"The power generator underneath is what builds up the energy to launch the projectile," Sylvia said. "She's deliberately overheating it. When it reaches the redline, it'll detonate."

"April," Juan said, "it looks like you're building to a generator overload. You need to power down now."

"I have to admit, you people are good," Jin said. "Sorry. I've put the cycle on automatic. Nothing can stop that now."

Juan looked at Sylvia, who nodded in agreement. He mouthed "How long?"

"Two or three minutes, max."

That didn't leave them enough time to get aboard and evacuate Jin before the trimaran exploded.

Juan put his hand over the mic and said,

"Stoney, move us away from the *Marauder.*" He removed his hand. "April, there's still time for you and your men to get off the ship."

"No one is getting off this ship. It would jeopardize my husband's mission."

They wouldn't be able to question anyone. Jin would go down with her ship, and they would be left no closer to finding out what the target of Polk's mission was.

Juan could keep her talking, but he'd never get the truth out of her, not without their tranquilizer darts like the ones Linc had . . .

That thought gave him an idea. Linc was the best marksman in the crew.

"Get me Linc on another line," he told Hali.

Juan had just come up with one of his infamous Plan Cs. This one was a literal longshot.

When Juan called, Linc was sitting with his back against a concrete slab, drinking from his water bottle and arguing with MacD about how long the surrender would take.

"Linc here, Chairman."

"Is your tranquilizer sniper rifle intact?"

"Yes."

"I need you to use it immediately."

455

Linc frowned. "On who?"

"On Jin. She's on the bridge of the *Marauder*. Can you make the shot?"

Linc didn't ask the Chairman why. He snatched up the rifle, loaded a dart, and knelt behind the broken slab he'd been leaning against.

He put the scope to his eye. At this range, the back of Jin's head was a pinpoint.

"She's three hundred yards away," Linc said. "That's beyond the spec range of this rifle, but I can try."

"You'll only get one attempt," Juan said. "If she sees a stray dart fly by her, she'll duck down, and you won't get another shot."

"Doesn't matter. I only have one dart left anyway."

"Then make it count. We don't have much time."

"Understood."

Linc threw some dust in the air. The wind was blowing slightly right to left. He made an adjustment on the scope and lined up the shot.

He held his breath and hoped that Jin didn't move. He squeezed the trigger.

The rifle bucked, and he saw Jin go down, but he couldn't tell if it was because she was hit or missed.

"I took the shot," Linc said.

"I saw," the Chairman said. "I'll let you know in a couple of minutes whether it got her to talk."

For a moment, the line to the *Marauder* was silent.

"April, are you with me?" Juan asked.

"I'm here," she answered.

At least she was still on the line. Either the dart hit her or it didn't.

"What's Angus Polk's target on New Year's Eve?"

"Sydney," Jin said, slurring the S. Linc's aim had been right on the money.

"Who in Sydney?"

"The city."

"I know that's a city," Juan said, exasperated.

"I think she means the whole city," Sylvia said, blanching at the idea.

"Do you actually mean you're going to use the Enervum gas against the entire city of Sydney?" Juan asked.

"Yes."

"Why?"

"The global expansion of China. And money from my stepfather Lu Yang, nine hundred and eighty million dollars in a locked cryptocurrency account. Passcode

Enervum143. Don't have the account number memorized. Where's Angus?"

"He's gone."

"Gone to Sydney," Jin said as if just realizing it.

"Yes. How will the attack happen?"

"What attack?"

"The attack on Sydney. Focus, April."

"Timer set to launch rockets at midnight. They explode all over Sydney. Millions paralyzed overnight. Ten major newspapers cover the story the next day. That unlocks the account and we get the money."

"Antidote," Murph said.

Juan nodded as he saw the white spot on the center of the *Marauder* growing brighter by the second.

"April, do you have any of the Enervum antidote?"

"Not in me."

"I mean, did you make any of the antidote?"

"Yes. Enough for nine thousand people total. Half on the *Marauder,* half with Angus. Angus is in Sydney."

"Where does Angus have his batch of the antidote?"

"On the cargo ship in Sydney."

"Where are the rockets?"

"On the cargo ship in Sydney."

"Anytime now," Sylvia said as she watched the overheating trimaran.

"What's the name of the cargo ship?" Juan asked Jin.

"The —"

Her voice was cut off as the plasma cannon power generator went critical. A massive fireball tore the trimaran in half, causing the screen to go white with the heat bloom. A second later, the shock wave rattled the *Oregon*.

Eric switched the view back to the color camera. The burning bow and stern were the only surviving parts of the *Marauder*. They went under mere seconds later.

Juan checked his watch. They had just over twenty-four hours before the midnight fireworks show the next day.

He threw the headset back to Hali. "Tell Max to pick up the shore party and get back here on the double. Eric, as soon as the doors of the moon pool are closed, set course for Sydney, maximum speed."

# SIXTY-FOUR

*Sydney*

Polk's plane landed at Kingsford Smith International Airport at sunset, and when it was taxiing on the tarmac, he noticed a voicemail from his wife, which was unusual because she preferred to text him. He listened to the message, perplexed and concerned by the odd tone in her voice and by some of the things she said. He was upset she wouldn't make it for the New Year's Eve rocket launch, but he'd be sure to record it for her.

When the plane reached his waiting car, they unloaded four large aluminum boxes containing the Enervum antidote. Each held a thousand vials of the serum in packs of twelve. Given the sales estimates, every pack represented a value of six hundred thousand dollars, which meant he had to keep the cache in a safe place aboard the *Centaurus* where sticky hands couldn't get to it.

He was driven to a dock at Walsh Bay, where a speedboat was waiting for him. His crew transferred the cargo and cast off, almost immediately passing under the world-famous Sydney Harbour Bridge. Polk could make out tourists wearing blue and gray jumpsuits walking along the girders below the bridge, on their way to climbing up the arched truss that spanned the structure. Tomorrow on New Year's Eve, the Bridge Climb would be closed down in anticipation of the colossal fireworks show that would be launched from the arch at the stroke of midnight.

Even at night, boats filled the harbor. Ferries, yachts, and sailboats of all sizes took advantage of the warm summer evening. On New Year's Eve, the harbor near the bridge would be crowded with pleasure craft hoping to get the best view in the city.

Next they passed the sails of the iconic opera house, which were lit in a dazzling white. The promenade in front was crammed with people taking pictures of the scenery and enjoying the ocean breeze. There would be even more viewers packing the area to watch the fireworks tomorrow night.

Lu's reasoning for launching the rockets at exactly midnight, besides his desire for

461

theatrics, was to maximize the number of people outdoors when the gas was dispersed. Polk imagined the optics of hundreds of thousands of paralyzed residents lying out in the streets on New Year's Day.

Five minutes later, they approached the far end of the harbor where it turned to exit to the Pacific. The anchored *Centaurus* came into view behind Shark Island, home to a small park for picnics and parties. Around them overlooking the harbor were some of the most expensive estates in all of Australia. It was very likely that some of the customers for the Enervum antidote would be people living in those villas and mansions.

As they rounded the island, Polk saw a boat lashed alongside the *Centaurus*. It had MARITIME painted on the side. He was alarmed to realize that it was a boat from the Port Authority of New South Wales.

When he reached the *Centaurus,* he climbed on board, letting his men haul up the boxes of antidote. He asked where he could find Captain Rathman and was told that he was on the bridge.

Polk looked at the men transferring the boxes. "I'll come back to secure these. If I return to find any of the contents missing or broken, I will hold every one of you responsible."

He took the external stairs to the bridge. When he got there, Captain Rathman was speaking to a man in a shirt with the Port Authority logo on it. It was clear the captain was nervous, despite the fake smile that was plastered on his face.

"I'm Alfred Johnson," Polk said. "I'm with the importer receiving this ship's cargo. What's this about?" His hand rested on the Glock pistol tucked in his waistband.

"It's nothing," Rathman said. "Just some confusion about our crew."

"I'm Paul Smythe," the visitor said. "We've had a report that a man was found floating in the open ocean north of Brisbane."

Rathman shifted uncomfortably.

"What does that have to do with the *Centaurus*, Mr. Smythe?" Polk asked.

"When this man was rescued, he was speaking in Chinese. He said only one sentence over and over."

"What did he say?"

"The people who plucked him out of the sea thought he was saying, 'The centaur left me.' But the Border Force district office in Cairns had his words professionally translated. He was actually saying, 'The *Centaurus* left me.' We thought he might have fallen overboard from this ship."

"And I've just shown Mr. Smythe our manifest," Rathman said, pointing to the logbook Smythe was holding. "As you can see, we arrived in Sydney with our full complement of crewmen."

"Did this man say anything else?" Polk asked.

"Sadly, he died before he could say any more or reveal his identity," Smythe said.

"What an odd situation."

Smythe looked at Rathman with an unconvinced expression. "Why do you think he was saying 'The *Centaurus* left me,' if he wasn't from your ship? It seems like a strange thing for a dying man to utter."

Rathman shrugged. "We were traveling in that area a few nights ago. Perhaps he saw us pass by and was upset that we didn't see him."

"I suppose that's a possibility. But he must have fallen off some ship to be that far out in the ocean."

"I hope you're able to solve the mystery someday," Polk said.

Smythe handed back the logbook. "Everything seems to be in order." He began to walk out, then turned and said, "How long will you be in Sydney?"

"Just another day," Rathman said. "We set sail on January first."

"Then you'll be able to enjoy the fireworks while you're here. This year I understand it will be even more spectacular than ever, something truly to remember. Good evening, gentlemen. And Happy New Year."

Polk glared at Rathman as Smythe left. When the official was out of earshot, Polk said, "Tell me what happened."

Rathman cleared his throat. "We did have a man fall overboard. It was during that storm. I thought he was a dead man for sure, so I didn't turn around to search for him. It would have delayed our arrival in Sydney."

"And you just admitted the ship was in the area where the man was found."

"He probably would have found out anyway."

"Do you realize how dangerous it is to have the authorities snooping around on this ship?"

"I doctored the manifest, just in case," Rathman said. "He seemed satisfied that we never had that man aboard."

"Are there any other surprises I should know about?" Polk demanded.

"We rechecked the cargo when we lowered the anchor," Rathman said. "All of the pallets weathered the storm intact and without damage."

"And you have no other missing crewmen? No errant radio calls that might be investigated?"

Rathman shook his head vigorously. "Nothing like that. There shouldn't be any more interruptions."

"You should be glad that crewman died before he could divulge anything else," Polk said. "Otherwise, I'd make this more painful."

He drew the Glock and put a bullet in Rathman's chest. He keeled over, and Polk bent down to make sure he was dead.

When Rathman's pulse ceased, Polk stood and told two of the men to take his body to cold storage.

As it was, he didn't need the irresponsible captain anymore. The *Centaurus* was never leaving Sydney Harbour.

# SIXTY-FIVE

*The Gold Coast, Australia*
While the *Oregon* raced south toward Sydney, Juan briefed Langston Overholt on the events of the last few days. The aristocratic CIA official nodded silently from the wall screen of Juan's cabin until the end.

"Unfortunately, I don't think we have enough hard evidence to convince the Australian Defence Force to mount a raid," Overholt said. "The best we could hope for would be a thorough search of the ship's cargo."

"We can't take that risk," Juan said. "An inspection might prompt Polk to launch his rockets early. Besides, we don't even know the name of the ship."

"I believe I can help on that front. As you requested, I had the NSA monitor networks for the key words you suggested. They got a hit on Nhulunbuy. It seems a private yacht picked up a stranded man in the middle of the Coral Sea. He died from a shark attack, but before he succumbed to his injuries, he repeated the following phrase. 'The *Centaurus* left me.' His possessions included a matchbook from a tavern called the Lazy Goanna in Nhulunbuy."

For the first time, Juan felt a ray of hope. "That's where we met Bob Parsons. Was the man from the town?"

"The authorities circulated his picture there, but no one knew him. However, we ran him through the CIA's database. Facial recognition identified him as a former soldier in the Chinese Army who subsequently worked for a private military contractor known for its brutal operatives and their willingness to do exceedingly dirty work if the money was right. The firm was owned by Lu Yang."

"That can't be a coincidence."

"I agree."

" 'The *Centaurus* left me,' " Juan repeated. "Did he fall overboard from a ship called the *Centaurus*?"

"That was a theory of the Australian authorities, but the ship's manifest listed no missing crewmen."

"Where is the ship now?"

"Its location is the reason I brought this incident to your attention," Overholt said.

"The *Centaurus* is currently anchored in Sydney Harbour."

"The Coral Sea is on the shipping lane between Nhulunbuy and Sydney, and falsifying the manifest to cover up a crewman's disappearance is not difficult. The *Centaurus* could be what Polk had been calling the *Shepparton,* but it's a thin connection."

"Hence my reluctance to involve the Australian authorities. Broadcasting our concerns to the general public would be even worse. Panic would ensue, and any effort to evacuate the city would be futile. As you said, it might also cause Polk to act prematurely. If he is determined to attack Sydney, I'm afraid it's up to you and your crew to stop him."

"Not just stop him," Juan said. "Jin said he has thousands of doses of the antidote on board with him. We need to retrieve them, or Murph and the others who've been paralyzed by the Enervum gas will stay in that condition forever."

"When do you arrive in Sydney?"

"Not until tomorrow evening. It'll be barely enough time to mount an operation before midnight."

"I'll leave it to you how to proceed," Overholt said. "But the first priority is stopping the launch of those rockets, even if it means destroying the antidote along with the ship. Five million paralyzed Australians would not only be a horrific tragedy, it could also irrevocably alter the balance of power in that region of the world."

"Understood," Juan said. "I'll keep you posted."

Overholt hung up, and Juan called Eric.

"There's a ship anchored in Sydney Harbour. It's called the *Centaurus.* Is there a way to see it?"

"It shouldn't be too hard to tap into the cameras used by the harbor's vessel tracking system. Give me a few minutes and I'll get back to you."

Two minutes later, Eric called.

"Got it. I'll put it up on your screen."

Although it was nighttime, there was enough ambient light to make out the ship's silhouette easily. It was a break bulk freighter with four cranes mounted along one side of the ship.

"The *Centaurus* looks a lot like the *Shepparton,* doesn't it?" Eric said.

"Yes, it does," replied Juan. "That has to be Polk's ship. I'll tell Maurice to put more coffee on. We've got a long night ahead."

Planning each component of the operation didn't allow for much sleep, so there were a

470

few bleary eyes when Juan called everyone to the boardroom for the group's mission briefing the next evening.

"We all know what's at stake in this operation," Juan said, glancing at Murph. "Because of our late arrival in the Sydney area, we're not going to be able to begin the assault until 2330 tonight. That gives us only a half hour before the scheduled midnight launch of the rockets. Our objective is to get on board the *Centaurus,* secure the antidote, and disable the rockets if possible. We'll use a similar boarding tactic to the ones we used with the *Dahar* and *Shepparton.*"

"But with no tranquilizer darts," Linc said. "I used the last one on April Jin."

"What are the rules of engagement then?" Raven asked.

"We'll have to go in fast and hard," Eddie said. "Based on the man who fell overboard, we believe that the crew is made up of mercenaries who are military veterans. According to the manifest filed with the Sydney Port Authority, there are eleven crew on board. Polk might bring some people with him, so we're hoping to encounter fifteen or fewer hostiles. We can't afford an alarm to sound, so we'll be taking out each of them as quietly as we can. We'll be armed with suppressed weapons, but don't use them unless you have to."

MacD, whose arm was in a sling, turned to Raven. "Ah will let you use my crossbow one more time if you promise to bring it back in one piece."

"I will treat it like it's my own," Raven said.

"But to be clear, it's not."

Raven simply shrugged, her lip curled in amusement at his possessiveness.

"I will be leading the mission," Juan said. "Raven, Eddie, and Linc will be joined by Eric and Sylvia."

That raised some eyebrows.

To head off their questions, Juan continued, "We don't know what kind of weapons system Polk is using to activate the missiles, so we need technical experts on site to give us the best chance of disarming them. Normally, that would mean Eric and Murph."

"Unfortunately, my hover chair isn't ready yet," Murph said.

"Sylvia has similar expertise as her brother, so she volunteered her services for this operation. Instead of our custom earpieces, she'll be wearing a comm headset. She will also be unarmed, so I'm assigning Linc to stay by her side."

Sylvia looked sheepish. "I may do research for the Defense Department, but I don't work with small arms. I never actually fired a gun until Eric took me to your shooting range this morning."

"She was a pretty good shot," Eric said.

"But I'm not trained in handling them like you all are," Sylvia said. "I wouldn't want to shoot one of you by accident."

"Max will take command of the *Oregon*," Juan said. "Polk might recognize the ship, so we'll plan to stop seven miles outside of Sydney Harbour and come in on the *Gator*."

Linda raised her hand. "I'll be piloting this time."

"I want to point out something," Eric said. "As good as we are, Sylvia and I may not be able to disarm the rockets for a multitude of reasons. What happens if we can't?"

Juan looked at Max, who said, "Then I sink the *Centaurus* before the clock strikes midnight."

"Sylvia and Eric have modified the rail gun controls to be operated by Murph," Juan said. "All he has to do is lock in on the target and fire. He'll be able to do that with a single finger."

"With my help," MacD said. "I'll be on the *Gator* with Linda. Even though I've only got one arm, I can point a laser designator

473

at the hull. As I understand it, the rail gun targeting system will automatically adjust to fire at whatever I point at."

"Just don't sneeze," Raven said.

"Sink her?" Linc asked. "Why not just blow the ship out of the water?"

Murph grunted aloud. "Uh-uh." Then he used his voice box to say, "Gas cloud."

Sylvia nodded. "If the rockets detonated simultaneously, it would form a toxic cloud that could still poison a significant portion of the city."

"Once the ship is sunk," Eric said, "the water should absorb the Enervum gas even if there is a subsequent explosion."

"Polk would want to keep something as valuable as that antidote secure," Juan said. "The two likeliest places to stow it would be in the galley refrigerator if he needs to keep it cool or in the captain's cabin if he doesn't. Our plan is to sweep the accommodation block, check the galley, and then take the bridge. Once we've captured or killed Polk, his men might give up or attempt to escape. If they don't, we'll need to fight to the bitter end. Any questions?"

No one spoke. They all wore serious and determined expressions.

"Then let's begin to gear up," Juan said.

"We leave the *Oregon* an hour before midnight."

# SIXTY-SIX

*Sydney*

From his perch on the *Centaurus*'s bridge, Polk should have been enjoying the New Year's Eve light show. It had begun at 9:30 p.m. with a minor fireworks show for children who couldn't stay up until midnight, followed by the Harbour of Light Parade in which boats strung with colorful lights sailed through the harbor.

Instead, he continued to regularly phone and text his wife. She hadn't responded since her last voicemail to him, and now he was beyond worried. All contact with the *Marauder* had ceased. He feared some kind of catastrophic accident with the plasma cannon.

Polk considered calling off the rocket launch, but he would feel foolish for aborting the mission if he found out later that the trimaran had a simple communications malfunction. He trusted that Jin would be true to her word and arrive before dawn to celebrate their newfound riches with him.

It was nearing 11:30 p.m. Time to prep for the launch. He pressed the buttons that activated the huge doors that covered cargo bays three and four, the ones closest to the bridge. They folded up to reveal two cavernous openings. From this vantage point, he couldn't see the holds' contents, but he knew what was inside.

Each bay held one hundred and forty-nine rockets loaded into vertical tubes. The individual rockets would be guided by inertial navigation systems and GPS signals to their detonation points over Sydney. They were spaced out to cover the maximum area when they exploded, dispersing the Enervum into the air. There was almost no wind tonight, so the gas would achieve its maximum effectiveness. Only the most outlying suburbs of the city would be spared.

Since the *Centaurus* would be at the epicenter of the attack, Polk and his men would need protection from the gas. A full-face mask dangled at Polk's waist, as it did for each of the mercenaries on the ship.

Sydney's vessel tracking system cameras would record the launch from the *Centaurus,* leaving no doubt about the origin of the attack. Thanks to some anonymous tips from Jin and Polk, news sites around the world would have the basic story by January first, providing the key words they needed to unlock their money.

He just wished he could share this moment with his wife. The lack of contact with Jin continued to gnaw at him. He looked at the security chief.

"Make sure everyone is armed at all times," Polk said. "We can't take any chances from this point forward. If any boats approach between now and midnight, kill everyone aboard."

"Yes, sir."

Polk picked up a thick metal case, set it on the console, and opened it. Inside was the control panel, with buttons and switches labeled in both Swedish and English. Embedded in the case's lid was a large touch screen. Above it was "MR-76 Launch System."

The case controlled the Swedish-made rockets, wirelessly connected to the launch system hidden in the cargo bay.

Polk removed a key from the chain around his neck. He inserted it into a keyhole marked with three settings. OFF, TIMER, and ACTIVE. OFF meant the rockets were inert, TIMER was for a countdown launch, and

ACTIVE allowed him to press the red LAUNCH button, firing the rockets immediately.

He turned the key to TIMER. The touch screen lit up. He tapped on the screen to enter the countdown, synchronizing the timer with his watch so that the rockets would ignite at exactly midnight. Then he selected LOCK OUT ALL CHANGES. Now only the countdown timer appeared.

Thirty minutes to go.

He withdrew the key. At this point, the only way to stop the launch was to reinsert the key and switch it to OFF. Even if someone threw the entire control case into the harbor, the countdown would continue.

Polk didn't completely trust Lu's mercenaries, even though they were all set to get a share of the profits if the attack was successful. There was always the possibility that one of them was a saboteur.

He walked out to the bridge wing and chucked the key in the harbor. Nobody was going to stop the launch now.

"Bring five men and come with me," he said to the chief mercenary.

He took them down to cargo bay four. The rockets were arrayed in black tubes pointing straight into the sky. They'd already been uncovered and checked over earlier in the day.

At least Rathman had done his job to keep the cargo undamaged.

The seas between Nhulunbuy to Sydney could be rough, so each of the rockets had a safety pin to prevent accidental ignition. The pins were attached to red cloth ribbons marked REMOVE TO ARM.

"Take out of each one of these carefully," Polk said to the men, holding up one of the ribbons. "Then bring them to me and I will dispose of them." He planned to throw them overboard for the same reason he tossed the key.

In a ceremonial manner, Polk removed a ribbon, activating the first of the two hundred and ninety-eight rockets. He felt a tinge of excitement, knowing he was about to launch a New Year's Eve party no one would ever forget.

# SIXTY-SEVEN

At 11:31 p.m., Juan, dressed in black and carrying a suppressed Heckler & Koch MP5 submachine gun, pulled himself over the railing of the *Centaurus*. The ship's lights were on, but he couldn't feel the main engines idling through the metal deck.

Two of the ship's four cargo bays were open. That could only mean that the rockets were being prepped for launch.

As Raven's head peeked over the deck, he heard some footsteps coming from around the corner. He hissed into his molar mic the signal to halt. She stopped moving.

Juan unsheathed his KA-BAR knife and crouched behind a rope capstan. One of the mercenaries came around the corner, casually carrying a Chinese-made QCW-05 submachine gun with its own suppressor. He didn't seem too concerned about a possible intrusion. Juan grabbed him from behind, putting his hand over the man's mouth to silence him, and plunged the knife into his back. The mercenary struggled for a moment and went limp.

Juan hissed twice to give the all-clear. Raven finished her climb, followed by Eddie, Eric, Linc, and Sylvia.

Throwing the body overboard would cause too much noise, so Eddie dragged the body behind the capstan where they piled coils of loose rope over it.

Juan led them to the outer door of the superstructure. The accommodation block was five stories high. They would clear each floor one by one as they went up to the bridge.

On the first two stories, they quietly took out three men, one by Raven's crossbow, two by knives, hiding the bodies as they went. On the third level, a mercenary munching on a bag of chips came out of the mess and stumbled into Sylvia. Juan was surprised to see her kick the man in the groin before he could react. Linc finished him by bashing his head against the doorframe.

Despite the ruckus, no alarm was sounded.

They dragged him into the empty galley next to the mess. This was their first shot at finding the antidote. They all had packable nylon duffels to transport the amount they needed for Murph and the rest of the paralyzed people. Six hundred and fifty doses would be enough.

The walk-in refrigerator would be the best place to stow the antidote. Juan opened the fridge and didn't see any container that could have held a large supply of serum. Instead, he found a dead man with a bullet hole in his chest.

"Somebody made Polk mad," Eddie said.

"Too bad it isn't Polk himself," Juan said. "Let's keep going."

They continued up the accommodation block, killing two more hostiles before they reached the bridge. One man was there. He scrambled to pick up his rifle, but Raven put him down silently.

Eric and Sylvia rushed over to the console where an open metal case was sitting on top. Juan sent Raven and Linc to search the captain's cabin for the antidote.

"This is the rocket control panel," Sylvia said. "It's already been activated. Twenty minutes to launch."

"Can you disarm it?"

Eric shook his head. "There's no key."

Linc came over, his gun raised like he was ready to bring the butt down on the panel. "What about smashing it?"

"That won't work," Sylvia said. "The MR-76 launch controller is a two-part system. If we destroy this or jam the signal, it won't stop the countdown. We'd have to disable each individual rocket."

"She's right," Eric said. "The only way to do it is to find the key and turn this back to off."

"Could you pick the lock?" Eddie asked.

"It would be tricky, but we could try."

Eddie handed Eric his lock-picking set.

"We still haven't found Polk," Juan said. "He probably has the key. In the meantime, we can close the cargo holds to prevent the rockets from launching."

He pushed the buttons to close the two open cargo bay doors.

Raven and Linc returned.

"No antidote," Raven said.

"And we found a picture of the dead guy in the fridge. It was the captain."

"We have to find Polk," Juan said. He hadn't been in the accommodation block, which left the engine rooms or the cargo holds.

The bridge had a camera link to the engineering area. The monitor showed both the main engine room and the room with the auxiliary generator.

Juan peered more closely at the screen and

noticed something that caused him to tense.

"This ship has a citadel."

"A what?" Sylvia asked.

"A citadel is like a safe room," Eric said. "If pirates try to take over the ship, the crew can retreat to the citadel and lock it up tight. It's usually stocked with plenty of food and water for a long siege."

"If Polk finds out we're here and goes to the citadel," Juan said, "we probably won't be able to break in before midnight. Raven, Eddie, you're with me. We're going to secure the citadel. Linc, stay here with Eric and Sylvia while they try to disable the launcher."

They were already hunched over the control panel with the lock picks as Juan's group sprinted for the stairwell.

As Polk emerged from the cargo hold onto the deck with his men, the cargo bay doors were closing.

"What is that guard on the bridge doing?" he asked, jogging toward the superstructure. When he got near the door, he slipped on some liquid on the deck. He thought it was oil until he looked more closely.

The small puddle looked black in the low light, but it had the unmistakable smell of blood.

He followed the droplets and found a shoe sticking out from underneath a pile of rope. They uncovered the dead body of one of the mercenaries.

Polk glared with rage. It had to be the work of the same group he'd fought against twice already.

"We've got intruders."

He only hoped they hadn't taken control of the citadel. He took the dead man's submachine gun.

He glared at the security chief. "Take three men and secure the citadel. I'll take the other two and go to the bridge. Kill anyone you see."

Without waiting for a reply, he ran to the external stairs with his men and headed up to the bridge.

# SIXTY-EIGHT

The citadel on the *Centaurus* was adjacent to the main engine room in the bowels of the ship. When Juan, Eddie, and Raven arrived, the inch-thick steel door was wide open. The three of them swarmed into the large, noisy space, ready to take down anyone inside, but it was vacant.

The two-story room housed the auxiliary generator as well as basic controls for steering the ship and communicating with the outside world. On the far side of the room were shelves stocked with pallets of water bottles and ready to eat meals. Beside it were several storage lockers. Stairs led up to a second door exiting to the next higher deck. A ventilation hatch in the ceiling thirty feet above them was tied down by a taut steel cable attached to the wall. The intent was to keep pirates from opening the hatch and spraying the citadel with gunfire or dropping grenades through it.

"Where is everyone?" Raven asked.

"I don't know," Juan said. "But at least Polk didn't beat us here. That door looks like it could survive a nuclear blast."

He closed and bolted the door to protect their rear while they searched the room. Eddie took the stairs to latch the other door.

He was about to pin the latch shut so that it couldn't open when the door flew open. One of the mercenaries charged in with his submachine gun blazing, but Eddie was able to grab his arms before he could swing the weapon's barrel toward him.

They were still wrestling when a second man entered. Juan and Raven couldn't fire without fear of hitting Eddie, and the second man got off a volley in Raven's direction. Juan could see the rounds stitch across her chest, and she went down.

Eddie used his leverage to force his guy over the railing, but the mercenary wouldn't let go of Eddie. Together, they somersaulted through the air and landed on the steel deck, giving Juan a clear shot at his companion. He fired a three-round burst that snapped the man's head back in a red mist of blood.

Eddie and his opponent continued their vicious fight, but Juan couldn't go to his aid. Two more gunmen entered, this time more cautiously than the first two.

Juan dived behind the generator as bullets ripped into the metal. Raven, who was lying on the opposite side of the generator, groaned and grabbed her chest, her face a mask of pain. Juan reached out and snagged the shoulder strap of her ballistic vest, dragging her to him.

Juan stole a look over the top of the generator and saw the two men coming down the stairs. They sprayed the generator with rounds, causing Juan to pull back.

Raven pushed herself up with a grimace.

"Are you hurt?" Juan asked.

"Broken rib maybe." Juan didn't see any blood. The Level III plate on Raven's body armor had done its job, but she would have some nasty bruises.

"Can you fight?"

She scowled at him. "Oh, yeah."

"They may not know you're still alive. I'll give you an opening." He handed her his MP5 and drew his pistol.

"Ready." She crept to the other side of the generator.

Instead of looking over the top, Juan slid out on his belly, firing his weapon before he could see the target. He didn't need to hit them. He was merely the decoy.

The two men ducked to the side, firing

blindly at the source of his rounds. With their attention on him, Raven edged out and fired controlled bursts at each man. They were dead before they hit the floor.

Juan sprang to his feet and rushed over to Eddie. He was too late to help. Eddie had the strap of his MP5 wrapped around the man's neck. The mercenary was motionless, and Eddie dropped the man's head to free his weapon.

"Are you okay?" Juan asked, holding out his hand to help Eddie to his feet.

Eddie took the offered hand and hopped up on one foot.

"I think I fractured my ankle on that fall," Eddie said. "This guy landed right on it, and I felt it snap."

Juan helped him over to the stairs and sat him down on the first step. Juan didn't want a surprise repeat, so he ran up to the door, nudged the dead man aside, and dogged it tight.

He clicked his molar mic. "Linc, we've had some trouble down here in the citadel."

"I know," Linc replied. "We saw the whole thing on the monitor. Wish I could have been there to give an assist."

"You need to focus on getting those rockets deactivated. But we still don't know where Polk is, so be on the lookout."

"On it."

"Chairman," Raven called out to him. She bent over in pain and lowered her voice. "I think we may have something here."

Juan went back down the stairs and over to Raven, who was standing by the lockers. One of them was secured with a combination padlock.

"There's something valuable in here."

"Let's take a look."

Juan retrieved the portable bolt cutter that Eddie carried. It took several tries to cut through the heavy lock, but it finally came loose.

The locker opened, revealing that it was full from top to bottom with five large aluminum boxes.

Juan removed one of them and unlatched its clasp. It was crammed with smaller packs of plastic containers. He lifted the lid on one.

The pack contained a dozen vials like those used in hospitals for dispensing intravenous drugs. Each vial was carefully snugged in a protective cushion.

He plucked one of the vials from the container. It held ten cc's of a clear liquid. The vial was marked "Serum NVL." Juan remembered the same letters from the Roman amphora he tried to recover from the buried *Salacia*. *Nux viridi lucus* was the cure they had discovered for their own paralytic agent two thousand years ago.

"The antidote," Raven said. She turned to Eddie. "We got it."

He gave her a thumbs-up.

"Looks like we did," Juan said. "We'll need about sixty of these packs."

"These boxes are too bulky to carry."

"Let's start loading them into the duffels. With the cushioning, they should be able to survive some jostling."

Juan keyed his mic.

"Max, do you read?"

"Here," Max said. "Time's getting short. Thirteen minutes left. Do you have good news?"

"We do indeed," Juan replied with a smile. "Tell Murph that we've got his cure."

His good spirits were short-lived, however. A single word came through on his earpiece. It was Sylvia's voice.

"Gas."

# SIXTY-NINE

The attempt to pick the lock on the rocket launch controller had been going nowhere. Sylvia, looking around the room for a possible hiding place for the key, had suggested that the mercenaries they'd killed on the bridge might have had it in his pocket the whole time. Eric seemed convinced Polk would be the one who had it, but she thought she might as well give it a shot and search the dead man.

While Linc stood behind Eric watching all of the entrances to the bridge, and Eric stayed focused on the control panel, Sylvia had gone to the other side of the bridge where the mercenary had been dragged out of the way.

She was going through his pockets when the door on the other side of the bridge cracked open, and a canister was tossed through. It popped open and started spewing white smoke.

493

"Gas!" she yelled.

Linc didn't have time to react. The gas grenade had landed between his feet. He keeled over onto the floor like a cedar tree that had been chopped down.

Eric, who'd been crouched over the control panel, turned his head and then passed out, slumping across the console.

Sylvia watched all this happen with her breath held. She realized she couldn't inhale again or she'd suffer the same fate.

She snatched the dual-canister mask that was attached to the dead man's belt and pressed it against her face. When it was sealed against her skin, she used the remaining breath in her lungs to blow out forcefully, clearing the mask of any residual air and gas that had gotten trapped inside.

She finally inhaled, expecting her world to go dark. There was no wooziness, so she must have acted in time. She drew the straps over her hair, ripping off her headset as she tightened the mask.

Through the window in the upper half of the door, Sylvia saw two of the mercenaries looking at their handiwork. She knew that as soon as they saw she was unaffected by the gas, they'd kill her.

She'd only fired an MP5 submachine gun once in the *Oregon*'s armory, but it seemed

494

simple enough. Literally point and shoot, with a minimal kick even on full auto. A QCW-50 was lying beside the dead mercenary. She hoped the Chinese weapon was just as easy to operate.

She picked it up at the same moment the two men saw her. She flicked the safety, put the gun to her shoulder, aimed its red-dot sight at the window and yanked the trigger, holding it down without letting go.

Bullets tore through the glass, hitting both men. She knew the weapon had a fifty-round magazine, but she was still shocked at how fast they were used up. The gun clicked empty just a few seconds later.

The door was pocked with bullet holes, but she seemed to have hit her targets. Both of them were down, which was fortunate since Eric hadn't taught her how to reload.

She got to her feet, concerned about Eric and Linc, when she locked eyes with the man whose image had haunted her since the sinking of the *Namaka.*

Angus Polk pushed the door open, a look of anger on his face and a gun in his hands. Sylvia had a split second to sprint for the stairwell before his bullets started slamming into the bulkhead behind her. She dived and rolled down the first flight of steps to the landing, smacking hard onto the floor.

Despite the jolt of pain in her back, she willed herself to her feet and ran down the interior stairs without looking back.

Polk didn't recognize the woman who'd just killed two of his men, but he'd soon find her. Based on how wildly she'd shot and the fact that she'd fired the entire magazine on full auto, she didn't seem like a pro. He looked forward to hunting her down.

But first he had to open the cargo bay doors again. With eleven minutes left to launch, they were the only thing standing between the rockets and all of those citizens out there waiting to celebrate the new year.

As he walked to the control panel, movement on one of the monitors caught his attention. There were three intruders dressed in black inside the citadel, as well as four corpses of the men he'd sent to secure it.

One man was seated on the stairs, while a man and a woman were kneeling by the lockers.

They were rooting through his supply of the Enervum antidote, stuffing the packs into bags. The man had paused his work and seemed to be talking to no one in particular.

Polk looked at the intruder who was slumped over the bridge console and noticed that he was wearing a tiny earpiece. His friends in the citadel must have been wondering why they'd lost contact.

They wouldn't have to wonder long, but they wouldn't be going anywhere, either.

Polk brought up the fire control system on the touch screen and selected the option operating the emergency fire doors in that area of the ship. Thick fireproof panels began to slide together. The man in the citadel got to his feet and ran to the door, but he wasn't fast enough. The room was sealed. Polk finished by locking out manual override at that location.

Now no one would be entering or exiting the citadel. It was secure, but not airtight. They would be gassed along with everyone else in the city once the rockets went off.

Polk activated the intercom to the citadel.

"Whoever you are," he said, "your friends are unconscious and paralyzed by Enervum up here on the bridge. I hope you now realize what a mistake you've made coming onto my ship. Just hang out there. You won't have to wait long."

Once Jin arrived in the *Marauder* — and he still held out hope that she would — they'd go down with the *Centaurus*.

Even as the three captives listened to him, they began to pry at the doors. Let them try all they wanted, Polk thought. Those doors wouldn't budge unless they had a jackhammer.

He still had to open cargo bays three and four. He pushed aside the unconscious man on the console to get at the switches. He flipped them, and the huge folding doors began to rise again.

Once they were in place, he pounded the switches with the butt of his rifle, hopelessly jamming them so they couldn't be used to close the doors again.

Now that those tasks were taken care of, the rocket launch was assured despite the intruders' best efforts.

He inserted a fresh magazine into his weapon, turned to the stairwell, and went in search of his quarry. Now it was just him against her.

# SEVENTY

The *Gator* idled a hundred yards from the *Centaurus,* only its cupola poking above the surface. MacD was checking over the laser designator. It looked like a giant pair of binoculars, except with three lenses instead of two, the third being for the laser itself. MacD would hold it up to his eyes, and whatever he was looking at was what the rail gun would hit.

"The doors are moving again," Linda said from the cockpit.

"What?" MacD said.

"The cargo bays are opening."

MacD went forward and crammed himself into the tiny space with her. The *Centaurus* loomed like a leviathan, filling the window. Sure enough, the doors above the cargo bays closest to the superstructure were in the upright position.

MacD listened in as Linda tried to make contact with the bridge of the *Centaurus.*

"Eric, come in," she said. "What's going on up there?"

There was no response.

"Chairman, this is Linda. Come in, please."

"Juan here."

"We've lost contact with the bridge, and we can see that the cargo bay doors have opened again. They can launch the rockets."

"We just heard from Polk. He claims that he got Linc, Eric, and Sylvia with the Enervum gas."

"We didn't see a rocket go up."

"He must have used a grenade or smoke canister. But we're locked into the citadel at the bottom of the ship. We're trying to get out, but we're not having any luck. This place is sealed tighter than Fort Knox."

"Can we do anything? Should we try to get aboard?"

"No," Juan said. "Stay put. We need you out there to target the *Centaurus*."

MacD looked at Linda. "Ah'd rather go and fight."

She returned his gaze with a resolute expression. "The Chairman knows what he's doing."

It was only when Sylvia had gone down two levels that she noticed that one of Polk's rounds had nicked her leg. She'd left tiny blood droplets behind her, like a trail of bread crumbs, leading Polk right to her.

There was no point in hiding. In less than eight minutes, the rockets would launch unless she could stop them somehow. But with Eric and Linc paralyzed, and Polk in pursuit, it seemed hopeless. Even if she got another submachine gun from one of the other dead mercenaries, she wasn't sure she could defeat a former police detective in a shoot-out.

Still, she had to try something. If he was following her blood trail, she might be able to use it to lead him to her.

There was a fire ax on the wall. She took it out of its cradle and got a feel for its weight. It was heavy for her, but she thought she could get in a solid swing.

Sylvia walked to the next corner and went around it. She put her back against the wall, the ax tight in her hands, and waited.

She kept the mask on in case Polk threw another grenade. She tempered her breathing so that the sound of her mask filter was as muted as possible. Polk would be breathing harder in his own mask because he was on the move, so she hoped he wouldn't hear her.

She didn't have to wait long for Polk. The

distinctive Darth Vader wheeze of his breathing slowly grew louder as if he were taking his time stalking his prey.

She'd only get one swing, so she had to make it count. The awful breathing sound got closer and closer until it seemed like he was right around the corner.

Without waiting for Polk to show himself, Sylvia swung the ax as hard as she could at chest level.

A hand came up to deflect the handle, but in his shock at being attacked Polk misjudged the angle. The razor-sharp edge sliced across his wrist, cutting deep, before embedding itself in the wall.

Polk let out a scream as blood poured from his ruined wrist. His hand dangled uselessly.

In a fit of fury, he forgot the gun and lunged at Sylvia with his good hand. He grabbed on to the canister of her face mask. He yanked her toward him, his eyes wide with rage, a terrifying sight through the eyeholes of his own mask. With the rubber seal loose now, only the straps were keeping it on her head.

Sylvia strained to pull the ax free, but she couldn't get it out of the wall. If Polk got any presence of mind back, he would let go of the mask and grab her around the throat to choke the life out of her.

She angled her head so that the straps came off, and she fell backward onto her rear. So did Polk, who landed on his wounded arm and let out an agonized shriek.

Sylvia took advantage of the distraction and ran for it. As she neared the end of the corridor, bullets whizzed by her, but Polk's one-handed aim was wild.

She went down the next hall and realized she was near the mess and galley. Polk wouldn't give up until he found her, so she decided to make it easy for him. After all, she wasn't wearing a mask anymore, and he knew it.

# SEVENTY-ONE

Eric woke with a start. His face felt like it was pressing against some buttons. He opened his eyes and saw that he was lying across the bridge control console. He racked his brain but didn't know how he got there. Even worse, other than his head, he couldn't move.

The last thing he remembered was tinkering with the lock pick set to try to abort the rocket launch. Then everything was a blank until this moment.

Out of the corner of his eye he saw Linc lying on the floor. He was conscious and blinked at Eric, but he said nothing.

On the floor next to him was the cylindrical canister of a smoke grenade.

That's when Eric realized they must have been gassed. In addition to paralysis, one of the symptoms was short-term memory loss. Murph hadn't remembered losing consciousness, either.

Eric lifted his head as much as he could, but he couldn't see Sylvia anywhere. The lock picks were where he'd left them, jutting out of the rocket control system keyhole. The display in the case's lid was still counting down to midnight.

Movement on one of the bridge monitors caught his attention. He could see the Chairman and Eddie pounding at a door, trying to get it open. They were trapped in the citadel by the fire doors.

Eric tried to move his arms, but the best he could do was bang his hand against the panel. There was no way he'd be able to release them.

Then he made one other disturbing observation. The switches controlling the cargo bay doors had been destroyed since he'd been gassed.

He had to warn someone. Although he couldn't form words, Eric could still move his tongue. He activated his molar mic to contact the *Oregon.*

The only thing he could do was click his tongue against the roof of his mouth.

"I'm getting a strange signal over the comm system," Hali said from his post in the *Oregon*'s op center. "I thought it was static, but . . ." He sat up straighter, excited. "Wait.

505

It's Morse code."

Max sat forward in the captain's chair. "Put it on speaker."

A series of tsking clicks tapped out a pattern of dots and dashes.

"That's Eric," Murph said, adding a "Woohoo" cheer for emphasis at hearing from his friend. Although all three of them knew Morse code, Murph spoke the words aloud as they listened.

*"Eric here. On bridge. Linc alive. Paralyzed by gas."*

"So Polk wasn't bluffing when he told Juan that everyone on the bridge was gassed," Max said.

"What about Sylvia?" Murph asked, his brow knitted in concern for his sister.

*"Not here. Where she?"*

"We don't know," Max replied. "We haven't heard from her."

*"Are cargo doors closed?"* Eric asked.

"No," Murph said. "Open."

*"Can't close. Switches broken."*

"Then we can't stop the rocket launch," Hali said. "Not even if the Chairman gets out of the citadel."

"Put me in touch with Juan," Max said. "We have to let him know."

In the citadel, they'd been trying to open

the doors for minutes now and had made no progress. Eddie was trying to activate the manual controls that had been disabled from the bridge. Juan had his knife jammed into the crease between the fire doors that had come together at the main entrance. His efforts to pry them apart hadn't produced even an inch of movement.

He called out to Raven, who was working on the door the mercenaries had used.

"Any luck up there?"

"Nothing so far," she said, her voice straining as she attempted to wrench the door open. "It's hard to get much leverage when your rib is digging into your lungs." But she kept at it.

Juan looked at his watch. Eight minutes before midnight.

"Juan, I've got an update for you," Max said in his earpiece.

"Go ahead."

"We've heard from Eric."

"I'm glad to hear he's alive."

"So is Linc, but they're both paralyzed. Eric says the cargo bay doors can't be closed again. The switches were sabotaged."

"Is Polk still on the ship?" Juan asked.

"Linda hasn't reported anyone leaving."

"And Sylvia?"

"We've lost contact with her. Can you get

507

out of the citadel?"

"It's not looking good on that front."

"Then we're in a bit of a pickle, aren't we?" Max said.

"Seems like it."

Juan considered their options. Disabling the rockets wasn't going to happen, and now they couldn't even contain them on the ship.

The backup plan to get the antidote off the ship and have the *Oregon* destroy the *Centaurus* once they were safely away wasn't in the cards, either.

He couldn't have MacD and Linda board the ship. If they came onto the *Centaurus,* they could be killed by Polk or prevented from getting back to the *Gator.* Then there would be no way to stop the rockets and their payload of Enervum from devastating Sydney.

That left only one choice. Eddie brought up what Juan was thinking.

"How long do you think it will take for the *Centaurus* to sink?" Eddie asked.

"The rail gun shells travel at seven times the speed of sound. With that kind of kinetic energy against an unarmored ship, the rounds will probably rip through the side and down through the keel. With four or five well-placed shots, I bet she'd go down in five minutes or less."

Eddie nodded slowly and looked at his watch. "Seven minutes to go."

Juan looked up the stairs. "Raven, any chance that door is going to open?"

She shook her head. "Not without an RPG."

Juan leaned back as he thought about what he needed to do. That's when he noticed the ventilation hatch thirty feet above them. There was no way to climb up to it even if they could detach the steel cable locking it down.

But there was one other way to get to it.

"We're running out of time," Eddie said. "What do you want to do?"

"I've got an idea, but it's risky."

Eddie shrugged. "I prefer your risky ideas to no ideas."

Everyone in the crew knew what they'd signed up for when they joined the Corporation. They had lost crew members in the past, and their names were memorialized on a plaque in the ship's boardroom as a reminder of what they'd sacrificed for the ship, their crewmates, and the greater good. Juan knew there was a very good chance their names would be added to the plaque if this didn't work, but he didn't see any other way.

"Max, you know how you don't like my Plan Cs?"

"Yeah," Max said dubiously. "They're usually insanely dangerous."

"I've got another one now. You're going to hate it."

"Why?"

"Ask Murph what will happen if the *Centaurus* is underwater when the rockets launch without the cargo bay doors closed to stop them."

Max relayed the question. A few seconds later, he came back with, "He says the overpressure from the water in the tubes will cause them to explode as they launch."

"Then it looks like we have our answer."

"No," Max said when he understood what Juan was planning to do. "There's got to be another way."

"Afraid not," Juan said. "In fact, it's our only chance to escape. You have to sink the *Centaurus* immediately. That's a direct order."

# SEVENTY-TWO

The *Oregon*'s op center was deathly quiet. Max could feel Hali and Murph staring at him. He was focused on the main screen showing the feed from the Port Authority camera showing the *Centaurus* in the distance. He couldn't help but picture Juan and the others trapped in the depths of the ship awaiting their doom.

This was not the way Max had imagined the ship's maiden voyage would go. When they'd departed unexpectedly early from the construction yard in Malaysia, it was just supposed to be a quick mission to stop a terrorist attack. Now he feared he was about to kill his best friend.

"Are we really going to sink the ship with everyone still on board?" Hali asked.

"You heard Juan's order," Max said. He tried to sound reassuring. "Don't worry. He's not giving up. Neither should we."

"I know Sylvia is alive," Murph said. He

didn't have to mention that his own best friend, Eric, would also go down with the *Centaurus.*

"Juan will do his best to find Sylvia and get Eric and Linc out of there. Are you going to be able to do this?"

"Yes. Sylvia would do the same to save the city."

"Raise the rail gun," Max said. "Hali, get me MacD."

"Rail gun ready in all respects," Murph said.

The image on the view screen changed. The *Centaurus* now much larger, with the camera panning slowly from bow to stern.

"Are you getting the picture?" MacD asked.

"We see it," Max replied. "Murph has the rail gun armed and ready to fire."

"What is the target?"

"The waterline," Murph said. "Not the open cargo holds."

"Remember," Max said, "we want to sink the ship, not ignite the rockets. We'll fire five rounds. That should put her under quickly."

"I'll target three in the bow and two in the stern," MacD said.

The image slewed around to the bow. A green dot appeared on the screen. It was centered under the name CENTAURUS stenciled on the bow.

Max waited for Murph to confirm that the ship's computer had automatically calculated the proper firing solution for the round.

He remained silent. Max could see that his chest was heaving.

"Mark," he said. "We need to do this."

Murph finally said, "Target acquired."

"Fire."

The *Oregon* shuddered as the rail gun launched its tungsten shell.

"Round one away," Murph said. "Loading round two."

Linda had repositioned the *Gator* another hundred yards away from the *Centaurus*. MacD was standing in the hatch with his eyes focused through the laser designator.

With the *Oregon* seven miles out to sea it would take five seconds for the hypersonic round to reach the target. The shell was unguided, so it was on a ballistic trajectory. MacD didn't have to activate the laser again until he was selecting the next target.

Unlike in the movies, there was no high-pitched whistle to announce the incoming round. As if out of nowhere, a gaping hole was torn in the bow of the *Centaurus*. There was no explosive in the shell. It was purely a solid hunk of metal. The kinetic energy of the round did all the damage. Water poured through the black maw.

The sonic boom of the round's shock wave followed immediately after, rattling the *Gator.*

"Successful hit," MacD said with no satisfaction.

"Acquire target two," Max said.

MacD adjusted the laser sternward under the first crane.

"Ready."

"Firing."

MacD waited another five seconds. It was as if he had drawn a bull's-eye on the ship. The shell ripped through the hull like it was made of crepe paper.

The bow of the *Centaurus* was already settling into the water.

"Keep going," Max said.

The next round went under cargo bay two. Three rounds, three targets hit. If it hadn't been in service of such an awful purpose, MacD would have been overjoyed at the display of the Corporation's teamwork and engineering skill.

He moved back to the superstructure, placing a round directly below the bridge at the waterline. Finally, he hit the stern right above the propellers.

Normally, MacD would expect Max to say something like, "Nice work." That seemed inappropriate given the situation.

Instead, Max said, "We're done."

For a moment, MacD watched the *Centaurus* lowering into the water. At this rate, it certainly seemed likely that the ship would hit the bottom of Sydney Harbour by the time the fireworks went off.

There was nothing else they could do for the team on board the ship. He climbed down and closed the hatch above him.

Linda looked back at him from the cockpit.

"The Chairman has a plan," she said, as though she were trying to convince herself. "He always does."

"Ah hope so."

MacD's watch said four minutes to midnight.

# SEVENTY-THREE

Polk vowed to make that mystery woman pay for severing the tendons in his wrist, but he had to get the bleeding under control before he could continue his pursuit. He was almost done tying a tourniquet around his wounded arm when the first impact hit the *Centaurus.*

It felt and sounded like an explosion, but it wasn't midnight yet. He wondered if the rockets had launched prematurely. Then the ship was rocked by another blast, then another, each one getting closer until one directly below him knocked him off his feet. A fifth completed the cycle, and the ship went silent again.

Someone had fired on the *Centaurus.* That was the only conclusion he could draw. It had to be someone involved with these intruders. Thanks to those blasts the ship was now at an incline toward the bow.

The *Centaurus* was sinking.

He didn't care. The rockets would launch. Whoever was attacking him would be paralyzed by the Enervum. He would simply get in the free-fall lifeboat and wait for Jin to arrive.

With the tourniquet tight, Polk gritted through the pain and adjusted his grip on the submachine gun. The woman's blood droplets on the white linoleum were as easy to follow as a neon sign.

He tracked them through several turns, where they ended at the door leading into the mess. She had to be hiding inside.

Polk wasn't going to fall for another swinging ax. He had one more gas grenade, and he'd ripped the mask off her face. She was vulnerable.

It wouldn't be as satisfying to kill her while she was unconscious. Then he realized he'd have all the time in the world with her. He could wait until she was revived and paralyzed. Then he could do whatever he wanted with her.

Polk made sure his mask had a tight seal and nudged the door ajar with his foot. He grabbed the grenade from his vest and pulled the pin out with his teeth. He spat it out, released the handle, and counted.

When he got to three, he tossed it through the gap in the door and let it close. It

517

popped and then hissed as it began spewing gas.

He waited a reasonable amount of time, hoping to hear a thump as the woman fell. But she could have been cowering in a corner or hiding in the fridge. If the door to the refrigerator was closed, he would simply open it and let the gas in to disable her.

He heard nothing. She had to be unconscious by this time. Nonetheless, he'd be careful. For such a small woman, she was feisty, and she'd already tricked him once.

He pushed the door open, crouching as he entered with the gun leading the way.

White mist filled the room. He swept the mess, but the tables were empty, and the floor was clear. She had to be in the galley.

The door was open, which meant the gas had filled both rooms. He cautiously approached the opening.

Nobody jumped out or swung an ax. He went in and noticed the refrigerator door was open wide. He didn't have a view of the interior, but if she was in there, she should be out cold already.

He edged in farther and saw a sight that made him smile. A pair of boots stuck out from behind the cook's island.

Polk eagerly went over to appreciate his handiwork, temporarily forgetting the pain in his arm.

But when he rounded the island, he was shocked to see a mercenary, the smallest in the crew. His feet were smaller than Jin's.

Then with horror, Polk realized something else. The gas mask that should have been hanging from the man's belt was gone.

Polk had fallen for Sylvia's trap perfectly. She figured he'd be so excited to see her prone body that he wouldn't notice the difference in the boots she wore and the ones on the dead mercenary she'd dragged behind the cook's island.

With the borrowed mask firmly on her head, she sprinted out of the galley refrigerator and leaped onto Polk's back, wrapping her arm around his neck and her legs around his waist.

He was thrown off balance by the sudden weight shift and staggered backward, firing the submachine gun at the ceiling. Some of the bullets ricocheted off the hanging iron pots, but none of them hit her or Polk.

First, he tried to turn the weapon to shoot her, but he couldn't get the right angle. He dropped the gun and crushed at her fingers in an attempt to get her off.

Sylvia cried out as he increased the pressure, but she didn't let go. With her other

519

hand, she pried at the edge of his mask and peeled it away from his face. The ambient air was now seeping into the mask, unfiltered.

She didn't need to get it all the way off his head. Sylvia just needed to outlast him. The second he drew in a breath, he was done.

He must have realized what she was doing because he slammed her back against the refrigerator door. A jolt of pain lanced through her spine in the same place where she'd fallen down the stairs. Still, she held on, keeping a gap in the mask.

Sylvia wanted to enrage Polk, to get him so blinding mad that he'd forget what danger he was in. She knew exactly what to say.

"You haven't heard from your wife, have you?" she yelled. "That's because she's dead. At the bottom of the ocean with the *Marauder.*"

Polk didn't cry out, but Sylvia could feel him tremble with anger. He rammed her even harder against the door and at the same time yanked her leg to the side. The combination was enough to make her lose her grip. She fell to the floor.

Polk turned around and glared down at her, his furious eyes wide behind the mask,

520

which was now sealed against his face again.

"I'll kill you for that," he growled, his chest heaving as he could finally draw a breath.

"You forgot to clear your mask," Sylvia said.

All of the air that had contaminated the inside of the mask when she unsealed it was still in there. She hoped it was enough of a dose.

Polk looked horrified as he realized that she was right. He reached down for her, but his eyes rolled back in his head. He keeled over right on top of her.

Sylvia struggled to push him off, rolling him onto his back.

She rapidly searched his pockets for the key to the rocket control system, but the only thing she found was his phone. Maybe he had an app to deactivate the rockets and abort the launch.

She pulled his mask off and put the phone in front of his face. The phone unlocked, and she quickly set it so it wouldn't relock.

Even unconscious, Polk continued to scowl.

"That's what you get for messing with my family," she said.

She hopped to her feet and sprinted for the bridge.

# SEVENTY-FOUR

Juan's plan to get out of the citadel depended on the ship sinking because there was only one way to get up to the ventilation hatch thirty feet above them in the ceiling. The room would have to flood as the ship sank, buoying them up until they could open the hatch. The fireproof door on the main level of the citadel wasn't designed to be waterproof as well, so that's where the water would enter the room first.

The problem was the cable securing the citadel's ceiling hatch to the wall. It was an inch thick, with a huge nut and bolt holding it tight. The eyebolt attaching it to the wall was halfway to the ceiling, far out of reach. The only thing tall enough to stand on were the food shelves, but they were on the other side of the room and bolted to the floor.

Juan wasn't going to attempt to loosen the nut and bolt. That would take far too long while they were floating on the surface of water flooding into the chamber. Instead, he was going to blow it in half.

He, Eddie, and Raven had taken off their heavy body armor and dropped their weapons, even MacD's crossbow.

"He's never going to forgive me for this," Raven said.

"I'll buy him a better one," Juan said.

The only thing he refused to give up was the duffel with the antidote vials inside. He had it slung over his shoulder.

Juan could tell the ship was already going down at the bow. All of them were standing at an angle, and the guns on the floor slid to the front of the room.

He bent down and pulled up his pant leg to expose his combat leg prosthesis. He opened the secret compartment holding his ceramic knife and .45 ACP Colt Defender. He left those in place and took out a packet smaller than a deck of cards and closed up the leg.

The packet contained a plug of C-4 plastic explosive and a remote detonator. The gray putty was moldable and could be formed into any shape. Juan hadn't wasted the charge on the fireproof door because the detonation would have only put a hole in it, not opened it.

The panels of the door creaked and deformed until water began to gush through the seals, forced into the citadel by the outside pressure until it became a torrent.

The water level rose at what would be an alarming rate in any other circumstance, but in this case, Juan was frustrated at how slowly it was filling the room.

At last they were buoyant, impatiently treading water as the water covered the shelving units. Food packets, soda cans, and water bottles drifted around the room.

Then the lights went out and the room went silent. The water had shorted out the auxiliary generator.

The battery-powered emergency lighting kicked on, giving the room a ghostly feel.

The water level height was accelerating now. Juan wouldn't have long to attach the C-4. As soon as he could reach the eyebolt, he slapped the plastique onto the cable fitting and mashed it in until it completely surrounded the metal. The final step was inserting the tiny detonator.

"Get ready," he said to Eddie and Raven, who were treading water on the opposite side of the room.

Juan swam over to them and counted down.

". . . three . . . two . . . one."

They all took a breath and submerged,

with Juan holding the remote detonator above the surface. He pressed the button, and a loud crack echoed through the chamber.

He surfaced to see the severed end of the cable dangling in the water.

"That's our cue," Juan said.

They swam over and grasped the cable, letting it guide them up as the water continued to flood in. The surface was now tilted at a crazy slant as the *Centaurus* settled by the bow.

When the water was three feet away from the ceiling, Juan kicked himself up and grabbed hold of the latch. He gave it a twist. It didn't move.

The hatch was locked.

When Sylvia got up to the bridge, the first thing she saw in the dimly lit room was Eric looking at her with alert eyes. She went over to him and gently ran her fingers through his hair. He gave her a crooked smile.

He made a clicking sound, and Sylvia instantly recognized it as Morse code.

NICE TO C U.

She grinned at him, although all he could

see was her eyes through the mask. "You, too."

## HEADSET.

Sylvia had completely forgotten about the headset she'd thrown off when she'd put on the gas mask. She went and retrieved it, stopping to bend over and assure Linc that she'd get them both off the sinking ship somehow. However, given that Linc weighed twice as much as she did, she had no idea how she was going to do it.

She fitted the headset over the gas mask and spoke loudly so that her muffled voice could be heard.

"Hello, this is Sylvia. Is anyone out there?"

A few seconds' pause made her wonder if it still worked.

"This is Max. Your brother looks very relieved to hear you. Where are you?"

"The bridge of the *Centaurus.*" She went back to Eric and glanced out at the deck. Water had covered the front half of the ship and was now starting to pour into the first open hold like Niagara Falls.

"You need to get out of there. We're less than two minutes to midnight. Can you stop the launch?"

"No," Sylvia said.

"Where's Polk?"

"Paralyzed. He didn't have the key, and there's no app on his phone to control the rockets. I checked on my way here."

"Then just get off the ship," Max said.

"I can't move them both out of the bridge."

"I'll see if help is on the way."

"Tell them not to come into the bridge. There still might be residual gas in the air."

She got Eric under his shoulders and lifted. For a slim man, he was heavier than she expected. Linc would be impossible for her to budge.

As she lowered Eric to the floor so she could get a better grip to drag him, she heard Max calling for help.

"Come in, Juan. Come in. Juan, are you there?"

# SEVENTY-FIVE

Juan heard Max say that Sylvia was up on the bridge with Eric and Linc. He just couldn't respond. The water had reached the hatch, so he was fully submerged. No matter how hard he tried to turn the latch, it wouldn't open.

He swam over to the small bubble of air that had formed in the corner of the tilted room where Eddie and Raven stayed above the surface.

"I can't get it open," Juan said. He shrugged off the duffel and handed it to Eddie. "This is too buoyant for what I'm about to try."

"What are you going to do?" Eddie asked.

"Blow the lock apart."

"It looks too thick for your forty-five to penetrate," Raven said.

"That's not what I'm using," Juan said. "When you hear the blast, swim for the hatch."

Juan took a breath and dived back under. He paddled over to the hatch and turned upside down.

The other weapon in his combat leg was a single shotgun slug in his heel. It was only for use in dire emergencies. This qualified.

Keeping himself inverted underwater was no small task. He had to keep clearing his nose with air so that he wouldn't inhale the seawater. And his natural buoyancy meant he had to hold on to the steel girder beside the hatch to get his foot in the right position.

He made sure his heel was snug against the latch. His lungs were screaming at him, but he wouldn't get another chance at this. He pulled the trigger.

The shell fired with a loud thump. Juan turned right side up and inspected the hatch in the low light.

The latch was shattered. He pushed against the hatch, and after a moment of resistance, it flew open.

He kicked himself up and out and found that he was on the stern deck behind the superstructure. The surface was already awash.

He looked down at the hatch to see Eddie's and Raven's heads pop up. He took the duffel from Eddie and then lifted each of them out.

He shoved the duffel into Raven's hands and said, "Help Eddie get to the *Gator*."

Then he turned and sprinted up the exterior stairs, taking them two at a time.

At the top, he saw Sylvia straining to pull Eric out of the bridge. Two dead mercenaries blocking her way didn't make the task easier.

She ripped off the gas mask and handed it to Juan.

"He's in there."

Juan put it on, noting that only the upper parts of the *Centaurus*'s cranes were now sticking out of the water. One minute left.

"Will the water short out the rocket ignition?" he asked.

"I doubt it."

"Get some life jackets. Locker one level down."

She dashed down the stairs.

Juan went into the bridge. Linc was on his back.

"Lying down on the job, buddy?" Juan said.

Linc responded with a hearty groan. Juan didn't know if that meant he appreciated the joke.

Juan reached under the shoulders of the massive Navy SEAL and pulled him to the exit. When he was outside, he laid Linc down and tossed the mask aside.

Sylvia came back with four life vests. They put them on Linc and Eddie first, then donned their own.

By this time, the bridge was only thirty feet above the water instead of sixty.

"All right," Juan said to Sylvia. "Jump. Be ready to assist Eric."

She nodded. Without hesitation, she climbed the railing and leaped into the water below.

Juan easily picked up Eric. "Time for a quick swim. Hold your breath."

He tossed Eric into the water. The moment he landed, Sylvia came over to him to make sure she got his head above the surface.

Linc was going to be a tougher one to deal with. Juan bent over and pulled Linc's arm over his back and put his shoulder against Linc's midsection. He then squatted the entire two hundred and fifty pounds into a standing position.

Juan edged over to the side with his rear toward the railing. As soon as he felt the steel, Juan tipped over backward just like he did when they were scuba diving off a boat.

The two of them tumbled through the air and splashed into the water.

531

In less than thirty seconds, two hundred and ninety-eight rockets were set to detonate virtually under their feet.

Polk's eyes fluttered open, and he wondered why he was wet. Dim lights shined from the corners of the room. His last memory was that he'd been looking for that woman. He'd entered the ship's galley and saw the mercenary's body. Then he had a vague recollection about his wife, but that was all he remembered.

The only sound was the water rushing to fill the room. The air was ripe with the salty tang of seawater.

And then he realized he was no longer wearing his mask.

He tried to get to his feet, but his legs wouldn't move. His arms would only make jerky movements.

He was paralyzed.

He'd been exposed to the Enervum gas. It had to be that woman. Somehow, she'd outwitted him. He didn't even know who she was, but he couldn't hate her more.

Water quickly rose around him. He thrashed his arms, but they were useless. He tried screaming for help, but he could form no words. His voice became the distressed wail of a terrified animal.

Polk continued his pitiful cry until it was doused by the water covering his face.

# Seventy-Six

The *Gator* motored over to where Juan was
holding up Linc. Next to him, Sylvia was
treading water with Eric. Eddie and Raven
had already been picked up by Linda, and
they were on the deck with MacD.

They came alongside and pulled Eric out
of the water, then Sylvia. Linc was next.

Finally, Juan kicked himself onto the deck
and followed the others in, grabbing a metal
handhold, like the others had, while keeping a grip with his free hand on Linc's life
jacket to keep him from falling back into
the water.

"Go, Linda," he shouted.

She gunned the diesel, and the *Gator* rose
until its hull was gliding across the surface.

Behind them, the superstructure and
cranes of the *Centaurus* were all that was
visible as water bubbled around it. The Sydney Harbour Bridge and opera house
gleamed in the distance, framing the hun-

dreds of sailboats and pleasure yachts that had gathered to observe the New Year's Eve celebration.

"Midnight coming up," MacD yelled over the wind. "Five . . . four . . . three . . . two . . . one . . ."

Fireworks shot up along the entire arch of the bridge in a glorious display of color. Glittering showers of sparkling crackers rained from its side.

Not three hundred yards away, the last of the *Centaurus* disappeared into the harbor. To punctuate its demise, a bright flash erupted underneath the surface as hundreds of rockets detonated simultaneously. A volcano of water exploded upward, lifting a dome of white foam into the air. It collapsed upon itself, sending out waves that diminished in size rapidly as they rippled in all directions.

The water settled again, and the flash vanished as suddenly as it had appeared.

Linda slowed the *Gator* and brought it to a stop.

"Are we clear?" she yelled.

Juan breathed in. He didn't feel light-headed or woozy.

"How does everyone else feel?" he asked.

All of them were sopping wet except for MacD. Nobody was shivering, though. Even this late at night, the air was warm and pleasant.

"Other than my ankle killing me, I'm fine," Eddie said.

"I think the water neutralized the gas just like we expected," Raven said.

"Come on up and join us, Linda," Juan called. "The weather's beautiful."

They were still catching their breath, not ready to do the hard work of lowering Linc and Eric into the *Gator*. So Raven and MacD propped Linc against the cupola to make him more comfortable while Sylvia cradled Eric's head in her lap. Even though he was paralyzed, he seemed quite content.

Linda climbed up through the hatch and looked them over.

"You guys are a motley sight," she said. "Is everyone okay?"

"Some better than others," Juan said. "We've got a few injuries that will need tending. Eric and Linc got hit by the same gas that paralyzed Murph."

"Oh, no."

"There is good news. I hope."

Juan took the duffel from Raven and unzipped it. He took out one of the plastic packs. He opened and removed one of the vials.

It was unbroken, just like all the others.

"This is the antidote," Juan said. He looked at Linc and Eric. "Hopefully, you won't be in this condition for very long. As soon as we get back to the *Oregon,* we'll give these to Julia. She's going to have a busy night."

The fireworks kept going, the pops and bangs a familiar and heartwarming sound.

"When you told us to sink the ship," MacD said, "Ah was sure we wouldn't be seeing y'all again. Ah didn't like being the one sending you to the bottom."

"That's the Chairman's Plan C for you," Eddie said. "Victory snatched from the jaws of defeat."

Juan nodded. "Max is going to read me the riot act when we get back."

"Speaking of jaws of defeat, what happened to Polk?"

"I don't know."

"I do," Sylvia said. "He went down with the ship."

"What did you do to get away from him?" Juan asked.

"I gave him a taste of his own medicine."

Something caused her to jolt. She fished around in her pocket and pulled out a phone. She let out a sigh of relief.

Juan was curious about what could be so

important about her phone. "Did you miss a call?"

"This is Polk's phone," Sylvia said. "I used the face unlock feature while Polk was unconscious. It's still open." She tapped on the screen.

"Ah have that model myself," MacD said. "It's waterproof down to two meters."

"When I was looking through it earlier, I flipped through his open apps hoping to find one that controlled the rockets. I didn't have any luck, but something in the notepad app caught my attention."

She turned the phone around to show Juan the screen. There were two lines.

CroesusCoin account number
9038 4734 2218 0635

"Remember when April Jin was drugged," Sylvia said. "She told us that a crypto-currency account would be unlocked after the attack was successful. She said it contained nine hundred and eighty million. She even gave us the password."

"Enervum143," Juan said.

"The only problem is, to unlock the account she said ten news sites had to carry stories about the attack."

The word "attack" reminded Juan of

another terrorist incident they'd foiled recently. It gave him the inkling of an idea, but he didn't want to get everyone's hopes up if it didn't work.

MacD looked around as if he were searching for harbor traffic, but the area around the *Gator* was clear. All the boats were gathered by the Sydney Harbour Bridge to watch the fireworks, which continued to light the sky in a festive display.

"We can't stay here forever," he said. "I expect we'll see the Sydney Police and Port Authority boats making their way in this direction any time now. We're probably on camera right now."

"I'm sure we've got a few minutes," Juan said, leaning back on his elbows. "And we're too far away to be identifiable by the port's cameras in the dark. We'll see the boats coming and be submerged by the time they arrive. Until then, let's just rest for a few minutes and enjoy the show. I have a feeling it's going to be a very happy new year."

# EPILOGUE

*Malaysia*
*Two Months Later*
Juan had a tradition when the *Oregon* was getting ready to embark on a new voyage after a long stint in port. He liked to do a walk-through just to keep himself familiar with every corner of the ship and connect with the entire crew. Sometimes, like today, it took a few hours. It was a big ship, and his people were proud to show off their individual domains to him.

He'd brought the *Oregon* back to Malaysia to complete the outfitting that had been abruptly paused before Christmas week. The crew finally got the well-deserved holiday vacations they'd been denied, and he'd had time to bring the ship up to full operational status.

The day was hot and humid, but at least the blazing sun wasn't cooking him as he completed his tour by walking the deck. An

540

enormous construction shed covered the ship to protect the workers from the elements while they were making repairs to damage caused by the *Marauder.* It also meant the ship wasn't exposed to any prying eyes from the outside.

The work was now complete. All systems were in place, a full load of ammunition was aboard, and the weapons and tech were fully upgraded and ready for battle.

Juan noticed a familiar face by the port gangway.

"Sylvia," he said, "I'm glad I saw you before you left. We're sorry to see you go."

"Thanks. I appreciate all you've done for me. And Murph."

"You've been a valuable part of the team. We couldn't have done any of it without you. I wish I could convince you to join us."

She smiled. "That's a generous offer. I won't rule it out completely in the future, but not right now."

"Are you off to the States?"

She nodded. "Thanks to the money we recovered, my research has now been fully funded for the next three years. I should be able to get it back to where it was within six months."

When Juan knew he had access to the account Lu had left to Jin and Polk, he'd pulled some strings with the Senators whose families the *Oregon* crew had saved in Bali. With Overholt's assistance, they cleverly leaked information about the *Centaurus* and Enervum gas. News organizations around the world had carried stories about the botched terrorist attack on Sydney during the New Year's Eve celebration. Lu had been shrewd in setting up his plan, but he never thought to stop the payout if the articles included the word "failed."

Not only did the key words unlock the money but they also set in motion a series of events that would have led the Chinese government to send a million of its citizens to Australia if they had really been needed. But with the attack unfulfilled, the Chinese government had to strenuously disavow any involvement with Lu's scheme, driving the Australians to even closer ties with their western allies.

The vast sum of cash had been divvied up among Sylvia's research, a compensation fund for the families of those killed by Lu, Jin, and Polk, and a bonus for the Corporation that substantially fattened their retirement accounts and paid for all of the *Oregon*'s needs.

"Will we be seeing you again?" Juan asked.

"Not if I have anything to say about it," a

voice called out from behind him.

"You don't," Sylvia yelled back.

Murph skated up to them on his board and kicked it into his hand. His hair was as untamed as ever, and he was back in his uniform of black jeans and T-shirt. This one had been given to him by Sylvia. It read WORLD'S OKAYEST BROTHER. His recovery had taken a bit longer than Eric and Linc's because he'd been paralyzed for a greater period of time, but he'd gotten back on his skateboard as soon as Doc Huxley had allowed it.

"I thought you were gone already," Murph said. "I said good-bye to you fifteen minutes ago."

"I'll miss you, too, you goofball. But I'm waiting to say good-bye to someone else."

She smiled, and Juan turned to see Eric walking toward them in his button-down and khakis, beaming as he looked at Sylvia. Murph rolled his eyes at Eric's mooning.

"Chairman," Eric said, "everything is ready for our departure."

"Thanks, Stoney. Sylvia, it's been a pleasure. I'm sure you won't be a stranger."

"Not at all. I have lots of reasons to come back." She planted a big kiss on Eric, probably to freak out her brother, which apparently worked.

"Oh, that's disgusting," he said, throwing down his skateboard. "I'll see you in the op center after I go throw up." He skated off as fast as he could.

Juan's phone rang. It was Max.

"What's up?"

"I need to see you down in the boardroom before we head out."

"On my way." He hung up. "I'll be going, too. Stoney, don't take too long." He winked, and Eric blushed. When Juan walked away, he still had Sylvia in his arms.

As he entered the superstructure, he heard gales of laughter coming from the stairwell. On his way down he met Eddie, Linc, Raven, and MacD going up. Eddie and Linc had a large cooler slung between them.

"Where are you cackling crows going?" Juan asked.

"To the bridge," Eddie said. "We're the phantom crew today."

Since the *Oregon* was actually operated from the op center, no one was needed on the bridge when they left port, but it would look awfully odd to observers in the harbor if it were empty.

"We thought we'd consume some refreshing beverages while we're there," Linc said.

"Raven was just telling us about the time she was in a bar outside of Fort Bragg,"

MacD said. "Ah wish Ah could have seen those good ole boys' faces when you whaled on them out of nowhere."

"Apparently, they'd never met a military policewoman before," Raven said. "After that, they never wanted to again."

That brought a new round of laughs, and Juan waved them on their way. He went down and entered the hidden portion of the ship.

Julia nearly bumped into him as she rounded a corner, her eyes intent on her phone screen.

"Oh, I'm sorry," she said, startled.

"No problem," Juan said. "Engrossing read?"

"It's an email from Leonard Thurman at the Royal Darwin Hospital. Everyone afflicted by the Enervum has made a full recovery."

"That's good news."

"And he says that the nut extract might have other interesting medicinal uses. Several research studies are underway."

"At least Murph and the others didn't go through all that for nothing."

"And can you please get through today without sending me any new patients?"

He smiled at her. "We're just leaving port, but no promises."

She chuffed at him and went back to her reading. Juan continued on to find Max waiting for him at the door to the board-room. He held out a card to Juan.

"This was forwarded to us courtesy of Langston Overholt," Max said.

It was a postcard with a picture of a red crab on the front. Juan flipped it over. The caption said, "Christmas Island, Australia." The card was addressed to Captain Juan Cabrillo at the Pentagon.

Dear Juan,

I hate using email, and I remembered you were a Navy man, so I thought the Navy would get to you eventually. Just wanted to let you know Renee and I are happily reacquainted. Don't know what you're doing, but it can't be as good as where I am right now. Thanks for saving my life and giving me a new start.

Take care,
Bob Parsons

"You never told him you weren't actually a Navy vet?" Max said.

"I didn't see a reason to spoil things by saying I used to be a CIA operative," Juan said. "Is this why you asked me down here?"

"Nope. In here."

He ushered Juan into the boardroom. There was a black silk cloth draped over something on the wall next to the plaque honoring the *Oregon*'s fallen crew members.

"You've been decorating?" Juan said.

"I wanted to surprise you." Max whisked away the cloth to reveal a shiny golden *aquila*. The eagle with its wings spread was identical to the one they'd recovered from the Roman bireme.

"Did you make this?"

"No, the Italian government sent it to us as a thank you. Gold-plated, of course. They weren't going to give us one made of solid gold like the original."

Juan had decided that the *aquila* belonged back in Rome after being away for two thousand years. He'd arranged to have it returned as long as it was displayed in a museum, with credit given to the archaeologists who discovered the wreck of the *Salacia* in the first place. The ship was now the site of a massive excavation that was revealing previously unknown details about Roman culture.

"I thought it could be the *Oregon*'s new standard," Max said. "But we certainly couldn't mount it on the jackstaff."

"This is a great place for it," Juan said. He thought it represented the gallantry of the *Oregon* crew well, especially those who had given their lives in its service, like Jerry Pulaski and Mike Trono, whose names were on the plaque beside it.

"Shall we set sail?"

"I thought you'd never ask," Max said, practically rubbing his hands with glee at the thought of taking his updated toy for a spin.

When they entered the op center, they were greeted by Maurice, who was holding a tray of champagne flutes.

"I thought it appropriate for you to celebrate this sailing since we didn't have a proper send-off the last time," Maurice said. "Dom Pérignon. I chose the year to honor the christening date of our previous ship."

He handed Juan one of the glasses.

"Thank you, Maurice," Juan said. "Very thoughtful of you."

Max took one and went to his post at engineering. Maurice then gave a glass to Linda at the radar and sonar station, Hali at comms, and Murph at weapons. Only a single person was missing.

Eric rushed into the room and grabbed the last champagne.

Maurice cleared his throat and handed Eric a bright white napkin. Eric stared at it in confusion until Murph chuckled and said, "You've got lipstick on your face, lover boy."

Eric blushed again and wiped off the telltale red marks. Maurice held out the tray for him to discard the napkin.

"Bon voyage, Captain," he said, and then left the room with patrician grace.

Juan went to stand in front of the main view screen and had Hali pipe in, by video chat, Eddie, Linc, Raven, and MacD on the bridge, Julia and her staff in the medical bay, and every other crew member, to join in for a toast.

"They say a ship is only as good as her crew," Juan said. "I couldn't agree more. I'm proud to say that the *Oregon* has been, is, and always will be the finest ship afloat."

He held his glass high and was matched by the others.

"Fair winds and following seas," he said.

The rest of them gave a rousing "Hear! Hear!" and drank.

Hali switched the view back to the external cameras and the bridge crew took their seats.

"Ship status?" Juan asked as he gazed at the construction shed exit on the main view screen.

"Weapons are stowed and secure," Murph said.

"Engines are operating normally and at your command," Max said.

"The port has given us clearance to leave," Hali said.

"Boat traffic has made way," Linda said. "The route out of the harbor is clear."

"Lines have been cast off," Eric said. "We are ready to depart."

Juan sat down in his chair, the place where he always felt the most at home. The light ahead seemed to beckon them.

"Take us out, Mr. Stone," he said. "It's time to see what the *Oregon* can really do."

# ABOUT THE AUTHORS

**Clive Cussler** was the author of more than eighty books in five bestselling series, including Dirk Pitt®, NUMA® Files, *Oregon®* Files, Isaac Bell®, and Sam and Remi Fargo®. His life nearly paralleled that of his hero Dirk Pitt. Whether searching for lost aircraft or leading expeditions to find famous shipwrecks, he and his NUMA crew of volunteers discovered and surveyed more than seventy-five lost ships of historic significance, including the long-lost Confederate submarine *Hunley,* which was raised in 2000 with much publicity. Like Pitt, Cussler collected classic automobiles. His collection featured more than one hundred examples of custom coachwork. Cussler passed away in February 2020.

**Boyd Morrison** is the coauthor, with Clive Cussler, of the *Oregon®* Files novels *Typhoon Fury, Piranha,* and *The Emperor's Re-*

*venge,* and the author of six other books. He is also an actor and engineer, with a doctorate in engineering from Virginia Tech, who has worked on NASA's space station project at Johnson Space Center and developed several patents at Thomson/RCA. In 2003, he fulfilled a lifelong dream by becoming a Jeopardy! champion. He lives in Seattle.

The employees of Thorndike Press hope you have enjoyed this Large Print book. All our Thorndike, Wheeler, and Kennebec Large Print titles are designed for easy reading, and all our books are made to last. Other Thorndike Press Large Print books are available at your library, through selected bookstores, or directly from us.

For information about titles, please call
(800) 223-1244

or visit our website at:
gale.com/thorndike

To share your comments, please write:
Publisher
Thorndike Press
10 Water St., Suite 310
Waterville, ME 04901